War of the Shattered Moon

The Wishkiller Saga, Vol 2

G. Scott Huggins

Copyright © 2025 by G. Scott Huggins

All rights reserved.

No portion of this book may be reproduced in any form without written permission from the publisher or author, except as permitted by U.S. copyright law.

Contents

To Ben Pittman, the first re-reader of my work.

Prologue

Crown Prince Abzalm's steps echoed stiffly through the bare stone of the Divine Hall. He forced himself to maintain the even rhythm, despite the pain, setting the pace for the six guards that walked behind him. Always, always behind him, as much a reminder of his subservience as of his station. Until today. The watery sun shone through the black glass of the hall, fretted with warm gold, leading ever onward.

Onward to the Scintillant Chamber, and the guard that stood before it.

Abzalm stopped, as he had for so many years before that figure. It was robed in blackness, a cloak of shadow that seemed to grow out from the very floor and walls of the Hall. Only the masked face gave it definition: the face of a young man in his middle thirties, the very prime of life. The face of a man who had once lived.

"My lord the Prince." The voice came from behind the mask, accompanied by a bow from the neck.

"Admit me to my father," Abzalm said.

"My lord," the figure said, as if reading from words engraved upon the inside of the mask, "he has not permitted you admittance. Even if you have chosen to obey his command and mask yourself before the Eternal King, as is proper."

The same words Abzalm had heard for years. Except for the reference to the mask. Abzalm smiled beneath it. His dim reflection in the black glass of the Hall betrayed nothing, though they did catch the slight grin of the captain of his guards tightening, shifting his eyepatch ever so slightly. "Of course. All things must be done according to the will of the King. And when was the last time my father spoke to you, Bishai?"

If the guardian of the door felt surprise at the use of his name, so long unuttered, he did not show it. "That is irrelevant, my lord. He has not admitted you."

"If it is irrelevant, then you have no cause to deny me an answer, servant. When did he last speak with you?"

After a brief hesitation, the guardian said, "It has been over a year since the King Eternal last favored me with his spoken notice, my lord."

"Then how can you know he will not wish to see his son?"

"He has not admitted you, my lord. His last orders upon the subject were quite clear. If I break his ordinance, and he orders me justly to die, how should I gainsay him? The word of the King Eternal is law."

"So it is," said Abzalm. "But how, if the King has no word?"

"The King Eternal always has a word. Even if it was his last. My lord."

"So you have said. By no word of the King except his own, you keep him in the Chamber Everlasting, denying any other entrance, except those you say he admits. And those are his lowliest servants, his handmaids and valets. The lowest-born men and women who infest the Great Palace."

"Such were his orders to me, my lord."

"So you have said." Abzalm paused. "All things transpire because of what you have said. The absence of the King's voice lends a great deal of power to all the things that you have said, Bishai."

"According to the will of the King Eternal," the guardian said, blandly.

"So you have said," Abzalm repeated, "but what if you say untruly?"

"My lord?" replied the guard, his voice dropping dangerously.

"No man can know whether you say truly," Abzalm said, in a voice that was almost a whisper. "No man, not even the Crown Prince of Men, can verify what you have said. So, I name you a traitor, who has usurped the throne of the King Eternal, ruling it in his stead."

"I have issued no command of my own," said the Guardian, his shadow-wrapped hand going to a sword-hilt of ebony, capped with a ruby that glowed at its pommel.

"Except to keep me from my rightful throne."

"Your accusation is improper. And unworthy of my faithfulness. You have no rightful throne, my lord, while the King Eternal reigns."

"But does he reign? Or does he merely exist? Or is he dead?"

"That is not possible, my lord. You know the Wish of the Eternal King was granted. As was your own."

"Yes," whispered Abzalm. "When I was too young to know even when I wanted. What a fascinating way to geld one's own son that was. Truly, I have already had my Wish." He stepped to the side, from between the guardian and his own escort. "But now I have had his."

The Guardian's mask swiveled to look at the captain of the Crown Prince's guards. To meet his gaze as the man raised his eyepatch. For the first time, the voice behind the mask betrayed emotion. Shock.

"What would induce you to do this?"

"What else?" asked Abzalm. "Access to the *Kahlid-ranym*. For a Wish of their own."

The captain moved. It was too fast for any human eye to follow, and yet the Guardian's own sword cleared its sheath before the flashing blade struck. Then the shadowy shape fell apart, its head and shoulder cloven from its body.

Of course, Abzalm's captain had been younger. Abzalm lifted the mask and, despite his knowledge of the creature who had worn it, recoiled anyway.

Much younger.

He took his own mask off, then, and let them clatter to the floor together. Conscious of his duty, the youngest of his guards leaped eagerly forward to the door. "No!" roared Abzalm. The young man froze, his expression aghast.

Gentling his voice, Abzalm said, "I will do you the honor of allowing you to open a thousand doors for me, and your name I shall never forget." He removed a lighter mask from his coat and fitted the smoked lenses of it over his eyes. "But this door I shall open myself. Gentlemen, remember: close your eyes. There is no danger within that I cannot face alone."

Seizing the doors, Crown Prince Abzalm thrust them open, and entered the Scintillant Chamber. His guards shuffled in behind him. One of them — possibly the same he had just rebuked, screamed and fell to his knees. *Ah, well,* thought Abzalm. *I suppose he can Wish for new eyes.*

Around the very edges of the obsidian lenses, Abzalm could sense the deadly brightness of the chamber. The Scintillant Chamber, wished into existence as a single diamond. The rays of the climbing sun turned it into a dazzling brightness worthy of only one man.

The man who lay in the bed at the center of the brightness. The man only Abzalm could see, who twitched feebly beneath his blankets, and his visored crown. "Hail Joram," said Abzalm, venom lacing every word, "King of Men Eternal, brother of Raham, son of Salnum. Hail, Father."

The creature in the bed exhaled a rattling breath.

"The word of the King Eternal of Men is law!" Abzalm thundered. Then he sat on the bed. "But that wasn't a word, was it, Father?" he continued conversationally. "I'm so glad you instated the custom of adopting your descendants. Otherwise, I'd be stuck here trying to remember how many 'greats' go before the 'grand.' This is much simpler." He lowered his voice to a whisper. "My father — my *real* father, whom I loved, and died but one more sad man in a long-forgotten line of princes while you doddered on — sends his regards."

The shape in the bed croaked. In a furious motion, Abzalm tore the crown off his head.

Half the scalp came with it.

Maggots crawled on the skull of the King Eternal. Bone showed through a withered cheek. Diamond-shattered sunlight poured onto the milky eyes, and despite their clouds, the withered throat pulsed and croaked in pain. Abzalm rose and turned his back on the twitching thing.

Closing his eyes, he removed his mask and placed Salnum's Crown on his head, the golden visor with its eagle's beak settling over his upper face. "King Joram has abdicated," he said. "You are all witnesses."

"We are all witnesses," the captain boomed. He dropped to his knees, eyes still closed. "Hail Abzalm, King Eternal of Men." His men repeated it.

"King Eternal," Abzalm repeated in a whisper. "Not a title I insist on, so long as I can be King for what length of time it pleases me. Fetch a rug."

It took his guards some time, working blind. "You cannot die," Abzalm said to the gulping creature as they wrapped it. "So, you will be buried alive, here in the Kalidranym, the Eternal Waters. In as fitting a place I can contrive, forgotten by all. And the last sight you will see — well, the last sound you will hear — is the scraping of the stones as we place them back over the corpse of the father you and your brother contrived to murder. In darkness for far longer than you lived in light."

The guards hoisted the body, too weak now even to shudder.

"Long live the King," Abzalm whispered.

Chapter One

46th of Spring, 312 Exodus

"All right, Aethal," said Farnan, removing his cloak and handing it to Osric. "What's it all about?" Aethal's valet spirited the cloak away into a garderobe and wordlessly invited them to step into the parlor.

"I've been invited to masquerades before, and I've been invited to evening tea before, but I generally don't get invited to a masked evening tea, and I've certainly never been escorted to one by a Wyrmguard before." He glared through the door where the one called Irontooth now stood watch. "And no offence, but if I were to be so invited, I'd hope that my host would be more... well, 'essy.'"

Aethal gave him a look. "Essy?"

"Yes. As in, a host*ess*. Because it sounds a delightful tale to open a tryst, but this," he spread his hand at the ale, sausage and cheese, "Well, it looks to be of the finest quality, but depressingly masculine, you know."

Aethal sighed. "Sit down, Farnan." He waved at Osric. "That will be all."

Farnan sat. "What's up, O Last Sword of the King?"

Aethal waited until Osric was truly gone. "Farnan, the masquerade does have a practical purpose: I don't want it known who's visiting me."

"Aethal, you're in the middle of the Hydraxis. Anyone can tell who's visiting you."

Aethal shook his head. "Only the King can command the Wyrmguard to tell me who they're escorting, and I'm hoping it won't occur to him to do so."

Farnan gave Aethal a sidelong glance and put down the ale in the middle of a sip. "Why are we keeping secrets from the King, Aethal?"

Aethal sighed. "The King is upset with me, Tyrsen. He thinks I have designs on the Lady Ardyth, and he wants her for Eraad."

Farnan rounded his lips in a silent whistle.

"Exactly. He thinks to offset My-Father-The-Chancellor's power by making alliance with the Westerend. Obviously, I intend no harm to his majesty, but I'd prefer that he not have tales brought to him about me — or you — sneaking out of the Hydraxis in the night."

Farnan rolled his eyes, "We're sneaking out of the Hydraxis in the night? Why?"

"Because as helpful as our new friend Guardian Magnei may turn out to be," Aethal said, "we can't afford to lose sight of the other resource we've been tracking."

"Malcoor, you mean?" asked Farnan. "But everyone at court knows he's missing, and the King has ordered him found! Why are we sneaking around under the King's nose for that? Are you afraid he'll commend you?"

"Tyrsen, don't be dense," Aethal said. "If Malcoor disappeared, it's because he's afraid someone is looking for him. Old as he is, would *you* bet against him having an agent in place here? To warn him in case we, or anyone else, got close?"

"But..."

"And if, instead, he *was* disappeared, do you think his captors — or his murderers — will want either of us to find evidence of their crimes?"

"Obviously, no. You suspect anyone?"

"Ilferth Simon wouldn't be pleased if we found him." Again, he puzzled over Ilferth Simon's strangely conciliatory visit last night.

"Thought you said you'd convinced him of something," said Farnan, obviously considering the same visit.

"I don't want to bet on it. I don't think my father will want him to turn up, either. That both of them have spies in the Hydraxis is certain. So eat up. It's time for a stroll in the Madlands."

***

The Madlands of Maednac Serpiin, capital of Verlaen, opened around them into an endless maze of alleys between warehouses, dingy flophouses, and shuttered shops, clothed in aromas of sour sweat, salt sea tang, tar, varnish, smoke, and the piss that ran down the narrow gutters. These were the slums of Maednac Serpiin, the rooms to let for sailor rats and army brats, where the crews of the Fleet slept and fornicated between voyages, and their wives and mothers raised up the next generation of human grease that made the kingdom run.

Aethal Paaling, Last Sword of the King, led his men through them with torches held high. Not because they needed the light to see, not these men. They needed to be seen. Their message needed to be seen, as surely as the beacons lit on the turrets of the Hydraxis and the outer wall of Maednac Serpiin needed to be seen as a talisman holding back the threat of the Lotus. *These are the king's men, and more than men. Touch us, and die.*

The Wyrmguard drew stares, and sent the few men they met into a furtive scurrying, an obvious desire to be elsewhere. "If you had to bring Wyrmguard," murmured Farnan, noticing the activity, "then why these two? I mean, I suppose this Irontooth is all right, but how old is *this* poor bastard?"

Aethal looked at the older Wyrmguard. The man was old, with iron-gray hair and a tough wiriness that bore not the least suggestion of softening. "Answer the Lieutenant, ah…" He had still not learned all of their names.

"Goldhammer, Last Sword," said the man.

Aethal looked at the gun. The hammer of the weapon was not made of gold.

"Your mount is old, Goldhammer," said Aethal. "Far older than usual, for one who must protect the King."

"It was a whim of the Last Sword but two," said Goldhammer. *Jehan Alfing's predecessor, then*, Aethal decoded this. "He bound my mount for a long sentence. He was not so old, then. The time is nearly up, but he said that the oldest Wyrmguard should have the oldest mount."

"I thought Wyrmguard were all the same age," said Aethal.

"The Last Sword has not read carefully in our book," said Goldhammer, just a touch of rebuke flavoring the words. "The Table and Forge of our making were Wished from the Well. But we were made over hundreds of years in the city of Nadesh Cor. Until the Wish-Kings fell, and their great fastnesses in the Northern Dark collapsed."

"Why are you called Goldhammer?"

"Another whim, but this of him who commissioned me. It is forged into me, that I shall strike hardest when loaded with balls of gold. A cheap metal, but my maker thought it more beautiful than lead. For this reason," Goldhammer continued, "I slept many years in our chamber, dismounted, ever since my first mount died, defending Maednac from an assassin's blade. Gold is not popular for bullets."

Aethal shook his head. Always, there was an element of madness about the living guns. In the warm drizzle coating the streets with moisture, the five men came to a halt before a wide, sliding door.

"That's it," said Sergeant Falk, his voice flat and flavorless as the rain.

Aethal drew a long breath. Behind this door, large enough for two wagons to pass through abreast was a clue. A clue that might lead to the missing General Malcoor.

Malcoor, who had gone missing at the same time the Lotus had reappeared, threatening to corrupt and destroy Verlaen, last kingdom of men.

Malcoor, who had seen the Lotus over twenty years ago, and had lived to tell the tale.

There was a man-sized door set into the large one: it had been split into an upper and lower half. Aethal pounded on it. For a long time, nothing happened.

Just as Aethal was drawing breath to order the door forced, the upper half swung open a crack. A face in shadow froze at the sight of the uniforms.

"And what would ye fine gentlemen be wanting with the likes of me?" The voice was pale, soft and gray, with the strong brogue of the Madlands.

Aethal said nothing, but placed Westerend's half-coin on the edge of the half-door.

There was a long, indrawn breath, and the door jerked open involuntarily. In the dim light, Aethal could just make out a face lined with scars, if not age, beneath a mop of ragged brown hair.

"Ye'll be wanting our hospitality, then," he said, as though the words were being pulled from him. "And would do us no small favor to be coming inside quickly." The door was opened. Somehow, Aethal now noticed, the coin had vanished, and Aethal moved in, followed by Farnan, the two Wyrmguard, and Falk.

They were in a cavernous, dark space, and their guide raised a lantern, conveying them through narrow corridors walled off by crates and barrels. When they stopped, he gave a rapid knock on an unseen door and fumbled for his keys, opening it into a dingy parlor lit by small, clouded-glass windows. It was furnished like a bazaar, with wall-hangings in a dozen styles covering the cracked plaster walls, floor strewn with rugs and mats, and a scattering of chairs and sofas. Aethal just had time to wonder why their host had knocked on a door that he opened himself when the man stepped and twirled, hand reaching behind his back. Aethal sidestepped, clearing the door, and the Wyrmguard stepped through behind him, hands on the butts of their pistols. Farnan and Falk were right behind them.

Covering the five men were three big bravos holding blunderbusses whose barrels were large enough to swallow a child's fist. Their host grinned and opened his mouth to speak, when one of his enforcers said to Irontooth, "Shit in the Well, Samal, I never thought I'd see you..." he trailed off, eyes widening, then stared at their host, who scowled.

"Rukh! Earn yer copper!"

Rukh just shook his head. "Not for this. You ain't got enough copper in the world for this. That's Wyrmguard, that is. And I ain't gonna be one of 'em." With exaggerated care, he eased the flintlock hammer down, and stepped back through the door, clearly poised to run. The other two did the same. Their host deflated. When his hand came out from behind his back, very slowly, it held only keys.

Now, Aethal could see him clearly. He was not old, but he looked as though he'd lived through two youths to get to a wiry, weathered middle age. Beneath the traceries of scars, one of which looked as though it had gone to the bone, his face was pale and gray. Carefully, he went to a drawer and opened it. On a small table, he laid the coin, two halves joined to make a copper circle.

"I never thought the likes of you would bring that token to me." He gazed at his guests. "You're not bloody Commodore Malcoor. Or anyone else we've ever broke coin with."

Sergeant Falk took two steps forward. When he spoke, it was in a broader Madland's brogue than any Aethal had ever heard from the big man's mouth. "And yer not the one as broke this coin with the Commodore, neither, boy," the big man said, softly. "And ye'll honor that coin, Hurkin, or I'll see you broke. Under the Gun or on this floor, it makes no nevermind to me."

The man's shoulders slumped. "All right. It's the guns, isn't it? Yer here about the guns."

"About? And what the hell are you about, ye shatter-skulled fool?"

The voice boomed from above, like the cry of a guttersnipe's god: raucous and deep and full of wrath. The Wyrmguard casually turned in its direction, which was through a trapdoor in the ceiling which Aethal had utterly failed to notice. Heavy steps preceded the voice's owner down a staircase that was quite concealed from view behind packed crates.

If Hurkin was one of the Madlands' crimelords, the man lurching down the stairs was its crime king. With a face whose lines and seams were accented by wisps of white beard, the old man speared Hurkin with a gaze that radiated pure power.

"The coin's the coin," he said. "And it buys the favor." He swept the intruders with a glance and locked eyes with Aethal. "And if ye took it from him and he told ye what it meant, then any debt I owed him is paid in full. And more so." he added in a growl. He turned his attention back to Hurkin. "It doesn't buy the blabber of idiots! Now get out. All of you! Out of my sight until ye remember yer wits!"

Hurkin and his bravos vanished. The old man stood before them. Now he turned his attention on Falk. "Yer brothers and sisters are well. Sergeant. But it's been a long time since I've seen you at home."

"Not long enough, *Yakuz* Skraalen." The big man's voice was back to its clipped, military tones.

But the old man nodded. "I see."

Aethal maintained a blank mask. "Tell me about the guns."

The man nodded. "In good time, Last Sword of the King. May I offer you refreshment? My son's discourtesy is a shame to me in my old age."

Aethal cocked an eyebrow at Sergeant Falk.

"It's safe, sir," he said, tonelessly. "Poisoners don't last long here. Bad for business."

Aethal nodded. The old man rang a bell. Before they had seated themselves, silent street urchins had come in with sausage and cheese and amber beer in cloudy glass mugs. Skraalen settled himself back on his chair with a kingliness that Paitir would have envied.

"I told my son it would draw trouble, but the money was too good to pass up what with Discipline this and Discipline that choking off a man's trade."

Aethal's lip curled. Of course, the extra scrutiny would make it harder on the criminals of Maednac Serpiin. Even Lotus, it seemed, brought a kind of benefit. "What a shame for you; do go on."

Skraalen snorted. "Oh, don't think I don't see the value in it, Last Sword. Leafeaters don't buy nothing but Lotus, and then they die. I wouldn't have had ye here if it were up to me, but now ye are, let's talk honest. You know I didn't become *Yakuz* and get rich by being a fool, aye? Well, I know you didn't get that sword dropped across yer back by being one either. Let's both of us talk with that in mind."

Aethal nodded. Skraalen continued: "I don't break Discipline, because one day it would cost me everything. But keeping it, Last Sword, that's costing me now. So, when Hurkin starts telling me there's a sudden market for guns, I listen. Lotus don't grow out of the barrels of guns, at least, though I know it grows in anything that lives or ever did. And there was a market for guns, oh, yus there was. Lots of guns. For the last two weeks it's been like a bloody masked parade down here. Every day, another buyer. Sometimes two. But now it's coming to my mind that the buyers of these guns might not share my view of the costs of breaking the Discipline."

Aethal felt his blood chill. "Who is buying these guns, Yakuz Skraalen?"

The old man raised his eyebrows. "Call them sort of colleagues of mine, though they'd turn up their toes and die rather than admit it. It's been an entertainment in these hard times to watch them conceal names, playing at my end of the business as though it were their own — while all the time despising *me* as a pretender among them." He turned to Falk. "Sergeant. Do inform yer boss there of my other interest in this city."

Without taking his eyes from the smuggler lord, Falk said, "*Yakuz* Skraalen is also the Madlands' delegate to the General States."

"Its only delegate," laughed the old man. "Just like any other town, for all that we've ten times the throats to feed. Well, ye can't hardly have the likes of us casting votes equal to any ten shires of the Bowl. We might get ideas above our station."

Farnan looked uneasy, but Falk's face was carved red brick. Yes. Here was a wound in the kingdom that ran festering and deep. The Madlands, mainstay of

Verlaen's Fleet, had never enjoyed the prestige even of the settlers in the Grain Sea that now fled the Lotus.

"You're saying that your fellow delegates — the members of the General States — are buying guns. Guns you've helped smuggle in," asked Farnan.

"Until I put a stop to it. Or thought I had. They took exception to me asking questions. Now, it's true I usually *don't* ask them. But this sort of thing might affect my entire business. You know, those bastards were actually surprised! They thought they could all buy their guns from me and I wouldn't notice. So it seems Hurkin has tried to continue the business, by not asking my questions. "Like 'what for?' Which they'd answer, were I a *gentleman* like they are."

"They won't tell you," Aethal said.

Skraalen nodded. "Now, it might just be that these guns are for their own villages. Any man with sense is scared of the Dead Man's Salad. But all those hamlets and towns have different numbers of men. So, why're they buying them in five-score lots, more or less? And that gets me to thinking, maybe there's a less savory use for them."

"Where are they taking them?"

"Now *that* I truly don't know," said the old man. "I can't watch every man. But it smells of what my honorable colleagues call knavery when it ain't them doing it, and that's why I'm telling you. You see, we in the Madlands go out into the wide sea, and work out their guts fighting and harvesting more Wellspawn than these Bowl-dwellers or Grain Sea farmers imagine. The Well's real to us. Its spawn takes our sons now and again, and leaves our daughters widowed. So, while I ain't averse to spitting in the eye of the law when it suits me, I'll not sit by and see them as are rich, fat and happy do it because they're too lily-livered or too stupid to know that the Wellspawn's deadly to all of us. You take my meaning?"

Slowly, Aethal nodded. *I may have found the most honest man in Maednac Serpiin, and he's a professional criminal.*

"What do you know, then?" asked Aethal.

"I can give you a list of names," Skraalen said. "I trust you realize it may not be complete?"

"Of course," said Aethal. "But I am curious, sir: what else do you intend to do about it?"

"Fight. After I've reminded my son of the value of my sort of Discipline," he said, giving the word his own special pronunciation that made Aethal very glad it wasn't aimed at him, "we'll keep our guns for ourselves."

"But their numbers will of necessity be limited," said Aethal. "I'm new at police work, sir, but your supply of... businessmen... must be limited. Or you could not keep it even an open secret."

The old man nodded. "That's so. What do you have in mind?"

"You must know who the loyal families of the Madlands are. You could arm them. As you have said already, there are far more of you than of any other shire in the Bowl."

"That would expose me a great deal," said the crime king. "And cost me more."

"Additionally, of course, the crown would be pleased to know of the loyalty of the Madlands in the present crisis," Aethal said. "I think you would find my cousin Paitir most grateful. Both to the Madlands and to you."

"Pardons all around, eh?" said the old man tolerantly.

"Rather more than that, sir," said Aethal. "A title, if it comes to that."

Farnan's eyes popped out. Sergeant Falk's face went white. Even Skraalen's froze into immobility. Then he laughed, long and loud and harsh. "I suppose next you'll tell me that I'll be welcomed into the nobility with open arms as an honored peer of the realm!" His voice was jolly, but under it was a current of fire.

Aethal snorted quietly. "Sir. I am the son of a Lord Paramount. The Lord Paramount Wrackberg, at that. I know the limits of what I promise. No. You'll be spat at and hear whispers behind your back from the first time you dare show your face in court until the day you die. As the first Wrackberg was. You know the story of the Wrackberg, yes?"

Now the old man settled back, the fires in his eyes banked and active. "Yes," he breathed.

"Not for you, *Yakuz,*" Aethal said. "But for your son." Aethal paused, thinking of Hurkin. "Perhaps a younger son. And his children."

The old man's eyes lit. "Aye. Perhaps. Your word on't?"

"My word," said Aethal rising. His host rose to meet him and spat in in his palm. Aethal took the wet, horned hand in his own. "Well, ye've a good beginning with the first families of the Madlands, such as we are."

"With you, sir, I'm sure we do."

"Aye, with me. And with the Sergeant, here. The Falk family's as proud — and large — a line as ye'll find in our warrens. Ain't that right, Sergeant? Looks like ye'll work with me again after all."

Falk's face never unfroze, but he gave a slow nod. The Yakuz looked at Aethal. "Well, we'll be in touch. You to your Discipline, and I to mine."

***

Back out in the Madlands, evening was falling, and the alleys lay in deepening shadow. Farnan said, "Wish me dead, Sergeant, I never knew you had such extensive family connections."

"As the Lieutenant says, sir," said the big man. It was as though a statue had spoken.

"Sergeant," said Aethal, "Just what..." *is it between you, Skraalen and your family?* he'd been going to say. But just then, Farnan pointed:

"Aethal, what's that?"

A crowd was spilling from the end of an alleyway, their backs to Aethal and his men. A cry of pain sounded from somewhere around the corner. The cry was overtaken by a masculine bellow of rage and ended in a solid smack of flesh on flesh. Aethal broke into a run. The five of them pushed their way through the onlookers. Behind a wide, open window whose sill was draped with carpets, a woman peered fearfully, two small children huddled at her side. On the ground in front of the small shop, spitting blood, rolled the shopkeeper, gasping for breath. A watchman in the solid blue of the Crownguard's uniform stood over him with blood streaming from his nose. Another watchman held a wild-eyed girl, no more than seventeen, with red-blonde hair, who was frozen stiff in terror while tears ran down her cheeks.

"Corporal, who are you, and what's the trouble here?"

The watchman swung around on Aethal, raising a gloved fist with brass studs sewn into the knuckles. He dropped it, recognizing Aethal instantly, and ripped off a halfway presentable salute. "Corporal Lorch. On patrol. Suspected case of Lotus, sir," he said. There was a murmur from the crowd. "Carpetman here tried to fight us." He prodded the shopkeeper with the toe of his boot.

"Spit in the Well, man, lower your voice!" hissed Farnan. "You want to start a panic?"

Lorch looked bemused. "What panic, sir? Ain't nobody panicking but the farmed girl, here."

Watching the girl, torn between pity and fear, Aethal was dimly aware that Lorch was right. The name of Lotus had not put the crowd to flight. They were watching. Eager. His stomach twisted.

The girl sobbed. "I'm not a Leafeater, milord!" she screamed. "Haven't had nothing green since the Lotus came back! We're good people, milord, and my father, he's a good man!"

Aethal stepped close to the corporal. "That girl isn't farmed," he said, raising his voice.

The corporal looked sullen. "With respect, how do you know, sir? Discipline says look in her eyes."

"The Last Sword knows because he is the man who found the Lotus in the Grain Sea," said Farnan, pitching his voice to carry. The crowd murmured again. Some edged closer. "You'd do well to listen."

"Anyone who's eaten Lotus wouldn't panic," said Aethal. "More likely they'd laugh as you dragged them away. But we must still observe the Discipline, as you so rightly point out." Aethal took a lamp from the shop window and knelt by the girl, who was watching him through puffy eyelids, fighting back tears.

"Open your eyes, girl," he said. "You're not farmed and I know it. Look at me."

The girl opened brilliant green eyes, and Aethal froze. Only for an instant. *Of course, the color's natural*, he thought. He looked closely. "Have you never seen anyone with green eyes before, Corporal?" he snapped. "Lotus *moves* in a farmed man's eyes. Let her go!" he barked at the man holding her. His hands sprang open and she ran into the shop, weeping.

The horror of it opened in Aethal like a belly wound. *How many of us have green eyes? How much Lotus could hide there? And how many might be jailed — or worse — just for that accident of birth?*

"The Lord Low Jailer said anyone with the color was to come with us," protested Lorch. "Discipline says so. Anyone with green eyes, you hold them a full day."

"Any man who *passes your watch*, Corporal, you hold him a full day. The Third Discipline. Now did she try to pass a watch-point, or is this her house, where everyone knows her, down to the color of her eyes?"

The corporal looked away.

The shopkeeper struggled to his feet. "They was just gonna take her milord," he wheezed. "My daughter, to th' Winery cells. I was gonna go too, but they shoved me back."

Aethal looked the shopkeeper in the face and turned back to the corporal with mounting rage. "Why didn't you take this one too, Lorch?" he said softly. "Look at his eyes. He passed them on to his daughter. Why not him, Lorch?"

Lorch muttered, "Coulda come back for him later if she was found farmed, sir. Didn't see the need."

"You don't see the *need?*" Aethal roared. "You're patrolling these streets, harassing anybody with green eyes that catches your fancy," *Any desirable body, more likely.* "And you find a girl you *say* you have reason to believe might be farmed and you don't see the *need* to hold her father as well?" The corporal stepped back before Aethal's fury. "As it happens, I do see the need, Lorch," said Aethal, deliberately looking at the man's codpiece. "To place you under arrest. To the Winery. Let's all go there together. Because the Lord Low Jailer and I need to have a talk. About you." *And about proper training. Again.* He thought he'd set fear into his little brother the last time they'd spoken. It seemed he was mistaken. *And it seems that Ilferth Simon may be telling the truth. About this, anyway.* He signaled to Farnan who unslung Crow, holding it at port arms; not exactly threatening, but ready to hand. Aethal and Falk did likewise, and Lorch and his fellow watchman moved out ahead of them, misery in their faces.

Corporal Lorch protested, "But the rest of the patrol, sir. How will my lieutenant know where we've gone?"

Against all odds, the man actually had a point. Aethal's own orders were very clear about what had to happen if any member of a patrol actually disappeared on duty. *Which is why they aren't supposed to split up like this.*

Aethal was saved from having to answer him by the rest of the patrol, an officer and two more prison-guard club-wielders, rounding the corner in front of them. Stumbling to keep up, another man in dockworkers' clothing was being hustled along. He carried an iron-shod pole with a lantern atop it. The lieutenant wore City Watch blue-and-whites, and looked scruffy and bored. On seeing Aethal he straightened, and gripped his short, twin barreled shotgun more tightly. The man's expression hardened.

"You," he called to them. "What business have you interfering with my...?" Aethal could tell the exact moment that the man recognized him. Or perhaps it was the Sword he recognized.

"Good even, Lieutenant. How goes the watch?" said Aethal.

"Last Sword," said the lieutenant. He gulped. My, uh, my Lord, I, uh..." Aethal knew what was going to come next. This was the look of a junior officer who was going to do his duty even though it might incur the wrath of as senior an officer as he could imagine. "My Lord, I must log your name, and look into your eyes."

"Last Sword of Verlaen Aethal Paaling. Lieutenant Tyrsen Farnan, my aide-de-camp. Sergeant Bedar Falk. And two Wyrmguard." He allowed himself a cool smile at the indrawn gasps from a couple of the men. The lieutenant swallowed.

"Go ahead and look, lieutenant." Aethal gestured to the lantern-holder. "But first, who is this man?"

"Oh, he's nobody, sir. Gutter-trash we picked up..."

"Why is he with your patrol?" Aethal cut in, seeing the flash of resentment in the man's eyes. "I had not thought we needed gutter-trash in the City Watch." The resentment spread to the watchmen's eyes.

"No, sir," said the lieutenant, clearly agitated by Aethal's mere presence, let alone his questioning. "It's just that standing orders from the Lord Mayor are to supplement the City Watch whenever possible by using prisoners. Saves paying them, sir."

"And what is your offense, man?" said Aethal.

"Don't know, milord. I was walking home when they grabbed me..."

"No backtalk, you," snarled a trooper, shoving the man hard.

"Trooper," said Aethal coldly. "Did you just interrupt the man who was answering my question?" The trooper shrank back, and his comrades stepped a little away from him. Aethal looked away, pointedly. "Continue."

"Just walking home, milord, and they grabbed me and shoved this pole in my hands and said I'd got to follow them all night. Just finished doing for my sister while her man's a-ship, helping with the kids after the dockwork was done." He yawned mightily. "Work starts at sunup, milord, and I'll be fallin' down come morning, milord, if this patrol goes all night like they says."

Aethal fixed the officer with a stare. "What's your name, Lieutenant?" he asked.

The lieutenant swallowed. "Gehlen, my Lord."

"Is this lantern too heavy for one of your men to carry?"

"No, my Lord!"

"Then let this man go home, and get some much-needed rest. After you look into our eyes. With the lantern."

"I'm sure that's not necessary, my Lord," Gehlen stammered.

"It is necessary." Aethal spoke in a flat voice. "It was apparently necessary for Corporal Lorch here to examine this girl, here and suspect her of being a greeneater, while she was helping to shut up her father's shop. Therefore, it is certainly necessary to examine us." He beckoned the luckless corporal and his partner over, then pulled the lantern down to the level of his face. "Look into my eyes. They should be blue. If they were green naturally, you'd have to hold me for a day. Aren't those your orders, Lieutenant?" He didn't wait for the other's jerk of a nod. "But I'm lucky; they're blue. Are they blue all the way around?" He looked each man of the patrol in turn, in the eye, including the dockworker. Then he motioned to Farnan. His own brown eyes alight with mischief, Farnan allowed himself to be put through the ritual silently. Then Falk. Then the Wyrmguard.

Gehlen made one more attempt to placate him. "My lord Wrackberg, we know you. You were the one that discovered the Lotus. You couldn't..."

Aethal gripped the younger man's shoulder. The man went quiet, his face tensing under the pressure. "I didn't discover the Lotus. The men who did are dead. We discovered *them*, Lieutenant. And that only makes it more likely that we're leafeaters. But we're not, as you all can see." The crowd was silent, watching this interplay.

Aethal gently lifted the lantern from the dockworker's unresisting hands. "Go home, docker. Sleep this night. And thank you for your service." The man nodded, staring at Aethal like he was Salnum himself, or some other Well-sprung wonder. Then he faded into the crowd.

Aethal hefted the lantern on its pole and motioned his men back. "Don't mix in, and fall back three paces," he muttered.

"Rank hath privilege, eh?" Farnan whispered back. Aethal glared at him.

"Tell me about the Lord Mayor's orders, Gehlen," Aethal asked. Gehlen's face was pasty in the dim light. He knew that the axe was about to fall — or perhaps had already fallen, and required but the slightest motion on his part to tumble his head from his shoulders.

"He gave them when the prison-guards and Temple guards were ordered to City Watch duties, my Lord. Any time we made an arrest, the prisoner could act as pole-bearer to save the wages."

"And that man was arrested, was he?" asked Aethal. "For being on his way home? Or did your men simply draw lots to see who'd carry this tonight and get to go hit the sack early?" There was no answer. All the watchmen stared resolutely ahead.

"So the patrols run more efficiently, and everyone's happier," said Aethal. "Including your captain, I'd wager. I see."

Gehlen smiled. "That's it exactly, my Lord."

Aethal sighed. Gehlen was a City Watchman, not an army officer. Any cavalryman who heard a captain say "I see," in the tone Aethal had just used would have been quaking, not grinning.

"Lieutenant Gehlen, why are you here?"

"We're on patrol, sir." Now the man was puzzled.

"And what are you patrolling to find?"

"Anyone touched by Lotus, sir."

"Good. And how will you discover them?"

"We shine the lantern in their eyes, sir."

"And if they run?"

Now Gehlen was confused. "We'd chase them, sir."

Aethal nodded. "And how do you know the difference, Gehlen, between a Lotus-eater trying to stay hidden and an honest man running away because he doesn't want to spend all night carrying a pole?"

"I..." the words caught in Gehlen's throat. "I don't know, sir."

"Gossip and complaining spreads even faster than Lotus, Lieutenant. In the Army or the Watch, we simply beat the shit out of complainers until they stop. This is a city, though, and you can't stop the dockers from complaining at their work any more than you can keep them from drinking after it. Tomorrow twenty men will know what you were about to put that man through, just for running afoul of your patrol. Tomorrow, ten of those men will run from you so it won't happen to them. Will you catch them all? All, Lieutenant? Because if even one escapes, then you won't know whether you've got a petty criminal or a Lotus Eater on your hands, will you?"

Gehlen was breathing hard now. "No, sir. No, I won't."

"That's right, you won't," said Aethal, in a more conversational tone of voice. "So, you'd better confine yourselves to using prisoners who are actually guilty of something, hadn't you?"

"Yes, sir."

"Good, because when you do that," Aethal said, "all you have to worry about is something like this." Aethal bent and whirled, sweeping the bottom of the pole around in a full circle. Four men went down, including Lieutenant Gehlen. Lorch managed to keep his feet until Aethal whipped the iron-shod end of the pole into his stomach, sending him to his knees, gasping for breath.

"Stay down!" Aethal roared. The four prison guards froze on their knees. Aethal reversed the iron lantern and slowly brought it to Gehlen's flushed, staring face. He spoke softly, trying not to look at Farnan, who was trying to look stern but not wholly succeeding. The crowd watching them cheered and hollered at the show. When the noise died down, Aethal spoke, pitching his voice to carry.

"There are men in the Fleet who are trained to fight on five-foot seas against the Weedrats and the Wellspawn they hunt. They manhandle ships' masts and spars in far worse weather. Try your little impression trick on one of them, and you could all be dead if you're foolish enough to put him in your midst and arm him with an eight-foot war club. This is why we say, '*It is the Discipline. By Discipline we live.*' Have I made myself clear?"

Gehlen nodded convulsively. "Yes, my Lord."

Aethal threw the lantern to him. "I will be speaking to the Lord Mayor about this. And about you, Lieutenant. You will continue with your patrol, except for Corporal Lorch, who will accompany me to the Winery for his serious breach of Discipline. The prison guards, it seems, have the idea that being on a Lotus patrol means harassing people. I wouldn't let that happen anymore if I were you. Understood?"

"Yes, sir!"

"I will send you proper replacements as soon as I can. Dismissed."

Are all our Watches so blind? I thought we were better than this! *Am I only wasting good oil and wood to have set them patrolling the streets? Where is their Discipline? We can't teach them all.*

Even here, despite Yakuz Skraalen's *words, Lotus has been a danger to conjure with for so long that no one's really afraid of it. It's too big. Like the Well itself, it's a word to curse with, and a story to scare children.* Wish me dead, *we say. Or even,* Wish me live forever. *Is this how the world ends: suicide by disbelief?*

"Let's move." They turned for Maednac Serpiin and the Winery.

"Take point," muttered Aethal to Farnan. He dropped back to walk beside Sergeant Falk. "Did these men go through your training, Sergeant?"

The big man nodded. "Or one of my cadre. Or Maednac's Own. No man goes out on Lotus patrol without going through it"

"Then what do you have to say about Corporal Lorch's behavior?"

"About what I'd expect from one of the Lord Low Jailer's men, sir. The City Watch washouts go into the prisons. But we had to train them, too. He's been through the Discipline and had his chances same as the others. You want any more use out of him, then shoot him as an example to the rest." His voice was cold and hard as stone.

Aethal ordered Farnan to go on to the Winery. Then he stepped into an alley and lowered his voice: "Sergeant, I expected soldiers trained in the Discipline, not wreckage to be thrown away."

"Then you shouldn't have sent me trash, sir," Falk replied, evenly. "Did you expect that when you raised the cry of 'Lotus,' every Madlands gutter-snipe would rise to his duty like a gentleman? That's not what training *does*, sir. Training only tells you whether a man can do what he has to without breaking. It doesn't change what he is inside, or what he *will* do given half a chance. That only comes out in the field and the streets, and then you've got a choice of how to use what you've got. Well, you've got Lorch, and a lot of men like him. Use him like the lord you are. Just like you've used the rest of us. You've had plenty of practice. Don't stop now. You've got two kinds o'men in this world: men who fight Lotus, and men who feed it. That man's soul is a farm for Lotus whether he ever takes a bite o'the leaf or no. This is fighting the Lotus, and it looks like dead men. Don't shy away from it because I've suggested you get yer white fingers dirty."

Aethal stepped closer. "Are you a judge of men's souls, now, Sergeant? I already have too many men fighting other men. I have, in that tower," he pointed up at the Hydraxis, "a great many fools, blaming the Lotus on one another. The Lord Chancellor blames the Conversant. The Conversant blames the King. The King, to his credit, has laid no blame yet." *Except upon Maednac, and praise the Moon-that-was no one else seems to have heard about that.* "What shall I do? Use them all? Put them all to the Sword, as leafeaters?"

The two men stared at one another. Finally, Falk spoke, and his brogue was gone. "You talk of men blaming Lotus on men as the work of fools? Then how foolish is it to blame men being men on the Lotus, Captain? This kingdom's used Madlanders whether we ever wore a uniform or not. Skraalen knows it: we're loyal to King and City, yes. Because anywhere else we go, we're spit on. Only the Fleet loves us. Only the King will have us. Unless we're low enough to work for the likes of Skraalen, that is. You really think all those men in the Fleet are volunteers? Open your eyes. The Lotus? It's the latest excuse to use us."

"You know it's not an excuse, Sergeant."

The Sergeant stepped forward like a mountain. "Oh, yes, sir, it *is* an excuse. And all the greater an excuse for being a real reason. It becomes an excuse the moment any one of us is thrown on a ship or into a patrol, just because it's *easier* to do it to one of us than it is to do it to anyone else. The Green Death may kill us all in the end, but these excuses kill us from the beginning. You need us, but you'll use snakes like Malcoor and Skraalen to gather us for you like a bloody harvest of rats: squeezed dry and broken. And then you'll honor the snakes. You're offering them titles. And after this is over, I and mine get to touch our caps to the man whose money we've been too proud to touch."

The bitterness in Falk's voice was a live thing, reaching out to coil around Aethal's guts. He swallowed. "All right, Sergeant," he said softly. "You are, after all, the one man I know who can tell me how to deliver your people. How to give them something more than an excuse for the use I must demand of them."

Falk looked up at him with eyes hard and scarred as the stones they stood on. "Captain, I took you for a bastard, that day when you blasted half that town to the Well and shot poor Harry Godwin through the head. But I took you for a man: because you brought us out of that damned inn — until I saw your knees turn to water before your father. Why should I take this as anything more than another chance for me and mine to have to finish what you've started?"

A hollow pit opened in Aethal's stomach. He had known, in the moment of its happening, that some choices, even some hesitations, were beyond redeeming.

So don't hesitate this time, the thought cut across his consciousness as abruptly as if it had been Gun's, but the voice was his own, now.

"No reason, Sergeant. I don't have any more damned excuses for myself or for you. Or for what I did. We may none of us finish what's been started. But you know what the Lotus means, whether it's an excuse or no. And you're not going to make it worse for your people than it is now by fighting it."

Aethal could feel Falk looking him up and down. "We'll see, I suppose," he finally said.

"So, what's it going to be, Sergeant? We both know what's before us. We both know I can use you. Only you can tell me whether you're going to be useful. And I need you being useful. What will it be?"

Falk gazed at him. "You have something in mind, sir."

Aethal laughed, and it was a fey sound. "I have a number of things in mind, Sergeant; they flow from my brain like Wishes from a fool."

"Just fight, sir. And let *us* fight. I don't know what they teach in nobles' houses. But just fight. Like you did in Everview when you cut your way through to us. Like you did when you led us down those stairs. There was a man worth following there, for a few minutes."

Aethal smiled hollowly. "Just a few minutes, Sergeant?"

Falk snorted. "Damn few officers worth following even that long, my Lord. And we all know it. Stop fighting, and you've already lost, and they'll desert like that coward Maednac before they'll follow you down one street of this city."

Aethal stood rooted to the street. "You... dare call Maednac a coward, Sergeant?"

"Ran away, didn't he?" said Falk. "Empire's gone."

Aethal nodded, dizzy with hearing his own thoughts, and the king's, echoed here.

"We all die. My folk know that. If not the Green Death, then something. You don't ask if you'll win. You fight. And if you're alive at the end, you won. Does the King know that, my Lord? I know what King Maednac did about the Lotus. What will this King do?"

Aethal replayed the scene of the last king, standing before the image of the first king. A hurled crown, clattering off into the darkness... "You may find this King more of your mind than you know, Sergeant." A smile forced itself to his lips. "Now let's catch up. Double-time."

They trotted after their prisoner and his guards.

***

It was full dark when they reached the Winery. Farnan was waiting for them with the prisoner by one of the stone towers that supported the Winery's bulk. "The Lord Low Jailer of all Verlaen declined to see us. I didn't actually ask, at that. I just got an order from these to 'go away.' I think that means to piss off, doesn't it? But since I have Wyrmguard, and he has..." he looked the two Crownguard at the Winery gate up and down, challengingly, "this... I thought I'd rather not. What do you think?" he asked Lorch. Lorch said nothing, but looked straight ahead as if hoping the world would vanish. The other moaned. Farnan continued. "Aethal. You said Aerhan would never find a post to match his talents!"

Aethal grimaced. "I said I doubted father would let him sink low enough to find the position worthy of him, but I'm forced to admit that he managed."

"Seems safe enough," said Farnan.

Aethal drew him aside, ten paces from the arched prison door. "That's what worries me. Aerhan didn't ask for this position; it's not obviously powerful. As far as I can tell, it's not powerful at all. It's nowhere near glamorous enough to suit him. Which means my father picked it for him. And that troubles me."

"Why?"

"Why would he want his favorite son in it? No idea. But he does; that's enough." Aethal released Farnan, who nodded. They approached the guards.

"Corporal," Aethal said to the soldier on duty, "We're going to see Aerhan. Pardon me, Lord Low Jailer Aerhan Paaling of the Wrackberg. Is he about?"

The soldier nodded, but blurted, "Sir, the Master of the Royal Dungeons has left strict instructions that no one disturbs him."

"Corporal," said Aethal quietly, "I am sure that the Master of the Royal Dungeons must also have left strict instructions that no man under his command is to use Lotus as an excuse to take unwilling women into his cells, and yet that is what we caught your fellow here doing. My brother will not take kindly to this, and more importantly, neither do I. Now, move."

"Yes, sir!" The corporal braced to attention.

"Corporal, secure the prisoner!" bawled Farnan. "Double time!"

At the top of the winding stone stairs, they followed the corporal down a long corridor lined with open-work wooden cells. The odor of unwashed bodies and chamberpots was palpable. Their heels threatened to slide on the warped and sticky planks, but they walked past the cells, nearly all of which were empty. No doubt they were out repairing the king's roads or working his mines.

"You think Aerhan will come down on him?" Farnan said, as they climbed more stairs.

"Our prisoner? If he doesn't, I'm coming down on him. I'm not about to sit idly because it suits him to play Little Gold God of a castle, even if it is a prison." Perfumed candles burned in this stairwell, somewhat keeping the sewer reek at bay, though the effect was mostly to make the candles smell as if they were about to spoil.

Aerhan's chambers were on top of the Winery, in the old observation turret, and the Greater Moon shone through the window, drawn to let the sea breeze in. Aethal did not bother to knock. Aerhan was writing at his desk. When he looked up, his face twisted in anger.

"How dare you force your way up here?" He yanked the bellpull by his desk sharply, and a sharp alarm-tone sounded. "Lotus notwithstanding, it gives you no right to run through my jurisdiction without so much as a by-your-leave. Get out at once; I have things to attend to."

"But Lotus gives you and your men the right to pull girls off the street because they have a convenient color to their eyes?" asked Aethal. "Farnan, the Sergeant and I have just seen how your men look for Lotus, Aerhan. This one, I'm shooting in the morning." There was a scuffle of feet behind him as a quartet of Aerhan's jailers answered his summons. He raised his voice. "For violating Discipline, Corporal Lorch, you are summarily sentenced to death."

Aethal kept his face a mask of stone, but his guts twisted, watching the man's face turn to pasty dough, lips working soundlessly, tears streaming down his face. "You men," Aethal said to the four jailers, whose eyes were wide with terror, "are just in time to escort this man to a condemned cell." *Or to face Wyrmguard,* did not need to be said. They swarmed their former companion and dragged him away just as he started screaming.

Aerhan flushed, his voice sullen. "*You* speak of Discipline. I'll have you know that trespassing in his Majesty's prison is a crime itself."

"I bet it's not one you charge many people with," quipped Farnan. "Aren't most of them trying to get out?"

Suddenly, Aerhan smiled up at him. "Oh, yes. We lose a lot of prisoners that way," he whispered. "A man tries to escape, you can't let him go. Lives might be in danger. They leave us no choice." Slowly, he pulled out a pistol. Ebony chased in copper, and an aluminum-plated barrel. "Why, I even had to shoot one myself a few nights ago. Crazy, breaking out in full view of the Master of the Royal Dungeons."

He brags about shooting unarmed prisoners, thought Aethal. The implication shot through him. When he spoke, his voice was chill: "And how crazy was General Malcoor?"

Aerhan flushed red. "Crazy enough, but I didn't shoot him. No, I'm afraid I have no idea where he is. I doubt he'll ever be found."

"Really?" said Aethal. "Curiously defeatist attitude. The King might not like it."

"Yes, he's quite upset. I shall no doubt have to offer my sincerest apologies," Aerhan spoke the words as if they tasted bad.

"It's not going to stop, Aerhan." Aethal advanced on his brother. "You keep acting as though we're going to forget the General. That you'll be allowed to cover it over. It won't be allowed, this time. I won't allow it."

"*You* won't?" Aerhan looked up fearlessly. "What more are you going to do, Aethal? You've searched my dungeons. Westerend *helped* you search them, for all the good that did. And you found nothing." And he smiled again.

"Well," Aethal whispered, "perhaps we haven't been searching the right way. Perhaps we should be searching your memory." He raised his fists. He'd wanted to take Aerhan apart for a long time, and five years in the Cavalry had given him the training to do it. Aerhan's right hand — with the pistol — rose.

"Do it and you're a dead man," warned Aethal. "I won't be able to save you."

Aerhan looked at the pistol in his hand. Then he looked at the two Wyrmguard.

"They look a little long in the tooth for Wyrmguard. Slowing down, maybe?"

Aethal stepped back. "If you want to duel it," he said, "Be my guest. That one last died defending Maednac himself."

Aerhan looked at the weapon again. "You defended Maednac?" He tried to make it a sneer, and half-succeeded.

"In this very fortress." The Wyrmguard might have been commenting on the weather.

Aerhan snorted. "Not very well, obviously, if your mount was slaughtered. How did you manage to get the poor bastard killed?"

"The fortress was just being completed, and Maednac had come to inspect it. He walked from this tower down to the ammunition pits. It was one of the native workers who sprang at him from a cornice. He thought Maednac's forces would bring the Lotus from the Empire with him. I interposed my mount and killed the assassin in my mount's dying moments. Maednac was pleased. But even his pleasure did not attach me to a new mount. Gold is not popular for bullets."

So long ago, and this creature remembered it like yesterday. But there was no soul in the retelling. No memory of Maednac the man. And why should there be? Something itched at Aethal's mind, but he couldn't place it.

He turned to his brother and Irontooth. "Take my brother to apartments in the Hydraxis. See that he is placed under arrest…" Aethal stopped. Aerhan had turned quite pale. Under threat of arrest in comfortable rooms? With father available to, more than likely, countermand Aethal's order? Surely not. Why would talk of arrest wipe that smug grim off his face?

It exploded in Aethal's mind like the sun. "Goldhammer. There are no ammunition pits in the Winery."

"Not now. But when this was a fortress, before the guns had been removed, there were two, below the towers."

"Show me," Aethal breathed. "And Irontooth, take my brother with us. Hold him. And if he tries to say a word to anyone but us, shoot him."

It didn't take long for Aethal to find the vast trap doors; they covered nearly half of the tower's width, so big you could step right on them in the dim light and never know you were on a door at all. They had no bolts in the floor, but two crowbars hung on the walls, inserted through knotholes, brought the floor creaking up. Aerhan, subdued but defiant, gazed into the hole.

Signaling for a torch, Aethal and Goldhammer descended into the darkness. The staircase descended further, but Aethal stopped at the small door set in a corner cell beneath the stairs. Pulling out Aerhan's keys, he opened it, holding his breath.

A tall, thin man in uniform blinked away from the light.

"General Malcoor, I presume?" asked Aethal, hardly able to wait for the reply.

"You've already presumed enough for ten lifetimes, Paaling," came the growl of a man who was in great thirst. "What more do you want?"

Aethal held the torch closer to his face, so that the General could see him. "I am not your jailer, General. In fact, I want more than anything else to set you free."

Malcoor blinked, and turned toward the light. "The voice is the same," he said. "But not the face. Not quite. Who are you, boy?"

"Aethal Paaling, House Wrackberg," said Aethal, going to his knees, so he could get at the General's manacles. "I was under your command, once."

The General moved back. "Oh. *That* Paaling. Not a bad soldier. But Paaling, still."

Aethal laughed softly. "We can none of us help our relations, can we, sir?" The old general glowered at that, and Aethal knew he had been understood. "But I am the Last Sword of the King in my own right, and His Majesty desires to see you at once. Indeed, we have all been looking for you these past weeks."

"The King and I have never been friends, boy," said Malcoor, but he let Aethal unlock his chains. "Not since before you were born. If he wanted to see me, well... it isn't as though he didn't know where I was. What does he want me for? Verlaen invaded and all hope lost?" He barked a humorless laugh. Then saw the expression on Aethal's face.

"What has happened?" said the general, finally.

"Lotus," Aethal said.

Malcoor swayed, and leaned against the cell wall for support. "Who did it?" he asked.

"We don't know. But we need all your help, sir. I must bring you before the King."

"If the King wanted me, surely all he had to do was send for me," said Malcoor, acidly.

"No, sir," said Aethal. "I am afraid you were never arrested. You were kidnapped. Please, follow me."

Aethal climbed from the pit, fury building as his eyes fixed on the creature calling himself his brother. "Why, Aerhan?" he asked.

Aerhan's breathing came fast, and his eyes darted from side to side, seeking an escape. "I have nothing to say to you," he breathed.

"You are the greatest traitor in history," Aethal said. The words felt unreal. He'd never had any use for his brother; he'd suspected his brother of knowing something. But *this...* "You'll speak soon enough. It's the only reason I'm not having you shot right now. Goldhammer, bring me those manacles. When we get to the Hydraxis, throw him in his own dungeons there. Alone. And tell his majesty: We've found General Malcoor."

Chapter Two

46th of Spring, 312 Exodus

In the Sky Chamber, Aethal watched his father's humiliation before the King of Verlaen. For such a long fall, it took surprisingly little time.

"So, the lost is at last found," said King Paitir. He looked from General Malcoor to his Chancellor, like a starving man marooned for a month might look at a landing ship. His lips trembled, though whether in rage or relief or fear, Aethal could not have said.

Paal's brokenness and silence was unnervingly pathetic.

"Your Majesty," he began. "Aerhan..."

"I am not prepared to discuss that creature at this time, Chancellor," said the king. "He shall have a trial in due time. And then he shall have justice."

"Yes," husked Paal. "Of course, Sire, by your leave, I have the duty to... to inform my son of the consequences of his actions. I must tell him."

The king nodded. "I grant your request."

Paal bowed stiffly, and left.

"General Malcoor." The king turned to him, and water stood in his eyes. "Beyond hope, you are returned to us."

The General's mouth tightened. "Then hope is suddenly closer than it used to be. Your Majesty. Had you desired my return from beyond hope, you had only to send to the Pass. I was there all the time."

The king laughed briefly, a flat, humorless bark. "And when we did send for you, on quite another matter, you vanished. A week ago, I had visions of offering half my kingdom for you to come back and aid us. I never dreamed to find you in my own dungeons. Certainly not after your own patron had searched them." Paitir's gaze turned upon Aethal. "I am most curious, Last Sword, as to how that was possible."

"Your Majesty, Aerhan had discovered disused and forgotten rooms in the Winery, which he had converted into secret cells. He was holding the General there." Aethal related how Goldhammer's clue and Aerhan's own carelessness had led him to find the General.

"Why?"

Aethal shook his head. "I do not know why. He would not say."

"Give me some time with him, Your Majesty," said Malcoor, softly, fixing the king with burning eyes. "He will say."

Paitir met Malcoor's gaze. "We shall consider this. But now, we have more important things to discuss. Please, General, sit. We do wrong to keep you in discomfort." He ordered refreshment brought. "I would like you to consider yourself our honored guest. Rooms shall be made available to you in the Hydraxis, and we shall keep you from them no longer than necessary. If you find yourself wanting for anything, you have but to ask."

"Uncle!"

The cry of joy burst from Ardyth, who ran into the chamber as fast as the door could be forced out of her way. Behind her was Lord Westerend, his face open and dazed, his eyes locked on his brother as though he were a ghost who might vanish from sight. Two Wyrmguard moved to intercept Ardyth, but desisted at a shake of Aethal's head.

Malcoor embraced his niece, a tear running down his face. "Ardya, child." He said the words over and over, like a mantra against...

Thirty years of house arrest, doubtless, thought Aethal. Eventually, Malcoor disentangled himself from his niece, and embraced his brother. Aethal looked away, not sure whether to be embarrassed or envious.

Finally, Malcoor looked back up at the king. "Your pardon, Sire." They all sat. "I hope you will not take it too much amiss," said Malcoor, "if I say that I am not interested in half your kingdom. I understand its value has been dropping rapidly since my arrest." The king winced at this, but nodded.

"General, I will not pretend that you owe us or Maednac's Line any particular affection, but you have been a loyal officer in our service for forty years. And the Lotus is no respecter of persons. The people of the kingdom need you."

"I have always served them," said Malcoor, stiffly. "What have you done thus far, Sire? Have you given the Fleet orders to prepare Verlaen for evacuation?"

King Paitir returned his gaze. "Evacuate where, General? Did you find some place for our people in your voyages? A safe haven for a colony that you did not mention to us?"

Malcoor's face closed. "I disclosed to your Majesty the condition of all the lands that I found in my voyages. All of them." His jaw clenched. He sat rigid in his chair. "It was by your majesty's command that I sailed West of the Prime in search of the Empire's Treasury. And it was your royal pleasure to reward me for my success and for my loyalty by removing me from my Fleet command. If I had found any such paradise, I would have returned to it."

"Then where would you lead us?" asked the king. "How can we evacuate Verlaen to sea? We need more than that, General. My Last Sword said that there was evidence that you discovered... that you might have... a cure for the Lotus?" Paitir's voice was strained to the breaking point with the hope of it.

Malcoor froze. Unblinking, he said, "And how would he know?"

"It was my doing, Joseth," said Vaughan. "I had to make them understand how much we needed you. And the Last Sword has been... honorable toward us. Tell them now what you have withheld all these years. Tell us where to find the cure for Lotus."

General Malcoor's face went milk-white. "Vaughan. You didn't," he said. "You didn't tell him about that? You swore!"

Vaughan looked surprised. "I had no choice! And I could tell them nothing more than they knew…"

The king interrupted: "Name your price, General, and I swear it will be given you." He was pale, but still. "My life for your revenge, if it please you. But help us now."

Malcoor's eyes glittered as he met the king's gaze. Then he rose, looking around the room, as if seeing it for the first time. "You think I would ask for your crown, Majesty? Or, the Well drown us all, the head beneath it? I am not so kind." He stared out the huge windows. "You ask the price," he said softly, "for my aid. Then here it is: I knew there was something wrong when the arresting soldiers came for me, but I truly thought that it would just be a matter of a few bribes and threats. Peculation, that was the charge, was it not?"

"Yes," said the king.

"That charge is to be dropped, and a formal apology delivered to me by the crown," Malcoor said. "This, and the news of my unjust seizure by Aerhan Paaling will be made public in as many ways as you can think of. As well as my promotion to Grand Admiral."

The king stared at him. "There is no rank of Grand Admiral," he finally said.

"There is now," said Malcoor.

The king let out a slow breath and then said, "I think it may save quite a bit of time if I simply revive the rank of Warmaster."

Aethal's heart faltered. With that, Paitir had just given Malcoor charge of every armed man in Verlaen save the Wyrmguard alone, and a title unused since the building of the Hydraxis.

Malcoor nodded. "There is one more thing." He stepped forward. Aethal caught his breath. Malcoor had always possessed a commanding presence, but the reserve and distance Aethal had come to know in his time at the Pass had fallen from him like a cloak.

His lips turned up, and he looked at his brother and niece. "You will remove the stain of bastardy from my head. You will say that evidence has been discovered that I am a legitimate son of Westerend." Triumph shone in his face. "Do all this, and I am yours to command."

Aethal blinked. Bastardy could *not* be legitimized. It was an eternal stain on the soul. The king looked stunned. "Do you have such evidence?"

"Of course not. It is not for me to discover, but for you to fabricate. The method I leave to you."

"It will be done," said Paitir steadily. "I have manufactured bigger lies for worse cause."

"I will have your word upon it," said Malcoor.

"By Maednac's Sword and Name, and before these witnesses I swear, all this you have asked shall be done." The king gave the words of the formal oath.

Malcoor sat, and stared at the king with the same look Aethal remembered from his days as a young officer at the Pass. "Where is the Lotus, and how contained is it?"

"The Lotus is among the Grassworms of the Grain Sea. General Jeharok is trying to hold it back, but some of the clans have broken through and are in the Grain Sea itself. Tomorrow, an army will leave for the Pass. It will destroy the clans that have broken through, and then proceed to the Treeline, where it will force its way through the clans blocking the road to the Westerend. With the Skysil forces coming down from the north, we should be able to burn them and the Lotus out."

Malcoor nodded. "We may need to burn the Grain Sea entirely," he said.

The king looked at him. "I have considered that. General Jeharok himself has already suggested it, and may be doing it. But the cure, General? Surely we do not need to take such drastic measures now that we have it."

Malcoor sighed. "It is not as easy as that, Sire. The cure my brother told you of has both limits," he looked as if he had bitten into something bitter, "and a price."

"I have promised to meet your price!" King Paitir cried in anger and despair.

"Not my price," Malcoor said. "Its own. And that is why I never told anyone — not even Vaughan — where or how I found it." When Malcoor's silence threatened to stretch on, Aethal took the old journal from his pouch.

"It was here, wasn't it, sir?" he asked. He handed it to Malcoor, turned to the page showing the Lotus grown large as a Keepwood.

Malcoor took the book, face open in wonder. "You knew the significance of these, boy?"

"It's why I've been looking for you all this time, sir." Aethal said. "We thought that for you to get so close, you must have discovered something."

Malcoor laughed, a black, bitter sound. "Oh, yes, I discovered something. Do you know where this is, Last Sword?"

"You're on the shores of the Republic, General."

Malcoor gave him a long look. Then he nodded.

"The Republic. Which I was investigating at the Chancellor's orders." Here he looked hard at the king.

"Since you were never charged with the crime of violating Maednac's Ban and sailing West of the Prime," said the king, coolly, "I cannot write you a pardon for it, unless you wish me to charge you and then pardon you. Pray go on, General."

Malcoor frowned, then nodded. "As you can see, I was right. If there were a cure for Lotus, it would be in the Free Republic." Aethal got the distinct impression that he was listening to the resolution of an argument that had begun before he had been born. "But as with the Lotus, the agents of the Republic got what they Wished for, and not what they wanted. When we approached the shoreline of Ys-Grillaf, the Republic's ancient seat, I saw no trace of Lotus, yet we had seen the smoke of fires off its shore. Being neither reckless, nor a complete fool; without those signs, I should never have dared a landing. That picture," he gestured to his journal, "was drawn later. Off another shore."

"Soon after our landing, we were met by... people," Malcoor hesitated, and a strange look came over his face. "Of a sort."

"What do you mean?" asked the king, obviously torn between curiosity and impatience.

"Forgive me," Malcoor said. "I never have decided whether they were people in our sense of the word. They have been much... changed by their homeland. But that is not important. They speak a pidgin of Vaerlaisni which made talking with them possible, and they took me to their homes. They were not afraid of us, you see... afraid!" Malcoor gave a short laugh, with tears in it. "But of course you don't see, I haven't come to that part, yet."

"Are you feeling quite well, General?" the king asked. Incredulity was in his voice, and indeed, Aethal had to agree that the General seemed like a man on the verge of hysteria. Lord Vaughan touched his brother on the shoulder.

"He's been under enormous strain, Sire," the Lord of the Westerend said, half-reproachfully. "If it weren't for the crisis of Lotus, this man should be in bed." But Malcoor waved him away.

"It's all right, Vaughan. It's just... I never did talk of this with anyone. We didn't even speak of it among ourselves, those of us who went. It's harder than I thought it would be." He drew in a deep breath.

"They took us to their homes, to bargain with them. To trade. But before we went, they gave us — they insisted that we share — the *yasnuum*. That's what they call it, in any case. Otherwise, they said, the Green Madness would take us. You can imagine that we did as they said."

"Indeed," muttered Vaughan.

"Despite that, I have to tell you, we were all more frightened than we'd ever been in our lives," said Malcoor, "And I set a guard on the boats to leave without us, should we fail to return. And we made the most solemn oaths that we'd shoot each other, should we eat of the Lotus. And then we ate of the *yasnuum*. And we weren't frightened anymore."

Malcoor looked each of them in the face. "You may think that was a fine thing, but I tell you, it was terrible. All my fear, all my hope, all my anger, all my," he groped for words, "heart. It was gone within seconds. Melted away. I still knew who I was, and why I was there, and that the Lotus was dangerous. I knew I could die in the next hour. But none of that mattered. It was as though my very soul had been killed within me."

"Then we followed the people to their village, and we walked among the Lotus."

The king and Lord Vaughan drew in breath. Ardyth clutched her father's arm. Even Aethal felt his lips draw back. *But it's not possible that Malcoor brought it back, not thirty years ago.*

"You see why I never mentioned this," Malcoor said, grinning like a skeleton. "The Lotus grew in vines and thick clusters of leaves all around the village. We walked among it, and smelled it. You can't imagine what the smell is like."

"I don't have to imagine it," said Aethal.

Malcoor stopped. "Indeed?" he said softly. "Then you're a good man, Aethal Paaling. As for the rest of you, I hope you never can. But despite the smell, we felt no hunger for it whatever. Yet all the while I knew without a moment's doubt that I would have filled my belly to bursting were it not for the *yasnuum*. But that was not the worst."

Malcoor's voice was quiet, his words measured like the steps of marching men. "I saw them harvesting the Lotus, as we would harvest grapes. Did you know that the Lotus bears fruits? I imagine no one does. By the time the stuff is mature enough to bear them, normal men would already have been killed by eating the leaves. But it does. I watched that fruit being eaten. Being squeezed for the juice. Silver-skinned fruits with deep purple flesh. They roasted them. They wrapped meat with the leaves. They pounded the stalks to flour and made them into bread."

Aethal saw the dread that he felt crawling up his spine mirrored on the faces of everyone in the room. But Malcoor continued. "They offered it to us, of course. And of course, we refused. They could not understand why. The *yasnuum* would keep us from harm. And we could see it was true. They were perfectly reasonable. Reason rules. How could it not, when the *yasnuum* removes all passion, all fear from among them? And that was perhaps the most terrible thing. I refused to eat the Lotus only because of my oath. Because I knew that breaking it would disgrace me in the eyes of my men, and degrade my authority. Not because I was afraid. I could not be afraid. Not even when I sat down to negotiate with the man whose eyes were green with Lotus."

"But you said it protected them!" said Ardyth. Her voice was loud in the chamber.

"Yes," her uncle said. "It does. And the most horrible punishment they can inflict for a crime is to withdraw the *yasnuum* from one of their number. Their chief bargainer had suffered this fate, for a time. He told me all about it, when I challenged him. I thought that they had told us a lie, and therefore could not be trusted. But he explained everything. He had nothing to hide. He felt no shame. He felt nothing at all."

Malcoor turned to Vaughan. "What I told you, all those years ago, when I was drunk and you visited me in the Pass was true. There is a cure for Lotus. But you see why I did not go into detail, brother. The cure is... its own disease."

Aethal's mind spun. "Then it won't work on anyone who has already become infected by the Lotus?"

"No, it works perfectly," said Malcoor. "It will keep him alive. It will stop the madness of the Lotus. It just doesn't kill the Lotus that has already grown. It will hold the Lotus in check, as long as you keep taking it. The *yasnuum* will even stop the Lotus growing, if you plant it right."

"God-Beyond-The-World," whispered the king. "God-Beyond-The-World, I don't know whether to grant you land and titles or have you hanged for treason. Why didn't you bring it back?"

"I did, your Majesty," said Malcoor.

The silence was absolute.

"What?" said Paitir.

"I brought it back. All that I could. I filled my pockets while my hosts were not looking. None ever suspected. Not even those among my own crew. In its raw state, it looks very much like rock, for all that they grow it."

"Then you can grow this thing?" cried the king, voice wild with hope.

"No, your Majesty," said Malcoor, softly. "They would not sell that secret. Not for any price. They claimed it was the legacy of their people. Theirs alone. They meant to keep it. And so, when our bargaining was completed, and I had what we had come for," he looked hard at the king, "I led my two companions, the only others who had seen these people and tasted the *yasnuum*, aside from the path. And then," Malcoor trembled as he spoke, "I drew my pistols, and put a bullet through each man's brain. Then I told the crew that they had been murdered by our hosts, and I alone had escaped, that there was nothing but savages on the island."

"But why?" Aethal wondered who had spoken, and realized it was him.

"The *yasnuum* made it all so clear. I knew that they would speak of what they had seen, and that I would not. The *yasnuum* removed all the guilt or feeling that would have made me hesitate an instant. For I knew that if people once believed that there was any "cure" for the Lotus, they would never listen to any warning I could give. They would consider all the wealth of the Empire, and would risk their very souls to reach the *yasnuum,* thinking it would let them plunder in safety. But the *yasnuum* is guarded by the Lotus itself. Imagine what could happen if we tried to steal it and failed. Imagine what could happen, if we succeeded. I have. Many, many sleepless nights, I have imagined that.

"But yes, I brought back some of the *yasnuum*. I never spoke of it... except the once, to Vaughan. Hoped he'd forgotten. I have it hidden away. But nothing I have done for thirty years has induced it to grow. Perhaps the soil is not right, or the weather. Or perhaps — heh — perhaps it *needs* Lotus nearby to grow. Whatever the truth, I was never tempted to go back, even if I could discover the secret. The risk was too great that someone — perhaps even I — might come back with a cargo of Lotus."

"Perhaps that is what happened," said Paal. They had all been so engrossed in Malcoor's story that none of them had seen the Chancellor come in.

Malcoor's head whipped around. "I told you I was the only one who knew the secret, Wrackberg! Or do you mean to suggest that I managed to get all the way back to the Glorious Republic while being exiled to the Pass at the same time?"

Paal held up a hand, "Peace, General. I meant no such thing. If you had brought back the Lotus thirty years ago, we would have known it then. But the *yasnuum*, as you call it, is there. The Lotus is there. Other things... are doubtless still there. Assuming you kept your word, all these years..."

Malcoor shot to his feet. "I'll not take that from you, you lying get of Well-spawned bastard!"

In the silence that followed the deadly insult, Chancellor Paal only blinked. "Are you quite finished, General? You couldn't goad me into a duel thirty years ago, and you'll not goad me into one now. I was going to say that whether or not you kept your word given all those years ago, it was always possible that others could discover what you discovered. Also, for what it's worth, I agree with your reasoning. You protected us from a great evil."

"What?" said Malcoor, clearly puzzled by Paal's unexpected support.

"What is all this about?" demanded Aethal, frowning. "Ever since the General disappeared, I've been hearing dark hints about his Fleet career and this mysterious voyage he made before I was born." His father was staring at him. "Yes, Chancellor, I have sources of my own." He wasn't about to bring Uncle Pyk into this. "Now obviously the General — or Commodore — didn't give you his word to keep the cure a secret, because no one but Lord Vaughan knew about it. So what was it that was so damned important that he got exiled for it?"

All four of the older men stared at him as though the furniture had spoken.

Finally, his father spoke. "There's no harm in telling him, now." Paal picked up Malcoor's journal, turned to a page near the back, and faced it out.

"There it is. He drew it himself." His finger touched the twin peaks of green in the background. "What do you think these are?"

Vaughan looked blank. Aethal had no idea what his father was talking about. But Paitir's jaw was set, and his eyes sad. "The death of the kingdom," the king muttered. "Almost as surely as the Lotus."

"They're grass-covered mountains," said Aethal. "If they're covered with Lotus, it's no more dangerous than the Lotus here," he stabbed a finger at the foreground.

"Hah!" snorted Malcoor. "Look at the scale, boy. Any mountain that tall would be bare rock and snow at the summit. But those mountains conduct the sun's heat too evenly for that."

What was green that would conduct heat? The answer overwhelmed him. Not...

"Copper," said Malcoor. "That's what we went out for. That's what those... people sold us. Worthless to them. Riches beyond measure to us," he breathed. "And that made me too dangerous to send to sea again, didn't it, Majesty?"

"Yes," King Paitir breathed, eyes hooded.

"But..." spluttered Vaughan, "The nation would be rich! You exiled him for finding the greatest treasure in the world?" He echoed Aethal's thoughts.

Paitir laughed, almost a cackle. "Oh, yes. Rich. You see now why I need Paal Haerling as my Chancellor after all; *he* understands. Too well, perhaps, but he understands." Paitir flipped a coin through the air at Aethal, who caught it. It was a big copper coin, a Royal Tree. "Take it, Aethal. As a gift from your King, a reward for a job loyally and well done."

"Thank you, Sire," Aethal began. "But I..."

Paitir had a double handful of the coins in front of him now; he had emptied his purse. He tossed one to Flintmaw, who caught it mechanically. Before Aethal could protest that Wyrmguard had no use for money, the king flung another coin at Lord Vaughan, and one at Ardyth. They both caught the coins reflexively. The one aimed at Malcoor, Aethal noted, he let fall with a glare. The king snorted. "Not enough, my General? Then perhaps a special coin for you. It's not a bribe, nor a payment; put your sour face away, but catch this."

The throw was short, though the coin looked like all the others. Malcoor had to take a step forward, and then nearly dropped it. It had the reddish sheen common to the rest of the coins. "The King, passing false coin, your Majesty?" asked Malcoor. He passed it to Aethal. The coin was as heavy as lead. He bent it, and the metal gave easily. Copper plate fell off the coin as fine dust, revealing... "Gold?" Aethal said, puzzled. "A gold coin?"

"Yes," said Paitir. "Your father tells me we might actually be able to use it as currency again, of a sort. Cheap coins only, of course, worth much less than copper. But gold isn't very common in Verlaen, though it's flashy enough that there's tons of it about in manufactured form. We might be able to do it."

"No one would accept a gold coin," Ardyth whispered.

"Which is why we decided against it," replied the king. "The people would panic if we started issuing gold coin, and trade would go to hell. What we needed was copper."

"And the price was increasing. Still is. Has been for years. Verlaen relies on the Fleet for so many things: whale oil, serpentsblood, krakenfish, and our own coastal trade, as well as keeping the Weedrats from raiding the coast or from uniting against us. If we want to keep the Fleet at sea, we've got to be able to copper their hulls. Otherwise, you get barnacles and hellborers, and then you have to build new ships every year.

"So, when Commodore Malcoor found this book..."

Aethal started. "Found it?"

Malcoor nodded. "Oh, the back half is in my hand, that's plain enough, but the front isn't mine. It's a log from an Imperial Fleet blockade runner. It makes reference to copper-smuggling from the Republic. Just west of the Prime. They made runs there several times."

"When he brought it to us," Paal continued, "The King and I decided that our need was great enough that we would risk an expedition to find this copper mine. We did not expect such an embarrassment of riches. Obviously, someone, long ago, Wished for untold riches. When the Empire found it, they had the sense to keep it very, very secret. Otherwise, it would have ruined them. As it would us, if anyone tried to mine those mountains. And that's assuming the copper would be *all* they brought back."

The king looked Lord Vaughan in the eyes. "Against the better judgment of my Chancellor," he said, "I let the Commodore live. None of the crew knew what they had found, since your brother was smart enough not to land, once he discovered what they were. Now I wonder if some of them suspected anyway. But there was no need to make a martyr of him and start wild speculations as to why."

"Or a civil war," growled Lord Vaughan.

"It was simply made known that he was in disfavor. Perhaps, though, Paal was right after all. Perhaps someone tried for those mountains and found something else there." He trailed off, looking into his own private green hell.

"And now that they have found it," said Paal, "we may as well take advantage of the fact."

King Paitir looked at Paal. "What exactly are you suggesting?"

"General Malcoor has discovered a cure for Lotus. Of a sort. Certainly something far more useful than anything we now have. Given the," he hesitated. "Given the consequences of his return to us, it is perfectly understandable that he kept the knowledge from us.

"The Guardians of the Well have proposed that we send an expedition all the way to the Dark Continent, which no living man has ever seen, to find the lost Kalidranym, the location of which we have only the vaguest guess, and to Wish in the Well. The Church has promised to oppose this, and the idea would face grave opposition from many of our own people, who will not understand the far greater danger that the Lotus poses until it is too late.

"On the other hand, the source of the *yasnuum* is closer, and is known. What exactly do we fear from sending our Fleet there? That they will not return? The

Fleet is not useful against the Lotus anyway. That they will bring back Lotus?" He smiled without humor. "I suggest, your Majesty, that *Admiral* Malcoor return to the Republic, and bring us back this defense."

Malcoor's face might have been a statue's. "You have no idea what you're asking. Truth to tell, I'd rather go on the Guardians' mad expedition to seek the Well. You've no idea what the *yasnuum* feels like. What it does to you."

"No, General, we don't," Aethal heard himself say. "But I know what the Lotus does to you. I've seen that. I've done everything but *tasted* that. I'll risk the *yasnuum*."

Malcoor nodded. "It may be possible. We'll lose men. A lot of men. But give me the Fleet, and I may be able to bring you back the *yasnuum*. Enough to let us destroy the Lotus."

"Joseth," said Vaughan, "Is that really possible? To bring back enough of this protection for all of Verlaen?"

"Of course not," said Malcoor. "Despite the fact that the smallest taste will protect a man for a full day. But we don't need to protect all of Verlaen. We need to protect the Army that's fighting the Lotus. So, you will all have to hold until we return, and we must start as soon as possible."

"As soon as possible had better be 'in the morning,' said Lord Vaughan. "Joseth needs rest, though the damned fool won't show it. And so do we all."

"Agreed," said the king.

***

Aethal escorted General Malcoor from the king's presence, telling two Wyrmguard to take him to his new quarters. "Do you really think that is necessary, Wrackberg?" the General asked.

"Most necessary, sir. It is by his Majesty's request. Goldhammer will even serve as your food-taster. I do not intend to lose you again."

Sergeant Falk rose as they left the Sky Chamber. "My Lord, your brother's adjutant was Major Varth of the City Watch. I have alerted him as you requested. He reports that he is ready to assume command as Acting Lord Low Jailer."

Aethal shook his head. "I know Varth. And I know why my brother chose him as adjutant. He can have his command for the day. But we're going to replace him. I think Lieutenant Farnan can do this job. Send him to me. And well done, Falk."

Falk saluted. "Yes, sir." He turned to go.

"Mr. Falk." The sergeant stopped at the sound of Malcoor's voice. A wintry smile touched Malcoor's lips. "It is you, isn't it? I see you found a place to serve His Majesty after all. The new rank suits you."

Falk's stare back at the General was cold as the sea. "As does yours. *General.*"

Never taking his eyes from Falk, Malcoor said to Aethal, "Last Sword, would you please have the sergeant make the arrangements for my Fleet uniforms in the morning? I'm sure he has lost none of his skill over the years. And I'll need a roster of Fleet Captains, so I'll know what we have to work with."

"Sir, no, sir." said Falk.

Aethal blinked. "Sergeant," said Aethal. "You were given an order."

Falk faced him. "Sir, no, sir. I cannot serve under this man."

Malcoor inclined his head. "I shall leave the matter of insubordination for you to deal with, Last Sword. Good night." Trailed by the two Wyrmguard, Malcoor walked out.

"Sergeant Falk, have you gone mad?" Aethal asked.

"Perhaps, sir." the big man stared hungrily at the door after Malcoor. "But whatever you choose to call it, I cannot serve General Malcoor."

"Explain yourself, Sergeant," Aethal said. "You're a soldier of the King, and General Malcoor is his officer."

"An officer. Yes, sir," said Falk. "And an officer's honor is in his words and his deeds. Sir, I will obey any other officer you care to name; their deeds and words are not in question."

"Sergeant, a soldier making an accusation of that sort about an officer had better…" He thought back to Falk's words. They were straight out of the King's Regulations, from the Officers' Code. "He called you, 'Mr. Falk,' Sergeant." He looked the man in the face. "You were an officer?" The Sergeant looked away. "But not in the Army. I thought it was strange, finding a Madlander in the cavalry. You were a Fleet officer. Under Malcoor."

The sergeant was silent.

"What happened, Sergeant?"

"With respect, sir," said Falk, "I think I've caused the Last Sword quite enough embarrassment. I'd take it as a great favor if you would simply assign me back to the cavalry."

Aethal backed Falk up against the wall, and was surprised at how easy it was. "Sergeant, I need you because I trust you and I need him because of where he's been. I will damned well have both of you, and I will go to the Well before I suffer one more breath of this cloud of secrecy that everyone seems determined to wrap around Commodore Malcoor's last mission. Talk!"

Falk looked daggers at him, and his mouth worked, while his eyes darted back and forth. Aethal relented. Whatever was about to come out, here, a hallway wasn't the place for it. "My quarters, then. With a drink. I owe you that and more." Mutely, Falk followed him.

***

Falk sat across from Aethal with a brandy in his hand and began his story. It was little more than a mumble at first, and Aethal had to strain to hear.

"It was forty days after our last landfall that the lookout called 'land ho,' and reported sighting an island. That's when the trouble began for true. The weather held, you see. Held good for days on end. The sea smooth beneath the wind. The ship running fine. And ahead of us, the island.

"Always, the island was ahead of us, you see. At first, the men didn't even know what they were frightened of, but it didn't take long. You see a coastline, it's sure you'll make landfall the next day, or if the mountains upon it are very tall, or the winds very bad, the day after that.

"We kept that island in sight for a week. And she didn't grow much larger, but she wouldn't go away. The sailors now, they began to curse and be afraid. Some said it was a ghost island: a Land of the Dead in the middle of the ocean, and we'd best turn back. Some said it was Leviathan, the great creature of the deep sea. And some said we were trapped in an enchanted calm, and that the feel of the wind and the snap of the sails was just a Wellspawned dream. Well, they hadn't the training, of course. But the lads and I knew. All of us midshipmen knew, at least part of it, and that was the most frightening part.

"We knew when the navigation lessons had stopped, two weeks before. We knew when the mate began locking up the sextant and the astrolabe. And every night we knew when the stars came out, and there on the edge of the northern horizon were constellations we'd never seen. And even the common sailors noticed how the sun was straight east and west at twilight.

"We were at the Equator. Some whispered that we were West of the Prime, and had broken Maednac's Ban that had held good three centuries. We scarce dared whisper it to each other. We didn't know exactly where we were, because you can't fix longitude at sea. There's no way but the coastline and dead reckoning to know how far you've gone to the west, but we were still going that way, and no soundings were being taken. We wanted to be told we were wrong, somehow. We wanted the stars to come right. We wanted the island to go away or come closer. Me and Elfred, my best mate who I'd shipped with, whispered about it most nights, but we hadn't the nerve to do or say anything.

"It was Haans that first dared to ask the third mate, to find out what had happened. He was the senior of us; it was his duty and right, so he told us, being the son of a margrave.

"He came back down in the middle of the night. Woke us up. His face was red in the lantern light, and he was breathing hard. Through his teeth, he told us that not one of us was to whisper so much as the word 'stars' aloud. Then he lay back in his hammock and bit back a scream. When we tried to help him, he swore at us and said he'd beat us to a pulp. But the next day, I saw the stripes of blood that had soaked through his tunic. He'd been beaten by the mate just for asking.

"Another day went by, and now we could see the island. Only it wasn't an island, it was a land, and what we'd seen for the past week-and-a-half were two mountains behind a low hill. They went up and up, like the peaks around Skysil Bay, only where they have snow on their crown, these mountains were green all the way up.

"We could see the shore when we dropped anchor for the night. That day, just before dawn, Malcoor landed with two young officers and two men. Haans... was one of the officers. Senior midshipman. And all day, we waited. Then, we heard the shots. Two of them. Beat to quarters was sounded and the whole ship roused. Well, Malcoor came back, with the two men. But the officers were gone. Very pale he was, his face dead as a doll's. An hour later, we'd turned around and were making for home. We were told that we had what we'd come for. But what was it? One small chest. It was locked in the hold with a twenty-four hour guard.

"For a few weeks, things improved. The winds held good, and the strange stars shrank below the horizon. We were on the Western Whale Road when we found the guard dead. His throat had been ripped out and there was a hole in the chest the size of a man's head. The sailor who found him said there hadn't been nothing in that chest but some old rocks and shards of what looked like a shell of some kind.

"Malcoor told us that we had to capture that thing. That it was worth a king's ransom and that there'd be a reward for any men who brought it to him... and the yardarm for any man who killed it. He armed us with clubs and nets and sent us all through the hold to hunt it.

"For the next week, we played hide-and-seek with it. Men saw it behind boxes, or on barrels, but it was too fast to be caught. No one could agree on what it looked like except that it was scaly and fast. Some said it was the size of a cat. Others, the size of a dog. Finally, one of the old gunner's mates took a shot at it, but it scampered through the porthole. Malcoor gave him twenty lashes. For shooting at it. Then we didn't see it anymore.

"Most thought it had jumped overboard, but there were the holes in the ship's stores. Food eaten. Malcoor was getting more and more nervous, though the bastard tried not to show it. Finally, he ordered the whole crew to search the hold at once, but nothing came of it. Half of us thought the missing food had been stolen by greedy bastards who'd figured they could blame it on the thing. We'd been out a long time, and all the best food was being rationed by then.

"Then men started to disappear."

Falk took a deep breath.

"The first man went while on watch one night. Fallen overboard, maybe. But then a man disappeared from his hammock. Malcoor doubled the guards. Pairs of men began to vanish.

"Then one day, shots echoed up from the hold, and Lieutenant Svinning ran up, his face white as death, burst into the captain's cabin. Malcoor came out, said we had a mutiny on our hands, and that our own men had taken the hold and the lower gundeck. Malcoor ordered us to retake the ship. So, we formed companies to do just that."

Aethal's stomach crawled, imagining it. The worst kind of shipboard combat, just as bad as the fight at Everview's Inn had been, but instead of Lotus, the ever-present fear of whatever it was Malcoor had been hunting — and God-Beyond-The-World what was *wrong* with the man? — leaping out at you during a fight. A fight against friends, only in a mutiny you couldn't tell yourself that they were infected with Lotus and you were giving them a merciful death. No. That battle would have been sheer and terror-filled slaughter.

"After that fight," Falk said, "we each controlled about half the ship. But we were on quarter-rations because the others," and Aethal noticed that Falk did not say *mutineers,* "had most of the hold. Of course, they had *it* as well. Sometimes at night we could hear them screaming. And firing. I think they hit it, because there were times when the screams weren't human."

"Malcoor," Falk's face twisted with hatred. "Malcoor, he laughed during those times. Said they deserved it for mutiny. He ordered the foredeck battery loaded with grapeshot for the mutineers, and the rear loaded with harpoon shot. In case it changed its mind."

"He was still trying to *capture* the thing?" asked Aethal.

"Oh, yus, he was. It was valuable, and there were always more men in the Madlands. He knew he couldn't hold out, so he ordered our course changed for the Westerend. That night, Lieutenant Svinning and twelve more men deserted him and went belowdecks. They said Malcoor was taking the thing to his patron, Lord Vaughan, and was planning to set up the Lord of the Westerend as a King.

"Well, it went on that way for the next two weeks. We were hungry, and the ship was slowing. Malcoor couldn't understand why we weren't making headway. He even wondered if somehow the others were dragging chains into the water to slow us down. Swore he'd hang every mother's son of them when we made the Twin Fans."

Falk breathed out a long sigh, and his eyes looked into the past. "I don't know what changed its mind. Perhaps it just finally thought it didn't need to hide anymore. I'm sure it thought. That much I know, because it struck just as we were changing the watch. First, we heard the screams from the lower gundeck. And then it burst through the *Webstalker's* hull like it was sailcloth. It was the color of water and sky and it swarmed over the deck. We put bullet after bullet in it like pinpricks. Three times long as a man, with that tail that could cut you in half in a blow. It was hungry, too. It ate men as it killed. Malcoor was screaming at men to get to the guns, to fire. Well, the harpooners couldn't miss at that range. One spear got its wings and pinned it to the deck. The other hit it in the gut. And that's when it flamed.

"The sails burned like lamps in the night. Fire like a hose spraying burning water. It was the first time I ever thought the word *dragon*. And Malcoor just stood there, watching his prize burn his ship, with his mouth hanging open, as it twisted on the foredeck. Then the other battery fired."

By the Well, Aethal thought. *Grapeshot fired along the deck of their own ship.* The deadly hail of lead balls would have blown anyone caught between them and the dragon to bloody fragments.

"By dawn," Falk said, "we had the fire out. The ship was a hulk. All the masts cut down. Half of us dead. A third of the rest were dying. Burns. Shot. But the others were all on deck and now Malcoor had them where he wanted them." The venom in Falk's voice was corrosive and quiet. "The next day, Malcoor had the surviving officers line up on the deck. Officers who'd fought for him on one side, and the... the ones who'd fought belowdecks on the other. Only our line was armed. Said that there was no place for mutineers in the King's Fleet, but that the men had only been following officers' orders, and the officers deserved a clean death for their courage."

Falk drew a long shuddering breath. "Two of them took the hint and just... walked backward into the sea. "The others, well, Malcoor ordered us to take aim. But no one would do it. No one except Commander Maedening, his first officer. He took five pistols and put a bullet through each man's skull. Even the middies, younger than me."

"Elfred?" Aethal asked, softly.

"No. I never saw him again. I don't know whether he was eaten, burned, or jumped overboard to get away. But Maedening would have shot him along with the rest. And Malcoor was willing to sacrifice any number of us to get his prize to the Westerend. We drifted for the next two weeks, with only the current to bring us closer to Verlaen. Then a Fleet Frigate found us.

"They arrested all of us, even Malcoor, when we got to port. No charges, though. After a long time, we were told that Malcoor would never command a ship again. We were made to swear, on pain of death, never to discuss the voyage, or aught that happened on it with any man."

"Then why are you telling me now?" asked Aethal.

Falk looked straight through him. "Would it have mattered before now? Malcoor brought back a terror, but it wasn't Lotus. I thought he was dead and his soul rotting in the Well's Core. Hoped so. But when I was an officer, I swore to protect Verlaen. And you and the King are going to send him out to save it. The King already knows his man. But I figured you should, too.

"When I was released, I resigned my commission. Enlisted in the cavalry. As long as Malcoor was an officer, I swore I'd never be. We only found out about his "promotion" later. And I vowed three more things. I'd never again step foot on a ship of the Fleet, nor ever again serve Commodore Joseth Malcoor."

Aethal let out a breath. "What was the third thing?"

"Taken care of years ago, sir," Falk said calmly. "Captain Maedening was never careful about where he went to drink in the Madlands."

Aethal swallowed. "All right, Sergeant. You won't serve under him. I promise. Dismissed."

"Yes, sir." Aethal watched him leave. *And I thought that finding General Malcoor would be the beginning of the end of my troubles.* It never occurred to him to doubt Sergeant Falk's tale. Falk had never been forthcoming, but never dishonest. His tale explained too much and matched Uncle Pyk's story too well. *A mutiny, barely suppressed, and Cousin Paitir caught between punishing Malcoor at the cost of the Westerend's rebellion... or punishing the mutineers and rewarding what might have been — but could never be* proven *to be —* treason. Had Malcoor meant to carry that dragon to the Westerend, to use as a weapon? Or had he simply been desperate to make landfall? And how was there a dragon anyway? Hadn't Magnei said that they were all Wished dead, long ago?

It was too much for him tonight. Aethal sought his bedchamber. What he could be certain of was that the questions would still be there in the morning.

Chapter Three

47th of Spring, 312 Exodus

In the cool light of dawn, the Hydraxis boiled with the controlled chaos of men and animals. The men of the Royal Army were ready to move out against the Grassworms. Against the Lotus.

If only the same could be said of the member of the Royal Line that was under his charge, Aethal would have felt better. "Your Highness," said Aethal, trying to keep the impatience from his voice, "The General and his officers await your pleasure."

Eraad shot him an annoyed look, but finally said to his valet, "You know the rest of it. Get moving."

When they arrived, the other officers braced to attention with fixed smiles on their faces. Only Malcoor and General Vaagen dared to give the prince hard stares. "Now that we are all here," Vaagen said with some irony, and an even colder glance at Aethal. "We can begin. Colonel Jereg?"

The colonel, in operational command of the 1st Heavy Dragoons, officially Eraad's cavalry regiment, straightened. "The men are ready to march at your orders, sir. With your permission, I'll have scouting units before the vanguard. General, we are ready to accompany your lead regiment. Colonel my Lord, I expect you'll want to accompany us in the van?"

"Of course," Eraad nodded with bored grace.

Brigadier Garedder nodded. He was an older man, clean-shaven. He had a good reputation earned fighting the Grassworms, Aethal knew from his time in the Phoenix Lancers. Vaagen had chosen his men well. "My officers report ready to march. And we thank my Lord Colonel's father for the distribution of Greater Rifles. The units so favored are now fully trained with them."

Aethal let out a sigh of satisfaction mixed with anxiety. The Greater Rifles had always been the exclusive province of officers and specialist snipers. But now the riflemen of elite units like Maednac's Own and the First Dragoons were receiving them as well. And as soon as possible, the whole army would get them. That would not be for a long time, though. Aethal hoped it would be soon enough. Perhaps a tenth of this army's best units had them. Those men, however, would be able to hit the Grassworms from over five times their own range. If the Grassworms *were* infected with Lotus, that could mean the difference between life and death. Even better, Greater Rifles could cut them down long before the Banshees' death cries could be brought into play.

As if reading his mind, General Vaagen said, "Good. Last Sword, may I presume that the security matter has already been taken care of?"

"Indeed yes, General." Aethal had taken deep satisfaction in signing Colonel Sigrad's arrest order himself and sending it accompanied by two Wyrmguard. They would be back with the man by sundown. "Then do we occupy the pass in force?"

Malcoor turned to his generals, a lean smile on his face that Aethal had only rarely seen before. Usually at the end of a wargame that Malcoor had used to decisively thrash his young officers. The Warmaster's new command insignia gleamed at his collar. Once he had thought of it, the king had wasted no time in promoting Malcoor — his only general officer with experience facing the Lotus — to the rank of Warmaster, the first since Maednac's day. Far from showing any resentment at having his command taken from him, General Vaagen appeared relieved.

"We occupy in force just long enough for our supply train to catch up. Garedder, you'll have the garrison to augment your strength. And if any Grassworms elect to assault you there..." Garedder's answering smile was wolfish. The

Grassworms' real strength was in the Grain Sea itself. Without its long grasses to hide in, they'd be easy targets for Garedder's Greater Riflemen.

"We will then immediately march for the Treeline, to force the Royal Road and link up with the Westerend forces." He nodded to Colonel Varian. The big, balding officer bowed slightly from the waist. He had arrived in Cemetery Bay aboard Lord Vaughan's merchant ships, but from the man's bearing, you'd never have guessed he'd been crammed into overcrowded hulls for the past fortnight.

"Our forces will be in place on the Vestris crossings long before we arrive there. We'll break any blockade the Grassworms think they can mount."

"Good."

The door burst open. Flintmaw stood there, his face a mask. "Last Sword. Warmaster. My Lord Heir. Your presence is required at once in His Excellency's chambers. A courier has arrived to see the Imperial Governor, on Peril of the Well's Rising."

Aethal saw the leashed horror he was feeling reflected on every face. They followed the Wyrmguard from the room.

***

Flintmaw led them to the king's solar, adjoining his bedchamber near the top of the Ophidian. Upon entering the room, it was obvious that Paitir had just woken up. Servants were attending on him while the courier stood waiting. Aethal's father was also there. So was Uncle Pyk, looking only slightly less disheveled than the king did. Aethal took in the dirty and bedraggled figure and recognized the regimental colors of the Phoenix Lancers rifles. Then he recognized the man.

Canuta! The young man met his eyes and gave him a grim smile. He'd thinned and hardened in the past few weeks. *Lieutenant Canuta, now, indeed,*

Aethal noticed. But more than any promotion, the change in demeanor announced that this was no longer a boy. This was a veteran of hard fighting.

Seats were already prepared for them, and the king, looking as if he had not slept all night, motioned them into the chairs. "Tell them," he said.

"My lords and generals," said Canuta. "General Jeharok charged me to ride as fast as possible to you. He is abandoning the Treeline and making with all speed toward the Serpent's Pass. He is doing this to avoid being surrounded, cut off, and having his men turned into leafeaters."

"God-Beyond-The-World," muttered General Vaagen. Then he looked hard at the young man. "Give me a full report. What led up to that? As much as you know."

"Yes, sir. Two days before I rode out, the Grassworms launched a united assault. They'd been quiet since the General had ordered the prairie fires set. With no cover from the Grain Sea, those of us with Greater Rifles could shoot them down from almost a mile away in the daylight, and they knew it. The General even had torches out at night so they couldn't get too near. Then, one morning at dawn, we woke to find they'd sneaked up under cover of darkness, right to the edge of the torchlight and waited. They charged us. With more men than I've ever seen in one place. And not just men, either. They advanced..." He swayed on his feet, and Aethal could see how tired the young man was. He must have been riding for four days straight. Which meant his news was that old, of course.

Canuta straightened and forced himself back into the moment. "They advanced on both ends of the Treeline at once. In whole tribes. Even down to the children, sir. We couldn't hold. By the end of the first day, the enemy had taken four of the keepwoods and we were cutting the skyways between them. We could see they were sending men to get behind us. I don't think there can be any Grassworms *left* beyond the Treeline; they must all have joined in the attack. They fought like... I've never seen anyone fight like they do. They just keep coming."

Aethal closed his eyes against the desperate crack in Canuta's voice, but the young man held on, determined to get to the end of his message.

"They're tying leaves of Lotus to their arrows and shooting them at us," he said. "We're fighting with our noses plugged, but they're doing their damnedest to spread the stuff to us. Sometimes it works. They may have as many as a platoon of our own men fighting for them, now. Fighting for the Lotus. They're marching beneath its banner, my lords. It's... they're worshipping it. They have it on their banners. Pictures of it where they can't keep a sprig of it uneaten long enough to carry into battle."

"Piss in the Well," cried Colonel Jereg in the silence that greeted this revelation. "Isn't it killing them?"

Canuta nodded. "We can see the groves where they take the dead. They're the only green things for miles since the General ordered the prairie fires set, and they sprang up the next day. We tried to raid them and fire the Lotus itself, but with nothing else to burn... We had to give it up when we lost the raiding squadron. But Lotus is a slow death, and they're fighting us almost until they drop. And now..."

"Yes, what is it, Canuta?" asked Aethal, gently.

"They weren't just waiting during those quiet weeks. They must have been doing it at night while we couldn't see. They've been sowing the Lotus, sir. It's coming up like new grass under their feet. When I left, you could still see the bare soil, but it'll be like a green sea, now. Beyond the Treeline, the Lotus is all that's left." Despair was in his voice, and his face sagged. Aethal led him to a chair.

"Get this man a room and some refreshment," he muttered to one of the king's servants. "He needs rest. And we'll want to talk to him later." He straightened.

General Vaagen looked pale. He looked at Malcoor. So did the king. Malcoor cleared his throat.

"We will continue with our planned advance. General Jeharok's force will be falling back on the Pass. It can take up the garrison duty there; Jeharok's a good man; I trained him myself. Then our entire main body will march on the Treeline and reoccupy it. We will burn the Lotus out of the soil all the way to the mountains and the coast with the *yasnuum* we have to fortify us. And once we hold that, I shall return to Maednac Serpiin. Lieutenant, did the General receive any contact from the Westerend forces?"

Canuta turned at the door. "No, sir." His face twisted in an ugly expression. "They just said the same thing they always did. They couldn't break through. That's all their birds have said for months while they sat there safe in that little pass of theirs."

"All right. Dismissed." Canuta was escorted out. "Your Majesty, with your permission, I need Vaagen and the rest of the staff to see to the men." The king nodded, but his face was like an empty mask.

There was silence in the room for several seconds after the officers filed out. No one had told Aethal and Eraad to stay, but they did. Finally, King Paitir said, "Bring Lord Vaughan of the Westerend to me immediately." He looked at Malcoor. "How long until the Fleet can be ready to depart?"

Malcoor's lips twisted in frustration. "I've had time to do no more than begin to solve that problem, your Majesty," he protested. "If everything is in the readiness I can expect, and I have the men I require, then..." He paused in thought. "I may be able to sail within six weeks." The king gave him a cold stare, and Malcoor's face twisted. "Sire, may I speak honestly. And without ears to hear?"

The king dismissed the servants, all of whom looked glad to go. They'd heard enough to frighten them senseless.

"Sire," Malcoor said after they had gone, "I cannot promise that there are enough ships in the entire Fleet to bring back the *yasnuum* we would need to guard all Verlaen, now. While it was outside the Treeline and contained, then yes. But if the Grain Sea is turning into a field of Lotus, there may not be enough *yasnuum* in all the world. The orders I have just given are for us to retake the Treeline. But I can't give orders that will allow us to inspect the Outer Grain Sea. We haven't the men. And if we did, many wouldn't survive."

Aethal swallowed. The king looked ready to faint. A small thunderclap sounded from outside in the courtyard. Pyk raised his head.

"Then what shall we do, Admiral?" asked the king. "We must do something."

The door opened, and Lord Vaughan was admitted, preceded by a Wyrmguard. The king frowned. "Well, Lord Vaughan, can you explain to me why no attack has materialized out of the Westerend against the Grassworms?"

The Lord of the Westerend straightened and looked at the king sharply. "What?"

"You assured me more than once that your forces would march to the aid of the Royal Army at the Treeline."

"Your Majesty, while I am here in the capital there is little I can do personally to encourage my men, but... you say there has been no attack? None at all?"

"No. And I am still waiting for your answer."

Lord Vaughan looked, for the first time since Aethal had known him, uncertain. "I ordered an attack. There should have been an attack." His face twisted in frustration. "Sire, you must let me return to the Westerend."

"No, Vaughan, we need you here," said Malcoor, quietly.

"Joseth?" Vaughan's voice rose in disbelief.

"We need you here for the vote in the General States that you told me about. Your Majesty, I can see only one hope for us to defeat the Lotus. And that is to send the expedition to the Well that the Lord Warden of the Guardians has proposed."

Silence reigned in the room.

"You realize," said the king, "That Ilferth Simon has practically promised to denounce us all heretics who will bring the wrath of God-Beyond-The-World down upon us if we do this."

The Warmaster nodded. "The wrath is already here. Your Majesty, it's true, I didn't want to go and harvest the *yasnuum*. I wasn't certain it would succeed, but I was willing to try. Now," he shook his head. "It is simply a waste."

"And a voyage to the Well?" asked the king, his voice rising toward desperation.

"I don't know anything about that. But a Wish brought the Lotus. A Wish should be able to destroy it. If we can get there. And if any man can get there, Sire, I can. And if I do, I will save your kingdom." Malcoor's face was calm and composed, and utterly confident.

We're desperate enough to believe him, a corner of Aethal's mind thought. *We've nothing else to believe.*

"Sire, I believe that the Admiral has the right of it," said Paal. "Therefore, we will have to place the matter before the General States, according to Maednac's Law. Will you assent to it, Sire?"

King Paitir looked as if he were aging before their eyes, but he looked again at Malcoor and said, "Yes."

"Very well. Will the Westerend support the expedition?"

Lord Vaughan nodded grimly. "My brother will do all a man can."

"And the Skysils?" Paal asked Pyk.

Pyk's face was sheened with sweat. "That's not a matter for just me to decide," he said. "The Skysil domain's delegates are on their way to the People's Chamber. And the Well... is evil."

"Allowing Verlaen to be eaten by Lotus and its worshippers is a worse evil, Uncle," said Aethal. "What about the Skysil Lord Paramount's vote?"

"Lord Falaar must make that decision," protested Pyk.

"And do you not have a thunderbird to ask him?" pressed Paal.

"Uncle Pyk," said Aethal. "Do you believe that we can defeat the Lotus? Do you believe we can win against it, without the Well's Wish?"

Pyk opened his mouth and shut it.

"I know my Uncle Falaar," said Aethal. "He's a good man. But he hasn't been here, close enough to see what the Lotus is doing. He's given you full representative powers. Will you use them to vote against what you believe is our only chance to save us?"

Pyk straightened. "I am bound in honor to tell Lord Falaar what I know," he said. "But I believe I can promise the Skysil's vote."

"Good," said Paal. "That leaves us three votes: that of the Church, and the two of the People's Chamber. Both, of course, are determined by the votes of their assembled members, in theory, but Ilferth Simon has the Church too well in hand for there to be any doubt of its vote. Which leaves only the vote of the People's Chamber, headed by the Lord Mayor of Maednac Serpiin, to consider."

"Why consider it at all?" said Eraad. "Don't we already have four votes for the expedition? And isn't that all we need?"

"Yes, your Highness," said Paal, patiently, "But if you would do me the great courtesy of paying attention, this is not a simple matter of what is legal and within our rights. It is very much a matter of how much trouble the Church can make for us. If we go against the vote of the People's Chamber, then we — the King and the Lords Paramount — will be the focus of the people's anger and fear. If their own representatives vote for us, then *they* will fight when Ilferth Simon condemns us all as heretics."

"Why not simply arrest him?" growled Eraad.

"If it comes to that, we will," said Paal. "But what do you propose to do, Eraad? Arrest the Church? You'll have to arrest the whole population. When people are scared, they turn to God. Even a God-Beyond-The-World. If you plan on ruling these people, you need to see them for who they are and not for what you think you can make them. So, we must know how the People's Chamber *will* vote."

Eraad subsided, but Aethal remembered the guns that were being bought and stored. *And what will those men do if a vote does not go their way? And will they approve an expedition to the Well? Or not?* Again, he cursed the opportunity he had missed to see what might have happened at Llhawcae Cathedral if he had been a little more 'subtle', as his father had advised. Aethal leaned over to a Wyrmguard and muttered a command.

Turning back, Aethal said, "The people are frightened. I'm not sure even the Lord Mayor knows which way the men of the Bowl and the City would vote. If we can get him on our side, I feel we would have a fair amount of influence." *And his friendship with the Conversant is surely strained. Should Aethal tell them about the guns? No. Eraad at least, would be sure to overreact. And I don't know enough yet. Better to be sure.*

Paal frowned at him. "Rolf Hlafen is a jellyfish, drifting with any current that may take him."

"Can we get him into our current, then, Chancellor?" asked the king. A knock sounded at the door, and the Wyrmguard opened it, and took a small scroll over to Pyk, who frowned and began to open it.

Paal hesitated. "Perhaps. He is an ambitious man."

"The Westerend's delegates will arrive in days. I can explain the necessity to them," Vaughan said.

"The Wrackberg's delegates will understand as well."

Aethal sighed. His father had iron control over his people. And he had little doubt that his father would be capable of handling the Lord Mayor of Maednac Serpiin. It was time to be gone. "Eraad, the Generals are waiting."

The cry that sounded behind him was like nothing Aethal had ever heard from his uncle's throat. He whirled. "Uncle Pyk?"

Paal was already there, helping the shorter man into a chair. "Oh, God," he kept saying. "God-Beyond-The-World."

Paal snatched up the scroll where it had fallen, and Aethal remembered the thunderclap. That was a scroll carried by the fast thunderbirds of the Skysil Lords. It was what the Wyrmguard had handed him. Paal scanned it, and his hands dropped to his side.

"This," he said, "is a message from Thane Diarmed of High Reach. He is one of the Skysil delegates sent by Lord Falaar to represent the Skysil domain at the General States. He is now the only one left alive. The rest were shot at the Serpiin Pass. They were all farmed.

"It is countersigned by Major Kennering, and dated three hours ago. Apparently, the thane never suspected his three companions were leafeaters. But the Discipline caught them."

"Maednac's Name," whispered the king, and Aethal felt the shiver of dread run through the room. Lotus was that close.

Pyk looked up. His eyes were haunted. "The road they took," he said. "It goes through Telerat."

Aethal nodded. Telerat guarded the way into the Skysil domain. Any road to their lands went through Telerat. Did they pick up the Lotus there? Or later?

Or earlier? If it was earlier, then Lotus had already spread into the Skysil domain itself. "Uncle," Aethal heard himself say, "Send the bird to Uncle Falaar with the message. Write to him and warn him. Ask him what to do. The thunderbirds are fast, you'll know what the truth is by tomorrow."

Pyk nodded, and Aethal signaled the Wyrmguard to fetch him some wine. To Eraad, he said, "We are no more use here, and with this news, the Army must make all speed." The prince nodded. But before he could leave, Aethal felt a hand on his shoulder. He turned, and looked into his father's face. "Aethal," said Paal. "You're taking with you all the best armsmen of the Wrackberg, and their colonel's a good man. But he'll follow your orders in the field. I have so instructed him."

Aethal blinked. "He should be following Vaagen's orders, not mine."

Paal shrugged. "Then tell him that."

Aethal nodded. Then said, "Thank you, Father." Paal inclined his head. Aethal turned to leave and Eraad followed him.

Farnan met them in the courtyard. Aethal stopped and drew out the letter he'd spent the morning writing. "Take this to the Lord Mayor. But read it first."

"You want me reading the Lord Mayor's mail?" asked Farnan, with a crooked smile. Won't he be a bit put out by that?"

"I hope not, but he'll have to live with it. It's your promotion, Lieutenant *Colonel* Farnan."

Farnan's mouth dropped open. "Lieutenant Colonel? Have you lost your mind, Aethal, that's three ranks!"

"Unlikely, isn't it?" grinned Aethal, ignoring Farnan's grimace. "Yes it is, but I need you for it. This letter puts you in command of the City Watch. The first thing I want you to do is appoint an Acting Lord Low Jailer to replace my brother. The one commanding now is his creature; don't trust him. Keep them trained. Knock some Discipline back into them. Don't take any backtalk from the Temple or the Crownguard, and trust Falk and his cadre. I'm giving them all to you. I want the City Watch to be a credible defense force — all right, a *more* credible defense force — for this city by the time I get back in eight days' time." He would have to be back by then, no matter how this battle went. The General States required the presence of the Last Sword.

Farnan grinned, but there was a tension in it. "Aethal, you know the Lord Mayor won't stand for this. The City Watch is his, by ancient custom."

"This is not a time for ancient custom, Farnan," said Aethal. "It's time for men who are willing to do what's needed."

"What's needed?" said Farnan. "Just how hard do you want me to push, Aethal?"

Aethal swallowed. "With your liege lord's voice of the Wrackberg I order you," he said, "to do whatever you must to carry out these orders."

Now Farnan's grin showed teeth, and he saluted. "Yes, my lord." And he was off.

Aethal hurried to catch up to Eraad, who was talking with Malcoor and General Vaagen. "We will have to assume that the city itself may be farmed," Malcoor was saying. "So we ride to Telerat."

Aethal nodded. "To Telerat, then."

"To Telerat," a voice said behind him. Aethal turned. There was Pyk, on a hastily-saddled horse, still in his court dress.

"Uncle Pyk, you can't come with us like that!"

"I am the Thane of Telerat, boy. My place is with my people. There's Skysil troops in the Serpent's Pass that have been sent to fight the Lotus: who's going to lead 'em? Baggage can follow me. Now is this army doing something besides standing around, scratching its collective arse?"

General Vaagen inclined his head. "It will be good to have you with us, my lord." He turned to an aide. "Tell the vanguard to sound the advance."

But as the bugles sounded and the mighty army thundered into motion, Aethal could not help looking toward the distant mountains and thinking how very small the ranks of men looked.

Chapter Four

50th of Spring, 312 Exodus

The Royal Army spread out like a glittering carpet of men on the Hameward Hills. Telerat sat before them like a crown of stone on a deceptively shallow rise. Smaller than Maednac Serpiin, it nonetheless guarded the way to the highlands of the Skysil domain, and its gates were shut. The Skysil banner, the five-masted ship surmounting three white mountains, flew over its turrets. Beneath it, flew the city's flag: a black hammer on a rose field beneath two moons.

For three hundred years, the Skysils had guarded their privileges jealously. As the weakest of the Lords Paramount, they relied on the difficult terrain of the highlands no less than on their deadly pike-and-musket infantry to guarantee their rights. After their alliance with House Wrackberg, they had grown even more determined to show their autonomy.

Aethal and his four Wyrmguard escorted Prince Eraad to Malcoor's command tent near the artillery batteries. Pyk looked up at Aethal's approach. His eyes darted this way and that.

"Uncle Pyk? I thought you were riding to the gate?"

"They are sending an embassy," the old man said, grimly.

"But you are their Thane!" Aethal said, aghast.

"Aye," the old man said. "And they invited me inside the walls. Alone. When I refused, they said their embassy would come to parley with us."

"Parley?" asked Eraad, indignantly. "With the King's army? What is this? Rebellion?"

"I devoutly hope so, Your Highness," said Malcoor. "The alternative is far worse."

Eraad's mouth froze on an angry retort, and Aethal saw his own leashed fear reflected in the prince's eyes. In every eye. If, as the thane of Telerat, Pyk did not command the loyalty of the city, what else did?

"We are preparing to meet them," said Malcoor. "We will have an unbroken ring around Telerat in an hour's time. I will meet them with Colonel Jereg and His Highness the Crown Prince. Thane Pyk Imya Telerat will, of course, be with us. And you, Last Sword." Aethal nodded. "Sergeant," said Malcoor, "Equip these men."

A sergeant handed Aethal and the prince what looked like a hand-grenade. It was equipped with the same friction-primer fuse. But it was made of heavy paper. "Gentlemen, this is your Lotus flare," said the sergeant. "A sharp pull on the fuse will set it alight in two seconds. Throw it to the ground and it will burst into green flame and smoke."

Malcoor looked at each of them in turn. "We will not speak to this embassy unless they submit to the Discipline. If the Discipline reveals any of them to be leafeaters, we will open fire. General Vaagen, in that case you will order an immediate assault to seize the gates. I expect every officer and every man to do his duty."

A bugle sounded. "They come!" shouted a color sergeant.

Colonel Jereg looked stunned. "Open fire under a flag of truce?"

Malcoor looked at him. "Maednac's Discipline is quite clear, Colonel. There is no truce with the Lotus. A man who is infected will do anything to stay alive, anything to eat more Lotus, and anything to spread it to others. An assault on the gates will be a horror for us, but if they aren't really expecting it, we may carry them. Then we should be able to pick the city apart.

"But I can think of no greater disaster that could befall Verlaen in the next few minutes than for all of us to be infected with the Lotus. That is why General Vaagen is staying here. If the worst should occur, and they kill us all, at least our entire command structure will not be decapitated. Last Sword?"

Aethal turned to the Wyrmguard, and with a dry mouth said, "Wyrmguard. You will take charge of administering the Discipline when we meet the party from Telerat. You will shoot anyone who is infected, or becomes infected. Including his Highness the Crown Prince. Understood?"

The Wyrmguard called Everwar turned to him with the passive face he had come to know and dread. "We will obey your orders as the Compact permits, Last Sword. Our first mission must be to protect the Heir from infection. If that mission fails, we shall kill him."

Eraad looked pale and angry at hearing this, but it appeared that he also understood it, and he straightened. "I'll die by my own hand rather than eat Lotus, as should any man of worth." He stalked between the Wyrmguard to his position.

"There is one more thing, gentlemen," said Malcoor. He took from his pouch a small chunk of something that glittered dully in the sunlight. He broke it into pieces that resembled glittering grains of rice, and handed one to each man, excepting only the Wyrmguard. "This is the *yasnuum*." Aethal examined it. It looked something like fool's gold, but shot through with muddy brown streaks, and having a spice-and-earth smell about it. He had seen Malcoor bring the small chest down from his old quarters the day they had stopped at the Pass. "If the Discipline reveals any man to be farmed, eat this, and it will keep you safe from the Lotus. For a day. No more."

"Sir," said Aethal. "Should we not rather take this now, just in case?"

"No," said Malcoor. "Remember what I told you. The *yasnuum* takes away all human feelings. And I want all my powers available to me now. Especially the feelings."

They marched forward. Aethal felt the unreality that always descended on him just before a battle. Except for the silence and the army behind them, they might almost have been a party of picnickers. The breeze was cool and refreshing from the north, and the grass of the hills before Telerat was almost as good as a lawn.

The embassy from Telerat approached under a white flag. Aethal saw three men in civilian clothes. They were flanked by six soldiers in Skysil livery, bearing large-bore muskets. Aethal began to breathe a little easier. This did not look like an ambush. Not a good one anyway. *But leafeaters do not think like men.*

"Halt!" cried Malcoor, when the two parties were twenty paces apart. "Will you submit to the Discipline?" he called.

The men looked at one another. "Aye," called one.

At Aethal's signal, two of the Wyrmguard marched forward. The men flinched under their level gaze, but did not turn away. When they turned back to Aethal, he released a breath he didn't know he'd been holding. "These men are clean," said Everwar.

All three civilians were men in late-middle age. The leader, a thick, shorter man with a trimmed white beard, wore the mayor's badge of office. He bowed to Pyk. "My thane," he said.

Pyk stepped forward. "Cleidh," he said. He turned to Malcoor. "Warmaster Malcoor, may I present Lord Cleidh, mayor of Telerat, and Squires Geord Cailing and Seanan Uitling, two of Telerat's ealdarmen." He introduced the royal party in turn, then rounded on the Lord Mayor. "What is the meaning of this, Cleidh? Explain to me at once what is happening in my city!"

Lord Mayor Cleidh's face closed. "With all reverence, my thane, I cannot discuss this matter with you in front of men not sworn to follow Lord Falaar of Skysil."

"And why would that be, my *lord*?" snapped Eraad. "Is this treason?"

"My Lord Colonel," said Malcoor, reminding Eraad of his place. "This is a military operation, and you will conduct yourself accordingly."

Eraad subsided. But the Lord Mayor looked at Malcoor.

"We did not come here to have our loyalty questioned or our rights violated, General. Telerat is closed. For our own reasons. Which we will discuss with our thane. Within its walls, or not at all."

"And if your thane orders you otherwise?" asked Malcoor.

"I have yet to hear him do so."

Pyk reddened. "Have you lost your wits, man?" He pulled at the medallion around his neck and showed it, the brilliant colors of the artwork flashing in the sun. "This is the Skysil's personal sigil. I speak with his voice. Now open my city to the soldiers of the King at once so that we may be sure our people are safe from the Lotus!"

"Aye, you speak with the Skysil's voice," said Cleidh. "And you do it in the company of — perhaps even in the custody of — forces that may mean Telerat and the Skysil domain harm. If Lord Falaar himself gave me orders in such circumstances, my thane, I should answer him as I do you, and count it the highest loyalty to him and his people."

Pyk sputtered. General Malcoor said, "Has the Skysil domain or Telerat had declared any rebellion or committed any..." he grimaced and did not look at Eraad, "...treason against King Paitir? I wasn't aware of it. Why should this army mean you harm?"

"Why should this army be here at all?" snapped one of the ealdarmen.

"We sent you couriers with the news," said Malcoor.

"I sent you a thunderbird. And one to the Skysil as well!" snapped Pyk. "When he hears of this, I assure you that Lord Paramount Falaar will extract a reckoning for your foolishness."

"Couriers with the news," Malcoor repeated, as though Pyk had not spoken, "That three of the delegates from the Skysil domain to the General States arrived at the Serpent's Pass with their eyes full of Lotus. Surely you can see that we have some cause for concern. These men must have passed through Telerat."

"And?" asked Cleidh.

"Don't play with me, Lord Cleidh," said Malcoor, softly. "This is a matter of the Discipline. Lotus may be inside your walls, and I know exactly what that means. I will and must order my men to inspect this city so that we may turn westward toward our real foes and retake the Grain Sea and the Treeline from the Grassworm bands that now wander toward the Pass sowing Lotus every time they camp. But Telerat alone has twice the population of the remaining Grassworms. Neither the Kingdom nor the Skysil domain can afford the slightest chance that the Lotus has gained a foothold in your homes."

"Rejoice, then," said Cleidh, in a tone utterly devoid of joy. "There is no Lotus here. You may return to fighting your real foes. As soon as possible, by our preference. We cannot afford to provision your army. Since the loss of the Grain Sea, food supplies will be scarce this winter."

"You know I can't take your word for that," said Malcoor. "Discipline requires that we inspect your city. And I will enforce that, for your own safety."

"Yes, that is the one claim that would allow you to force our gates, isn't it?" asked Cleidh, anger cracking his expressionless façade for the first time. "And a very convenient one. All we must do is let in the royal army at our gates, and you will save us from the Lotus. Was not the Lotus discovered practically at the Westerend's back door? A month ago? And yet you are here, not there, on *your* home soil, Warmaster. You didn't confuse us with them, did you? It seems rather... selective... that at the first rumor of Lotus in the Skysil domain — Lotus that may have been picked up anywhere between here and the Serpent's Pass — an army appears within days."

"I can *get* an army here within days. It would take nearly a month to march this army to the Westerend with the whole Grain Sea between us, and you know that," snapped Malcoor. "And every hour you delay adds more time to that march; it's where we were bound before we discovered the Lotus in your people."

"A most convenient discovery. I have no proof of it."

"Cleidh," said Pyk. "Did the thunderbird deliver my message?"

"My thane," replied Cleidh, evenly. "I shall be honored to discuss the matter within your walls. Not in front of an army at our gates. And not while you yourself are in the power of that army."

"Are you calling me a traitor to the Skysil, you upjumped whoreson?" roared Pyk.

Cleidh's face reddened at the insult, but said, "No, my thane. I am suggesting that you may be under duress. If you wish to prove otherwise, you have but to come with us."

"You know we cannot allow that," said Malcoor. "There may be Lotus in Telerat. To allow anyone else to enter the city would violate Discipline. I certainly do not propose to allow the highest-ranking Skysil noble within two hundred miles to expose himself to such a risk."

"Just so, Warmaster," answered Cleidh. "Then do I take it you intend to besiege us?"

"I intend to inspect this city and go. A siege would cost time and lives I do not have to spend. And yet I cannot leave Lotus here, and I cannot allow it to enter or leave. For the sake of the kingdom," he paused. His voice softened. "My Lord Mayor, I beg you will not make me do this. We cannot waste time in suspecting one another of such foul motives. Not now. I have just marched from the Treeline, and I have seen the shattered remnants of the army that fought the Lotus at the Treeline. They've seen their brothers-in-arms die. And worse. General Jeharok is there, now, recovering his strength so that this army may fight while all Verlaen answers the call to arms."

The Lord Mayor's eyes darted from side to side. "And do you have any of this army with you?" he asked. "These brave men who fought the Lotus on our soil? Or were you the only one?"

Aethal stepped forward. "I have fought the Lotus," he said. "Look at me, my lord. I discovered it in Everview barely a month past, and already it has nearly engulfed the Grain Sea. I've breathed the stink of it, and I nearly ate of it myself. Whatever you remember of the stories of Lotus from your histories, my lords, the truth is far worse. Do you really believe that his majesty would simply invent the Lotus's presence in order to gull you? I am of the blood of the Skysil, and I tell you this is true."

The Lord Mayor seemed to consider this. Then his eyes hardened. "Your father is also the Lord of the Wrackberg. And you wear the King's uniform, sworn to protect his line. Meaning no disrespect to your blood, Last Sword, but you cannot speak as a Skysil, here."

"It seems that no one can speak as a Skysil here but you, Lord Cleidh," said Malcoor. "And that is also very convenient."

Cleidh made no answer, but only glared at him. "Your Highness," he bowed to the prince. "My lord thane, gentlemen. We have nothing more to say, other than to advise you that it is in your power to seek the real enemy you claim to fight."

"I have something to say." Eraad stepped forward. "You are a traitor, and you have dishonored my father's name. And if he listens to my counsel after this, then he will burn this city to ash for your treason!"

"His majesty is welcome to try," replied Cleidh, icily. "But we see no need to endure insult. If you find the courtesy you seem to have lately lost, General, you may call on us again." And the Skysil lords turned their backs on the army's commanders, and walked back to Telerat's gates.

***

In the command tent, Malcoor sighed heavily. "I could Wish in the Well that I knew whether they're actually stupid enough to think that we'd use Lotus as an excuse to take Telerat by treachery, or whether they're making excuses to hide the fact that they're infected. Thane Telerat, what say you?"

Pyk paused in his pacing. "I don't know! Cleidh has always been a stubborn bastard, but this...? I'd never have thought him capable of it. If I had, I'd never have left Telerat. Is it not possible that I could talk to them? I'd give you my word to return, and we might clear up the whole matter. There's men behind those walls who are loyal to me, not Cleidh, but they can't do anything if they don't know I'm here."

"Lotus keeps no man's word," said Malcoor. "If you should be infected, we would be even worse off. And even if not, you might still not be allowed to leave. They could restrain you and simply give orders in your name. That is why we follow the Discipline. Until we know that there is no Lotus in Telerat, only soldiers masked for inspection go into that city."

Malcoor looked at them. Then he turned to General Vaagen. "Have the mortars emplaced," he said softly.

Pyk's face drained of color. "Malcoor. You can't do that!" Aethal closed his eyes: the squat, heavy guns could throw bombs over the walls and turn Telerat into an inferno. There would be no escape for the frightened citizens inside. Every face in the tent grew grim, except Crown Prince Eraad's. He bared his teeth in a smile.

"I don't want to do that, Thane Pyk Imya Telerat," said Malcoor. "But if they will not allow us to inspect in the name of the Discipline, then it will be my duty to destroy them. According to strictest law, I should be doing it already. Believe me, Thane. It would be kinder than leaving Lotus in your city. Now, help me find a way *not* to do it!"

"Your thunderbird," said Aethal. The words came to him almost before he knew what they meant. "Uncle Pyk, you have a thunderbird in your personal baggage, do you not? With an attendant to care for it? In case of dire emergency?"

"Aye, the voices of the Skysils always carry them, but what's a thunderbird going to do? The people we have to talk to are right there!" he pointed out the tent flap.

"And Lord Cleidh said that he would not obey Lord Falaar himself if he were here," said Malcoor. "Even if a thunderbird could carry a man."

"Because Lord Falaar would then be in our power," said Aethal. "Those were his words. But, Pyk, if you could have Lord Falaar order them to open their gates to us, by thunderbird, they'd have no cause to suspect coercion. They know that Lord Falaar is safe."

Malcoor and Pyk both looked at him. "The message would be there in hours," said Pyk. "Telerat would have its orders in a day, at most."

"A day we can't afford," muttered Malcoor. "But a day that burning the city would not save us." Aethal winced at the cold-blooded calculation, but he was right. It had taken Jeharok at least that long to burn the far smaller Everview to the ground. "Good thinking, Last Sword. Do it." Pyk left the tent screaming for his attendants.

Malcoor's shoulders finally relaxed. "I hope this works. I'm going to order our chaplain to pray that it works."

"This Lord Mayor is guilty of treason," said Eraad. "And so are all his accomplices. They are breaking the Discipline, what's more. You heard the man: he as good as accused my father, the King of inventing the threat of Lotus!"

"Yes, he did, my lord Colonel," said Malcoor, patiently. "Because he is frightened. But we do not know what frightens him, yet. Is he a suspicious but honest fool, or is he so terrified of the Lotus that he dares not be honest?"

"He should be terrified of the King's justice!"

"If he fears that more than Lotus, your Highness, then his Majesty has done a very poor job of ruling."

"You dare speak of the King so?" said Eraad.

Malcoor fixed the prince with a bored stare. "Stand at attention when you talk to me, boy!" he snapped. He fixed Eraad with his eyes until the younger man reluctantly braced himself upright. "You may be my next King, my Lord Colonel. But your father knows well that he needs my services, so you'd better damned well listen. You are no less subject to Discipline than those men inside the gates of Telerat. You act like a spoiled royal child, and undermine our authority before them. It's not his Majesty I criticize, my Lord Colonel, it is you. You will be with us when we meet these men again, because they need to know that Maednac's Line is among them, but you will remain silent unless I directly order you to speak, or I will have you removed and punished for breach of Discipline. Is that clear, my Lord Colonel?"

"Yes. Sir." Eraad pushed the words out as if they hurt.

"Good." As if nothing had happened, Malcoor turned. "Colonel Jereg, we had better meet with the Lord Mayor once more. I want to know how he's going to react to this letter from Lord Falaar, assuming we get it. And... he and his people deserve to know what we will have to do, if he does not obey."

"Yes, sir." The colonel ducked out of the tent. Aethal followed him, heading for Pyk's tent.

"Aethal!" Eraad's voice rang out behind him. He turned to see Eraad standing beside the tent, glaring at him, and pointedly waiting. Aethal slowly walked back.

"Your Highness needs something?" he asked.

"Do you propose to say nothing while my own servants rebuke me?"

Aethal blinked. "What would you have liked me to say, Highness?"

"I expect you to remind them of the proper deference to their Prince!"

Aethal sighed. "My Lord Colonel..."

"Your Highness!" snapped Eraad.

"No," said Aethal, bluntly, and watched surprise blossom on Eraad's face. "Not here. Have you never been with your own army before?" Eraad did not answer. "These men are not your servants. They are your soldiers. A soldier's honor comes from doing his duty, not from his bloodline."

"They have no bloodline, most of them," Eraad sniffed.

"No, they don't. You have there something they can never match, so they guard the honor they *do* have all the more fiercely." Eraad stared at him, eyes sharpening. Now he was considering something new. Aethal pressed on. "My Lord Colonel, they are inviting you to share their honor by accepting your duties among them. It is a small honor returned to you in exchange for the honor you do them by being here. Part of those duties include obedience. They will obey you better if they see you obey."

"Really?" Eraad seemed both repelled and fascinated by the idea.

"Yes."

"Obedience is one thing," Eraad finally said. "But insult another. Malcoor impugned my dignity."

"Your Highness," said Aethal. "As the Last Sword, I am your royal bodyguard. I cannot guard your dignity. That is left to every man to do for himself, even for kings."

"I suppose you think it was an honor, the way he ordered me about?" Eraad said, giving him a calculating look.

"Part of a soldier's duty is to disobey the King, especially if the King gives an order that would place him or the realm in danger. And right now, allowing you to threaten the men of Telerat would do exactly that. You're making it easier for them to resist your father's will. If they think he means to kill them anyway, why should they obey?"

"They are infected with either Lotus or treason, and either way, those infections must be burned out."

"We cannot afford to burn them out if we can win them back to our side," pleaded Aethal. "And it is the Warmaster's duty to do that if he can. We know the men we met with are not farmed, at least. For my part, I hope a message from Lord Falaar will make them see where their loyalty truly lies. To Verlaen, and to humanity."

Eraad looked at him for a moment. Then a smile broke out on his face. "I see. Thank you, Aethal. We must always remember where our true loyalty is. I didn't see it before. But now I do."

Aethal blinked. He hadn't expected such a soft answer from the prince, but was coming to recognize Eraad's changes of mood as part of his character. He hoped that by the time he was king, he would settle down. *Of course, the overriding problem is to make certain that Eraad lives to be king at all. And that his kingdom does, as well.*

"I must have a word with Thane Pyk. Will you come?"

"Of course. It's always worth seeing a thunderbird. But Aethal, are you certain your Uncle Falaar will give Telerat the necessary orders? We have not seen him in court in some time."

"Uncle Falaar is estranged from my father, not from his majesty. And not from common sense either. He will do the right thing. And we'll have the response in hours."

"Of course."

Outside Thane Pyk's tent, a pair of Skysil-liveried servants coaxed the thunderbird out of its cage. They cursed and the bird protested in its eerily deep voice. Then it emerged all at once in a flowering of night-back feathers, clutching its handler by both shoulders and clacking irritably. Aethal and Eraad stared.

The thunderbird was the largest and fastest bird ever to fly. It spread its wings and hissed, revealing dark gray feathers shot with silver. Its black top feathers drank in the light and its steely talons dug deeply into the leather armor covering its handler's shoulders.

At rest, its body was squat and compact, looking the very antithesis of speed, but Aethal knew that the bulk was pure flight muscle. The bird took a tremendous breath through its huge nostrils, and Aethal saw the slits at its shoulders open as it flexed its legs, looking for all the world as if it would carry off the man it perched on as prey.

The falconer's partner drew what looked like a giant black pearl from a pouch and held it up by a great perch set in the ground. Clacking, the bird hopped and glided to its beacon. The beacons were what made the thunderbirds so useful. Unlike pigeons, who had only one home, and would fly back to their nests only, every thunderbird, on reaching maturity, coughed up a single black beacon-pearl. From that time on, it would fly from its beacon to its home. They could span the island of Verlaen in a day, and were among the House of Skysil's most jealously guarded secrets, for they allowed Skysil armies unmatched coordination over long distances.

Pyk came out of the tent and nodded to Aethal and Eraad. "My lords." He handed a thick message cylinder to the falconer, who began the tricky process of tying it to the bird. He handed another scroll to Eraad. "Take this, if it please you, your Highness. It is a copy of the letter I have just sent to my lord of Skysil, asking him to order the city council to open its gates to your father's forces."

"Thank you, my lord Thane," said Eraad.

The Thane of Telerat took the beacon from the handler. Then he spoke a word. The thunderbird leaped forward, beating the air with great flaps of its mighty wings. Up and up it rose, laboring for every foot of height.

When it was high enough that it looked like a toy, it circled once and then pointed toward the distant mountain fastness that House Skysil called home. With two powerful beats of its wings, it shot forward and then, with the clap of thunder that gave the birds their names, shot off, streaking toward the north. The peal of its passage echoed across the hills.

"They'll not miss that in Telerat," snorted Pyk. "Now, let's go to tell them."

***

The delegation that met them this time was larger. Malcoor had insisted that all the Ealdarmen of Telerat be included this time. "It will also tell us, perhaps, whether there are any Ealdarmen that are strangely missing. Won't it, my lord Thane?"

"Aye," Pyk had said, shifting uncomfortably at the thought.

"But mostly, you can be sure that in any council of ten men, some will dissent if you give them a reason to," Malcoor had said. "Let them have a quarrel within their own ranks to divide them, and see how fast they open those gates to us. General Vaagen, are the mortars in place?"

"Yes, sir. We can begin reducing the city in minutes."

"I don't think we'll have to. But, gentlemen, all my orders from before stand. At the first sign of Lotus, we open fire."

Now the ealdarmen of Telerat stood, enduring the Discipline. As before, some stared past the Wyrmguard, and others flinched away, but all eventually were pronounced clean.

"Lord Mayor," began Malcoor. "I trust that you and your men heard the thunderbird."

The man looked wary. "Aye. What of that?"

Malcoor turned to Pyk. "My lord Thane?"

"I sent a message to Lord Falaar," said Pyk. "He, at least, you will admit, is not subject to the power of the King?"

The Lord Mayor nodded cautiously. "I suppose he is not."

"I have asked him to send, in his own hand, an order to you to open my gates, and allow the Warmaster to inspect Telerat. You do know Lord Falaar's hand?"

Lord Cleidh looked ashen. "I know it."

Pyk pitched his voice to carry. "Then the question before us, Lord Cleidh, is whether you will obey a direct order from my liege lord of Skysil, once you have received it?"

The silence stretched.

From the back of the Telerat delegation's ranks, Aethal thought he heard one of the ealdarmen hiss, *"We can't let..."* before the man was roughly silenced by Squire Uitling.

"What assurances would I have," said Lord Cleidh finally, "that the message that arrived would be the one I would see? You know Lord Falaar's hand, too, Thane Pyk."

"And you think I could forge it?" scoffed Pyk. "Shite in the Well, man, you know *my* hand. Do you think I could forge aught?"

The ghost of a smile flitted across the Lord Mayor's face. Pyk's handwriting was legendarily unreadable. But the mask returned instantly.

"You might have forgers in your train, my Lord. The King could certainly afford to employ them, if he thought they would get him what he wants."

"Now you're quibbling, Cleidh," Pyk said urgently. "You can leave an agent to watch for the bird. Hell, you can stay yourself, and..." He trailed off. The Lord Mayor swayed on his feet.

"Is there really Lotus in my city?" Pyk whispered.

The Lord Mayor's mouth worked. "My Lord Thane," he began. "It is not..."

He was interrupted by a tearing noise, and then a loud hiss.

Eraad's flare was in his hand, the fuse lit, and he looked at Aethal with an unholy grin.

"No!" screamed Malcoor. But his voice, loud and desperate as it was, was a small thing on the vast plain before Telerat. Equally uselessly, Aethal leapt at the prince just as he threw the flare in a gentle arc onto the grass, twenty feet distant, where it flashed into green fire, the smoke billowing skyward in a venom-green tower.

dodge right! Aethal's reflexes twisted him to the side just as the pistol in Eraad's left hand coughed, and searing fire flashed beneath his ribs. He hit the prince and bore him to the ground.

And a hundred artillery pieces fired as one.

"Treachery!" cried the Lord Mayor.

aethal! weapons! Aethal reared back and drove his fist into Eraad's face as hard as he could. The shock of it traveled up his arm. Rolling to a crouch, he had the Greater Rifle off his back, just as a ripple of fire tore over his head. One of the ealdarmen whirled on him, and Aethal fired, dropping the man with a bloody hole in his chest. Two of them. Aethal couldn't tell whether he or the Wyrmguard had fired first. Two of them had tackled the prince and were dragging him, screaming, up the slope toward the gun batteries. The other two were firing into the desperate Telerat delegation with a methodical snap of bullets as rapidly as they could rotate the chambers of their weapons. Aethal used the covering fire to reload. Lord Mayor Cleidh dived at Pyk with a snarl on his face. Pyk stood frozen in horror as the first cannonballs struck high on the walls of his city, bringing down crenellations and turrets in showers of mortar and stone.

"Traitor!" the Lord Mayor screamed. Aethal rose, interposing himself, and drove Gun's butt into the man's chest. A shot sounded, far too close, and Colonel Jereg fell at Aethal's side, blood running from his mouth. Most of the Telerat delegation were running for their own gates, now, and Aethal heard the trumpets sounding the charge behind him.

"Fall back! Fall back!" Malcoor was screaming. Aethal snapped a shot into Jereg's killer. Then he threw Gun to his back and drew the Last Sword. The Lord Mayor rolled to his feet with a snarl and came up with a pistol in his hand, aiming at Pyk. Reflexively, Aethal struck. The pistol spun away, leaving Cleidh to stare at his own hand, hanging by a thread of skin. Aethal ended it with a stroke.

"Help me!" cried Malcoor. Aethal bent to lift the still form of Colonel Jereg.

"Run, Uncle Pyk," Aethal gasped, lifting the colonel. "Wyrmguard. Covering fire!" The three of them staggered backward, up an eternity of green lawn. Shots from the Wyrmguard behind them snapped out, and then they, too, were helping lift the colonel's body. Horses and men thundered past them, in full charge.

At the command tent, they were met by a squad of guards. "Get this man to the surgeons!" snapped Malcoor. He and Aethal lowered Colonel Jereg to the grass. For a long moment, Aethal stared down at the man, not much older than he was himself, trying to believe that he saw any sign of life in the wax-pale face. There was none.

Aethal turned away and looked down on the city of Telerat. Musket fire poured from its walls, slashing into the infantry charging up their slopes. Larger puffs of wall-mounted cannon showed erratically. Another volley from their own lines echoed across the field, and a defensive turret erupted in stone chips and dust.

"We might still carry the walls," Malcoor muttered. Aethal could see a dozen scaling ladders going up even as he watched. Jereg's cavalry had dismounted and were using their Greater Rifles to shoot the defenders from the wall, but without their colonel, they hadn't deployed as well as they should have. Then Aethal realized what was wrong.

"Why aren't they using their Greater Rifles for long-range covering fire?"

"This isn't a planned attack," growled Malcoor. "This was a counsel of desperation. So, they're fighting the way we've trained them for the last fifty years!"

And they're attacking a walled city. Even Greater Rifles can't shoot through that sort of cover. In horror, Aethal saw that the pike-and-shot squares of the small Skysil contingent had not attacked, but stood in formation, watching the slaughter of their countrymen. *And what is their commander thinking?* Whatever he was doing, he wasn't obeying orders to attack. As he watched, they began to move. But not toward Telerat, or back toward the rear of the army. They were marching north, into the hills around Telerat. Back to the Skysil domain.

We've lost them, Aethal thought, numbly.

General Vaagen ran up to them. "Warmaster! Last Sword! Is it treachery?"

Malcoor whirled on him, and Vaagen, old campaigner that he was, stepped back from the rage on the lean face. "It is treachery, General. Great treachery. Bring me the Prince at once!"

Aethal turned to Everwar. "Bring the Crown Prince to the Warmaster. Carry him bodily if you must."

In less than a minute, Eraad was stumbling between two Wyrmguard with an expression of outrage on his face. Blood was running freely from his nose. "What do you mean by having these things drag me across the field? I was..."

"Shut up, Your Highness." Aethal hadn't known he was going to say the words until he did. Then Malcoor was there, advancing on the prince like death.

"What have you done, boy?"

Eraad glared at him. "I punished them for rebellion and treason. They were hiding the Lotus and defying the King! We were going to have to attack them anyway. I just did what you feared they might do to us: decapitating their command. They should fall apart easily enough, now. You said so yourself. If we took the gates by surprise..."

Malcoor seized Eraad by the collar, and turned him to face the walls of Telerat, where gunfire sparked and gouts of smoke marked the impact of their own cannon fire. "Does that look like they're falling apart, you Well-spawned bastard? Does it? You killed their leaders under a flag of truce and are attacking their homes. They're going to fight to the last man!"

"They were hiding Lotus!" yelled the prince. "There's no truce with Lotus! You said it yourself! Unhand me!"

The Wyrmguard moved.

"Belay that!" Aethal spoke sharply. "The Prince is not being hurt. The Prince is being taught a lesson." *The Prince tried to kill me.* The thought wouldn't become real. Eraad twisted in Malcoor's grip and shot Aethal a look of pure hatred, but it slid off like water.

Malcoor did not notice. He took Eraad's head in his hands and forced him to face the city. "The attack you just launched was meant to ensure that we could not be thrown into total confusion if we were betrayed by *them*. We hadn't prepared the men! We hadn't planned the assault. Our only hope now is to carry the gates by surprise!"

Involuntarily, Aethal looked at the walls of Telerat. He could see the king's banner up in two places, now, but the musket fire from the walls was still heavy. Surprise had bought them a place on the walls, but he'd never seen an all-out attack against any position as heavily defended as Telerat. The dead and wounded lay in a carpet before the walls, and his stomach turned.

"They were going to tell me everything when you threw that flare," Malcoor hissed. "Those men you just had shot were not farmed, and if any of them survived, they will never meet with us again. If Lotus is in that city, we will have to root it out ourselves, and every man's hand will be against us. You have betrayed Verlaen more thoroughly than any thousand leafeaters and, my Lord *Prince*," he made the word a curse, "I shall charge you with treason and violation of the Discipline accordingly. The penalty for making a false report of Lotus infestation is death."

Incredibly, Eraad drew himself up. "I did *not* make a false report. The Lotus is in that town, and we will find it. And I am the Crown Prince of Verlaen; I *cannot* commit treason or violate the Discipline. Maednac my ancestor created the Discipline, and it is my right to decide when it applies. It is your privilege and duty to serve me!"

"And these men?" whispered Malcoor. "These men you sent to their deaths? Was it their duty to let you throw their lives away for nothing?"

"When we find Lotus inside the walls," Eraad fumed, "I will expect your apology, Malcoor."

Malcoor screamed in rage and swung his fist at the prince. Everwar blocked his fist with his own. "Warmaster," he said, as if he was discussing protocol in the capital. "I cannot allow you to strike the Imperial Governor's Heir in such a manner. It is against the Compact. You could injure him."

Malcoor stepped back, breathing hard. He looked at Aethal. "I have no time for this," he said. "I have to see if anything can be salvaged from this debacle. Last Sword, conduct the Prince to where he will have a good view of the consequences of the exercise of his *rights*." He stalked off.

"Old fool," Eraad muttered. He made to leave.

"Wyrmguard, hold the Prince," Aethal said.

The Wyrmguard took Eraad by the upper arms. "Aethal, have you gone mad?" Eraad asked. "Let go of me! I said let go!"

Rage coursed through Aethal at every beat of his heart. It surprised him vaguely how ice-cold it was. "You tried to kill me, Eraad," he said.

"You jumped on me!" Eraad snarled back. "What was I supposed to think? You killed Jehan Alfing for the same thing!"

It almost made sense. Eraad had been there for Aethal's bloody succession to this post. *Only I hadn't drawn the Last Sword. And you had that pistol ready in your hand.* Eraad was frothing with anger. "Why didn't they stop you? Why won't they obey me?"

"I spent the lives of my men in the streets and buildings of Everview to bring you and your father the news of Lotus, Eraad," Aethal said quietly. "Because of the Discipline. I ordered them into danger because of it, and in the end, I had to shoot a good friend. Because of the Discipline." Lieutenant Godwin's face, composed in desperate courage, floated in his mind's eye. "And now, you have thrown men just like them into that hell," Aethal pointed at the battle, "and exposed us all to the Lotus, all because you. Have. No. Discipline."

Eraad opened his mouth to reply, but Aethal didn't let him. "Take the Prince," he said, "to the surgeons' tents. He will watch the battle from there. You will force him to observe until I come for him. He is not to be allowed to move from that spot. If he can no longer stand, you will hold him on his feet. This is for his own protection. Am I understood?"

"Yes, Last Sword," said Everwar.

"Let me go!" screamed Eraad, as the Wyrmguard began to march him off. "Let me go! You are *my* Wyrmguard! *Obey me!*"

"Stop!" said Aethal.

The Wyrmguard stopped.

"Please explain to the Prince," said Aethal softly, "what is happening."

"According to the Compact," said Everwar, "The Wyrmguard are charged to preserve the life of the Imperial Governor and his line. We may accept no order that would endanger the Governor or his line. The Last Sword struck you to preserve your life and his own. The Wyrmguard do not answer to you unless the Imperial Governor and the Last Sword are not present. In the absence of the Imperial Governor, the Compact dictates that we obey the Last Sword, unless he should deliberately place you in danger. His order is not dangerous to you."

They dragged Eraad off, still protesting.

***

By the time Aethal caught up to Malcoor and Pyk, they were surrounded by messengers. Most were waiting for Malcoor's orders. One was finishing his report. "Brigadier Garedder reports he has control of the walls and gates, but the enemy is contesting every street leading to the town center. The scouts — the *scout* that returned reported there was some sort of barricade near the center of town — but we don't know what they could be protecting there. He said some of them were firing *into* it."

Malcoor nodded. "What's his estimate?"

"We can't push any force inside the walls without heavy losses. The enemy counterattacks every time our fire slackens, and they've shot two men under white flags."

"Determined to make us pay for our sin, I suppose," said Malcoor. He let out a sigh, then he raised his voice. "Take this order to all your commanders. Our forces will disengage and retreat to the mortar pits. They will form defensive lines there. All infantry will use their Greater Rifles to kill anyone who emerges from the city bearing weapons. You may accept the surrender of any civilians who offer it so long as you are confident in your ability to impose the Discipline. Otherwise, you will shoot to kill."

"Lieutenant," Malcoor said, to a young man at his side. "Tell the cornets to ride to the mortar pits. All of them. Tell them to deliver this message: Stormfall. Tell them, Stormfall."

"No! Warmaster, ye cannot do it!" shouted Pyk. "Not the whole town. Ye..." He stopped. Looking twice his age, Pyk straightened and then dropped to his knees before Malcoor. "Please, sir. You can do what you have ordered. But I beg you not to. I beg you in the name of God-Beyond-The-World. Take the city. Occupy it. Save it from the Lotus. Do not destroy it."

For the first time since Aethal had first seen him as a young cadet, Aethal saw Malcoor's face soften. "Thane Pyk Imya Telerat, I can save your city. No one knows it better than I do. But I also know that if I do it, I could be giving this same order from the Westerend to Maednac Serpiin itself, and still lose Verlaen. I dare not take that chance. I am sorry. But I have seen what the Lotus can do when people *can* live with it. And it's worse than what I have just ordered."

The couriers departed in silence with their faces turned away so that they would not have to see the Thane of Telerat sobbing with his face in the dust. Aethal led him away before the first bombs arced out over the city, and called the surgeons to commandeer enough brandy to drink his uncle unconscious.

Chapter Five

55th of Spring, 312 Exodus

"Sir," said Osric. "You must wake up. Please, sir." His valet looked worried.

Aethal woke from confused nightmares of fire and horses to muscles that screamed in protest, and a head full of fog. Yes, he had to wake. Stumbling out of bed, he croaked, "Bath."

"Already drawn, sir." Bless Osric, towels and hot wine were waiting for him.

This was the waking world, then. There had been no baths in his nightmares. Otherwise, the world was much the same. And it would have to be dealt with. The General States met today. And there were matters to see to before that. "Summon Colonel Farnan," he said, after a pull at the wine had banished the rasp from his throat. "And find out how Thane Pyk is doing." Osric froze, nodded jerkily and left.

Aethal winced at the heat of the tub and the ache in his joints. The news of the battle at Telerat must be all over the city by now. Aethal had no idea what time it had been when he had stumbled to bed. They had arrived well after dark. He only remembered Paitir's shattered expression as he'd told him about Eraad's disgrace. He'd had to tell him three times. Or was it four?

Sire, Eraad is under arrest for Breach of the Discipline. He gave a false signal of Lotus that resulted in the razing of Telerat.

Then he'd had to tell the story. All of it. All the while watching Paitir's eyes flick to the two Wyrmguard flanking him, as if hoping that one of them would contradict him. Finally, when Aethal had finished, Paitir had not been able to resist asking.

Wyrmguard. Is all this true?

All that the Last Sword has said is true, Your Excellency, Everwar had said. He might have been confirming Aethal's attendance at a staff conference.

But Lotus was, in fact, in Telerat? Chancellor Paal had asked, then.

It was, Malcoor had said. *But the Prince could not have known of it at the time. None of us did. He committed gross insubordination and violated the terms of the parley.*

Yes, that had been confirmed by Squire Cailing, who had run from his burning city with the half of his family he had been able to find, out of the horrors of the mortar bombardment. Through his sobs, the man confirmed that Lotus had been in Telerat for a week, and that they had discovered it growing in the Temple. He swore that they had it under control, and that all the leafeaters were either dead or barricaded. One of the priests had gotten out clean, but others were farmed.

The survivor had sworn that the king had ordered that any town infected with Lotus was to be destroyed, and its people burned. The ealdarmen had told the people it was a plague, while desperately trying to destroy the infection. And then the royal army had arrived before they could finish it. So, they had panicked, refusing to admit the truth. To save themselves.

And who knows if anyone ran from the city, carrying the Lotus in a family member they did not want to see killed?

There was no Lotus in Telerat now, of course. There was no Telerat for there to be Lotus in.

It had taken two days for the army to crawl back to the Serpent's Pass. Two days of listening to Eraad protest his innocence and scream threats whenever anyone but the Wyrmguard approached him. Eventually Malcoor had ordered him held away from everyone else, and threatened to lock him in the root cells of the Pass keepwoods for the night if he wouldn't shut up. Aethal almost wished he'd carried through on that threat, and that Jeralta's unknown assassin still lurked in the great tree. It would have simplified a great many things.

There had been no question of moving on to the Treeline. Razing Telerat had run them out of ammunition. More supplies would be needed before setting out against the Grassworms. And more men to replace the Skysil troops that had abandoned them.

Until they knew what the Skysils would do about Telerat, no decision could be made. Aethal felt nauseous. His Uncle Falaar was a proud man. What would he do when he heard that his third-largest city had been burned at the whim of a fool?

Malcoor had left Vaagen and Jeharok guarding the Pass, while he consulted with the king. *I owe his Majesty this report in person,* he had said.

Today we try to convince the General States that we must go to the Well in order to end the Lotus at its source. He could not linger in the bath, even if the water could be kept heated. He rose, dripping, and made himself presentable. He could not appear weak today, not when Malcoor and the king would be carrying such heavy burdens themselves.

Osric entered as Aethal was pulling on his boots. "Last Sword? Your breakfast is ready and," he trailed off. "And Colonel Farnan is here. He's... there's two other men with him, sir."

Aethal frowned. "Did you ask their names?" Osric hesitated. "I'm sure Farnan has good reason for bringing them. Show them in. And offer tea."

Aethal greeted Farnan, Sergeant Falk, and, as it turned out, Magnei, in his parlor. "Gentlemen, I hope you will not think me rude if I break my fast while we talk. It's like to be my only chance to eat. Sit. Tea is coming."

A hollow grin was on Farnan's face. "Wish me dead, Aethal, I'm glad to see you at last. It's been a long week without you, and when we heard the news from Telerat," he trailed off. "How bad was it?"

"It's hard to imagine it being worse. However, I suppose it's best you hear it from me than that you hear rumors." Beginning with their arrival at Telerat,

Aethal told the entire story, leaving out only Eraad's attempt on his own life. He had not even told the king that. He wanted to consider the matter more before acting on it. Farnan's face fell, and Magnei, who was already looking worried, went pale. Sergeant Falk merely looked grim.

"Magnei, you are my Lotus Expert. Malcoor thinks that your expedition to the Well is our only chance, now. Is he right?"

"Last Sword, I have been honest with you from the beginning. While I was always glad to hear of a new weapon against the Lotus, the Lord Warden sent me because he believed that I was correct in my analysis. Only a Wish can stop the Lotus. If it was true then, it is truer now."

Aethal nodded. "Thank you." He turned to his friend. "So cheer me up, Farnan. Tell me everything you've done with the City Watch since I left."

Farnan pursed his lips. "I'll have to be honest, they're better than I thought. Training and patrols are going smoothly." Farnan ran down a list of various checkpoints in the city. All were in order. "I've been working with Major Ganling of the Temple Guard to ensure that his Lotus patrols are working smoothly. That's seemed to calm matters down on the streets."

"The Temple Guard has taken over the Lotus patrol duties? Entirely?"

"Not entirely, there weren't quite enough to do that. But mostly." So, Ilferth Simon's recommendation was good. "If it's working, then it's working." He hadn't meant to implement it quite so quickly, however. Osric came in with the tea and placed a cup in front of Farnan. Falk accepted a mug and saucer, and Magnei turned faintly green and pushed his saucer away.

"Be careful, there, Osric," Aethal said.

"Sorry, my Lord," said Osric, wiping up the tea he had sloshed over Aethal's plate.

"It is working, sir. When the Church took over the Lotus patrols — the day you left — the people stopped resisting. The Church asked them to turn over the weapons they did have. Appealed to them in the name of God-Beyond-The-World. I always knew the people of this city had quite an arsenal, here, but I've never seen so many of them. I wouldn't have believed it. It's been good to have them off the street, frankly. Everyone's a little less jumpy. They're not afraid of being seized for a night's hard patrol anymore, or, ah, anything else."

"Good to know." One less nightmare to endure.

"And we just finished moving our own armories there yesterday."

Aethal felt his head jerk up. "You what?"

Farnan narrowed his eyes. "Aethal? We finished moving our armories to the Churches."

"Why in the Pit of the Well would you do that?" Aethal asked.

"Aethal," repeated Farnan. "You ordered us to. Just like you ordered us to hand over the patrol duties to the Church. All those dispatches from Telerat."

Aethal felt his mouth hang open. "I never sent any dispatches."

"But, Aethal, Osric handed me every one of..."

Then Sergeant Falk threw his scalding tea at Aethal's face.

The throw was high, and Aethal managed to duck out of the way with only a searing trail of drops burning through his hair. Osric cried out in agony.

danger behind!

All of Aethal's instincts screamed for him to come to his feet and face Falk; he knew how deadly the man was. But Aethal's long trust in Gun won out, and in a smooth motion he pistoned his legs against the table, sending himself flying into Osric's legs. Both men hit the tea cart in a shower of crockery. Osric cried out again, whether because he hit the floor or landed on hot tea Aethal could not say. A metal shape spun away from his hand and struck the divan. Aethal recognized the dart gun, a one-shot weapon slightly longer than a man's hand. Almost silent, it was only accurate out to ten feet. Horror flooding him, he rolled over and looked down at Osric, whose face, already contorted in agony, seized up again in a rictus. Sergeant Falk had stepped on his left hand.

"Who bought your life and honor, Osric?" he asked, feeling the same awful detachment he'd experienced in Everview and in Telerat. "What were they worth?"

"Very little, compared to the whole world," Osric whispered, staring at the ceiling. He gasped in agony again. Aethal drew breath to tell Falk to ease off.

Falk's foot was no longer on Osric's wrist.

"Even less compared to my soul," the servant sighed.

"Tell me who sent you," said Aethal.

you know already.

Gun did not understand the value of witnesses. It understood efficiency in killing.

"Tell me!"

"I must respectfully refuse, my Lord," gasped Osric, his face now turning purple. "You see, I drank a cup of tea as well..."

It took five minutes more for him to die. Even before that, Aethal had turned to his companions. "Can I at least hope that no one drank the tea?"

"It was too hot yet," said Farnan, as if poison crossed his plate every day. Shock.

Magnei was staring across the table. "Always hated the stuff," he muttered. Then he collapsed, shuddering.

Falk rounded on him. "Were you splashed?"

Aethal held up a hand. "No, Sergeant, if it was contact poison, we'd both of us be dying. Magnei is not a soldier. Well done, by the way."

"Thank you, Sir."

Aethal summoned a Wyrmguard. It was Flintmaw. "Take the remains of this tea to the Royal College to identify the poison, along with the dart-gun. I'd like to learn our enemy's weapons, even if we cannot identify him," he said.

"We know already who he is, Sir." Falk's words and tone were such an exact reproduction of Gun's that Aethal found himself staring. "Only Ilferth Simon's man would go down thinking of his worthless soul."

"And now he has all our guns? All the Watch's guns?"

Farnan slowly nodded. "Not all of them of course. The men on the walls are fully armed, but all those inside the city store their weapons in the Church depots. Spit in the Well, Aethal, I thought you'd *ordered* me to..."

Aethal held up a hand. "I'm not interested in recriminations, now. We get them back as soon as we can. If Ilferth Simon is indeed behind this, he'll expect us all to be dead. We'll pretend that nothing has happened and see if that provokes our Conversant into doing anything even more foolish. Farnan, in case it does, turn out the City Watch. All men on duty. Double the Guards on the Hydraxis. If Ilferth Simon is desperate enough to try this already, how desperate will he be if this vote goes the way I think it will? I don't want us surprised."

Farnan rose. "Yes, sir."

"How many weapons does the Church have?"

Sergeant Falk answered, "To hear Major Ganling tell it, he thinks we've taken the weapons off the streets of Maednac Serpiin. We haven't. At best, we've got the bullshit that people keep around their homes to scare away burglars. Pistols and shotguns that haven't been fired in years. But Boss Skraalen, well," he fished in his pocket. "He promised you a list. Here it is. Not all of these shipments have names attached to them, and damn few mean anything to me."

Aethal took the list. He felt his guts churn.

"Sergeant, these are some of the most powerful men in the Bowl. Easily half of them will be casting their votes in the General States in two hours' time."

"None of those guns are in the Church armories. They're no Greater Rifles, but they're deadly enough for all that. And Ganling doesn't have a clue where they are. The man's a fool."

Something in his voice made Aethal's ears prick up. "I hear a 'but' on the end of that assessment, Sergeant."

"But everything seems to be going very smoothly for him. Like the Colonel said: the moment his men took over, the problems we've had with Discipline and resistance vanished. Oh, a few incidents, but nothing like what we'd been seeing. It's as if people were just waiting for him to do what he did. It feels bad."

Aethal frowned. He'd learned to respect the Sergeant's feelings. But he had no time to analyze them now. "I must attend upon the King. Skraalen will be here, too. You talk with him. And then I want those weapons back in our possession."

Falk rose. "Yes, sir."

"Flintmaw," Aethal said, "Keep my guest safe. He is to have two Wyrm-guard with him at all times. After that, attend me. I shall be in the Thane of Telerat's apartments." Bracing himself for the ordeal to come, Aethal went to meet his uncle.

***

The guard outside the Thane of Telerat's rooms wore Skysil purple-black-and-white. Upon seeing Aethal, his face hardened. "I will see if the Thane has time for you," he said. After a longer pause than usual, the guard returned, and Aethal was admitted. A serving girl led him through the parlor and into the Thane's bedchamber, where the older man looked up at him through bloodshot eyes from where he lay sprawled in a chair. He was draped in a bathrobe, and already had a cup of wine in his hand. Around his neck hung Pfyfr's torc, slightly askew. He blinked in the sunlight.

"What d'yer want, boy?" he asked.

Aethal felt his heart sink. Uncle Pyk looked utterly defeated. *He had to watch us burn his city to the ground. What more defeat is possible for him?*

"Uncle Pyk, the General States meet in an hour," he said. "Your servants should be getting you ready." He turned to the valet who was passing through. "Get your master's clothes laid out." The man nodded and disappeared.

"Ain't going to the General States, boy. No point."

Was the man really that far gone? "Uncle Pyk, it's your duty. You have to cast the Skysil's vote!"

Pyk looked at him with a watery, empty gaze, and then said, "Leave us. All of you." The servants scattered. Pyk picked up a scroll from a sideboard.

"This was waiting for us, boy. It arrived by thunderbird two days before we did. You can deliver it for me to the General States. Or to the King. Or to hell." He threw it, and Aethal picked it up from the floor. It was brief:

To Paitir Eadmunding of House Maednac,

We have received concurring testimonies accompanied by many pieces of evidence that your forces did, five days past, treacherously attack and destroy our city of Telerat, even while negotiating with its chief citizens under flag of truce.

We therefore declare that by this act, you have shown yourself to be a tyrant, a murderer, and a coward. And taken together with your unwillingness in times past to acknowledge, much less redress grievances suffered by our house and realm, must consider that you are unworthy of the ancient respect due your great ancestor, and find you unworthy to bear the title of King of Verlaen.

Nevertheless, by reason of the great crisis which confronts our peoples, so long as we cohabit this land, we will have peace with you, if you have the wisdom to accept this, and will receive your ambassador if he is sent to us at our court where we now reign as King of the Skysil Dominions.

Delivered by thunderbird into the hand of our Servant, the most noble Thane of Telerat

King Falaar I

Aethal's guts churned. *Secession. Civil War. No.* "Uncle Pyk, the King didn't order this. He didn't do it..."

"He ordered it," said Pyk, harshly. More quietly, he said, "He ordered it when he sent that jackal that calls himself his son, with cannon. To invest my city."

"Eraad isn't the King. You saw what he did. The King hasn't pardoned him." Pyk laughed, and there were sobs in it.

"So that monster will face justice, then?" he asked. "Can he? He's the King's only child, boy. Maednac's line is ended, one way or another. No Skysil will ever follow that bastard. But it doesn't matter. Skysil is out of the kingdom, and I'm not staying in the same building with that murderer a moment longer than I have to. I was only..." he stared at his wineglass. "I don't know what I was only," he muttered. "I'm going home. If I have one. My hunting lodge in the North Peaks, perhaps. The Wellshite didn't burn that, at least."

"Uncle Pyk," Aethal said, forcing himself to calm, "All of Verlaen hangs on this vote. The Guardians tell me we have no hope to stop the Lotus by our own efforts anymore."

Pyk's lips trembled. "Piss on Verlaen."

"Uncle Pyk, hear reason! If Lotus was in Telerat it may be in the rest of the Skysil domain, too. If we're to save anything from the Lotus, we have to send someone to the Well, and by Maednac's Law, we can only do that if the General States agree."

"Then let them agree," Pyk said. "The Skysil domain isn't part of your General States anymore. Your uncle's made himself king, and king or lord, I'm his man. So, I've no vote and no business here."

Aethal lifted the parchment. "Pyk, you know I honor Uncle Falaar. He gave me my chance to be something more than just the son of my father. And I know why he has done this. I was there, Pyk, and I know why you want to join him. But you can't. We can't go our own way, fall apart before the Lotus. Not because of Eraad. We must stand together before it as men. Or every city in the land may suffer the same fate as your people of Telerat. Please, Uncle. Don't make that more likely. Don't let that be Telerat's legacy."

Pyk was finally listening, and the water stood in his eyes. "But I have no power to do aught, Aethal. Don't you see? The Skysil vote is water."

"But it isn't," said Aethal. "Uncle Falaar didn't revoke your ambassadorial power. You still have this." He touched the torc about Pyk's neck. "Yours is the voice of the Skysil. Whether he acknowledges it or not. And more. Because if

Uncle Falaar is in rebellion, and his brother Galenn with him, then you are the rightful Lord Paramount of Skysil, by all the laws of this kingdom."

"That's treason, Aethal." Pyk shook his head. "I'll not betray my cousin," he got out, tears running down his face. "Not even for you, Aethal."

"No. What Eraad did was treason. What Uncle Falaar is doing, by all the laws of the kingdom, is treason, however good a reason he has for it. What you are doing, by casting the Skysil's vote, is remaining loyal. It's taking your last chance to save him, King or Lord, or traitor or whatever men call him. Your people are gone, and your city. No one can bring them back. Save others from joining them."

Pyk blinked, and the tears flowed down his face. Finally, he nodded.

Aethal raised himself off the wall. "Thank you, Lord Pyk," he managed.

Pyk clutched the torc that his lord had sent him just weeks ago until his knuckles whitened. "For Telerat," he whispered. He continued whispering it as Aethal summoned the servants to prepare him for the assembly. "For Telerat. For Telerat."

***

At the bottom of the great keep of the Ophidian, central tower of the Hydraxis, Aethal entered the Red Chamber in full dress uniform. Gun and the Last Sword rode on his back, and his metal was polished to a mirror sheen.

The walls were covered with the arms of the Houses Paramount and their vassals. As was the tradition, the Wrackberg and the Skysil retainers sat to the king's right, the Westerend sat to the king's left, so that the king might look down on his lords as though they were a stylized map of his realm. Directly behind them, the Single Moon of the Church graced the doorway, and to either side on the great rear wall, hung the banners of the towns and shires of the kingdom, representing the common folk.

The chamber should have been filled. But because of the Lotus, only about half the seats in the back of the hall were occupied. Too many had been unable — or unwilling — to travel. Most of the seats belonging to the Church were filled, as the Conversant could appoint his own representatives. All the Wrackberg vassals were in attendance. The Westerend seats held a good dozen of Lord Vaughan's. Aethal looked down at the Skysil seats and winced. The three men, whose companion had been found farmed and then shot according to the Discipline. They sat alone: it seemed the rest of the delegates feared that Lotus might be contagious by mere association.

All eyes looked up at Aethal when he entered beneath the Royal standard and took up his station before the throne.

Vermilion shimmersilk curtains were drawn aside from the stained glass, allowing the multicolored light to play on landscapes painted by some of the kingdom's finest artists. Aethal recognized a Kaanleva oil that was doubtless beyond price, showing Maednac's Bay before the Wrackberg had even been raised. Green hills rolled away to the sea, undisturbed. On either side of Aethal, a pair of heralds emerged silently with their cornets. They blew a high, clear chord. The last of the delegates had arrived. Now the General States would convene, for the first time in living memory.

Lord Mayor Rolf Hlafen entered, trailed by a ceremonial pikeman in a blue tabard adorned with Maednac Serpiin's key-and-lock sigil. A Greater Rifle rode upon the pikeman's back. It was Farnan, of course, in charge of security. He gave Aethal an almost invisible nod. The Lord Mayor strode to his seat at the front of the Commons, for whom the Lord Mayor by tradition spoke, exchanging nods and a rare smile with his fellows.

Ilferth Simon swept in next, in full Church regalia. His rich, black robes were of silk lined with sea-otter fur. The shimmersilk moons on them seemed to flow as he moved, like pools of quicksilver. He was adorned with the other symbols of the Church: silver shields of polished aluminum at his shoulders, and over his face, the half-mask of the Conversant's office: aluminum polished to mirror-brightness. Four Church riflemen marched behind him. Aethal felt Gun tense in his mind.

ware now. lesser rifles, but the greatest of them, surely. Aethal nodded. The rifles would be made by master craftsmen. Each had two barrels. One would be smoothbore, loaded with shot. The other would be rifled, the equal of anything short of Gun itself. Aethal watched the Conversant's hands and face. *Are you surprised to see me, Holiness?* But Ilferth Simon gave no sign.

The Lords Paramount entered next. First Pyk, looking grave, but dressed in his court finest. Aethal met his eyes as he bowed to the king. Next entered Lord Westerend, his face as expressionless as Ilferth Simon's mask. He took his seat without looking at the throne. Last was Chancellor Paal, who entered nodding to his own vassals, but continued up the steps to the dais, taking position before Aethal in preparation for performing his office. He gave an unobtrusive hand signal to the heralds.

The cornets played the high counterpoint descant that was the anthem of the Kings of Verlaen. According to tradition, it was the last bars of the fanfare of the old Emperors, in a minor key. Behind Aethal, four Wyrmguard escorted King Paitir to his throne.

Paal tapped his staff of office on the bloodstone floor. "In the name of Paitir the Second, King of Verlaen and Steward of all the Fallen Lands, in this three hundred and twenty-third year since Maednac's Landing, let this General States of Humankind be assembled a fifth time before the throne, and their will be done. May the One-Beyond-The-World favor us."

And it was done. What was decided here, now, would bind the kingdom. "Would the Conversant with God-Beyond-The-World do us the honor of praying before this Assembly of His lost children."

Ilferth Simon rose and advanced. The Chancellor gave way before him. His voice, when he spoke, was sonorous. "In the Name of God-Be-yond-The-World, Whose Name is hidden from lost mankind, all shall kneel."

Aethal knelt. Chancellor Paal knelt. Behind him, Aethal could hear the king kneel. The Conversant alone remained standing. In the silence, a keening cry filled the air. Aethal could not help himself. He looked up for the source of the sound, and realized that it was the Conversant himself who was crying out. The keen modulated suddenly into words.

"O Holy One, Who long ago gave us the Wish we asked for, and denied us Yourself until we should prove worthy, we ask: do not deny us the wisdom to obey You in all things this day, as You have revealed them to your Servants.

"Once, O Lord of Heaven, the heart of the King was turned from Your light, and in his pride, Salnum sunk the Well, because it seemed to him the best of things. Allow our King and these his servants, to make a better choice, though it be a hard one, and seem hopeless. Amen."

Aethal blinked. Was that Prayer? It had sounded like any political speech he had ever heard. But he had no time to wonder, for his father was speaking.

"His Majesty has called the General States to hear its assembled wisdom. The matter is to determine our response to the threat posed by the Lotus, which even now grows within our borders. His Majesty wills that you first examine the testimony of certain of his subjects, who have studied the Lotus and fought it."

"A point of order, Chancellor." The Lord Mayor of Maednac Serpiin rose. "Before these General States deliberate, I must ask whether the rumors we have heard are true: has the Lord Paramount of the Skysil domain rebelled and declared himself King? And if so, then why is his representative in this chamber?" A chorus of agreement broke out at these words from the Commons.

Chancellor Paal's staff slammed into the stones for quiet.

"If you want an answer," Paal said, in the acid tones for which he was famous, "you must consent to hear it." The uproar calmed. "It is true that Lord Falaar has raised his banner in rebellion against His Majesty. But his ambassador, the Thane of Telerat, is His Majesty's loyal vassal, and has been confirmed by His

Majesty as the Lord Paramount of Skysil, until and unless the Lord Falaar be reconciled to the throne. Does that satisfy you, Lord Mayor?"

"It begs another question, rather," the Lord Mayor replied. "Seeing as the cause of the Lord Falaar's rebellion is, by all accounts, the destruction of Thane Pyk's city of Telerat, has His Majesty yet determined what shall be done about the conduct of his son, the Crown Prince Eraad?"

The Commons exploded with noise again. This time Paal simply stared at the Lord Mayor until silence fell. "What does that matter have to do with the purpose for which these General States were convened, my Lord Mayor?"

Lord Mayor Hlafen barked a short, humorless laugh. "The Commons think they have a right to know, Chancellor, if His Majesty is trying to buy his son's pardon and the vote of the Skysil's delegates with a Lord Paramountcy! Is Thane Pyk being compensated for his loss with a greater prize?"

Now the whole chamber exploded. Aethal felt fury erupt in him at the accusation. But it was nothing compared to the white rage on Thane Pyk's. He was being wrestled back to his seat by his three vassals, and his knife was bare. "You bastard! You bastard!" he screamed, and the words were audible even over the roars of "Shame, shame!" from the other delegations.

"Lord Mayor, you are out of order," said Paal, when Pyk had been restrained and he could again be heard.

"Is it out of order to know what favors may be exchanged for what votes? Let the Crown answer now: is the Crown Prince to be charged with Breach of Discipline, the penalty for which is death?"

"That is not a matter for discussion in these chambers, Hlafen," said Paal.

"I move we make it one, Wrackberg!"

"It is a matter for a military court."

"A Breach of Discipline goes beyond that, Chancellor, and you know it."

"There was no Breach of Discipline," Paal replied. "The Crown Prince disobeyed the direct order of Warmaster Malcoor, his legal superior, and he will be charged with that crime."

This time, the reaction was an astonished murmur, and Aethal barely kept his mouth from falling open. *No Breach of Discipline? What in the Well are you playing at, father?*

"No Breach of Discipline?" echoed Hlafen.

"The Crown Prince gave a signal that there was Lotus in Telerat," said Paal. "By the testimony of the civilians who sought refuge with our forces, there was indeed Lotus in Telerat."

Aethal felt his face grow brick red. So, he was using that defense. Eraad hadn't known of the Lotus in Telerat; at best he'd made a wild guess and gotten lucky.

The Lord Mayor wasn't swallowing it either. "Have you already held the trial, and I've not heard? How was this determined? Or..." he paused dramatically. "Is it possible that there is another motive here? Have you made your own bargain, Lord Wrackberg? Your son awaits his own trial on the serious charges of kidnapping and treason, does he not? Have you and the Crown agreed to ransom one another's sons?"

If the Lord Mayor had hoped to goad Paal as he had goaded Pyk, he was in for a disappointment. "Your speculations are baseless and waste this Assembly's time," said Paal, in a bored voice. "I have no son but Aethal Paaling, the Last Sword. If you have a motion, make it, or sit down."

"Very well: I move that the General States try the Crown Prince for Breach of Discipline and high treason."

"Second!" cried Pyk. "You bastard!"

Aethal's breath caught. So that was the Lord Mayor's game. He'd scored Pyk's vote for the price of an insult, and Uncle Pyk was far too enraged and devastated to see it. But why was he so determined to press this now?

"It has been moved and seconded that the General States bring the Crown Prince to trial for his actions at Telerat. I shall now request the votes." He looked the Lord Mayor in the eyes. "It is the privilege of the Commons to cast its votes first. Lord Mayor, poll your delegates."

Hlafen turned to his delegation. "All in favor?"

"Aye!" The shout rebounded from the chamber's walls like thunder.

"The Commons casts two votes in favor, by acclamation," said Paal, cutting off Hlafen before he could speak. "Your Holiness, please poll your delegates."

The Church's vote was much quieter, but was also unanimous. "The Church votes no," said the Conversant.

"My Lord of Skysil?" asked Paal.

"Aye," grated Pyk, teeth bared.

Paal did not poll his delegates. It was the privilege of the Lords Paramount to overrule them, and Paal did so. "The Wrackberg votes no. My Lord of Westerend?"

"The Westerend votes no," Lord Vaughan said, in a colorless voice.

What's wrong with him? Aethal had never seen the tough Lord of Westerend look so subdued.

"Your Majesty?" asked the Chancellor.

"No," said the king, in a voice full of shame. Aethal felt both revulsion and sympathy for the man, but there was nothing he could do.

"By a vote of four to three against, the motion to try Prince Eraad in the General States is quelled. Now we may return to the original purpose of this Assembly.

"We have known of the presence of the Lotus in Verlaen for two months. In that time, it has consumed the minds of the barbaric tribes of the Grain Sea, and driven our forces from the Treeline. As yet, the Lotus has not penetrated the Westerend or the Serpent's Pass to threaten the bulk of our population. At the moment, General Vaagen is rallying the Royal Army for the purpose of taking back the Treeline and exterminating the Lotus and its leafeaters once and for all. Nevertheless, it has been proposed to the Crown from sources whose credentials cannot be ignored, that the King take the extraordinary step, for the first time in our history, of violating Maednac's Ban, and sending of an expedition to Salnum's Well, for the purpose of Wishing..." even Paal's dry voice stumbled at the word, "Lotus to be destroyed."

The Red Chamber exploded in voices. Aethal frowned. Was his father *trying* to turn the General States against the idea? He'd supported it himself.

Paal spoke over them. "The Crown calls to give testimony and be examined, Warmaster Joseth Malcoor of House Westerend."

This title was greeted with a few murmurs. Obviously Malcoor's new legitimacy had its doubters, but every voice was silent when the Warmaster entered. Aethal watched him walk down the length of the Chamber, every inch a commander of men. He stood before Paal and bowed from the neck. Paal returned the bow. "Warmaster," he said. "You may address the General States."

Malcoor turned to the assembly. "I have served His Majesty as a general officer for nearly forty years," he said. "In that time, I have fought no foe so implacable or terrifying as the Lotus. The Lotus turns friend to foe, and suborns all his talents to one singular purpose: eating and spreading the Lotus. The Lotus-Eater does not fear death, and does not fear pain. If the Lotus was Wished from the Well, as all our tales assure us it was, then we must call upon the same source to destroy it. For I tell you now, I do not see any other hope for our victory."

"Why do you think we cannot hold as we are?" asked Paal.

"We've lost our main source of food. The Grain Sea cannot simply be replaced. But even if our Fleet can make up the difference by its harvest of the oceans, I give us a year. Two at the outside. We cannot retake the Grain Sea."

"Why? You were not so pessimistic even two weeks ago."

"Two weeks ago, I had promise of help from the Skysil and Westerend domains. The attack from the Westerend failed, and the Skysils intend to fight us. If I advance into the Grain Sea, I will have to reckon with the possibility of an attack through the ruins of Telerat. If I guard against that, I will not be able to advance. It's true we are still mustering our strength, but the men of the Bowl will only double what I have available to me now. We have lost half of our land in a month. But there's a greater reason we won't hold."

"And why is that?"

"Because we are not perfect, Chancellor. I know the men of Skysil. They aren't fools, and they knew to keep the Discipline. But Lotus got into Telerat anyway. If we think it can never get into Maednac Serpiin, then we are the fools."

Paal nodded and turned to the Assembly. "Are there any questions that any present would put to the Warmaster?

Not a man stirred. Apparently, the very thought of violating the kingdom's most ancient law had stilled their tongues. It certainly chilled Aethal's blood.

Paal was speaking again: "The Crown calls to give testimony and be examined, Guardian Magnei in the name of the Lord Warden Cledan."

Dressed in his cassock, Magnei made a pitiful figure in the midst of the General States. The delegates stared at him as though he were actually a beggar with the temerity to walk through their midst. He bowed low before the Chancellor, and even lower to the king.

Paal nodded to him. "Guardian. You may address the General States."

Haltingly at first, but with increasing fluency, Magnei began to repeat the story he had told Aethal. He spoke of the Dragon King, and the power of the Well. The men in the chamber sat in silence.

"My Lords Delegates, we have been taught by the Church that the Well is evil, and so it is. But my Lords, killing is evil, and the Church does not forbid us to arm ourselves against evil men. We do not condemn as evil the man who kills in defense of his home. My Lord Warden begs you, rulers of Verlaen, to send us, if none else can be spared, so that we, at least, might fulfill our ancient vow, and guard mankind one last time from the Well." He sat.

Paal spoke in the silence that followed. "Would you support and accompany Warmaster Malcoor to the Well?"

"I would," said Magnei, almost too softly to be heard.

"Based on the Guardians' knowledge of the Well and its works, is this expedition a wise measure?"

"No, my Lord Chancellor. It is the *only* measure that will succeed."

"Why?"

"Because based on our knowledge of the Lotus — and the latest news we have from Telerat — my Lord Warden and I both believe that the Warmaster is very optimistic in his estimate of our ability to hold out against the Lotus."

"Even prepared against it, and with our full strength assembled?"

"Especially with your full strength assembled," said Magnei.

For the first time, Paal seemed uncertain. Only a touch, but to Aethal, it was like a shout.

"Why do you say that?"

"Lotus uses your own strength against you. Every man you field against it is one more field for the Lotus to take root in. Yet you dare not fight it with less than your full strength. Once your full army is mustered, I think we will be very fortunate if Maednac Serpiin survives a year."

Paal left off. "Do any present wish to question the Guardian?"

Ilferth Simon rose, and Aethal could see Magnei's knees begin to tremble.

"Isn't it true," the Conversant said, in deadly chill tones, "that you are a Sindrinker, like your Lord Warden?"

"No, your Holiness," said Magnei, barely audible, but with no tremble in his voice. "I do not believe that heresy, and neither does he."

Paal stepped between them. "Your Holiness, you are out of order."

The Conversant looked as if he would speak, and then seated himself.

"Seeing no further questions," said Paal. "The General States, as required by Maednac's Law, will now consider whether the Crown may violate Maednac's Ban and send Warmaster Malcoor on a mission to the Well, whose purpose shall be to Wish for the death of the Lotus."

The Conversant rose, and his face was like thunder carved in stone. "The Church shall speak," he said. The Chancellor nodded.

The Conversant turned to the room, and when he did spoke, his voice was so soft, Aethal almost had to strain to hear, yet everyone did: "I know all of you, my Lords. I know the King. I know his servants. It is my business to know them, and I know their intentions are good. But more than that, it is my calling to know the mind of God. And if our sad history has taught us anything, it is that good intentions are not sufficient to excuse disobedience of God.

"You intend to call on the Well to save you from itself. God, though He is beyond the world, will never permit such a thing. The very nature of the Well will prevent it." His gaze swept each of them in turn. "Do you drink poison to save yourself from plague? Or do you purge yourself? Purging is the only cure for Lotus that God will permit. You have asked me to pray for our salvation from the Lotus, the spawn of the Well, and with the same breath you call on the Wyrmguard and your Greater Rifles — in this very room — to protect us from God's Judgment with mockeries of men's minds, and now to contest His Judgment by deliberately, with full knowledge of your sin, going to the Well for the salvation that only God can give."

He pointed to Magnei. Aethal tensed. "This boy and his Lord Warden remind you they have an unfulfilled vow. I remind you that they have a shattered vow. How many died when the Apostate spoke his last Wish, and drove men from the Dark Continent forever? How many have died for Salnum's pride and sin?"

Ilferth Simon stared at Magnei. "You do not fulfill a broken vow to God, Guardian. Once it is broken, there is no returning. You must suffer His judgment." He lifted his gaze to the king. "And it is better to accept His punishments cleanly than to die further soiled in sin. To speak otherwise is heresy, and God will not honor it. I ask the delegates here to quell this motion, and preserve themselves in the sight of God."

He sat. In the silence, Paal rose again. "Does any other delegate wish to address this Assembly?" The silence stretched. "Then, My Lord Mayor, poll your delegates."

Hlafen rose. "Gentlemen of the Commons, you have heard the testimony given to this Assembly. It is a rare and fearsome privilege to be a part of it. Maednac, in his wisdom realized that there were times, and there were questions for which the judgment of one man was not sufficient. The King's judgment, and that of his line has been called most grievously into question today, and when the Commons asked to review that judgment by conducting the trial of his son, His Majesty refused to trust us with it. I say that if anyone has earned distrust today, it is His Majesty and this wild plan that is as likely to doom us as to save us. But that is not my decision to make alone. Gentlemen, how many of you are in favor of this expedition?"

The vote was not by acclamation this time. But Aethal could see clearly that at least three-quarters of the Commons voted Nay, more than sufficient to cast the Commons' two votes against the expedition. He looked amid the delegates and found himself staring into Skraalen's seamed and pinched features. He nodded, even as he cast the Madlands' vote for the expedition. Aethal recognized the men voting "no" the loudest. Most of their names were on the list Skraalen had passed through Sergeant Falk.

"The Commons votes against this expedition, Lord Chancellor," said the Lord Mayor.

"Your Holiness," said Paal, "Poll your delegates."

The Conversant turned to his priests, and the shout of "No!" resounded through the Chamber.

Aethal forced himself to calm. *Now we come to those in favor.*

"My Lord Skysil," said Paal.

Pyk rose. "The words of God-Beyond-The-World are for priests and for them that have no other hope, but my lord father's Church Overseers always said that for a man who can fight, a keen edge and a true strike are the proper prayers." He bowed to the king. "The expedition has my support, and that of the Skysil's domain."

Paal acknowledged this. Then he turned to Aethal. Walked toward him, and held out his staff of office. Blinking, Aethal took it. Paal then walked toward the Wrackberg's delegation. He was obviously preparing to cast his vote, but he had not bothered with this bit of theater before. Why now? He turned to the king.

"The Wrackberg votes no." The Commons erupted into applause.

Aethal felt his knees tremble. *What?*

The king rose. "Chancellor! What are you doing?"

"Your Majesty, as your Chancellor, your will is my command, but as Lord Paramount of the Wrackberg, I and my House cannot support this expedition. No force sent to the Dark Continent can possibly penetrate to the Well. The Well may be closed beyond all reach. The Lotus demands more of our forces every day, simply to keep it contained. Any serious expedition would require men and arms we cannot possibly spare. But despite the Guardian's words, I do believe that we can keep it contained, if we commit every man to the effort, and keep the Discipline. I would dissuade you from this expedition by words, your Majesty, but if I cannot, then I have a duty to my House to dissuade you by its vote."

King Paitir's mouth worked. "You spoke in favor of this expedition in my chambers just days ago when the Warmaster recommended it. You lied to me."

"I have changed my opinion based on the new evidence we received from the Warmaster and the Last Sword when they returned last night. It is obvious that Lotus is far too dangerous to be fought with Wishes and hopes. Only practical defense will save us. This is my vote, Sire. The General States have convened to give you the counsel you wanted. That was the purpose of this body."

When the king spoke, his voice was grey. "I will have your Chancellorship for this, Paal."

Paal nodded as though he had expected nothing else. "I am sorry that my honest counsel has displeased your Majesty. The Wrackberg votes no." He climbed the steps and took his staff back from Aethal's nerveless fingers.

"My Lord Westerend," he said.

It was all Aethal could do not to sink to the ground. The motion was defeated, but the vote had to play out.

Lord Westerend came to his feet. He did not look up. "The Westerend also spoke in the King's chamber just days ago, in favor of this expedition," he said, looking at a paper in his hand. "But we can no longer do so."

"Vaughan!" The cry came from Malcoor. *What?*

"Indeed," Lord Vaughan went on. "The Westerend would never have assented to such a mad plan but for the threats of coercion leveled against our House. Two weeks ago, in order to compel our cooperation with his plans, the King himself sent his Wyrmguard, led by the Last Sword Aethal Paaling House Wrackberg," Vaughan looked at Aethal for the first time, finger and lips trembling with fear, "to kill Westerend retainers on Westerend soil, threatening both my life and the life of my daughter and heir. As she is now removed to a safe place, and these General States may bear witness to my testimony, we may now speak out against this heinous misuse of royal power."

Aethal swayed on his feet. What was he doing? Vaughan dared to use his own plan to ambush Aethal as an indictment against him?

"What is the meaning of this, Vaughan?" The king was on his feet. "You gave me your word! These are lies!"

"Vaughan, have you gone mad?" General Malcoor strode over to his brother, who pointed. In a moment, the General was spun around and slammed against the wall of the chamber by Vaughan's Westerend bodyguard. His delegates were looking at him and at the king in horror. Some of them had hands on their swords.

"And as *we can now prove these events,*" Vaughan went on, his voice rising higher, "the Westerend votes no, and moves that these General States immediately order the dismissal, arrest and imprisonment of Aethal Paaling House Wrackberg until such time as they can examine the evidence for these charges, and to bring him to trial once they have done so."

What proof? Aethal thought, wildly.

"The motion is seconded," said the Lord Mayor, rising, to the shouts of approval of his own delegates.

"Your motion is out of order!" cried Paal, losing his composure at last. "The vote must be completed before any new motions are entertained!" The uproar grew louder, and Paal stared at Aethal. For the only time in his adult life, Aethal regretted not confiding in his father, who had no idea what Westerend was talking about. Reflexively, he hammered on the floor for quiet. "The Westerend votes no!" Lord Vaughan shouted, and silence fell.

Aethal looked down at Lord Vaughan. The Lord Paramount would not meet his gaze. "I have learned to expect my father's betrayal, Lord Vaughan," he said. "But I thought that you were a man of honor."

There was no reply. Paal turned to the king. "Your vote, Sire," he said, mechanically.

"The Crown votes aye," said the king. A useless gesture, now.

Paal turned back to the Assembly. "By a vote of five to two against," he said. "The proposed expedition to the Well in violation of Maednac's Ban is quelled."

Westerend rose again. Paal had no choice but to recognize him. Aethal listened with numb ears as the charge against him was repeated and seconded by the Lord Mayor. The roll call of votes rang out like bullets.

"How do the Commons vote?"

"The Commons cast two votes in favor of holding Aethal Paaling House Wrackberg for trial."

"How does the Church vote?"

"The Church votes aye."

"My Lord Skysil?"

"Nay! And these charges are false!"

"The Wrackberg votes nay." Hoots of derision greeted this. Of course, it did not matter. Lord Westerend voted aye. Aethal did not even hear the king's useless vote in his defense. When the cheers and cries vanished, he found himself looking into the king's tired, old face.

"I will need your weapons, cousin." Aethal, as if in a dream, handed Gun and the Last Sword to his king. *How little time I carried it,* he thought. The Wyrmguard each took an arm.

"No!" Aethal looked up in horror at the shout.

Farnan was charging at the dais. His face was locked in a snarl. He hadn't bothered to unlimber Crow, but ran at the Wyrmguard with his pike leveled.

"Farnan, don't!" Aethal cried. But it was too late. Farnan lunged at Flintmaw, who dropped Aethal's arm and dodged the head of the pike. He brought the barrel of his pistol down on Farnan's head, and Aethal's friend dropped bonelessly. More Wyrmguard scooped him up, and carried him along with Aethal. Aethal tried to shout to his friend, but he was unconscious and moaning.

The Wyrmguard walked them down many flights of stairs. At the bottom, in the dungeons, they separated. Aethal was searched, despoiled of all tools, weapons, and possessions, and thrust into a cell. He asked them to leave the light in his cell, but they took it. They no longer obeyed him.

Chapter Six

55th of Spring, 312 Exodus

The straw in the cell stank of urine, but the smell had long since overloaded Aethal's nose, leaving only a dusty tang in the air and a permanent itch in his nostrils.

The dark was timeless and featureless. Feeling along the greasy straw had revealed to him the slop bucket, and the rings set in stones for chains. For all he could tell, he had been blinded. *No, I would surely remember that, at least. For the pain if for nothing else.* Insanely, he touched his eyes and felt them still intact.

Lord Westerend's face hung there before him, looking straight at the king, never meeting Aethal's eyes. *You thought you had Westerend as an ally. Yes, he trusted you, as no one has trusted a Wrackberg in centuries.* The voice sounded like his brother's. *You really believed him. What man would pass up the opportunity for revenge you offered? With one accusation, he destroyed the Wrackberg line, and you helped him to it by discrediting your father and jailing your brother. You thought Westerend was above all that, and now all is his.*

Are they such great actors then? he asked himself. *Am I the only man so foolish, that I cannot see their duplicity?* He would have sworn that Malcoor's shock, at least, had not been feigned. Certainly, his father's had not been. Nor the king's. *Fool,* his inner voice said again.

The silence was broken by approaching footsteps, and a light, so dim that at first, he thought he had imagined it, but soon the oil lamp burned with a warm yellow light that threw shadows through the knots and joints in the solid door.

Aethal picked himself up by rings he found set in the stones, and felt one of them give a tiny fraction. Before he could consider what that might mean, however, the door opened into his cell. Aethal shielded his eyes against the dim light. It sat at floor level, and the silhouettes of men who entered wore jailers' uniforms. Then Aethal froze, catching sight of the length of chain in the hand of the larger man.

"What are you doing?" Aethal snapped, ashamed at the rise of his voice on the last word. "I am a Royal kinsman. I have not been found guilty of any crime." Aethal though he heard the man with the chain snort. They came on.

Aethal charged the chain-bearer, who pulled back and swung the chain in a whistling blow. Aethal tried to catch the middle of the chain, but his eyes had not yet adjusted to the light, and the man jerked back further, shortening the arc of the swing. The heavy links struck Aethal on the elbow, numbing his arm to uselessness and making him cry out in pain. Before he could react, the other man had kicked him in the groin and followed up with a blow to the jaw that filled the night of the cell with bursts of colored light. He seemed to be floating in a room stuffed with cotton while the two men locked ankle irons and manacles on him and threaded the chain through the rings on the walls. There was something important about one of the rings, Aethal remembered, but in the haze of pain could not think what. Something thumped lightly into the straw in front of him.

Then they were gone, leaving Aethal leaning against the tepid stone of the cell, breathing hard. Through the door, Aethal heard the ghost of a conversation.

"...member what you're told, wormy... no talking to him," said a high, mocking voice.

"Shut up... crazy? ...'s get out of here," said a softer, lower voice. "Hate those things. They never forget, you know."

"...can't do anything ...out orders. Can you?" A long pause. "See?"

The footsteps retreated. But a dim light remained. Dimmer.

Had they really left him under the care of one of his own Wyrmguard? Aethal raised his head. His hands were bound in front of him, with about six inches of chain, and yard-long chains on either side fastened each arm to a ring directly behind him. Another yard of chain ran from each ankle to the same ring.

"Wyrmguard," Aethal called. There was no reply. Nothing to indicate that anyone was there. Except the light. Even Wyrmguard needed light to see, and such a dim light would not destroy its night vision. *Doubtless if there is a Wyrmguard there, it's been ordered not to talk to me.* Aethal wondered if there had ever been any Last Sword with a shorter tenure.

Aethal could not lie down without having his arms or his legs suspended in the air. He could sit, but his wrists dangled in front of him, as if he were pleading for mercy. Then Aethal saw what his visitors had left him. After picking the dried blood from his nostrils, he could smell it: a bowl of fishy gruel, thick with rice. There was no spoon, and Aethal drank it off before it could entirely cool. It was still tepid and bland, tepid like the cell and the wall. Just enough to raise a sweat and for the sweat to trickle down his back, itching in all the places he could not scratch. He felt a tightening in his throat, and wanted to weep. So close. Now, what would the king do? What would Uncle Falaar do? Would they really fight over who ruled Verlaen while the verdant tide of Lotus rose and drowned all civilization? How long would it take? How long would they leave him here?

The Wyrmguard outside the door would not obey him, and would not speak to him. Very well. But it would surely report what he said, whenever it was relieved. Even Wyrmguard had to eat. If it reported he asked for news, would someone give it to him? The king was not cruel, whatever else he might be. He raised his voice to shout, but no sound came. His throat tightened in fear. *No.*

He tried again, and this time there was no mistaking it. Only the weak sound of exhalation escaped him.

Dumbworm. In the gruel.

Memory flooded him, of another cell, and Jeralta's face trapped in a rictus of horror, the corpse's hands stretched out toward the intestines that had spilled on the floor.

It seemed to Aethal that he went mad then. He screamed for some time, gulping air and shrieking it out again, but he could make no sound. He rattled his chains until his ears rang, but of course, the Wyrmguard would not see that as any threat to him... if indeed there was a Wyrmguard and it had been ordered to keep him safe. He pulled at the ring that bound him, and found that it gave the slightest fraction, but no more than that. Finally, exhausted, hands and ankles bleeding, and breathing in gasps, he fell against the wall of his cell.

He could not tear his eyes from the door. Vengeance or mystery would come through it soon. *It takes a dumbworm three days to starve.* He remembered that much from his instructors on Wellspawn in the Army. He would never last that long. His murderer would surely not wait.

Timelessness and darkness had passed. Aethal's muscles already ached in the weariness of maintaining the same position while his mind roamed through memory and terror. The waiting had begun.

***

Aethal slumped against the wall. He thought it was night, because he had dozed a dozen times, but whether night or the next day, he could not know. Each time he had awoken in terror, but still the door had stayed resolutely shut, the steady light from the dim lamp gliding ghostlike through the cracks in the door. The last time he had dreamed he was choking and had awoken sobbing, but still no sound came from his throat.

He could feel the worm; he was sure of it. The slightest tickle at the back of his tongue. Unreachable. By experimentation he had discovered that by exhaling noisily, he could form words with his lips and tongue alone, though each one required nearly its own lungful of air, to speak in a loud whisper. Doubtless how Jeralta's torturer had gotten any information he wanted. He had tried a dozen times to attract the Wyrmguard's attention.

"Help! Murder! I! Am! Dying!"

But there was no sign that he had been heard, or that anyone was there at all. Perhaps there was nothing, and the conversation of his jailers had been for his benefit only. But no; that way lay madness. There had to be someone there.

There was a scrape of footsteps. The shadows of feet appeared at the door, and there was the clink of a key in the lock. The door opened.

Aethal had only a moment to see a bulky figure against the door. He tried to shout for help again, thinking that perhaps without the intervening door, he might be heard, but the moment he started, the door was flung to noisily.

He was alone with the stranger.

"So, you have discovered that you have no voice. But you can speak, after a fashion. If you try." A match flared too brightly in the darkness, and the stranger lit a small, oil hand-lamp. It threw shadows on the walls, but did not reveal the face of the stranger. A large man, though shorter than Aethal and of considerable girth. The voice was somehow familiar, but Aethal could put no face to the clipped, businesslike tones.

The stranger knelt, clearing a space in the foul straw with gloved hands. He set down the lamp, and Aethal could see that the man had drawn a scarf about his face, leaving only the cold gray eyes visible.

Who is this man?

"I will not insult your intelligence, Aethal Paaling of the Wrackberg," said the man. His voice was low. Far too low to carry, pitched to be muffled, inaudible to anyone but Aethal. "I know that you have already seen my work."

Aethal felt his guts contract and try to crawl up his spine. *Not like Jeralta, oh please...* He felt himself close to babbling. But another part, a colder part of his mind, filed the information. *This is Jeralta's killer, then.*

"I will also do you the courtesy of telling you that you will not leave this cell as a living man. It is, however, your choice whether you go to your death as a man, with the dignity and grace that befits one of your rank." He pulled from his cloak a long dagger with a spiderpearl set in the pommel and laid it down at his knees, just out of Aethal's reach. "Or as a quivering mass, unmanned in body and mind." From beneath his cloak, the man produced a large bundle with handles protruding from it. He laid it at his feet.

"What I need to know, Lord Aethal of the Wrackberg, is how you, and your father and brother, planned to take the kingdom."

Aethal felt his eyes bug out. The murderer shook his head. "Do not pretend surprise. My father already knows that your father has a spy — probably more than one — in his House."

His father? Whose son is he? Immediately his mind flashed to the answer: Westerend. *A secret bastard that he keeps on some sort of leash? He uses bastards just like tame dogs.* Even his beloved Malcoor, whose dream of leading an expedition to the Well lay in ashes. Did this bastard hope for the same reward of legitimacy?

The murderer continued. "You may or may not know the identity of these spies, but that is of secondary importance. Of much more importance is this: What does your father plan? My father has bought us a week in which to keep you safe here. You will be dead, of course, by the time that week is up, but before you are, you will tell me what his plan to become king is, and when you were to assassinate King Paitir. You will also tell me when Aerhan is to be released and what role he will play in the decapitation of the kingdom."

Aethal's jaw hung open. He didn't know whether to laugh or scream. Actually, he did know which to do, but he was certainly incapable of it. He gathered his breath and gasped, as loudly as he could.

"You're. Mad. There. Is. No. Plan."

Slowly, the murderer began to unroll his bundle on the straw. "I thought as much. It is easier to rob a bomb-spider of its pearls than to get a Wrackberg to let go of power. I plead with you, my lord. You have seen my work." The handles of the instruments lay all in a row. The murderer took out one, its razor-sharp blade glinting like a clouded crescent moon. He took out another that looked like a tiny morningstar with a cylindrical head and very long spikes. "I know where you got that ring on your smallest finger. Jeralta Stevning kept no secrets from me. Neither will you. Of course, I was constrained by time, then. With you I need not rush. What is the plan?"

Aethal felt himself almost ready to vomit. "Would. Tell. You. If. I Could. Father. Tried. Bribe. Me. With This." He held out the finger. "Kept. It. Told. Him. Not. His." Aethal drew in a great breath. "He. Didn't. Even. Save Me. From This Cell."

The man nodded. "A grave miscalculation, but good theater. You Wrackbergs must think you are the only people who understand subtlety. We shall see about that. But first, some unsubtlety." He raised the crescent blade and stood.

Aethal crouched, muscles keening in pain. He kept his manacled hands stretched in front of him. With luck, he might be able to tangle the man's blade, or better, his hands, when he lunged.

The murderer's foot lashed out. It caught Aethal in the right calf, and the overstressed muscle spasmed in a violent cramp. Hissing in pain, Aethal went down, and another kick connected with his left thigh. That cramped as well, and Aethal lay helpless in the straw, bands of fire arcing through his legs. Suddenly his hands were locked together in the big man's elbow. "I remind you that I can do this twenty more times if I need to," the man said, in a voice utterly devoid of emotion. The crescent blade flashed down. It bit into Aethal's left smallest finger, below the nail, and levered up, ripping the nail away. Aethal choked on the waves of pain that coursed through him. The murderer stood and waited while Aethal sobbed silently, clutching his maimed hand.

Eventually, he said, "Will there be anything else you would like to add, my lord?"

Aethal sobbed for breath. "Please. Tell. You. Anything. No. Plan. Just. Save. Kingdom."

"And how will you do that?"

"Send. Malcoor. Well. Wish. Miracle."

The big man paused. "You are a fool, or you think my father and I are." He took a blunt rod from the bundle, and approached. Aethal tried to face him, but the agony was too great. He flinched away. The man reached behind him, stuck the bar through the links of chain where they met the ring, and twisted, shortening all four lengths of chain, bringing Aethal even closer to the ring that held him. Cutting off more range of motion. His muscles cramped agonizingly.

"I can do that about twenty more times too," said the man, gathering up the bundle. "I shall leave you to reflect on this, and see if my father may allow more subtle methods of dealing with you. Oh. Yes." He moved a bowl filled with fragrant stew to within Aethal's reach. "You should eat. Keep up your strength. You see, I can dispense rewards as well as pain." He opened the door and was gone. Aethal collapsed as much as he could on the floor, his arms hanging from their chains, and knew he was a dead man.

***

Slowly, Aethal's muscles relaxed. His limbs were still sore, but compared to the fire that radiated in nauseating waves from his left hand, they felt like heaven. He could walk only on his knees without triggering more cramps. The dank straw shielded his feet minimally from the heat-sucking dirt floor. *A hot spring above and I'm shivering.* Aethal overbalanced and fell with his face nearly in the gruel. Saliva flooded his mouth. Despite the nausea, he was starving. *Eat now,* a voice seemed to say. *You're dead whatever happens, and the food might give you strength.*

130

But no. Food would give no strength against more of that sort of torture. Aethal picked up the bowl with his nine good fingers and laboriously dragged it over to the chamber pot. Tipped it in. *It's just about full now.* He could tell from the sound. *Daren't put any more there. If he shines that lamp on it, he'll know what I'm doing and force-feed me. Why isn't he?* Perhaps he thought Aethal did not know how long dumbworms lived without food. *After all, I ate the bowl with the worm in it without suspecting, didn't I?* His stomach cramped and he hated himself more thoroughly. He had thought himself beyond all need for vigilance, but he had been betrayed by his own thoughtlessness again.

He fell back into as much of a sitting position as he could get to. In the formless doze that comes to the exhausted, he met his brother, and Jeralta, and the two of them laughed at him and kissed each other like lovers, even though Jeralta dripped blood from a slit throat, and Aethal had wanted to say, *no, it was your belly that was cut, don't you remember how you died, you idiot?* Then Paal approached him, and presented the two before the king as his sons, Aethal and Aerhan, while Aethal could not speak, even though he had starved himself for a month.

"These things take time," Malcoor said, taking a bite of Lotus. "It's a shame we couldn't go, but the King thought it too dangerous," he said, as his skin turned green from the eyes outward, and green pustules erupted in bloody vegetation from his scalp and skin.

The scrape of boots woke Aethal from his nightmare. He had no sense of time passing. But he knew whose boots they were. He knew that he could not resist. *It is only my ignorance that frustrates his plans. If he asked anything I truly knew, I would tell him.* He shrank back into the wall. *So much, then,* he seemed to hear himself say, *for your belief that you could stand any pain. Any fear. Only those who know no pain and fear can say such things. Pain is all, and I cannot stand against it.*

The door opened. Shut. His torturer took two heavy steps forward. He lit the lamp and set it on the cleared space. His voice sounded thick and muffled, as if he had a cold. "I have something for you, Lord Aethal, House Wrackberg. "Something to eat. Would you like it?"

Aethal nodded, trying to show disinterest. He was ravenous, but he was hardly dying of starvation in just one day, or even two. *Is my captor a bit more stupid than I took him for? Why wouldn't he simply take my fingernails off one by one?*

Well, it hadn't worked for him, had it?

"Here it is." The man brought from beneath his cloak a small, clay pot with three pentagonal leaves just poking up out of the surface, hanging over the sides of the pot. With his gloves on, he bruised the leaf carefully, tilting the silver-bottomed leaves to catch the lamplight. The smell flooded the cell, pushing back the urine and the dust. It was as if the sun had flooded the cell with poisoned beams of light.

Aethal pressed his back into the wall and wept, tears running down his face. Lotus. In Maednac Serpiin. In the Hydraxis itself. After all his efforts.

"TRAITOR!" Aethal screamed into the cell without sound. "TRAITOR! LOTUS-EATING TRAITOR!" But outrage at this ultimate sin did not free him from the dumbworm, nor let his whispers pierce the door to the Wyrmguard. If there was a Wyrmguard. The perfume of the Lotus filled his head, and he inched forward, trying to get closer, to kill this man, who dared...

Aethal slammed himself back against the wall, realizing that he was advancing toward the Lotus, that the Lotus would use even his fury as a lure.

"Lotus-eater? Certainly not," rumbled the man. "Do you not like my present? I thought you were hungry. I could take it with me. Or I could leave it. And when I come back in a few hours — or tomorrow — you'll might be so much more cooperative. And this will go so much more quickly."

Aethal's heart raced. He had once resisted Lotus, by the grace of Gun and the stink of battle. By sheer horror. But now he had no weapon. No shield between his mind and the Lotus pot his torturer slowly pushed closer, just within his reach.

"Very well, my Lord. I give you good day." He turned to go.

"WAIT!" Aethal chose words, inhaling through his mouth, and as little as possible. "I. Will. Tell. You. Please. Take It. Away."

"Good." The man knelt. "What is your father's plan to seize the throne?"

Aethal's mind turned over frantically. "He. Will. Do. It. At. The. Launch. Of Malcoor's Expedition. Will. Send. Half of Wyrmguard. Away."

The mean leaned forward. "Really? Is that why you were chosen Last Sword?"

Aethal nodded, and breathed shallowly. "Yes. Other. Half. Gunned down. By Wrackberg. Honor Guard. Once. Back. In Hydraxis. Surprise."

"Obviously you were not chosen for brains." The man got to his feet. "Malcoor is in charge of no expedition. The Warmaster is being sent on the campaign against the Skysil rebellion. You are lying, Lord Aethal. Good day." He rose with the lamp, leaving Aethal alone with the smell of the Lotus.

Immediately, Aethal staggered over to the chamber pot. He held it to his nose and inhaled deeply. Urine and shit and rotting fish filled his nostrils. He vomited and cried tears of relief. The stink erased the Lotus from his brain, at least for a few minutes. Heaving the brimming bowl up, he hugged it tight to his chest, nearly choking with the smell. *This stench is life*, he reminded himself dizzily. For a moment, he forgot why in his revulsion, and he blessed that too, for he somehow knew that this shielded him from it. But soon he remembered the Lotus.

Minutes stretched into hours. Hours stretched into a blank nothingness, hunger and the sweet, compelling scent of the Lotus. Only the line of light under the door, the maybe-lamp for his might-be guard showed any sign of an outer world. And an obstruction in the line that had not been there before. The Lotus pot. He tried to hug the chamberpot closer to him, but his arms would no longer obey. They twitched, and he knew that if he did not set the pot down, it would soon spill, and the foulness inside would dry and dissipate, leaving him alone with the call of the Lotus.

He set the pot down, and a great weariness overcame him. He jerked his head up. He dared not sleep. How strong was the call of Lotus? Strong enough to penetrate dreams? Would he sleepwalk? Sleepcrawl? Sleepeat? He feared he knew.

There was only one answer. Taking a deep breath of the fumes of the chamberpot, Aethal crawled forward, reaching for the Lotus pot, to dash it against the wall. He crawled and reached, straining. Then he recoiled. The index finger of his left hand had brushed, not the pot, but what could only have been a Lotus leaf. Clutching the finger to him, he held it up to the dim light. The finger did not feel damp, nor did it have any stain upon it, so far as he could tell. But he couldn't really tell; the filtered lamplight was far too dim. He washed his hands in the foulness of the chamberpot, preserving only his mutilated finger, and then thrust them into his jacket pockets.

His left hand encountered a fine grain of rice. What had been in his pocket that...?

The *yasnuum.*

Aethal's heart pounded. The *yasnuum* that Malcoor had given him at Telerat. Too small for his captors to notice and seize. He pinched it in his fingers.

They stank of his own piss.

It did not matter. Aethal ate it, crunching it between his teeth. It tasted like sand, and earth and bread.

The world went... flat. It was the oddest sensation. The smell of the Lotus did not lessen, or recede. But it no longer seemed to matter as much. His hunger was still there, but now was more remote. Aethal wondered if it would have gone away entirely with a full dose. He was no longer terrified. Only a vague concern penetrated the flatness. He could think more easily.

His torturer had been too clever. He had placed the pot with exactitude: Aethal could reach the Lotus leaves, but not the pot itself. Precise. So precise, his positioning. Aethal tried to reach back for the bar the man had used to shorten his chains, but it was stuck fast, whether locked, or merely jammed, Aethal could not tell. There was no adjusting his chains. According to Malcoor, the *yasnuum* would make him immune. Did he dare sleep? There was one thing more he might try before that.

Slowly, stretching each joint to its maximum, Aethal lifted his ankle, and got it wedged inside the crook of his elbow so that he could not move. He could barely breathe, and the hours crawled by with his tortured muscles begging for release.

***

"You cannot win, of course,"

Aethal lifted his head. The cell was the same, but lit now with a silver light. He could pick out every detail of the straw scattered along the floor, and every knot in the door. But the Lotus was gone.

She leaned against the door, sitting there naked. Her eyes were green and milky, but they saw him. Her skin was veined with green, and even her hair was twisted with green filaments. Lotus in its last stages, when all else was eaten away, but her eyes found his, and she spoke in a perfect, low voice.

"Why do you fight me, Aethal?"

When she stood, he could see her body, the glory of it, tall and straight, her breasts perfect and pale. "It has been long since you have known peace. And you have never known the peace that I can give." She stepped forward.

"You are death," Aethal said. His voice made no sound, but she heard him anyway.

"All of life is death, Aethal. Men died before I was born from the Well, and they will die in my embrace no more surely. Why am I your enemy?" She took another step. "You see, you cannot answer."

"You eat people," gasped Aethal. "Slowly. You steal their minds."

135

"So does life." She leaned forward. *"Ask any of your people, dying of old age, what it is like. You are young; do not deny them my mercy. Is not mercy the greatest gift?"*

"No!" he choked. *"It is not the same. They leave. They left. Something of themselves. Behind. For their children. For their people. But you just eat, and leave nothing but yourself."*

Her tone imperious, she advanced on him. "Is that what dying children beg their parents for as they lie dying at the end of their brief days? Is it to leave 'something of themselves,' or to stay, and not to depart? In me all can stay. They do not all die. They are merely changed. Into me. Into myself. And I am eternal. I am the last queen of the world. Born of the Well, and of your people. We should come together, you know."

"Stupid," Aethal gasped. *His head was throbbing. "Not us. Our enemies. Wished you."*

"Poor fool." Her lips were almost touching his, now. *"You fight what you do not even understand. You were not there at my Wishing. You do not know what they wanted. Did they Wish for victory? Or for peace? For mercy? You cannot know until you have tasted. Taste, and understand."*

Aethal's heart threatened to burst, and he knew there was something wrong, but he could not breathe, and he could not move, and he was straining to move, and the lips came closer...

✳✳✳

Aethal woke choking against his wrist chains, right hand outstretched for the pot, fingers crawling towards it. He shrieked wordlessly and rolled back to the wall, muscles locked and cramping in rivers of white fire. He had saved himself. For now. But the *yasnuum* had worn off.

*****

Aethal clutched the chamberpot to his chest, breathing its rank odors when the footsteps returned. Reflexively, his fingers tightened, and he winced as his maimed left-hand finger touched the pot. The door opened, and his torturer swept in. He stood staring for an instant. Then he cursed and shut the door. There were three quick steps and the pot was kicked from Aethal's grasp, shattering. Aethal hissed in pain, agony lancing up his hand.

"Clever, Wrackberg. And strong, to hold out for so long." Again, the match-flare, and the lighting of the lamp. From where he lay on the floor, Aethal could see the man pick up the Lotus pot. "How weak are you, Lord Aethal? Perhaps the direct approach would be best after all." He stepped forward and plucked a leaf off the plant. *This is the last chance.* Desperation sharpened Aethal's mind, and the room seemed to get just a little brighter.

His captor kicked him in the belly, and Aethal rolled with it just enough to avoid taking it in the solar plexus. He dropped like a stone, and gagged. The hand with the deadly leaf descended, and with it his captor's face.

Aethal rose up, right hand stabbing for his torturer's eyes, fingers raking down. Surprised, the big man rolled away smoothly, but his veil dangled from his throat. Even the dim light of the lamp was enough to reveal his features.

"Sigrad." Aethal mouthed the name, but he didn't believe.

Sigrad crushed the leaf in his hand and put it down beside the pot. The deadly Lotus scent filled the room, but for once, Aethal paid it no mind. Neither did Sigrad. Under the mask, Aethal could see plugs of clay in the man's nose. He had not disturbed those in the slightest.

"Still a bit dangerous to force-feed, I see." Sigrad shuddered, ever so slightly. "We'll stick to subtlety for another day."

Aethal stared at the Colonel. This was the man that his father had thought was Ilferth Simon's mistake. Killed Jeralta under Aethal's nose. *Wait. Ilferth Simon's mistake? Not Westerend's. He's not Westerend's man, unless Westerend and Simon are together, but that's impossible. No confederate of Simon's would have even pretended to love a bastard brother. What has Simon got on Westerend?* The lack of knowledge tormented Aethal more than his finger ever had. Sigrad snorted. "Don't feel too bad, my Lord Aethal. Your father and the King, and the rest of the General Staff have been fooled for longer than you've been alive." His cold face assumed a bright, unfocused stare, laced with anxiety. "Terribly sorry about that, Captain. Hope that doesn't distress you in *any* way. I'll have the man imprisoned at *once*, and please give my regards to your lord father." Sigrad turned, placing the Lotus pot with the crushed leaf in it precisely at the limit of Aethal's chain. Then he left the bowl of stew directly in front of it. He turned and left.

Aethal waited in the darkness, breathing shallowly. When the footsteps had faded out of hearing, he crawled forward, holding his breath, and grabbed the bowl. Back at the wall, he tested the limits his chains imposed on his arms. He let his eyes adjust from the flash of light that the open door had revealed. There. That break in the light from the door. That was the pot of Lotus. *Only one shot at this.* When he was certain, he hurled the bowl of stew at the pot with all his strength. The clay vessels slammed into each other and the Lotus skidded far beyond his reach. Fish gruel lay spattered across the floor.

Aethal blanched. The meat and vegetables from the stew spread across the floor, their sight and smell obvious. Sigrad would know he was trying to starve the dumbworm. *He'll force feed me that, for sure.* Despair threatened. *No. Think.* Slowly, Aethal gathered straw, scattering it over the trail of gruel, and over the shards of the pots. Shards of the chamberpot lay within reach too, and some of the foul chunks within. He threw these, too... He waited. Waited until pressure built to pain he could no longer stand and finally released a stream of urine into the far corner of the room. There wasn't much; he was getting dehydrated, but he covered the gruel as thoroughly as he was able. *Two days' food gone,* he told himself. *One to go. I think.*

I surprised you today, Sigrad. And you, too, milady. He nodded toward where he guessed the Lotus lay. *You cannot break me if I have any hope. A soldier uses all the weapons he has, even the disgusting ones; the dishonorable ones. Just like you. Only better.*

***

It was one long sleep later that Sigrad came back. Since he had awoken, Aethal had tried to speak, but the dumbworm was as strong as ever. Now, with the familiar footsteps approaching, Aethal's insides knotted again. What if Sigrad noticed the stew, in spite of everything he had done? Aethal hung limply in his chains, eyes slitted, hoping that this time he might do some damage.

Sigrad stood silhouetted only for a short time, and made a sound of pleasure. "I have more for you," he said kindly. "More Lotus, my Lord. Would you like that?"

But then he noticed the smashed pot and grunted. "That's not good." He lit the match and the lamp. He came close to Aethal. "You are awake." The plugs were still in the man's nose, but he no longer bothered with the veil. "And not yet a greeneater, I see. Not that it matters. Ah." He saw the smashed Lotus, and picked it up, carefully gathering the loose dirt. He sniffed, and paused. Aethal stopped breathing. "Becoming rather filthy of habit, aren't we, my lord? No matter." He piled the dirt he recovered neatly, and placed it and the remains of the Lotus in a second pot with a new seedling in it, both in the same position he had always picked. "This stuff is almost immortal. It can live without sunlight or soil for two weeks, so they say." Then he picked up the shards of the chamberpot and carefully removed them from Aethal's reach. *So that's what he thinks I did.*

He turned to Aethal. "My father Ilferth Simon has a message for you."

"What. Message?" asked Aethal, when Sigrad refused to continue.

"His regrets. On the deaths of your cousins, Paitir the King, and Eraad the Crown Prince. He did all he could to save them, but the panic of the crowds was too much, and they were lost. Well, I wouldn't mourn Eraad too much, if I were you. He was quite willing to kill you in Telerat in exchange for no more than my father's promise to stop exhorting him to take holy orders. As though a promise to men were binding in the face of God's will! But as the royal idiot was incapable of even that, it matters little. As your father, Paal, and your brother, Aerhan, have been implicated in high crimes, and your uncle is too distraught to be troubled with matters of state, Lord Westerend asked before he left for home that my father assume the duties of Regent until a new succession can be established."

Aethal's world seemed to stop. Lost. All lost. Verlaen lost. No expedition. No Wish. Lotus in Maednac Serpiin. And Ilferth Simon Regent. How long would they last? A year? Even a month? Sigrad was still speaking. Why?

"What? Need. Me. For?"

Sigrad sighed. "Why for testimony, Aethal Paaling. Your father is technically next in line of succession. Obviously, if he were to be found guilty of conspiring against his cousin, he could not ascend the throne. So, the situation is as before. We do need your testimony, Lord Aethal."

"Given. It."

Sigrad leaned closer. "You're a loyal son, Aethal. No father could ask better. But you can't save him. If you testify, all three of you may be allowed exile. But if we must charge all three of you, it will have to be with high treason. You know the evidence we have on your brother; you collected it. We will have the testimony. From your mouth. Whatever it has eaten. Or not. Good-day." Sigrad left. Dimly, Aethal realized Sigrad had not left any food.

He knows I will break today. He knows it. It doesn't matter if the worm starves one day. Tears flowed down his face. *It really doesn't matter. They're all gone. I failed you, Paitir. And Ardyth, and Farnan, and Canuta, and all the Phoenix Lancers. Even the Wyrmguard. Failed.* There would be no last chances. No voyage. He was it and he had failed, and soon the Wyrmguard would be melted down, and Gun, and the keepwoods uprooted, and all works of the Well purged from the land. Except the Lotus.

Hopelessness fell down on Aethal like a drowning current of mud and filth as he sobbed, the Lotus perfume filling his nostrils, rattling his chains as if he could deafen the news away

Aethal sprang up into a tottering run. The woman had been right. Oblivion now was mercy. Only mercy. He dove for the Lotus, but slipped. His fingers brushed not leaves, but the pot, knocking it away by sheer chance and desperation. He went madder then, and pounded his fists on the floor, circling back and forth until he was spent, and muttering silently. Eventually, night closed in with nightmares dark and formless, but none to compare to his waking.

***

Aethal lay in the dark a long time. A new smell had been added to the maddening Lotus and underlying urine. His own blood, where the manacles and irons had bitten into his wrists and ankles. Aethal still wanted the Lotus, but the want was far away, now, held back however temporarily by shame. *So, I am no Lotus Eater, then.* He couldn't be. They had no shame, anymore, and he envied them. He coughed. Of course, the sound came out attenuated by the dumbworm.

Was it his imagination, or had the cough been more forceful? He tried to speak, but still could get no sounds out. What time was it? It felt like another day. He cursed himself for a fool. It could be anything. Anything could be anything, so far as he knew. Was there a Wyrmguard outside that door? On that all depended, for any other guard might be bought by Simon. And Sigrad might be telling the truth or lying. He had nearly killed himself for a lie. His shame bit deeper.

Just take a long time today, Sigrad, he thought. If he was right, the worm would die today. But would it matter?

All too soon, the footsteps sounded. Sigrad entered, and set up his lamp. He cocked his head and looked at Aethal. Perhaps he bowed a little. "I never thought anyone could get that close to Lotus and not touch it. Perhaps it's not all it makes out to be. Even my father makes mistakes." He reached into his cloak, and pulled out the dark bundle, spreading it out across the straw. "I'm afraid my father is in a bit of a hurry. I don't care to risk force-feeding you the Lotus, though I think I could..." he paused, and Aethal prayed to a God he had never really believed in, that doctrine said would never hear him. "...but I think his wisdom will guide me. So, we will go back to the basics." He produced the crescent shaped blade again. "Will you tell me what I want to know, Lord Aethal?"

"Yes!" Aethal gasped. It hurt to talk. He tried one of the stories he had rehearsed for the purpose of dragging out the time. "When I entered the Service..." Sigrad backhanded him.

"Don't try to spin me a yarn, Aethal Paaling. Will you tell me what I want to know?"

"Yes!" His throat itched like fire with the strain of the whispering. "My father raised me and my brother to hate one another in public. We have always worked together. When kidnapping Malcoor failed..."

In two lightning motions, Sigrad slashed with the tool. Aethal felt skin part along his jawline, two deep cuts.

"Aethal Paaling, you were the one who made that kidnapping fail. You have this last chance. Tell me your father's plan."

"Yes, lord!" gasped Aethal. His throat was burning now, a tickle driving him mad. "Please. He hid. Lotus. From the King. He planned. Aerhan. To send. To the Keepwoods. Arrest Malcoor." He told all he could invent, and Sigrad sat there, hand twitching. With no warning, his left hand shot out and caught Aethal's wrists.

"Jehan Alfing was a fool who thought that killing you and that sergeant would serve my father. Instead, he nearly wrecked all. I am not such a fool. You will learn," Sigrad said, his voice level, "that you have no escape." The blade bit and tore, and Aethal's ring fingernail was gone. He gasped a silent scream of agony, and began coughing.

"You will learn," Sigrad said, his blade biting deep into Aethal's fifth knuckle, "that you have no secrets from me." The blade began to travel upwards, grating, so slowly, on bone. Aethal screamed again, began to choke.

"You will learn," said Sigrad softly, and for the first time Aethal heard a real fury in the man's voice. "That I can flay you to the bones. And there will be no help. And your blood will wash me clean before the throne of God!"

He's going to peel my hands off, thought Aethal. *One finger at a time.* He shrieked soundlessly, coughed once, and blood and something small that wriggled fell into his mouth.

"Help me!" Aethal shouted, and his own voice sounded sweeter to him than a cavalry bugle.

Sigrad twisted around, his face a mask of shock, and Aethal spit the dumbworm into his face. With a cry of rage, Sigrad jumped up, flailing at his cheeks.

"Help! Wyrmguard! Guard! The prisoner is being murdered!"

Sigrad reared back, ready to plunge his blade into Aethal's heart. Aethal held his hands up futilely. Then dim light blinded him, and then a flash that rocked him back like a thousand suns. Sigrad fell past him.

In the doorway, his mouth agape, was a guard in Westerend livery, mace raised. Beside him, face expressionless, Goldhammer's mount looked in.

"Aethal Paaling. You need medical attention. You should not be chained." He turned to the Westerend guard. "Get help." The man turned and ran as if all the demons of the Well were after him.

What followed was like a dream. Goldhammer unchained him and dressed his wounds with strips of his own uniform. Aethal lay on the straw, exhausted, limbs stretched full-length. Only the sound of running footsteps brought Aethal blurrily to himself. "Goldhammer." He clutched the Wyrmguard with his good right hand. "Seal the room. Don't let anyone in. In fact, get me out."

"Aethal Paaling, it is the Imperial Governor's orders that you be confined here. I cannot obey you in this."

"You can and you will. Put me in any other cell you like, but seal this one and do not leave the door. That is Lotus." He pointed.

Before the feet could come any closer, Goldhammer had removed him and thrown him into another cell. The guard came running back with two more regular guards. "I brought the doctor, sir!" he said, "But sir, their lordships insisted on coming, too."

The doctor entered, looked at Aethal's hand, muttered an oath, and set to work. Aethal leaned against the stone wall of the cell, but raised himself as Ardyth Westerend came through the door. "My Lord Aethal!" she cried, and fell to her knees beside him. "Forgive me, Lord Aethal, forgive me!" She looked in horror at his face and hands. "He will be all right, doctor?"

"Yes, milady," said the doctor in a detached tone. "If milady could remove herself from the light." Ardyth stood, abashed. Then she turned to the door. "I am afraid he is wounded, my Lord."

Aethal raised his eyes to the door, and his jaw dropped. Paal Haerling of the Wrackberg walked in, his jaw set and his eyes steely. "But he is alive, and that is all that matters," he said, quietly. Then Aethal knew he was dreaming, for his father knelt to him. "I am sorry, my son. I came as soon as I could. I am only glad I did not come too late."

Aethal could only stare. "The King," he got out. "Is the King alive?"

"Yes," Paal nodded. "But in great danger, as is the entire kingdom, partly due to my own blindness. Pray God-Beyond-The-World I am not too late for that, too. Your expedition must go forward, Aethal, I see that now. But we must move quickly, and together, or Ilferth Simon will pull down the kingdom with him. I bring this message not only from myself, but for the King. From this moment forward, Aethal, you are again his Last Sword. And I will do all in my power to support you in his defense."

Chapter Seven

58th of Spring, 312 Exodus

The charred beef and sweet peppers that Aethal pulled from the crisp, brown parchment bag threatened to unhinge Aethal's knees after three days' starvation. His tender jaw forced him to chew slowly. Occasionally, a shooting pain lanced up Aethal's bandaged arm, and he had to slow down.

Ardyth, seated across from him, looked worried. Magnei, dressed in new clothing that somehow suggested Guardians robes, but neater and more like a military uniform, would not meet his eyes, sitting some distance away with a collection of books and papers. Malcoor dismissed the servants, and seated himself next to Aethal, and caught him looking at the young Guardian.

"He wouldn't have a cadet's uniform. Apparently, that violates a Guardian's oath, but I have no time to bother with such things, so we're all just pretending he's my aide. Boy's brilliant at remembering every little detail.

"But what we need to do now, Lord Aethal, is to catch you up on what's happened these past three days. You're the Last Sword again, so you need to know if anyone does."

Aethal raised a hand, "Where is my father? What changed his mind?"

"Hold on, boy," said Malcoor. "I know you're full of questions. Were it possible, I'd give you at least a day's bed rest to recover. But we're counting minutes now, and can't waste them. Your father is at the Wrackberg, mobilizing his reserves. Lady Ardyth, please explain to Lord Aethal your role in changing his father's mind."

Ardyth did not meet his eyes. "Do your wounds trouble you, Lord Wrack-berg?"

He tried to keep his tone steady. God-Beyond-The-World, she was beautiful. He would never again take the sight of a beautiful woman for granted. "Only as any wound might, Lady."

"Our house owes yours a debt of honor," said Ardyth, "and I do not see how we can repay that."

"Ardyth," said Malcoor. "We've little time. Tell him how it was."

She caught her breath, and turned half away from him, looking into the setting sun as though the reddening beams could cleanse her vision of some unwelcome sight. "My father returned from the General States drunk as I have never seen him. He stumbled in the door and I could hear him arguing with someone. It was Uncle Joseth. My father had the door slammed in his face and ordered Uncle Joseth thrown out. The same uncle he has wanted returned to us for almost thirty years! I asked him what was wrong and he flung me away. Almost as an afterthought, he ordered me confined to my chambers. And there I stayed. Stayed like a useless lump for two days, simply having meals brought to me and wondering what I had done!" There was anger in her voice. Not at her father, Aethal thought, but at herself.

"The rumors were already flying. The servants said that you had been accused of some dreadful crime and were awaiting trial. That the Chancellor was fallen from favor and a new one appointed in secret. That both the Chancellor's sons were to be beheaded along with him. What I couldn't find out was why. Why you, I mean," she said to Aethal.

"And then..." Ardyth turned away, and Aethal could not tell if it were to hide a snarl or a sob. "Finally, I could stand no more, and sent my lady in waiting to discover the truth of things, and if I might in honor help you, for I thought that I owed you no small debt for my release from that terrible Gun." She shuddered.

"My lady returned, her face pale, to tell me that you had been accused..." she fought for words. "By my own father! In *my* name! Of the most base acts and treachery!" She was weeping now, but spoke through her tears as though they were of no consequence.

"I did not think any more. It was like..." she paused, said quietly. "Like being part of the Gun again, only deciding for myself where to fire. I took a saber from its display rack in the dining hall; it had once served in a Westerend's hand; it could do so again.

"Before I knew it, I was at my father's door, facing the captain of our guards. He asked me what I was doing out of my chambers against my father's orders. I told him I was come to see my father. He said that the Lord Paramount was not to be disturbed under any circumstances." Ardyth's eyes flashed. "I told him that I was the Lord Paramount's daughter, not a circumstance. He offered to escort me back to my room, at which point I'm afraid I lost my temper. I asked him if he could really be certain of disarming me without one of us being badly hurt. He was my teacher in the blade, and we were both holding live steel. He stood aside." She showed her teeth in a humorless grin

"I found father slumped at his desk, staring at the wall like a dead man. For a moment I thought he *was* dead, by his own hand, for he made no sign that he had heard me. He was still drunk.

"He made no move until I touched him, and then he whirled like a man possessed, screaming at me to get out, that I did not know what I was doing, and that I would kill them all. That, 'He said so. He said he would farm them all.'"

"I was weeping by then, and asked him what he thought he was doing, to dishonor us so, and whom he could possibly fear so much. But he was still screaming that I had to leave before 'he' found out, that he could see all that we did. He... he begged me to leave if I loved him, if I loved the Westerend. And he kept looking over his shoulder at his desk, and the little table just beyond. That's when I saw it. A small black disc, just as big as a large man's palm, roughly cut around the edges, and mounted in a silver frame. But there was something in it, as when glassblowers encase objects in molten glass. It was just that sharp. And it was green." Her voice hardened.

"Father was still telling me to step away, that I had to listen to him. But he could barely keep to his feet, and I dodged around him easily. And then I peered into the stone myself and saw what was really in it. It was a single pot full of Lotus, somehow able to fit within a stone too narrow to contain it.

"I was never so frightened. At first, I thought that somehow the maker of this evil thing truly had encased Lotus in a glass, and my father feared that. But as I looked, the stone... drew my eye into itself, and I could see more, far more than I should have been able to in anything that small. I saw that the pot sat on a table. That the table sat in a room. That the room was some sort of cell, set high in a tower, with bars on the doors. And that the view from the window..." she stopped, and caught her breath. "The window looks out over a waterfall, deep in our territory, which feeds the river that flows out into the Twin Fans. Where all the Westerend is watered."

"My father caught me around the waist and again ordered me to be gone. 'He said that if any but myself looks in the glass, he will release the Lotus!' he cried. 'If we are silent for only a little while he will remove it.' 'Who has done such a thing?' I asked him, unable to believe what I had seen. 'The Conversant, Ilferth Simon,' he said, finally. 'We must do as he says. He has the power of God-Beyond-The-World, to bind or loose Lotus as he pleases, and we must join him. We have no choice.'"

Ardyth looked up into Aethal's face. "Please, Lord Aethal. My father is no traitor. He was trying to convince himself more than me, I could hear that in his voice. He is frightened beyond reason for the lives of our people. In truth, so am I. But they cannot live as hostages to a man who would threaten to unleash Lotus on us, even if he *can* do so.

"I snatched the glass and rode. I rode pausing only for the requirements of Discipline, straight to the Hydraxis, and brought the stone to my uncle."

Aethal's mouth was dry. Had Ilferth Simon been more attentive, she might have been intercepted and killed.

"My uncle, of course, immediately saw the King, who was meeting with Chancellor Pyk of Telerat, and your father."

Aethal stared. "Uncle Pyk is Chancellor?"

"Oh, yes," Malcoor interrupted. "When you were dragged away, the King stripped your father of his Chancellorship and appointed the only man who'd backed his expedition. Then he adjourned the General States. I believe when Ardyth arrived, the King and his new chancellor were having an interesting, ah, *discussion* with your father over some of his decisions as Chancellor." He smiled.

"But when your father saw the glass, he immediately locked it away," said Ardyth. "He seemed to know something of it. He was very frightened."

So was Aethal; he felt himself shaking. Lotus in the Grain Sea. Lotus in Telerat. Lotus in Maednac Serpiin, in the dungeons of the very Hydraxis. And now Lotus in the hands of a madman in the Twin Fans, home to the richest soil in Verlaen, aye, and the densest population, save the Bowl itself. *My kingdom is invaded, and not all the true men who serve it can save Verlaen against one mad prophet out to cleanse the world.*

"Where does he get this power?" Aethal whispered. "Is it true that Simon will know that you have seen this, or is it a bluff? A cheap trick of the blackmailer?" But it was a vain hope. Intuitively, Aethal knew: This was a piece of what his father had spoken of that first night Aethal had arrived from Everview, the source he had refused to disclose to Aethal upon their first meeting in the Hydraxis.

"I do not think it a trick, Last Sword," said Magnei. "The Well is known to have produced such things in the days of the Wish-Kings. It was thought that they were all lost, though; I have seen no record of the Empire having held any of them. The stones were often set up in a complex hierarchy, so that greater stones could direct and observe the doings of the possessors of lesser stones.

Stones Wished for later could be Wished independent of, dependent on, or interdependent with all previously existing stones..."

Aethal cut him off. "That doesn't concern me, Magnei. Does Ilferth Simon have one of these master stones, controlling all the rest?"

Magnei licked his lips. "If he has made this stone he gave to Lord Westerend show what he commands, then he must."

"Might this stone be at all useful to us?" asked Malcoor, deep in thought.

"No, sir," said Magnei. "The control will lie with the possessor of the master stone."

"The less Simon knows, the better," growled Malcoor. But if he can see out of the stone we have, he has to know something's up. How did you carry it to the King, Ardyth?"

"By horse," Ardyth said, puzzled.

"Not that," snapped Malcoor, "I mean how did you physically carry the Well-Wished thing?"

"In my saddlebag, wrapped in cloth."

Malcoor nodded. "Likely the only thing that saved you," he said, echoing Aethal's earlier thoughts. "That and your speed. If he could have seen where you were, he'd have sent men after you. Perhaps we'll get lucky, and he'll not have seen you snatch it. Perhaps he'll think Vaughan's only a gutless coward, too scared to view his realm's doom, but I wouldn't bet on it. How many of these damned things do you suppose he has?"

"There is no way to know, sir," said Magnei.

Suddenly, Aethal's vision darkened, and his breath caught in a flash of memory. "No," he said softly. "We don't know how many he has, but I can tell you that there are at least two others."

Even Magnei looked amazed. "Where are they?"

Aethal forced himself to breathe steadily. "One was in Everview, concealed as a penance icon worked of silver and obsidian. That's the message my father intercepted; the one telling of Lotus in Everview. The old bishop sent it to

Ilferth Simon." He swallowed, the memory of a swollen face and a blackened tongue floating up before him. "And the second," he looked at Magnei, "you have seen before. Around the neck of your own Lord Warden Cledan. The chain around his neck, which contains a disc of dark glass. *And which he clawed at, in my presence, but I was too blind to see it.* A present from Ilferth Simon, if I do not miss my guess. One which the Conversant was most happy to give, and which the Lord Warden never removes, neither day nor night. On pain of what punishment, I wonder?"

But there was no need to wonder. The drained look of horror on Magnei's face said all that was needed and more. "We have to save him," he whispered.

"The best way to save the Lord Warden and your fellow Guardians," said Malcoor, "is for us to take the Temple. I must get to planning the assault. Magnei, you're with me. Last Sword," he bowed. "Your counsel will be welcome."

"But how did you know to come and save me?" asked Aethal.

Ardyth frowned. "Only your father can answer that, Lord Aethal. As soon as he had locked away the stone, he had the King order the Wyrmguard to bring him Colonel Sigrad from the dungeons. The Wyrmguard came back and reported that Sigrad was not in his cell. Your father turned white then and set all the Wyrmguard, and all the Crownguard he could summon to bring you to him, and then to search the Hydraxis dungeons from top to bottom. When a guard reported back that *you* were not in your cell either..." she trailed off. "I have never seen a man fly into such a rage."

Aethal blinked. "I can assure you, milady that I was in my cell."

Malcoor snorted. "It wasn't the cell that was in the prison records. Sigrad obviously had those dungeons penetrated deep as the Well itself. Fortunately, we found you soon after when a guard led us to you. The rest, you know."

I don't know a damned thing, Aethal thought. *I'll have to talk with my father as soon as I can.*

"But sir," Aethal said, as they rose, "Where is the King?"

"As soon as he locked that disc of Ardyth's away," Malcoor replied, "Lord Wrackberg ordered Ilferth Simon brought to him. He urged the King to couch the message as an invitation, but to have him brought nonetheless. Have you heard from the Wyrmguard yet?"

"No." The first thing he had done upon receiving command of the Wyrmguard again was to order a room-by-room search of the Hydraxis for any other signs of Lotus. It would take some time: he had only twenty-four of them here. "Who was commanding the Wyrmguard in my absence?"

"His Majesty. He wouldn't appoint another Last Sword while you were under suspicion."

"And did Ilferth Simon come?"

"Of course not," Malcoor snorted. "He's sent one of his archbishops. I have no doubt that the man is having an unpleasant time trying to figure out what to tell a very angry king. And while your father is raising his own legion, I have Maednac's Own assembling in the Hydraxis, along with the City Watch."

Good. But Maednac's Own was one of the Army's smallest regiments. They were also the only regiment left in the Bowl. If the City Watch was backing them, then...

Aethal's mind caught up to him. "Sir, who is commanding the City Watch?"

Malcoor frowned. "The Lord Mayor took back command after Colonel Farnan was arrested. Since then, I haven't had much time to pay attention to City Watch affairs."

A cold spike of fear pierced Aethal's guts. "I need to know what he's done with them. How many do we have in the Hydraxis right now?"

"Sir, we have one hundred of the City Watch in the Hydraxis," said Magnei. The rest were withdrawn by Colonel Varth to watch the approaches."

Varth. Damn. "Sir," said Aethal. "The City Watch has very little in the way of weaponry. Someone sent false dispatches from Telerat in my name ordering Colonel Farnan to move the City Watch armories from Maednac Serpiin's Watch Stations to the Churches. Where the Temple Guard could keep watch over them, because the City Watch had proven to be too violent with the people. The Temple Guard has all the weapons that the City Watch is not actually carrying right now."

Malcoor had stopped in the middle of the corridor. "Why in the Name of the Well didn't you tell me this before?" he shouted.

"When, sir?" asked Aethal. "We only discovered the trickery a half-hour before the General States met, and then Colonel Farnan and myself were arrested!"

"What about you?" he whirled on Magnei.

In a small voice, Magnei quavered. "The Last Sword had ordered me not to discuss it."

Malcoor shook his head. "Damn. Nothing for it now." They marched on.

In the Hydraxis court, Malcoor was met by Colonel Henling. "Warmaster. Last Sword."

"Colonel. How do we stand?"

Henling gestured behind him where about five hundred men were assembling. Half were mounted, half afoot. All bore Greater Rifles, and gathered under the banner displaying Maednac's sigil, whose staff was topped with a hammered-silver ship. "Maednac's Own is at His Majesty's disposal. The rest of us will be here as soon as they are relieved of their guard over the city walls by the Watch."

Aethal looked about. "Is Colonel Farnan with them?"

Henling's eyes drew down. "I had assumed that Colonel Farnan had been released and reinstated along with the Last Sword, but the only officer of the Watch I've spoken with has been Captain Esterling."

Aethal turned to Malcoor. "Wasn't Farnan released along with me?"

"I don't know, Last Sword. I have had other things on my mind." Malcoor fell into a discussion with Henling over assault plans while Magnei spread maps on a camp-table.

Aethal called Flintmaw over. "Find Colonel Farnan at once, set him at liberty and have him brought here." Another thought struck him. "Flintmaw. Have you or any of the other Wyrmguard heard anything from Sergeant Bedar Falk while I was imprisoned?”

Flintmaw shook his head. “No, Last Sword. This soldier has not reported to any Wyrmguard unit.” And Aethal’s last order to him had been to meet with Skraalen. Two hours later, Aethal had been under arrest. *Falk wouldn’t have done anything stupid,* Aethal thought. *But the best man can be brought down by fate. Or treachery.* Falk knew how to work with Skraalen, but didn’t trust him. Therefore, Aethal didn’t either. But any man he sent to make contact with the Sergeant stood a much better chance of being hurt in the Madlands than he did of accomplishing anything. Aethal would just have to trust the old soldier. And wait.

Aethal eyed the men in the courtyard. The best trained soldiers in the Empire, yes. *But this is all we have with which to march on the Temple, humble Ilferth Simon, Conversant with God-Beyond-The-World, and bring him to justice, if we can?* Aethal remembered the hedges around the Temple. His thoughts ran cold. *If we cannot, we will have to burn him along with the Lotus.*

Aethal directed his attention to Malcoor’s plans, and said, “Sir, I think you’ll find those maps are out of date. The Conversant has planted...”

“Man-high hedges all around the Temple. I know. Show him the other maps, Magnei.” The young man bent, and took out a large sheet of paper. An intricate network of lines, converging on a building that was obviously the Temple, was traced on it. Aethal stared at it in wonder.

“Did you get this from my father’s agent?”

Malcoor snorted. “Your father’s agent got us into this mess by not telling us what he *did* know, and sooner. That’s drawn from memory. His.” He pointed at Magnei. “The boy is a walking library.”

“Sir,” Aethal said. “Is it possible to attack the Temple?” He looked up. The sun was setting in the west, and it seemed to Aethal as if the whole west of Verlaen was on fire behind the mountains surrounding the Bowl.

"Please, Last Sword," said Magnei. "You have to save the Lord Warden. You have to save the Order." Magnei's eyes showed white all the way around. "The world itself may be lost if Ilferth Simon succeeds!"

"I'm well aware of that, Guardian!" snapped Aethal. Then he softened his voice. "But we cannot save him by getting these men killed against an entrenched foe. However, the life of the Lord Warden will be a high priority, yes, Warmaster?"

Malcoor looked as though he had bitten into something sour. "Breaking through the Temple will require concentrated force if Ilferth Simon is as mad and desperate as I fear he is. We've got proof positive he's involved in blasphemy and treason."

"The Guardians might help us."

"Yes, sir!" cried Magnei. "Liberate us and we will fight!"

Malcoor stepped close to Aethal and squeezed hard on his shoulder. "If you don't know what hold Ilferth Simon has over the Lord Warden Cledan," he growled, "who's to say he wouldn't order the Guardians into the fight on the side of the Temple?"

"He would never..." Magnei began, but subsided under Malcoor's cold stare.

"He's already knuckled under to blackmail, boy. Don't tell me what he wouldn't do; he's already done it in the face of Lotus." Malcoor's disgust was palpable. "Here's some good news." He pointed. Aethal turned to the great gates of the Hydraxis, which were opening to shouts and the clatter of hooves.

In rode Paal Haerling, Lord Paramount of the Wrackberg, at the head of a column of cavalry, followed by a longer one of infantry, all liveried in scarlet and black. Aethal did a quick estimation. His father must have emptied the Wrackberg for this: there had to be about twelve hundred all told. He'd never been so glad to see his father in all his life.

"Now," said Malcoor grimly, "if these Wrackberg reserves are worth anything, we may be able to consider a real attack."

Leaving his force in the hands of their officers, Aethal's father dismounted, and walked towards him. He looked his son up and down. "Is there much pain?" he asked, stiffly.

Aethal nodded.

"I will speak with the King. You will do him no good as Last Sword if you are too exhausted to lift one. Perhaps you might have other duties, such as helping to prepare the voyage to the Well." Aethal regarded his father. Of all the alien feelings, his father's quiet patience with him was the strangest. Yet his words were jerky, as though they were being pulled from him to his own surprise.

"What changed your mind about that, Father?"

Paal came to a stop and looked past Aethal, as though seeing a truth in the clouds. "Not changed," he said, his voice strangely soft. "Say rather, awakened. By that rather extraordinary daughter of Westerend's."

Aethal nodded. Ardyth. "Extraordinary, yes." Paal's eyebrow rose, but he continued on as before. "I still think it may be a waste, and a dangerous risk. But that is beside the point. We must hold Verlaen together. I am willing to do anything toward that end."

"Even support the Westerend and Chancellor Pyk?"

His father grimaced. "Aethal, I am a practical man. I do not make a virtue of forgiving my enemies or a vice of holding grudges against them. Your uncle and Lord Westerend have been my opponents, but in the end, they are of noble blood, and understand what power is. Even your Uncle Falaar knows it. Perhaps this will bring him to his senses in time."

"Indeed," Aethal said, but his belly was heavy as gold at the very thought. The word from the Keepwoods of the Serpent's Pass brought back his earliest nightmare-visions of Lotus to mind. More and more commoners — and who knew how many refugee Telerati might be among the refugees from the Skysil-ruled Plateau? — were streaming towards the Pass, and being turned back from the refuge of the Bowl. With Greater Rifle fire, where necessary. Where the Plateau Road met the King's Highway, still more migrants joined them, fleeing the Lotus in the Eastern Grain Sea. At the last word, several thousand were encamped below the Pass, frightened and hungry. And some of them reported seeing horsemen — horsemen liveried in the purple-white-black of House Skysil — in the northern pass up to the Plateau. "Let us hope that Uncle Falaar has not also decided that his power can only be secured by a royal title." Would Paitir accept a divided Verlaen as the cost of fighting the Lotus? It could come to that. "If he wants to, he can press our own people forward simply by driving them into the army in the Pass."

"Falaar must know that Paitir cannot accept him as a Skysil king," said Paal. "He isn't mad enough to assault the Pass; even if he won, he'd slaughter his people along with our own and risk terrible judgment at home, where his power cannot be great."

"I never thought Eraad could be so mad at Telerat," said Aethal. Privately, he doubted his father's assessment of Falaar's following. He had lived with the Skysils, and Paal never had. The people were fiercely loyal to their lords, and considered themselves far tougher than the soft denizens of Westerend and the Bowl.

His father swore. "Eraad, that fool. He has nearly ruined all. I was fortunate to save him from summary execution. The General Staff will see no advantage in forgiving him, and the Well knows whether Pyk will intervene."

Aethal tried to keep his tone indifferent. "And Aerhan?"

"That's out of my hands, now," Paal said shortly. He sighed. "You couldn't know this, Aethal, but he did good work for me, in his own way. I fear that I failed him through being too indulgent of his temper. If both Aerhan and Eraad can be kept out of the public eye while we fight the Lotus — and teach them both good, sharp lessons — they might yet be redeemed."

"After their crimes?" Aethal turned on his father. "Why?"

"Because we need them," Paal answered. "The bloodlines must be secured. The Church and the Lord Mayor are desperately trying to undermine them so that they can seize power; you see that, don't you? I've been fighting that ever since Eraad's mother died. If you think that problem is bad now, it would be far worse with Eraad dead. We'd have a crop of assassins growing up as fast as Lotus to kill Paitir. They'd think the Lotus was their perfect chance to launch their coup. You know it's true."

Reluctantly, Aethal nodded. The General States had shown that if nothing else.

"Fortunately, our bloodline is better protected," Paal clapped him on the shoulder. "But I'm well aware of how easily I could lose you, too. I regret I have no other son like you. Or like Westerend's daughter, by the Well. I never thought to see *her* do more than glare prettily at me beneath over-curled hair at court balls. I certainly didn't expect her to show up at the Hydraxis gates after midnight, begging an audience with the King."

Paal started toward the low complex of barracks that bordered the Hydraxis' wall, and Aethal perforce followed. "And how did you manage that, exactly, Father? When I last left the King's presence, you were scarcely in more favor than I myself, though housed more comfortably, I doubt not."

Paal sighed. "There is a distinct difference between being out of favor and being under arrest. A wise man avoids both. You must tell me one day what substance, if any, lies behind Westerend's charge; young Ardyth is indeed brilliant, but naïve. She could not hide the fact that *something* went on at their Residence. But no matter. What has escaped Ilferth Simon, and possibly Westerend as well, is that the King has not dismissed the General States; what they have done they can undo. I offered to change my vote in the next session, restoring the vote in favor of the expedition."

"And restore the Chancellorship to you, as well?"

"Perhaps. I am glad you start to consider these matters," said Paal.

"That's not all I've considered. Father, you knew about Ilferth Simon's network of these Wellspawned vision discs. So, answer me now: if you suspected the Conversant of having planted Lotus in Verlaen, why did you say nothing?" said Aethal.

Paal's temper flared. "Pull the wool out of your ears and listen, Aethal! I said no such thing because I *didn't* suspect. I knew Simon was mad; not suicidal. My agent in the Church simply discovered that Simon knew of the Lotus. Which is how I knew."

"But you kept it from the King, Father!"

"I had no proof, then! If I'd gone to the King with that, it would have been the Conversant's word against mine that there even was such news. He'd have denied knowing anything, but the eye of suspicion would certainly have fallen on me. I would have had to announce it, and then my agent would certainly have been discovered and killed. All I could do was dispatch poor Jeralta to the Keepwoods."

"I trust you believe I had nothing to do with his death now?" said Aethal.

"Obviously." Paal looked uncomfortable. "Sigrad was one of my worst intelligence failures. Simon had obviously nurtured him for years, just waiting to use him as needed."

"How did he escape?"

"Ilferth Simon most likely suborned a jailer to slip him the key to his own cell. I'll have it out of them one way or another. Sigrad was a most resourceful man."

"Let us hope Ilferth Simon has no more such highly-placed and dedicated men," Aethal said. What promises, what rewards, could make a man swear to appear a fool for his entire life? Riches? Future power? Or simply a promise that his soul would walk in Deep Heaven with God after his death? Remembering Osric, Aethal shivered.

That danger would be as minimal as Aethal could make it. He would assign eight Wyrmguard to keep the king in view at all times, and act as his food-tasters and valets as well. That made Aethal feel almost safe. *Almost. Ilferth Simon found something that talks across leagues as fast as a man could speak to another across a table, and is ruthless enough to use Lotus as a weapon against his enemies. Who knows whether he might suborn even a Wyrmguard?* That was supposed to be impossible. Yet with the Well in the world, nothing could truly be impossible, could it? *While the Lotus was across the sea, we could pretend the Well did not exist,* thought Aethal, *and define what was possible. Now our illusory wall is breached, and we can no longer live by knowing what is possible; rather we must fear what may be possible. And that is too much for men to fear and yet live with.*

"Aethal," his father interrupted his reverie. "I tried to do what I thought was best for Verlaen, and for our house. It took Ardyth to make me see... to remind me... that sometimes a man must take great risks to do what is best. I could not do less. Nor will I."

Aethal looked at his father. He saw a weariness there; but, it also seemed, a strength, perhaps even humility. "Trust between us may take time," Aethal finally said. "But, thank you. Father."

Paal nodded. "And now, to battle." They turned toward Malcoor and Colonel Henling, who had been joined by two Wrackberg officers. Flintmaw hurried up to Aethal.

"Last Sword," he said. "There is no sign of Colonel Farnan in the dungeons. He was not found. The records indicate that he was moved to the cells in the Winery." Aethal looked toward the great gates just in time to hear Ardyth's shout.

"Look there!" she cried, pointing southward.

Aethal followed her finger. A red flare was rising below in the Madlands. Aethal looked down on it. "A patrol is in trouble," he muttered. It seemed to be close to Sergeant Falk's neighborhood. But other patrols should see the signal and converge on it. Any Lotus patrol could be mobbed by angry citizens. Which was why most of the patrols had been handed over to the more popular Temple Guard.

A cold sensation spread through Aethal's belly. His eyes leapt to the beacons. They had been lit an hour ago, bathing Maednac Serpiin in light, and signaling safety, as they had since Aethal had issued the order, on every tall building in the capital, spaced as evenly as the organic growth of the city allowed.

Only it seemed that there were rather fewer of them tonight. Aethal frowned. "I need a view from the Ophidian," he said, turning to leave.

There was another flash of red, a flare rising from the docks. Aethal froze. Right below the flare, before his eyes, one of the great lighthouses guarding the bay went out. A great cloud of steam went up.

Then another flare, near the Llhawcae Cathedral, Aethal realized. And another darkening of lights, this time all over the city. Two red flares. Three. Half a dozen.

"What's happening to the patrols, Last Sword?" asked Magnei. But when he looked to Malcoor, Aethal saw that the man's face might have been carven stone.

Suddenly, an out-of-breath messenger handed a note to Paal. He opened it and turned pale. Looking up, he said, "Warmaster. My source within the Temple has gone missing. I'm afraid it has been discovered."

"Wish me buggered!" swore Malcoor. "Will he hold out?"

"It depends very much on whether..." began Paal.

Aethal nodded, dreading the image he saw unfolding in his mind's eye. A cell. A man offered food. The taste of green and silver leaf. "No, he won't," Aethal said. "He won't hold out at all."

✳✳✳

"Closing hour!"

The shout rang out from the Ophidian, the hourly cry which all of the patrols were to echo as they heard it, so that all would know that the city was patrolled and safe from Lotus. There was a pause. The first white flare went up just a half-mile from the outer gates of the Hydraxis. *Signal not echoed.* Aethal watched white flares rise, one, five, a dozen, twenty. An ever-expanding ring of white fire, marching at the speed of the human voice, showing patrols not answering the hourly call.

And still there were far fewer than should have been. With the white flares, a handful of red flares rose, then went out. Aethal's mind froze. *They're supposed to converge on a patrol in trouble, or one not hearing an echo. Run towards a red or a white flare.* And there were at least fifty places to converge on. Were the patrols in trouble? Or were they suborned? *And those who are not suborned? What will they do?* He had given them no instructions for this contingency. He'd planned it to announce a warning from one location, not to respond to trouble in every place at once!

The city was still darkening. The signal fires were going out one by one. Here quickly, there slowly. "What does that mean, Aethal?" snapped his father.

Aethal turned to answer, not knowing what he would say. A last, bedraggled ring of white flares rose over the city, along the docks, almost halfway to where the Wrackberg sat shrouded in mist.

And fifty green flares rose over the city as one.

Ardyth screamed.

Lotus. In Maednac Serpiin.

"Lotus," whispered Paal, giving voice to the unspeakable.

Malcoor whirled on him. "Pull your head out of your arse, Wrackberg! D'you really believe fifty people found Lotus all at once and fired flares at the same instant! That's a signal to action, not for help!"

"But the people will think..." said Aethal.

"Damned right, that's what they'll think!" Malcoor shouted back. "And where will they go, in their panic?"

Aethal looked back at the city. The red and white flares were fading, but the green burned on. Below them, the beacon fires shone, in steadily diminishing numbers. But there was the Llhawcae Cathedral. And the Kirk of the Docks near the water's edge. And northwards, the High Temple, whose beacon shone off its Single Moon like a star.

"They'll go to church," he said.

Civil war had come to Maednac Serpiin.

Chapter Eight

58th of Spring, 312 Exodus

Under the red-bronze glow of Maednac's likeness, the Hydraxis braced for assault.

Two hours ago, Malcoor had sent out scouts. The one that had returned had reported masses of the population gathering, barricading the streets and squares, and especially the churches. And through it all, banners displaying the Single Moon of the Church. The other had been swallowed by the night. There was no hope of assaulting the Temple now; Maednac's Own had become the desperate defenders of the Hydraxis walls.

Aethal, with Gun and the Last Sword on his shoulders, walked the circuit of the Hydraxis. There were eight gates. Companies of men manned each one, with a few light cannon apiece. Light guns only. Maednac's Own had never been intended to take the field without support. Or to defend the Hydraxis unaided. The men were spread out. Much too far out. Only half of them had made it to the Hydraxis. The rest, they had to assume, had been surprised at their posts on the city walls.

The Hydraxis wall measures a circle one mile in circumference. With just under 2000 men, we have one man to defend every three feet of wall, thought Aethal. The wall was crenellated, but only five feet high. It had not been designed as a fortress. *Maednac Serpiin is a fortress,* Aethal thought coldly. *Inside the city walls, we would be safe from any foe. The walls are twenty feet thick, and bristle with heavy cannon to mow down any foe from without.* But Maednac's sons had never cared to arm themselves against their own people like the Emperors, or the Wish-Kings of old. What had once seemed a source of greatest pride to Aethal now smelled of rankest folly.

The Dragongate yawned before him; though it was only large enough to pass a single cart, it seemed large and vulnerable. The guards, wearing the ship-and-shattered star of Maednac's Own, shone their torches in a man's face. He looked into it unblinking, though he flinched at their grip on his arm. His uniform was half torn off, but it was plainly the gray-and-blue of the City Watch. The gate was hastily closed behind him.

Five seconds passed, and the torch was lowered.

Aethal looked at the newcomer. "Report," he said softly.

The man looked up at Aethal with fear in his light-brown eyes. "The South Watch post. Gone, my lord. Don't know what..." he swayed. "The lieutenant heard the call for Closing Hour, and I repeated it, just like always. I had the best voice; I'm the crier. No one answered from the Wall. And then the white flare went up, so we sent Davyd back to report, and the Lieutenant said we had to investigate the Wall's flare. So we double-timed it to the Wall, and there they were, just waiting. They wasn't Lotus Eaters, my Lord, they couldn't-a been! They were just calm and collected as anything. They were the *Temple Guard Patrol!* And they sent up the green flare while we were watching them. And then they shot us. Milord, my arm hurts real bad..." Aethal noticed the blood dripping from the man's sleeve, "...and I guess I hit my head, too, when they shot me, because the next thing I know I was heading here. I dunno where my mace went. Is it Lotus, milord?"

"No, soldier," Aethal said gently. "Go find a fire and food. You'll find those who can send for a doctor there, too."

The man nodded and staggered on. Aethal looked at the soldiers. "Fifth one in the last half-hour, sir," said the one who'd carried out the Discipline. Aethal nodded. The numbers were falling. Those who were loyal were mostly inside the gates... or did not dare to try for them.

"Any of them armed?"

"We had one officer who brought in his family shotgun," said the man. "And another who was... pretty bad. We called the surgeon ourselves for him."

"What happened?"

The soldier drew breath and looked blank. "The eye that they left him was green." Aethal swallowed. "It wasn't Lotus, sir. Sir?" asked the man.

"What is it?"

"*Is* it the Lotus? Out there?"

"No, corporal," said Aethal, for the tenth time, to the tenth man. "Not here. Not yet. It's a trick. Ilferth Simon is in rebellion against His Majesty. And if you are wondering whether to place your faith in His Majesty or the Church... well, His Majesty has not used a false cry of Lotus to panic the people to his side."

"No, sir," said the corporal.

Aethal clapped him on the shoulder. "Be strong and fight smart. His Majesty will need every one of Maednac's Own before this night is through."

"We Keep The Word, sir," said the corporal, giving the regimental motto.

"Good man." Aethal continued on his circuit of the wall, giving encouragement here, a minor correction there. *The eye they left him. During any other disaster, the people would all be flooding to the Hydraxis to receive the king's protection.* But the fear of Lotus kept the people indoors, and the Church spread the rumors were that the king and his son had led Verlaen into disaster and to civil war. *And the people brave enough to leave their walls in the face of the Green Judgment flock to the churches to hear more lies.* Turning his steps toward the Wagonmast, where General Malcoor had his headquarters, Aethal bared his teeth in a snarl. A small ring of watchfires still burned: around the city, at its gates, now doubtless in enemy hands. At the bases of church spires, which rose all through the city. From within a street of the Hydraxis to the docks of the Madlands, the watchfires burned. Aethal burned with resentment against the darkness of their minds, and their eagerness to believe in a God who would use Lotus as His tool.

From the interior of the Dragonmast, noise interrupted his thoughts. Barrels and boxes were being broken into, unloaded, carted outside. Aethal could see stacks of muskets and barrels of powder being counted and... he paused, checking the stacks of arms. *Matchlock smoothbores,* he recognized them. *Matchlock smoothbores, and God-Beyond-The-World say no, a ballista?* But there was no mistaking the giant crossbow. There seemed to be plenty of the wrist-thick bolts, at least.

Malcoor stood at a large table, with a map of the Hydraxis spread before him. Around him stood his father's Guards Captain and three officers. Aethal recognized Colonel Henling. Malcoor was addressing them. "The outbuildings must be used to reinforce our lines of retreat. When it is sounded, you will fall back along these lines to the Wagonmast, where we will form a new firing line. Dismissed, gentlemen."

Aethal approached him. Malcoor nodded. "Last Sword. How are the men doing?"

Aethal allowed an edge to come into his voice. "Well enough. They'd be doing better if you were seen outside, directing them. From where do you intend to command?"

Malcoor raised his eyebrows. "From right here, Aethal Paaling. I have no intention of leaving the Hydraxis unless we are victorious."

"The likelihood of that is diminished if you wait inside, sir." Aethal retorted. "What chance have we got if the men break and run because they're convinced you have no hope of victory? You trained us better than this, sir. You trained half the officers out there. Do you think we've forgotten?"

Malcoor's eyes were hooded. "Think more and remember less, Aethal Paaling. In wars, men die. Even Warmasters. And at the moment, you will have to pardon my saying so, I am the one man the Kingdom cannot afford to lose."

"Explain yourself," Aethal said.

"I'd have thought it was obvious," sighed Malcoor, "especially to the man who did so much to find me, but I'll spell it out for you." He lowered his voice.

"The expedition to the Well is Verlaen's last hope. The only reason it matters if we win today is because the expedition is lost along with us if we lose. If we win, it will still go forward, assuming your gutless father doesn't change his vote a second time. But, Last Sword, even if we win, Verlaen is lost. There is civil war in Telerat, and soon it will be in the Pass. My brother will be fighting Lotus in our homeland unless Ilferth Simon is bluffing in his threat to release it, and the fact that civil war and Lotus have both grown up right here suggests that this is a stupid thing to hope for."

Malcoor pulled out another map, this one of the Bowl and its encircling mountains. He pointed to the narrow defile that led through. "All our loyal forces are in the Pass, and cannot get here in less than two days, even if I dared withdraw them, which I do not. Your uncle is a dangerous and canny opponent, whom I would much rather not fight, but I daren't let his soldiers through, nor the refugees who seek shelter from those soldiers, lest Lotus Eaters come through with them.

"So, Aethal Paaling. You may not like what you hear. You may not like what I say. But at the moment, Verlaen's ultimate hopes rest on the voyage to the Well, and the voyage rests on the knowledge and experience of the one man who has even come close to making that journey." He bowed. "So for tonight, and for Verlaen, there is no man's life within this wall that I intend to guard more fiercely than my own." He turned away, calling for the quartermasters to attend him. Aethal felt sick. And yet he could not fault Malcoor's coldly logical reasoning.

"Last Sword!" a voice called. It was a young lieutenant dressed in Wrackberg scarlet-and-grays. "A man has come in at the Seagate. Badly wounded. Civilian. Calling for you, my Lord!"

Aethal held Malcoor's eyes for a smoldering moment and then broke off to follow his father's man. "Where does he come from?"

"The Madlands by his voice and tale, sir." He spoke with the feverish energy of youth seeing the real world for the first time, recognizing that it was far more than everything he had thought. "He's been shot at least once; I..." his voice dropped. "I don't think he'll live, sir."

Aethal grunted, and they broke into a run. In the quiet eternity of the bouncing, jarring run, Aethal noticed how slowly it was all happening. The spread of violence by lights and running men and word of mouth. *If I could be there. If I could be at a hundred places, I could stop this with just a few good men. A platoon, or less. But I can only run in this tar of night, and because of this, hundreds — thousands — will die.*

They reached the gate to see two men bending over a third, with bright lanterns set near the man lying down. He knelt, and in the instant recognized the heavy features of Sergeant Falk. His heart sank.

Except, as the man turned his head, he saw that it was not the Sergeant. It was only his face, echoed in slightly younger lines, on another man. This man's tunic was awash in blood, and his face was white even in the lanterns' glow. The man's eyes widened.

"Last Sword!" he gasped, and then curled in on himself, coughing blood and mucus. Eventually, the spasm subsided, but while it continued, Aethal had to endure the glare of the surgeon.

"Calm yourself," Aethal said, forcing his voice to obey that advice. "Tell me all, but softly."

The man began again, his face fighting the paroxysms of coughing that his wounds created. "Landen Falk, milord," he got out. "Bedar's brother. We've got... got two for you, milord. If you come. Kirk o'the Docks. Llhawcae. Ammunition. Plenty. Men. We need." Falk the elder's face twisted with the effort to speak, to breathe. His eyes popped wide open, clawing for Aethal's. "Lord! Family! There! Come soon!" Then he dissolved in coughing, coughing until there was no more breath in him, and the surgeon wrestled him down, until he was breathing in long, syrupy gasps.

Aethal turned away. He turned to the officer at the gate, a young captain, and drew breath to speak. He was interrupted by a cry from the walls.

"Infantry column! Infantry advancing on the south wall!" The cry rang out, and seconds later, so did the bells. They rang out steadily, ordering men to their places on the wall. Aethal climbed the wall and looked out.

There were indeed men marching toward the wall, out from behind the large, low bulk of the Admiralty building, but to call them infantry columns, Aethal thought, was being very generous indeed. They moved forward in a mass, grouping together in more-or-less evenly spaced blobs. Even from this distance, he could see that they had no concept of marching together. But they did carry weapons. What sort, Aethal could not say. Even as he watched, Aethal could see the royal standard being lowered from the roof of the Admiralty. But it was not removed. It was sent back up, below another flag: blue, with the bronze key-and-lock sigil of Maednac Serpiin's City Watch on it. *Hlafen*, Aethal thought, feeling his blood run hot. But it wasn't just Hlafen's insignia anymore, was it? There was a device over the top, in silver. Something like a chevron. *What is our Lord Mayor playing at?*

Far off, Aethal heard another cry, "Infantry! Infantry advancing on the east wall!" "Infantry advancing, west wall!" And finally, "Infantry. Rebel infantry advancing, north wall." Aethal swore, and hoped someone else was doing it, too, at the overenthused lookout. *They're not rebels yet. Not until we talk and someone refuses to lay down arms. But if we call them rebels, they surely will rebel in truth.* There was little option. By the Discipline, rebellion was death.

Another shout pierced the night: "Standard! Standard bearer at the north wall." Aethal's jaw set itself grimly. A standard. And at the north wall, that could mean only one thing: Ilferth Simon's Single Moon.

A young private in the uniform of Maednac's Own ran to Aethal and bowed, breathing hard. "By your leave, milord, the General's compliments and you are requested to attend him at the Dragonmast."

But there was commotion beneath the altered banner of the Lord Mayor. A small party had started out from it, beneath a white banner. Parley.

"Attend me," Aethal murmured, and the soldier swallowed. Aethal's own head swam a minute. A month ago, he'd have been guilty of gross insubordination for ignoring a general officer's order. Now he was in a separate chain of command. And he thought Malcoor would want to hear what the Lord Mayor had to say. Behind him, the streets filled with his men. Some few hundred wore the City Watch uniform, but behind them were thousands in civilian clothing, carrying all manner of weapons. No few of them carried shining rifles, the guns Skraalen had warned him about. They fingered their weapons nervously. *No veterans, these.*

Rolf Hlafen stood surrounded by an even dozen of his City Watch. The men carried, alternately, smoothbore muskets and shotguns. "Aethal Paaling," said Hlafen, and surprise colored his tone. Aethal clamped down on his rage, forced himself to study the man. *Surprised to see me alive, Hlafen? Is it possible that Ilferth Simon believes I am dead?* His left hand still throbbed.

"My Lord Mayor," Aethal said, deliberately putting on a friendly tone. "Shall I tell His Majesty how fortunate he is that you have brought these citizens, with all speed, to aid in the defense of the Hydraxis against the forces of the traitor, Ilferth Simon?"

Hlafen's face blanked, then shifted in calculation. He looked for all the world as if he were wondering if he could take advantage of Aethal's naïveté and simply march his troops through the gate. Then his mouth grew hard.

"My Lord Aethal Paaling, we are indeed come to offer our *loyal* aid to His Majesty in this desperate hour, despite his discourtesies and the fact that he has been beguiled by unwise counsels. We are here to remove those counselors."

"My Lord," said Aethal. "His Majesty has decided for himself whose counsels are wise. The King and the General States have spoken..."

"Yes, I heard them speak!" said the Lord Mayor, and his face was flushed. "They voted against this expedition. And yet we hear that they shall be called again, so that his Majesty, without the support of the people, and without the support of the Church, can push through this blasphemy with the support of the Lords Paramount alone! The Kings of Verlaen do not overrule the General States." Hlafen cried, pointing a shaking finger at Aethal. "It is Maednac's Law, that goes back three hundred years!"

"Maednac himself sided with the people against the Lords and the Church when they wanted the free farmers returned to serfdom, as it was under the ancient days of the Empire. Only in union can the States overrule the Crown."

"And they did," said Hlafen. "They did. The people of Verlaen are merely here to see that the laws are carried out."

Aethal lowered his voice. "And when the General States convene again?"

The Lord Mayor smiled thinly. "I cannot imagine why that should be necessary, Last Sword."

It was the wind that caught the tabard of one of the Lord Mayor's guardsmen and straightened it for Aethal to see. The bronze key-and-lock insignia reflected to torchlight dully, but above it, in silver, a coronet blazed.

"I see," said Aethal, looking at it. "A nice addition to your office. You have come to take the crown, then?"

Hlafen looked as though he would burst. "Support the crown!" he huffed. "The city of Maednac Serpiin supports the crown, as we have ever done, as you can see!"

Aethal leaned close. "If it is as they have ever done," he said, pitching his voice to carry, "then why change your banner? Is that coronet for the Lord Mayor you are? Or is it for the Lord Paramount you think you might become? What has Ilferth Simon promised you?"

Hlafen's face blazed with unbridled hatred and avarice. Aethal had struck home. *I am not my father's son for nothing, Rolf Hlafen,* he thought.

"The terms are these," Hlafen said. "The Lords Wrackberg and West-erend will retire to their estates at once. The King shall appoint Ilferth Simon as Chancellor, and myself as Warmaster. We shall at once purge Verlaen of its Wellspawn. And the Kingdom shall return to its ancient purity."

Ancient purity? Maednac himself had accepted the Wyrmguard's oath. There was no ancient purity.

"My Lord," whispered Aethal, this time for Hlafen's ear alone. "There is no reason in this. If we win, you cannot avoid the noose. If you win, you and Ilferth Simon together must still be weaker than any king in Verlaen's history *and then* you will still have to fight the Lotus. Accept the honored place that is yours by right and fight with us; not against us."

Hlafen hesitated then. For a moment, greed warred against fear. But too briefly. "No man can fight against the Word of God, Aethal Paaling. Not even the King." He turned away. "You force us to this," he said. "You and your Warmaster."

"Your choices are your own," Aethal replied. "When I saw you stand up to the Conversant in front of the King, I thought you were a man. But you were only a mummer, playing the role your master set for you. Congratulations, my Lord. You fooled us all. You will suffer the consequences of that treachery." But the words sounded hollow even to him.

When the party had left and the gate was shut, Aethal turned to the private who had summoned him. "To the Warmaster. At once!" They went off at a run.

***

Aethal found the General staring through him. "Where the hell have you been, boy?"

"Receiving the Lord Mayor of Maednac Serpiin. He was not in a listening mood. I don't know what hold exactly Ilferth Simon has on him…"

"If you'd been here when I'd damn well told you to, you might know! I have a parley delegation right outside the gate."

Aethal looked beyond the general. Below the standard of the Single Moon stood a white banner of parley. He did not recognize the man below it, though. "Why aren't you handling it, General?"

"Oh, pay attention, boy! What did I just tell you? Do you think Ilferth Simon is the kind of man to miss killing his enemy, by any means? After what you've seen?"

The Lotus floated up to Aethal in his memories, tainted with the smell of green perfume in the dark, and the look on Jeralta's dead face. "No," he said, and went to meet the embassy.

***

Obviously, Ilferth Simon fears the same, Aethal thought, when he failed to see the Conversant beneath his own banner. He wondered. If Ilferth Simon could be killed, would the insurrection fail? Or would he become a dead martyr, spurring on the people and the Temple Guard to heightened fanaticism? The man beneath the Single Moon banner was unknown to Aethal. He had no guards. Behind him, grim lines of men in black cloaks and carrying rifles waited. *At least a thousand of them. And when did the Temple Guard learn to fight?*

"I am Aethal Paaling, the Last Sword. Who are you and where is the Conversant?"

The smooth-faced young man looked back at Aethal, completely serene. "Out of range of the abomination you carry, and in congress with God-Beyond-The-World." He nodded at Gun. "I use no name. I am the Conversant's voice, as he is God's."

"I have a good idea what the Conversant will say," said Aethal. He relayed the message from the Lord Mayor.

"The Lord Mayor is an inexact man, whose understanding of God's will is minimal," the spokesman observed calmly. "In addition to those requirements, the Crown Prince Eraad will submit himself to the Church for purification, as is God's will. And the King will do homage to the Conversant. As a man should in the presence of the voice of God."

Aethal's throat froze. What Hlafen had wanted was bad enough. What Simon wanted was a theocracy.

"His Majesty is the King of Verlaen by the Grace of God-Be-yond-The-World. And no man will alter that, not even the Conversant."

"And if God has decided to alter it, Last Sword?" the nameless man said. "The Lotus has altered many things, and will alter many more. How can you be sure what He will alter? The Conversant can."

"The Conversant can be sure of what the Lotus will alter," said Aethal, "because he spreads it by his own agents. Did you know that, you who have given up your name? The Conversant is a tool of the Lotus. I've seen him use it myself."

The smooth-faced man smiled. "I see you do not understand. I am the Conversant's voice, but sometimes words are not sufficient to a voice that must make its meaning clear. When God speaks, the Conversant acts. Even so, when the Conversant speaks, I act." The man closed his eyes and made a convulsive biting motion. He looked at Aethal, and his eyes were steady.

Then they bloomed red and began to bleed. The man coughed just once, an explosive, red outburst that spattered the cobbles. Then he fell. *Poison. He took poison right in front of me.* The simplicity of the plan was beauty itself. *The Conversant will say we murdered him, and his men will believe Paitir a tyrant.* Again, he damned Eraad for making that story plausible. Aethal turned back to where Malcoor waited.

***

When he had heard Aethal's tale, Malcoor's face hardened. "The message is very clear. No quarter, then."

"We can expect none, certainly," said Aethal.

"I mean for them, boy," said Malcoor.

174

Aethal's jaw dropped. "Sir, if we show no mercy even to our own people, they'll never give up!"

Malcoor grabbed him by the arm. "This isn't about who gives up anymore, boy. You pay attention, now, or you're no good to me, the King, or anybody! Ilferth Simon has ordered his men to die for him."

"They can't all be like that!" Aethal broke in.

"They can all be infected with Lotus," Malcoor said, his voice dead. But he hesitated. "We'll take surrender if it's offered by a man who's thrown down his weapons. But we won't ask for it. Any man who crosses that wall with a gun in hand, dies. Now, get to your station. I want the Wyrmguard and City Watch assembled as a reserve. Now!"

Aethal turned away. In the distance, trumpets were sounding to receive infantry. He walked into the nightmare.

***

Aethal stood between Maednac's feet and surveyed the wall. The fire that burned there had long since been extinguished, as had all the lamps within the Hydraxis. Yet the ghostly light of the two moons, both full, bathed the court in shadows and silver-blue light.

On the southern wall below him, he faintly heard the shouted command: "*Present... Volley Fire!*" Four hundred rifles crackled out over a front nearly a quarter-mile wide. Then,

"*Fire at will!*"

The crackle of rifle fire grew continuous and sporadic. *Not even time for two volleys*, Aethal thought. Ilferth Simon had been right to launch his attack at night. The defenders of the Hydraxis were armed with rifles, which could hit a man at three-quarters of a mile in the hands of an expert sniper. Now, under the cloak of night and the cover of the nearest buildings, they were down to shooting at just under a hundred yards.

The light cannon on the walls, a pitiful half-dozen to Aethal's ear, belched fire, and now Aethal could hear the screams of men, and see the return fire's sparkle from below the wall. The smoothbore musket fire was barely aimed, but it was close now, and inevitably some of the men on the wall fell. *And we have no more. I hope Sergeant Falk is doing better than we are,* he thought. *They might as well be on the Dark Continent itself.*

The clash of steel reached his ears, and Aethal strained forward. Around the base of Maednac's statue stood his sixteen Wyrmguard. Goldhammer. Flintmaw. All the Wyrmguard save the eight surrounding the king. Encircling them stood the hundred men in City Watch gray-and-blues, along with a few in civilian clothes that had been armed from the Dragonmast's stores. The slow matches of their smoothbore matchlocks burned like sullen fireflies. They were his reserve, assembled from all the men who had staggered in through the gate since the flares had gone up. Those who hadn't been in on the Lord Mayor's plot. The gate was not broken yet; the small company drawn up just inside it had not moved to fire its pair of light cannon. But there was steel against steel on the wall. "Company, attention!" Aethal called.

From the other side of the Hydraxis, the fire was more intense. Maednac's Own were fighting at the Cragsgate, and their rifles spoke in unison. *The enemy has to charge out of the Garden Third there,* Aethal thought, but Ilferth Simon would be there, with his Temple Guards. Some of them would have rifles. And some might even have Greater Rifles. The greater skill of the elite unit would be needed to the north.

Here, as to the east and west, the Hydraxis would have to make do with House Wrackberg troops, and the City Watch. Aethal could hear the crackle of fire reach a crescendo as the Dawnsgate to the east and the Dwimmergate to the west fired volleys into the third charge of the night.

They have not broken through yet, thought Aethal. But even as the thought formed, he saw men falling back from the wall. He drew the Last Sword, and it shone in the moonlight. "At the ready..." he called.

Suddenly, his ear stung with the wind and buzz of a bullet. Maednac's statue rang like a bell. *down!* screamed Gun in his mind, and Aethal was rolling and behind Maednac's huge ankle in an instant.

The Last Sword lay on the granite base of Maednac's statue, glinting in the light. Gun was in his hands without Aethal ever knowing quite how it had gotten there.

sniper. admiralty roof.

Aethal froze. He had not thought that Ilferth Simon would waste any snipers along the south wall. The weaker Rolf Hlafen's troops were, the less chance he would be a threat after the coup.

"Last Sword," said Goldhammer, gesturing at the conscripts, "What —" The sentence was never completed. The side of the Wyrmguard's head blew out in a gout of blood. Men screamed, threw down their muskets, and began to run.

"Stand there!" Aethal roared. "Wyrmguard! Rally them! Seal the breach!" Aethal gestured, and pulled back his hand an instant before a bullet sparked off the granite beneath it.

It was terrifying. The Wyrmguard raised their weapons and fired as one. The eleven men who had run first staggered, then turned in stunned terror.

Their helmets had been knocked off by a single bullet each.

"Rally!" The Wyrmguards' mounts spoke in one voice, as well. The men picked up their helmets and guns. Slowly, then with gathering speed, Aethal's company reformed itself.

But there was still a sniper to deal with. One that killed Wyrmguard. Or their commander, for preference.

caution. we face now one of my own forging.

Ice flooded Aethal's stomach. A Greater Rifle here? That he was its target was obvious. It was equally obvious that he was the only one who could do anything about it.

if you are the sniper's primary target, you play into his hands, said Gun. *we will have to expose ourselves in order to counterfire.*

But the Wyrmguard cannot shoot at that distance. It was true. The Wyrm-guard had been Wished for countless ages ago, when volume of fire was more important than accurate shooting at a distance. Perhaps the Forge at Nadesh Cor, wherever that had been, could have wrought long-barreled Wyrmguard for this sort of work, but a pistol's accuracy was far more limited than a rifle's.

The reserve company was charging at the breach now, and lining up to fire. Aethal peered carefully around the statue's legs, just in time to see a Wyrmguard — he could not tell which one — fall.

Aethal knelt and aimed; this would be his one chance, between the sniper's firing and his reloading. Time seemed to slow, and it wasn't just the heat of battle and fear coursing through Aethal's veins that did it. This was a deep sniper trance, far deeper than Aethal had ever needed to go before. The night sprang out over Gun's iron sights, the silvery light of the moon drawing the Admiralty roof in charcoal and indigo, just barely above Aethal's own position, higher up the hill.

It was not magnified. Not really. But Gun's senses were not Aethal's and were sharp as only machines can be sharp. Aethal felt every tension in Gun's lock; brought the trigger to the instant before release, needing only a thought to break it. His heart slowed, breathing stopped. He felt the roof, with its spire and chimneys. Its flat surface. The very motions in the air, but those only in Aethal's immediate space, and so ignored. Aethal's sights slowly swept the roof. A chimney. The spire. A chimney. Too wide. *fire.* A flash. *too late.*

Fluidly and without thinking, Aethal fired, using Gun's recoil to swing him behind Maednac's ankle. He felt the sick, buzzing wave of the bullet pass through the space his chest had occupied a fraction of a second before. Fever-ishly, he reloaded.

the light outspeeds the bullet.

Gun's voice in his mind was like oil running down in the spaces between his muscle fibers, calming him. Who would be faster? And who could win, at this distance? Was it possible he had killed the man? No time to consider. Aethal flung himself down on his chest, peering into the night, over Gun's sights, looking for the chimney. Aethal could see the Admiralty building now in his mind's eye, clear as if at noon. The copper spire of the building over its faded yellow paint, and the roof studded with squat brick chimneys topped with wide, rusted pipes.

a trained sniper will move. This was an advantage Aethal did not have. He couldn't leave the statue of Maednac without dropping and worsening his angle of fire. *He won't move far*, he thought back. He wouldn't dare count on Aethal's being slower than him. *But he knows where I am, and might count on seeing the flash.* There was no way to stop that. At least two seconds, maybe three, before the bullet would arrive. It might be enough time. Prone, Aethal was harder to hit. And harder to move. Breathing shallowly, Aethal traversed Gun from chimney to chimney, seeing nothing.

Then the flash. Gun screamed in his mind to move, but this time Aethal overrode the weapon with smoothness born of practice. Time stretching out, barrel moving, correcting... *fire.* Aethal rolled like a madman, off the base of the statue and into the air. A flat *whack!* of lead on stone, and he flung Gun aside, fell, fell and slammed on his hands and knees to the cobbles. Scrambling up, he snatched Gun from the stones and raised it, empty, up to his eye, sighting on the place the flash had been.

There was a timeless pause. Dimly, Aethal saw the chimney the sniper had hidden behind. The chimney he had shot at, counting on the enemy, on his reflexes. A dark shape separated from the chimney, fell, and did not rise.

Aethal breathed again. Gun's bullet had passed through the flimsy iron of the chimney's upper pipes, and most likely the enemy's head or throat as well.

ware the wall. Gun's flat tone snapped Aethal back to the battle. Before him, his company was reloading their muskets at a glacial pace. The Wyrmguard stood on either wing of the double line, half of them methodically firing while the other half, machinelike, forced ball and powder into their cylinders. A ragged burst of fire rippled out from beyond the smoke in front of them, and half a dozen of his men fell, coughing and moaning. The back row faltered and stepped back in a raggedly line.

Rage filled Aethal, and he ran forward, Gun on his shoulder, snatching the Last Sword from Maednac's plinth. "Hold your line! Hold! Your! Line!" he shouted, turning men around with his bare hands. Over their shoulders, he saw a small knot of enemy musketmen facing them, reloading, huddling close together, just inside the wall. Behind them, in ones and twos, a small trickle of rebels climbed over the walls, brandishing clubs, knives, and makeshift spears. They fought blade-to-bayonet with the Wrackberg troops lining the wall. Beyond, torches flared at the Seagate.

"Load your weapons!" Aethal strode down the line, cuffing men frozen in shock. "Load them now!" Dazedly, men reached for their powder horns. Aethal shouted the cadence aloud. "Powder. Ram. Ball. Wad. Ram. Shoulder." He looked up. Perhaps half the men had followed orders, but by the Well, it would have to do. "Company, take aim!"

The half-dozen or so of the enemy were raising their muskets. One fired from the hip, and a man on the end of Aethal's line went down, gurgling. The men froze again.

"Take aim!" Aethal screamed. "Fire!"

A dozen of the old matchlocks spoke, stuttering as one slow-match after the other caught the powder. But half the enemy musketeers fell, and the rest broke. Wyrmguard picked them off.

"Fix bayonets!" The men fumbled for the old knives with the plug hilts, but Aethal wasn't about to wait. He snatched up the Last Sword in his left hand. "Charge!" And then they were running for the breach. Aethal fired Gun from the hip at an enemy pistolier and then he was through the howling mob, at the wall itself, watching the rebels fling down arms and retreat.

"Reload!" Aethal cried. "Stand to the wall and reload!" He surveyed the damage, and felt himself sicken. Dead and dying rebels and Watchmen littered the inner court of the Hydraxis for fifty yards in from where the wall had breached. The burning Seagate was being extinguished, but fire had blackened the heavy portcullis, and shattered timbers protruded from it like teeth in a dead man's jaw. Five more Wyrmguard were down, but Flintmaw was still with him.

"Hold here, Flintmaw." He went on to instruct the weapon to count the steps of the drill loudly and clearly to the men who were even now reloading their ancient muskets.

Aethal walked over to the dead Wyrmguard. To their mounts, he reminded himself. The Wyrmguard were still very much alive. Hesitantly, but deliberately, he closed his fingers over their barrels, and tucked them in his uniform belt. He recognized them. Pikesbane and Widower. He felt them clawing for a purchase in him, a place in a human mind as he touched them, but it was reflex, not deliberate. Had the guns truly wanted him, he would have been as powerless as Ardyth had been.

their hunger cannot be assuaged, Gun said.

What do you mean? he thought, leaving the two who had fallen, walking back to retrieve Goldhammer. But Gun was silent.

He had only reached the wall again when a young man, barely more than a boy, in a subaltern's uniform, ran up. "Last Sword," he said, striving for calm. "You are requested at the Dragonmast."

Aethal surveyed the wall. "Tell General Malcoor the situation is too unstable for me to leave."

The subaltern swallowed and bowed. "Begging your pardon, milord," he said. "But it was His Majesty who requested your presence."

Aethal nodded. Turning to Flintmaw, he said, "You're in command. Keep them here," and followed the young officer toward the wide tower of the Dragonmast.

***

181

Within the cavern of the Dragonmast, men continued to assemble old weapons and supplies. Looking younger than Aethal had seen him yet, General Malcoor stood at the head of a small, oblong table. At his right sat the king. For every year of his age Malcoor had appeared to lose during the fight, Paitir seemed to have gained two. He was shaking his head from side to side, as if the gesture could deny the carnage without, and yet he looked determined. At the king's right stood Pyk and Paal, both looking grim. To Malcoor's left, Major Caanling stood, looking pale.

"Where is Colonel Henling?" asked Aethal, after bowing to the king.

"He bought it," growled Malcoor. "Sniper. The enemy seems to have a handful of Greater Rifles." Malcoor's own Greater Rifle, Legate, had been sent for, and it perched on his back like a hunting falcon. "Caanling is doing a fine job. What's the situation to the south?" Malcoor asked.

Aethal reported on the Seagate's condition and the lack of reserves. "We may stand another charge," Aethal concluded. "We will not stand two."

"It's the same to the north," said the young major, who looked as though he were speaking out of a trance. "We've no reserves left to send."

"I thought you told me — all the cadre did — that the Temple Guard was useless in a fight!" said Aethal.

"They fooled us, Last Sword," answered Caanling, with a self-accusatory look that Aethal recognized. "They acted like green recruits, and some of them still fight like it. But they've a cadre of their own and they're better actors than we are. This was all planned. For some time."

"And we daren't strip the east or west approaches," said Malcoor. "They haven't tried to come over those walls yet, but they certainly will if they think they can."

Caanling struck the table with a fist. "By the Well's accursed pit, where are the loyal men of Verlaen?"

"At the Treeline," said Aethal. "At the Pass. On the ships of the Fleet and scattered throughout the city, believing they cannot win. They have not failed us, Major, any more than the dead have. They were out-organized." He dropped his voice, a great weight settling on him. "I was out-organized."

"What do you mean, Aethal Paaling?" asked Malcoor.

Aethal briefed Malcoor on his suspicion that the Conversant had been planning a revolt. "I had not yet acted on my suspicions. I was trying to make Simon think I knew nothing of it. And then I was arrested. It seems I am not a very competent spy. Only one church, maybe two, has been captured by Sergeant Falk and some irregulars. I received word that they've holed up at the Kirk of the Docks and are besieged; they may even be taken by now."

"Why in the name of the Well didn't you tell me, boy?" snapped Paal, old exasperation leaking into his voice.

"From the cell you allowed me to be thrown into?" Aethal asked. *And I didn't trust you any more than I trusted Ilferth Simon.*

"You should have —"

"You two can quarrel later," snapped Malcoor, leaning forward, his eyes agleam. "I'm more interested in the people holding this church. Enough men and ammunition — and *outside* the wall at that — could buy us some time." He paused to draw breath, looking at the ceiling. Then his gaze nailed Aethal to the wall. "I want them. Here. Now. Get them."

Aethal's mouth opened. "Sir, I have the word of a dying man who may even have been hallucinating..."

Malcoor pointed at him. "I'll tell you what I have that's not a hallucination. I have about a thousand men left to stave off seven thousand rebels. And they're bringing up cannon. Cannon they've stripped from the city walls. They're too heavy to move quickly, but they're bringing them. If we don't get someone else here to help, we will be fighting inside these walls before dawn and we will be marched outside them before noon to our gibbets. I need those men. And I need you to go get them for me."

Paal looked sharply at Malcoor. "The Last Sword's duty is to guard the King."

Malcoor rolled his eyes. "Wrackberg, you are an ass. What do you think I am trying to accomplish here? Your son will die very prettily at the King's feet, I am certain. I had rather have him return at the head of some more substantial forces than his own body."

Aethal nodded. *So, this is how I die.* "Have we any breaches in the enemy lines?"

It was Major Caanling who answered. "None. The encirclement is complete."

Aethal nodded. "General, I will need a company of men armed with Greater Rifles to accompany me."

Malcoor snorted. "Out of the question. Those men are all that's keeping the enemy off the walls right now. Your arquebusiers may have been facing Hlafen's cannon fodder, but we've got the Temple Guard to the north. They've breached us once. I don't mean them to do it again."

Aethal's frustration rose. "I cannot break through even the forces to the south with less than a company," he said, "or you might as well shoot us all right here!"

Malcoor's eyes swept the room. "Take the Wyrmguard."

Aethal yanked seven pistols from his belt, one by one and let them fall on the table. Except for the king, and Malcoor, the men in the room recoiled. "These are the Wyrmguard who have fallen," he snapped. "I have nine effectives left."

"I see twenty-four." Malcoor looked at the walls.

"Those are guarding the King!" cried Aethal.

"Wish me dead, it runs in the family!" shouted Malcoor. "The King will die if we are not reinforced. Use those men to guard the King by leading them to get my reinforcements."

"Sixteen or twelve, General, even Wyrmguard can't survive such odds."

Malcoor raised an eyebrow. "I didn't think Wyrmguard died."

"No, Sir," Aethal said softly, "but the men they ride do."

"But these seven are still usable?" asked Malcoor. "Good. Get more men."

"From where? There are no more prisoners to be bound under the Gun. What shall I do, ask for volunteers?"

"Yes," said Major Caanling, rising.

Aethal stared at the man.

"We are Maednac's Own regiment, Last Sword. We swear to die for the King. We Keep The Word. Unto death."

Aethal met the man's eyes. "It is possible that being a Wyrmguard may be worse than death, Major."

"Unto damnation, if we must. I am your first volunteer." He reached for a pistol. Malcoor knocked his hand aside. The major recoiled in fury. For a moment, Aethal thought the younger man might strike the Warmaster.

"I need officers, Major. Not martyrs. And we do have prisoners. Men can be bound under the Gun for treason."

"General," said Aethal. "Most of the prisoners we have, I cannot use. Not well. A Wyrmguard has no fear and feels no pain, but it cannot force its mount beyond his endurance." *Or hers.* Aethal shied from the sickening memory of Ardyth's glassy stare.

"I told you the Temple Guard had broken through once," Malcoor said. "We caught a few who weren't quite dedicated enough to fall on their bayonets for him. I hope Ilferth Simon will appreciate the irony. As for the rest," he turned to the major. "Call for volunteers. And return to your post. Send them along to the Last Sword."

Aethal turned to Paitir, who had stopped shaking his head, but continued to stare like a man in a nightmare. "Sire," he whispered. "Paitir, I am your Last Sword. If I do this, you may be killed."

A faint smile touched Paitir's lips. "Do you really think so?" he asked. "Go. It is my command."

Aethal stepped back and nodded. He gathered the three Wyrmguard to himself and replaced them in his belt. "Wyrmguard," he said, voice dry as dust.

"Come with me. To the Armory of the Thirty." And their steps behind him were heavy and quick as they left the king's presence.

Chapter Nine

58th of Spring, 312 Exodus

In the Hydraxis court outside the Dragonmast, the noise of battle was at its peak. It was there that Aethal met the Wyrmguard, all twenty-four, the new and the old mounts. They did not wear their uniforms any longer, neither the bright uniforms of Maednac's Own, nor yet the simple house uniforms that all Wyrmguard wore. Now they dressed in simple tunics of black and grey, the pistols carried at their sides.

They had decided that Aethal's men would break out the south gate. It was the most direct path to the docks. And though Hlafen had more men than Ilferth Simon, they were not as well-trained as the deceptive Temple Guard. Nor were they bringing up cannon. They either didn't know how to use them, or thought they didn't need them.

Aethal opened his mouth to speak, and found that he had nothing to say. It had always been his duty as an officer, to find words for his men before battle. Before he led them to face shot and shell and blade, to lend them courage under fire, or to take with them into the darkness.

But these were Wyrmguard. Their dedication was absolute, their fear nonexistent. And they could not be killed. And how Aethal wanted the old Phoenix Lancers Rifles with him now. *Farnan, where are you?* He reached into the place which had given him courage and comfort before, to pass along to his men, and met only the cold necessity of his orders.

They would have to serve.

"Wyrmguard. The King can no longer be defended by your wills, your bodies, or your fire alone," he said. "Today we must defend him by breaking this siege. We do not know how many we must fight through to get to the Kirk of the Docks. We do not know how many will be there to help us, nor whether they will need our aid first. But we will need as many as we can get.

"To that end, I give an order that may seem strange to you. Preserve your mounts! Dismounted, you are no use to His Majesty. If your mount should fall, and you acquire another, meet us at the Kirk. If there is no hope of that, then return here. Protect the King as best you can. And wait until we return. Do you understand?"

Twenty-four locks snapped open as one.

"Then we march. At the quick step!"

Aethal fell into the rhythm of the march naturally. Just as naturally, Gun fell into his hands, and he felt the weapon's mind slide into his own with a practiced smoothness, as surely as the trigger and barrel fitted into his hands. They marched southward, toward the Seagate, stepping with a precision that Aethal had never seen approximated by human troopers, let alone equaled.

He had never in his life felt so alone.

A subaltern in the uniform of his father's men ran up to him. "Milord Aethal," he said. "Seagate is under heavy assault. The portcullis is breaking under the blows. The cannon are in position, but may not be able to hold. The enemy is threatening to breach the south wall."

Aethal swore. "Reserves?"

"Committed long since, milord."

Aethal looked ahead. Just behind the lines, men were struggling to load makeshift bombs onto a few dozen ancient ballistae. A line of them arced up over the low wall, and half detonated in the air. The subaltern read his face. "They're keeping up some pressure on them, milord, but there's fighting inside the Wall."

Aethal nodded. "Double-time! March!" The Wyrmguard quickened step. "Alert the battery! We're coming, and we'll need that breach!"

"Yes, milord!" and the boy dashed off.

The Seagate loomed nearer with awful steadiness. Aethal slowly allowed himself to drop to the rear. *The Wyrmguard must be in front. These men, who know nothing of what they are about to do, who have no say in their bodies' deeds, they must bear the wrath of the enemy.* There was no way around it. If Aethal were killed, who would lead the attack on the Kirk, or break the siege of the Hydraxis? *And isn't that what Malcoor told you?* He thrust the thought from him.

Now the small knot of cannon was before them, and the gate yawned high. Even beyond that, Aethal could see the boiling chaos beyond the gate, with axemen and torch-bearers struggling to get at the heavy wooden portcullis while pikemen on both sides sought to thrust their weapons through the openings. Around the gate, musketeers feverishly reloaded and fired.

The captain of the battery saw Aethal and the Wyrmguard approaching, and his face set.

"Take aim!" Aethal heard the order given. At the same time, enemy fighters poured over the walls. "Fall back! Fall back!" Aethal heard the cries echoed around the courtyard.

But that was in another world now. His world lay only ahead.

The musketeers retreated from the gate, firing sporadically. The pikemen retreated in ragged lines.

"Battery one! Fire!" Aethal heard the shrill order from his left.

The cannon spat fire and thunder, and the gate dissolved in splinters and dust.

"Forward!" Aethal saw teams of men wheeling the light cannon dash past his Wyrmguard. It was time for the order Aethal had never, even after his impossible appointment as Last Sword, thought he'd give to Wyrmguard.

"Wyrmguard!" roared Aethal. "Fix! Bayonets!"

The Wyrmguard pulled blades from their belts blades and snapped them over the ends of their barrels. Each Wyrmguard pistol was now a two-foot stabbing sword as well.

Ahead of him, men writhed, dying. The splinters and cannonballs had plowed a channel through the enemy, but it filled with men who recognized that the Seagate was clear and open. They surged forward.

"Battery Two! Fire!"

The light cannon spoke, their flatter crack splitting the air. But these did not fire cannonballs. They vomited canisters of grapeshot. The men pouring through the Seagate exploded in fragments of bone and froth. They had just one more moment to await. One more space of time to look upon the ruins of men lying before them. And then Battery One fired again. Two more cannonballs crashed out, scattering the survivors of the grapeshot, and there was no more time.

"Wyrmguard!" Aethal cried, "Charge!"

Aethal realized he was the only one screaming, and stopped. All the men he had ever commanded yelled as they charged, to terrify the enemy and to bolster their own courage. But there could be nothing as eerie and terrible as the Wyrmguard's silent charge.

They were through the gate before they met the first men on their feet. Weapons rose to meet them with dreamlike slowness. Holes sprouted in their wielders' chests and heads. They fell. Others saw what they were facing and ran. Not one of them was shot down. The Wyrmguard saw no need.

Aethal had never known anything like it. There was no pause. No hesitation. Beneath it, all was the steady crack of the Wyrmguard pistols, as they took ground and left it behind them.

There was neither time nor need to give orders. He was in command of beings that had been old when the Empire had been young, and they had not forgotten any tricks of fighting, either as individuals, or as a unit.

But there were only two dozen of them.

Pikesbane went down with a bullet through the head. A deadly whizz sounded in Aethal's ear, and he turned to see Kindread staring up at him, a quarrel buried to the feathers in his chest. The face of a man Aethal had last seen eagerly taking up the weapon stared out at him. His eyes focused briefly on Aethal. "Already?" he said. And then he fell back, dead.

Aethal brought Gun around, shooting the crossbowman in the act of reloading. *ware right*! A huge man, shirtless and howling, jumped at Aethal, swinging a cleaver in both hands. Aethal parried and slammed Gun's butt into the man's knee, which shattered. He reversed Gun in time to skewer a City Watchman boring in with a mace.

Three more Wyrmguard were down by the time Aethal could look up again. They had nearly reached the street beyond the Admiralty building, which towered above them. Aethal reloaded Gun feverishly, looking for an opening. The Wyrmguard's charge was slowing. The flat cracks of pistol shots rang out less frequently as the weapons reloaded. If they were not careful, they would be trapped here by the enemy, converging from the left and right.

The counterattack of the Wyrmguard had stunned the rebels momentarily but the street leading to the Winery gate was filled with reserves, pressing to join the fight. To the left lay a narrow street that cut behind the Royal Library.

"Wyrmguard," he called. "Take that position!" And they were off again, reloading forgotten. Some of the Wyrmguard snapped out a few last shots, but most were blurs of flashing steel.

Aethal saw his two point-men go down. Everwar parried one pike with his blade and one with his other arm, but the third punched through his backbone. Aethal bayoneted his attacker through the throat, then ducked a sword blow. The man ducked, scooping up the pistol, and reared back to ram its bayonet through Aethal's middle. Then he looked confused, and Everwar returned to its place on the line.

If that happened more often, the casualties wouldn't matter. But the Wyrmguard were not being picked up as fast as they dropped. Aethal saw Widower stagger and fall to lie still. No one picked up the weapon.

Then they were clear and running down the narrow street. Continue, or give the Wyrmguard the time they would need to reload? *It's stupid to make your soldiers fight at a disadvantage.* But that cut both ways. Aethal didn't know what strength the enemy had in front of them. If he paused, they could be trapped here. If he didn't, the Wyrmguard would meet their next challenge with their chambers nearly empty.

"Reload!" The Wyrmguard ducked into doorways and nooks. There was no panic or fumbling. Alone of his command, Aethal felt fear. He peered into the darkness ahead. If they could once get past the rebel force, they could lose themselves in the streets of Maednac Serpiin and break out of the city.

The sounds of reloading stopped, but they were not free yet. The crack of muskets and the ugly whine of bullets came from behind them. "Move out!" Aethal cried. The Wyrmguard advanced up the narrow street. Now Aethal could see the other end. A small knot of enemy soldiers stood there.

"Fire!" Aethal ordered, and the Wyrmguard pistols let loose a withering barrage. Most of the enemy broke and ran, screaming, but the crackle of fire increased rather than dying down. A Wyrmguard fell, Aethal couldn't tell which. Then he looked back, and knew despair.

About three dozen city watchmen were running flat out down the street to take them in the rear. Aethal knelt, picked a likely-looking target for their leader. His only hope was to break their spirit. *Head shot*, he thought, and Gun corrected his aim. He fired.

The man dropped, but his followers were too frenzied to pause. Out of the smoke, a rider galloped up behind them on a single, black horse, and Aethal cursed his luck for having missed the more-important target. "Go!" he screamed.

Aethal and the Wyrmguard ran from their attackers. They burst out of the narrow street into a small plaza. Assembling before them was a rapidly-forming line of Temple Guard musketeers. Beyond them, empty streets that might as well have been on the other side of the world. They were trapped, caught in the open between two forces. Aethal had guessed wrong. Even if they could break through, they would not do so in time. Aethal felt like a spectator, and reloaded Gun in a mechanical trance sustained only by long training and hopeless resignation.

Without needing his orders, the sixteen surviving Wyrmguard advanced, firing in a deadly, unhurried cascade of shots. The Temple Guard dropped one by one, each man shot through the head. But it was too late. Their firing line was formed.

At least twenty of the Temple Guards' muskets — poor dumb weapons of wood, steel and powder — fired back, and the deadly hail brought down a third of the Wyrmguard. The rest kept up their steady fire, and the Guard began to waver, But Aethal could hear the bellowing charge from behind them and knew it was all over. The Wyrmguard turned to meet it. Aethal ripped Gun and turned to meet the onrushing City Watch, the moons' light glinting dully off pikes and musket barrels.

The horseman pulled up short in the mouth of the alley, right behind the City Watch. Then he threw a hissing, sparking object into their midst. Instinctively, Aethal threw himself down.

The grenade's thunder shook the ground. Rolling to his feet, Aethal saw the charging men scattering desperately in every direction from the unexpected attack. A dozen of them lay dead or stunned on the flagstones. A few hesitated, and were shot down by the unshakeable Wyrmguard, who were pouring the last of their fire into the shattered remnants of both Guard and Watch. Two Watchmen valiantly charged the horse, but the rider's bright blade flicked out and down. They fell back, clutching their arms.

Then two shots rang out, and the horse screamed; the rider was down, rolling free. Aethal ran forward. He knocked one man aside, stabbed another one with Gun's bayonet, and reached almost to the fallen rider before his feet were kicked out from under him. He rolled half upright and kicked back, missing. A mace came down at his head. Aethal parried with Gun, but the force of the blow rolled him over. Two men stood above him: the mace-wielder and a huge man swinging an ugly, spiked flail.

Another steady ripple of snapping fire, and the two men pitched backward. Aethal got up. The surviving Watchmen were running, running back toward the Hydraxis and the main battle.

Aethal stood, and bent over the fallen rider, who was already getting to her feet.

"Bastards! Well-be-swallowed bastards shooting at my horse that way!" Ardyth was dressed in soft black riding leathers, and her dueling saber was out. She looked around herself for an enemy, but there were no foes left.

Aethal was rooted to the spot. "Lady Ardyth!" he finally cried. "What in the name of *Wishery* are you doing here!"

"Defending the King. As you are."

"This is no place for a lady!" Aethal blurted. It was the only thing he could think to say, and sounded bloody stupid the moment he said it.

"This is a place for a Westerend," said Ardyth. "My father has dishonored our house by submitting to the blackmail of the traitor Ilferth Simon. Who else can cleanse the taint from our line?"

"Lady," said Aethal. "Your Uncle Malcoor..."

"Is dear to me above all men save my father," said Ardyth. "But I am my House's heir. And the honor of the Westerend will *not* be tarnished. My father taught me that. Uncle Malcoor would not allow me to fight inside the Hydraxis, so I left. I now place myself and House Westerend at your disposal."

"I refuse your offer," said Aethal. "Go..." he stopped. Go where? Go back? She'd be killed. Go into the city? She'd be killed or possibly worse.

Stonelock stepped up to him. "Last Sword, we have gathered what mounts were available and remounted the fallen. We must go."

Aethal looked about him. They were still out in the street, within sight of the battle. They could be easily noticed. He counted quickly. Thirteen Wyrmguard. Thirteen to break a siege of whose strength he knew nothing. And Ardyth, who looked up at him defiantly.

"I hope you can run," he said, and they moved off into the night. He felt he should have had something more profound to say, before they died. But there was no one else to hear.

***

The Kirk of the Docks stood practically on the water's edge, a massive square of thick stone. There were no crenellations atop it, though it bore a spire with the Single Moon atop it. Unlike almost any other cathedral this night, a watchfire blazed defiantly at the base of the spire. And above it flew the kingdom's flag.

The Kirk had been the first Church in Verlaen. Constructed of thick native rock, it had been designed to protect Imperial citizens before the Wrackberg had been raised, when Weedrats had raided into the bay, and the soldiers had withdrawn to the hillfort that would become the Hydraxis.

Now, looking down upon the great stone slab, Aethal felt as if gold had been poured through his guts. The force besieging the Kirk was little more than an afterthought: no more than three hundred men, perhaps as few as two. They crouched behind makeshift barricades, covering all the doors and windows. Because the Kirk had been designed as a fort, there were not many.

From here, Aethal could see the long poles of the erstwhile Lotus patrols now giving light to Rolf Hlafen's City Watch. The men were semi-attentive and not well-armed. They carried the same maces and pikes their fellows had, with a flintlock shotgun here and there. The real weapons were at the Hydraxis.

From where Aethal, Ardyth, and the Wyrmguard watched, atop a warehouse, they could see a group of Watchmen manhandling a ship's mast spar.

They hurled it against the Kirk's western door. For nearly a minute they heard the rhythmic banging of the ram on the door.

Then a staccato fusillade poured from the small windows. One man dropped, and an equally ragged burst of fire went up from the besiegers to the west. Aethal recognized smoothbore musket fire. *Damn fools to think that they could hit anything like that.* The best marksman in the world couldn't have put a bullet through one of the Kirk's small windows at anything over twenty yards.

Then a shower of objects fountained from the windows above the battering ram. The ramming faltered, and Aethal could hear curses and yells of pain. Following this came two bulky, sparking, hissing objects.

The men ran. Seconds later the grenades burst in gouts of fire. Obviously, the defenders had ammunition and powder, but little idea how to use it. If there had been very many of them, they would have broken out already. Sergeant Falk was there, but with how many men?

Three hundred men surrounding them. Maybe two. Badly trained and ill-motivated. Likely, Falk's irregulars could hold the Kirk all night. But they could not break out. And Aethal had thirteen Wyrmguard. Knowing what the answer would be, he had asked, "Stonelock. Advise me. What can the Wyrmguard do to raise the siege?"

"We can give our mounts and our lives in service to the Imperial Governor, as we have sworn by the Compact," he said, unblinking.

Aethal nodded. He raised Gun to his shoulder. With thirteen Greater Rifles, he might sow confusion and even panic by shooting into the besiegers from widely dispersed points. But the Wyrmguard, Wellspawn though they were, could not duplicate that feat.

In truth, Aethal was amazed they had come so far. If they had met a strong force at the defensible Winery gate, all would have been lost, for unlike the Hydraxis it had been designed to be impenetrable against an invading horde. But in their confidence, the enemy had left only a dozen men at each gate. The

Wyrmguard had made short work of them, taking not a single loss. And now this.

"Lady Ardyth," Aethal said. "It would be best for His Majesty," he continued, "if you return to your father, and explain what has happened. It may be that you can persuade Lord Vaughan to oppose Ilferth Simon's treachery, and fight for your people."

Ardyth's face was a torment of concentration. "And it may be that I cannot," she said, distantly. "It may be that I can... only do more."

"What more, milady?"

Her face was white in the moons' light. "Did it always hurt you this much, Aethal Paaling? To betray your father in the name of preserving the honor of House Wrackberg?"

The question sent Aethal reeling. "In truth," he stammered, "and as far as I can see, the honor of House Wrackberg is dead far beyond my power to bring it to life. My only honor is in defending the kingdom."

Ardyth swallowed and nodded. "Shall it be said that a Wrackberg knows more of honor than a Westerend, Father?" She spoke the words to the air. Then she turned a tear-stained face to Aethal. "My father has committed treason against the kingdom. I alone know of it. He taught me in case he should die, so that I might save my life and our house. But I cannot save them at the cost of keeping this secret."

Aethal listened, dumbstruck while she continued.

"After Uncle Joseth was practically imprisoned in the Serpent's Pass and your parents were allowed to marry, my father believed that the King and the other two Lords Paramount were plotting to destroy the Westerend. After all, the alliance was against us, and they had deprived him of his most trusted advisor. After that, my father never trusted any summons to Maednac Serpiin, and always brought his full contingent of household guards with him, fully expecting they might need to defend him to the death."

"Lady, this is no treason," said Aethal.

"Not then, no," said Ardyth. "But father knew that a hundred guards would scarcely allow him to resist. He would need far more to escape, and so he planned for his moment. Do you remember when you brought us news of the Lotus? My father offered to bring troops to aid in the fight. They arrived on ten ships our trading fleet while you were away."

"Yes, of course," said Aethal. "But all those units are loyally holding the Serpent's Pass, alongside the Royal Army."

"Such are their orders. But their ten trade ships are still here. Every one of those trading vessels is a disguised warship."

Aethal's mouth opened. That *was* treason. The Lords Paramount were not permitted navies, by Maednac's Law. "But Lady, why? Warships couldn't possibly force their way past the Wrackberg." That's why the artificial island had been *built.*

"But they don't have to force their way in. They are already inside." They had even asked *permission* to come inside, Aethal had realized. "The sailors are all my father's sworn men who have separate orders: upon his command, they seize the Hydraxis and hold the King hostage." Aethal lay back against the roof, head swimming. Ten converted trading ships? Inside the Bay?

"If your father could do this, why hasn't he done it already?"

"He never had any excuse to bring so many ships into Maednac's Bay before the news of Lotus. But father believed that whether the news of Lotus were true or not, the King would be forced to permit his ships entry. If it were true, he would need the men too badly to refuse. And if it were a lie, refusing would be a strong proof of it. He very nearly ordered the escape when we held you and Lieutenant Farnan hostage. Before I..." she trailed off, looking at the Wyrmguard.

"My lady," Aethal said. "With these ships and men, the Kingdom may be saved. If we do not, we are surely lost."

"And my father may die by the Last Sword you carry on your back when his treason stands revealed. That is its other function, is it not?"

Aethal's voice caught. He had nearly forgotten. It had not been used thus save a handful of times. But the Last Sword was also the Royal Executioner for those high nobles who were found guilty of crimes against the kingdom.

"My lady, I swear to you I shall do all in my power to convince the King to pardon your father."

"But you cannot swear to succeed."

Aethal could not meet her eyes. "No."

There was a moment of timeless silence. Then he met them again. "But this I swear. I shall not take your father's head. Not though the King himself should order it and my own besides. I shall die beside him, rather."

"Scant comfort that would be!" Ardyth dropped her voice. "But it is honorably done. I will honor my father's teachings rather than his fear. You shall have your ships, Aethal Paaling, for the King of Verlaen."

***

The merchant ship seemed dirty and unremarkable as a hundred others, though Aethal noted the placement of the low-slung ship that Ardyth had led them to. It was on the western end of the docks, as close as possible to the center of the bay. Well-positioned for escape, but also for an attack on the Navy Yards. Ardyth had insisted Aethal remain well back of her, when she approached the gangplank. It was manned by two sailors, and this in itself was remarkable. They appeared to be asleep, but they straightened the moment Ardyth's foot had touched the plank.

Ardyth's voice was low, but the water carried it well enough: "Get me Captain Guilorum. Immediately." One of the sailors bowed and left, moving more quickly than any merchant sailor would in port.

A brief wait. Then Gun said, *do not move.* Aethal yawned deliberately, giving himself the excuse to look upwards, into the tops of the sails, and saw shapes that ought not to have been there. Snipers in the tops.

A stocky figure of a man had appeared. "I be Captain Guilorum of the *Lass's Kiss*. What wouldja be wanting with me, pretty lady?" The words were drunken, with a broad Madlander accent. He peered past her. "And with a pretty company o' Watchmen there, as well? Is there a problem with yer manifest, me Lady?"

"No problem with the manifest," Ardyth said. "Just a special cargo. A cargo for the Wrackberg."

The man's easy, drunken composure vanished, along with his accent. "A cargo for the Wrackberg," he repeated. He stared at Aethal and the Wyrmguard. "Milady, what have you...?"

"They are part of the cargo," Ardyth said. "Not its recipients, do you understand? They are to be permitted aboard. For the delivery."

"My lady, does your father countenance —"

She cut him off. "If he did not, how would I know where to find you or what to say? Captain, there is no time to delay. You must have us aboard and send your messages to your fellow captains immediately."

Guilorum frowned. "You'll bring those men aboard. Now." All deference was gone. Ardyth nodded and beckoned Aethal up the gangplank. Moving slowly, Aethal complied.

At a gesture, he handed over Gun and the Last Sword. Before Guilorum could make a lethal mistake, Aethal said, "Captain, these are Wyrmguard. They cannot hand you their weapons. They are under my command," he raised his voice over the sound of sailors reaching for hidden pistols. "They will not shoot unless you attack."

"My Lady, this is treason!" Captain Guilorum cried, voice hoarse with dismay.

"No, Captain," she had said, "it is keeping faith." Quickly, she explained the situation. "If we do not go now, then the city will fall into the hands of Ilferth Simon and all will be lost."

"I never heard we had any quarrel with the Church," Guilorum had growled in return. "Only with Wrackbergs."

"Then hear this: Ilferth Simon is blackmailing your lord into treachery with the threat of sowing Lotus in the falls that feed the Twin Fans."

Guilorum's face slackened with fright. "Send out the runners," he whispered.

"Sir?" said a mate.

"Send out the runners, if you value your children's lives. And prepare for battle!" The ship exploded into swift, silent action.

"Now, milady Westerend," said Guilorum, bowing low. "Tell me: where do we really deliver our cargo?"

***

There was no sound but the creaking of ropes and the flapping of sails. No lights but the moons', now beginning their long fall to the western horizon. Aethal glanced at the quarterdeck, saw Captain Guilorum watching him, and, keeping Gun carefully pointed at the deck, looked back along their wake.

The rest of Westerend's ships formed two lines behind them. They were at the head, steering for the Kirk with its watchfires burning. Ardyth stood on the quarterdeck beside the captain.

Aethal wondered what was happening on the smaller line of ships, the three that sailed a hundred yards further out, too small for warships of any kind. He shuddered at the extent of Westerend's success. But the success had been well-earned. Standing on the deck, Aethal *still* couldn't see any guns except the small deck cannon that every trader carried for self-defense. And he'd *seen* that the ships had no gunports.

The crew did not speak except in hoarse mutters, and the ship rustled as if with the soft babble of ghosts, except that even only half-heard, the whispers were filled with purpose and tension. Powder and shot were brought up from below, muskets and cutlasses checked, and disguises cast off. Officers moved up the deck, repeating orders. Where they went, men stopped moving, and went still, knots by each of the small cannon. Under his feet, Aethal felt the rolling of heavy carts. An officer about his own age glided up to him. "The Captain orders you to take position... sir."

Aethal could hear the distaste in his voice, and the anticipation, but moved to the mouth of the forward hatch, where six Wyrmguard awaited him. The Wyrmguard would be in the forefront of the assault. He had insisted. And the captain had certainly not objected. They floated closer to the small ferry docks right next to the Kirk. The men of the City Watch crouched behind the barricades, talking and laughing, many sleeping, looking inward. Apparently, they had decided that the Kirk could not be broken tonight. A few peered out at them. There were shouts.

The young officer behind Aethal nodded at the captain's gesture and lit a rocket. It streamed up into the sky. Not red, not green, but a glorious blue and gold, unlike anything in the Navy's signaling books.

The three small ships behind them vomited flame into the night. "Wellspawn!" he shouted. They'd blown up. All three of them. They were lost...

"Not Wellspawn. Bomb ketches," said Ardyth, suddenly beside him. "Look." Now Aethal saw the falling shells, arcing over them with fuses lit. *God-Beyond-The-World. The Westerenders put mortars on* ships! "It's their only weapon," Ardyth said. "That's why they stay back."

"But how could you keep that a secret?" Aethal asked.

With a rattle and bang of wood, the two great boxes on their own main deck collapsed, folding outward. Aethal gaped. Four huge rifled cannon set in twin mounts, hidden until now, rotated on rails set into the decks, already primed and loaded. They were almost as large as the *Wrackberg's* guns!

"Fire!" roared Guilorum.

The sea was shattered by thunder. The deck guns sent gouts of flame into the barricades, which flew to pieces. The men manning them simply vanished. To either side, men fell bonelessly under the flail of the smaller cannon. Then the mortar bombs arrived, and the square around the Kirk was bathed in flame.

"Steady!" Aethal screamed over his shoulder to the Wyrmguard. The docks were getting closer. The next wave of mortars was already screaming overhead. They struck, practically on top of the barricades to the east and west, shattering them. Aethal filled his lungs and nearly choked on the powder smoke.

"Charge!"

Aethal snatched up a rope, and leapt. Behind him, he could feel the rush of feet. He was followed by six Wyrmguard and a company of Lord Westerend's personal guard, now dressed in their house uniforms of silver, black and green.

Aethal hit the ground, and swept out the Last Sword. Much as he would have preferred Gun, he needed Sergeant Falk's men to recognize him. The Wyrmguard formed around him. A third wave of bombs rained down, these on the other side of the huge Kirk, and Aethal staggered under the sound, but the Wyrmguard marched on, impassive. Just for an instant, Aethal felt a stab of envy of their utter fearlessness amid the carnage.

"Take the doors!" Aethal called, and they jogged onward. Around them, there was the staccato bark of musket fire, and the occasional clash of steel. The great ornate and bound doors of the Kirk loomed closer, and Aethal felt his hair standing on end. Just one overeager musketeer with better than usual luck...

He waved the Last Sword through the air like a madman. "To me! The Last Sword commands you! Tell Sergeant Falk! Sergeant Bedar Falk! Sortie for the King!"

An age seemed to pass. Twice, the Wyrmguard fired shots into the smoke at foes only they could see. But finally, Aethal heard the scrape of bolts being thrown back. A young man, holding a bayoneted musket in trembling hands, leveled it at Aethal's stomach.

"You are the Last Sword... milord?" He flushed as the automatic courtesy escaped him.

"I am."

He was gestured inside. Through a cavernous hall, Aethal was led through a scant number of similarly armed soldiers, crouched in the shadows. Near the back of the sanctuary, behind the hundreds of rough-hewn benches, the boy led Aethal up a winding staircase to the roof.

"It's him, Uncle," and now Aethal could sense the relief and excitement in the boy's voice. It went quiet.

"*Yakuz* Skraalen," he said.

Falk stood with his back to them, but now he turned, his features, as usual, carved from stone. Skraalen sat in a carved chair that had been set up beneath the eaves.

"Those your ships, sir?" Falk asked.

Aethal stepped to the sergeant's side and looked out over the battle. The barricades were gone. The gunfire was no more than a smattering of shots. The enemy was, to all intents, simply gone.

"They are," Aethal answered, "a friend's."

"Good friends, you have," said Skraalen, with a dry laugh. "It took you long enough."

Aethal ignored him. Falk said, "For a little while, sir, I thought you weren't coming."

Aethal said, "For a little while, I thought I wasn't either."

"Of course, I wasn't certain whether Landen got through to you."

"Landen..." said Aethal, "did all that he could, Sergeant. All."

Bedar Falk's eyes closed in pain, then opened them. "I'll have to tell his boys. Their father was the best I could send. Always could outrun any of us."

Aethal nodded.

"Sergeant, you have done everything I could have asked and more. And at great cost."

Falk speared him with both eyes. "And there's more to do yet, isn't there, sir?"

Aethal took a deep breath. "There is." He outlined the situation around the Hydraxis. "How many do you have, here?"

"Here and at Llhawcae?" asked Skraalen. "About two thousand."

Aethal's mind seized up. "Did you say 'two *thousand*,' Skraalen?"

Falk nodded. "Yes, sir. Most of Skraalen's boys and their people."

Aethal didn't know whether to kiss the man or shoot him. "Why were *we* rescuing *you*, Skraalen?"

Skraalen grinned. "My boys don't fight for honor and glory, Wrackberg. They fight for coin, and so's they can live long enough to spend it."

Aethal's jaw clenched. "For a man who wants to be a lord, you have a curious sense of honor, Skraalen."

Skraalen snorted. "For a man who wants to live to see tomorrow, you have a curious sense of bein' clever, me lord. I told you where those guns was, and you ent did nothing with it."

"I couldn't just arrest every name on that list!" Aethal snapped. Then he barked a laugh. "No, as it turns out, Skraalen, you're right. That's exactly what I should have done. Well, Sergeant?"

"Sir, Boss Skraalen's right: most of the fighters here are street toughs and enforcers. Skraalen's boys will be holy hell in a brawl, but not one'n a hundred can fire a musket more than once a minute. The rest are women and old men. I'm not even counting the boys. They'll charge for you, once. But they won't stand in the firing line. They're not fighting for the King. They're fighting for their lives. They'll save those."

Aethal's mind raced. "What else do you have?"

"The cellar is full of powder and shot. The Temple Guard was sharp, but they weren't expecting Skraalen to loose all of us at two Churches. They ran off and left us gunpowder and muskets aplenty. Just very few can shoot them worth a damn."

Aethal closed his eyes. Two thousand. Two thousand raw citizens with guns.

His eyes flashed open. "Can they carry heavy loads? And can they run?"

***

False dawn was in the sky when Aethal and his sweating followers burst up onto the Admiralty roof. Hoarsely shouted whispers filled the air. The Westerender sailors were breathing hard. Some of them seemed disoriented. And who could blame them?

The march had been surreal. Two thousand Madlanders filling the streets and shouting. Shouting to their neighbors. To their friends. To their fellow-workers. They had marched north. They had marched to the gate. And their numbers had swelled.

The cannon taken from Westerend's fleet and looted from the Winery's stores were set up. The cannoneers cursed their helpers, cursed the flat roof, and cursed the makeshift gun carriages. They would fire once: the recoil would shatter their mounts. Aethal was glad Ardyth was not here. But she had another errand, almost as dangerous.

She is where she is needed, he thought, forcing his eyes front. The wall of the Hydraxis was clear of men. They had been overrun. The court inside the shattered gates was thick with bodies. The defenders of the Hydraxis had not sold their lives or their positions cheaply. But cannon fire sounded from the north, and he could see the musketry of the City Watch crackling at the walls of the Dragonmast. From the crenellations came only a sporadic return fire. *We have very little time.*

Aethal ducked back down through the deserted Admiralty building. In the very street he and the Wyrmguard had broken through, he faced his men. And his women. And his boys. And his old men. They formed, not companies, but a great mass. Their front two ranks gleamed steel. Each of them carried a musket. On their backs, another musket, this one with a fixed bayonet.

On and on they had marched. A sprawling mass of men, women and children. They pounded on doors and shouted at windows. They were not joined at once. The city's fanatics had seized the cathedrals with Ilferth Simon and Rolf Hlafen. But one by one and two by two came the men who had stayed out of the way, those who had been afraid of greater numbers. They had seen that they had armed friends, and it filled them with courage. Up to the Winery itself.

There they had wavered a moment. It was the only way into the city proper and Aethal, dry-mouthed, wondered if their foes had been cautious enough to re-arm the deadly fortress, and were waiting to flay them alive with concentrated cannon fire.

But the fortress was still empty. And after Aethal's people left, it was even emptier.

Farnan had not been there.

Now Aethal looked at his forces. "Men and women of the Madlands!" he cried. "For generations you have fought in the vessels of the King. You have fought the Weedrats for mastery of the sea and after that you have fought the sea itself for its riches. This kingdom, the last kingdom of men, was built by you, and upon you. Today you fight not for your King upon the sea, but for your city, your lives, and for your very souls. The Church has told you that the King is a Sindrinker. That he has betrayed Verlaen, and God-Beyond-The-World, bringing Lotus to our shores by his sin!

"Madlanders! I stand before you today as one who has seen and smelled Lotus! It was sown by the hands of Ilferth Simon, who sought to make me a greeneater, and turn the Last Sword of Verlaen into a living infection, to walk your streets and kill the lot of you! Will you let him do it to your King?"

"NO!" The roar came from a thousand throats.

Aethal did not dare look back, but he knew that shout could not have gone unnoticed.

"What will you do?"

The officers and sailors of the Westerend's tiny flotilla led the crowd in their orders. "TAKE THE WALL! SHOOT! SHOOT AGAIN! CHARGE!"

Aethal nodded. He drew the Last Sword. "Wyrmguard, to me!" The thirteen remaining Wyrmguard ran to join him. Aethal looked at the sky to the west. It remained blank except for the two setting moons and the false dawn.

If Ardyth has not succeeded yet, we cannot wait for her, he thought. He raised the Last Sword. Brought it down.

Fifty cannon fired from the rooftops of the city. The shells struck well inside the wall, sowing fire and agony.

"For Verlaen and the Madlands!"

And three thousand Madlanders charged.

Then Aethal was running for the shattered Seagate, he and the Wyrmguard together. Madlanders poured through the Seagate like a tide, swarming over the Hydraxis wall. The enemy troops turned, frantically raising their guns.

Aethal never got to shout a command to fire. The ripple of fire from the untrained Madlanders on the wall was like the continuous ripping of an island-sized cloth. Only a few spurts of flame leapt back at them. Aethal heard screams through ears muffled by an ocean of noise. There was a longer pause while empty muskets were tossed aside. More screams as bayonets were wrestled around by amateurs, and their second guns were brought to bear.

"Fire!" screamed Aethal.

This time the sound was slower, a continuous rattle of sharp explosions. The men of the City Watch surrounding the Hydraxis fell atop their dead fellows like wheat before a scythe. Then Aethal found what he sought. The Lord Mayor's banner.

He and the Wyrmguard broke into a run and the Madlanders followed.

Aethal ran into the bewildered foe. But this fight, Aethal could already sense, was over. Caught between the unforgiving walls of the Hydraxis and the charge of a fresh, unexpected enemy, the men Aethal charged dropped knives, axes, maces, and even guns. Twice Aethal had to parry a blow, and twice more strike at men too slow or shocked to dodge. The Wyrmguard kept up a slow and steady fire upon all who stood in their way.

Rolf Hlafen's standard swelled in Aethal's vision. A small band of City Watchmen guarded it. Three of them brought up heavy shotguns, and fell with bullets through their faces. The rest fled. The standard wavered and fell.

One last man tried to flee. Aethal grabbed his cloak in his left hand and yanked him savagely backward. Rolf Hlafen, Lord Mayor of Maednac Serpiin, rolled on his back on the cobbles. He cried out, "Mercy! Mercy!" Aethal jerked him to his knees. His eyes stared from his head, like a man who had just woken from a pleasant dream to find himself in a nightmare. Everywhere, his men were running. Running away. Away from Aethal's Madlanders. "Mercy, Aethal Paaling. It was Ilferth Simon. He had me in his power! I didn't want to help him. I couldn't do anything to stop him. I wanted to, I swear. Oh, please, Aethal Paaling, mercy!"

Aethal felt his soul recoil and he raised the Last Sword high.

"I would have given you mercy at the beginning of this night," he said. "The only mercy I have left to give I hold in my hand."

The Lord Mayor's cheeks flushed. "You can't murder me here in cold blood!"

"I am the Last Sword of the King," Suddenly, Aethal felt tired. Tired of lies and tired of greed and filth. "I cut where the King commands. It is his mercy or justice that you must find. Not mine," he repeated. "Not mine." He lowered the blade.

The Wyrmguard came behind him, and pulled the Lord Mayor to his feet. "To the Dragonmast," he said. But even as he said it, a new fear swelled up in him. The south of the courtyard was theirs. Rolf Hlafen's troops were scattered. But the sky remained blank, and he doubted that Ilferth Simon's Temple Guard would scatter so easily.

Aethal forced himself into a jog. He was almost to the great doors of the Dragonmast when they began to open. Calling on a last reserve of strength, Aethal ran. "Come on," he cried. "We need a sortie. Clear them out while they're off balance!"

He needn't have bothered.

From out the huge doors poured the last of the Dragonmast's defenders, a thousand strong. General Malcoor was at the rear, just visible, but there at the head of Maednac's Own was the Major Caanling. And beside him, leading a column of scarlet-and-gray uniformed Wrackberg house soldiers, his father, wearing a half-helm and carrying a pistol.

His father saluted him. "The Wrackberg!" he cried.

"THE WRACKBERG STANDS!" chorused his troops.

"WE KEEP THE WORD!" answered Maednac's Own.

Aethal made his way to General Malcoor, who saluted him. "Aethal Paaling," he said slowly, "I thought the expedition to the Well was still in the planning stages. Wish me dead if I don't believe you've already been there and back. Where did these people come from?"

Aethal drew a breath, and felt as though his ribs would break. "From the Madlands that we had forgotten. From the Westerend we believed lost. From all the places we had discounted, sir."

Malcoor nodded. "Come with me. This battle is not over yet."

***

Aethal felt singularly useless as he trailed in the wake of his men. The only order he had given in the last five minutes was to a pair of servants to lock the lord Mayor in a Dungeon cell. Malcoor seemed to catch his mood. "You and I have done all we can for the moment. It's in the hands of the majors and their lieutenants, now. And more, their men."

The enemy was being pressed back. Malcoor said to him, "You certainly have upset our dear Conversant's master plan. I wonder if he's as much in the dark as to what you did as I was?" He pointed to the wall. "But he hasn't lost yet if he keeps his head and accepts his losses. He can still hold the north wall. Look."

Aethal did, and his heart sank. He could see the Madlanders waver before a fusillade. Their loyal troops — Maednac's own, the Wrackbergers, and Lord Westerend's sailors — had formed an unbroken line behind them. And now the Temple Guard was recovering. A wave of crashing fire plowed into the Madlanders. They wavered. "They'll break," said Aethal, too softly to hear.

"Yes, they will," Malcoor answered, nonetheless. "And we'll be just that much worse off. We'll have to retreat again to the keep itself. Aethal Paaling?"

"Yes, sir?"

"You haven't seen my niece, have you?" The old general's voice was heavy.

Aethal did not trust himself to speak, but could not ignore the question. Then Malcoor looked up.

A white flare broke to the west of the city. And another, further out.

Malcoor raised his eyebrows. "What does that mean?"

Aethal felt as though a sword had been pulled out of his chest. "That means, sir, that I have seen Ardyth. And so have you."

"What in the name of all Wellspawn are you talking about?"

Fifty horsemen rode out of the Garden Third, and charged along the western curve of the wall. Where they rode, the Temple Guard cast aside their weapons and fled. Desperately, the black-clad army tried to reform, to face the charge. A volley of guns from Maednac's Own ripped into them.

Then another volley of guns rang out from the orchard behind Ilferth Simon's main body. The Conversant's black-and-silver standard wavered. Another crash of fire, and the Guard abandoned the wall, flocking back toward their banner, which fell. Caught between Maednac's Own, the Westerend cavalry, and an unseen foe firing Greater Rifles, the Temple Guard broke, running northward.

From the field below, a shout of victory filled the early morning air.

"Fools." Aethal turned at Malcoor's mutter.

Aethal was taken aback. "What?"

Malcoor pointed. "That's not the rout they think it is. That's the Temple, that way! We need to follow them, catch them before we have to dig them out of that monstrosity!" He muttered a curse, seeing the men celebrating and cheering. "There's only so much men can do, though."

Aethal couldn't help it. "I suppose, in the end, they could only save King, Kingdom, and your ass. Sir."

Malcoor turned slowly. Then he cracked a grim smile. "You are learning, Aethal Paaling. Indeed, you are."

Chapter Ten

59th of Spring, 312 Exodus

The hedgerows in the courtyard of the High Temple burned, and the smoke of their burning rolled up to blot out the sinking sun. The aluminum-sheathed Single Moon looked down, an angry infection, reflecting red flames where it was not plated with soot. *It looks broken.* The screams had long since stopped, but the smell of burning meat and grass and wood hung heavy in the air with a horrible redolence. Aethal's stomach growled, and he thought he would vomit.

When the flames died, Malcoor would send in Maednac's Own. He would have no choice. And this time the slaughter would be total. The regiment had sustained almost half its strength in casualties the night before.

Once again, Aethal thanked all his fortune that Pyk had been with them the day they had gone to see the Lord Warden. Now, the hedges around the High Temple had been sown with stake-filled pits, and were swarming with Temple Guards waiting to sell themselves to defend each twisting foot of the maze.

Malcoor had solved the problem with the materials he had to hand. The old ballistae and catapults in the Wagonmast had rained bombs filled with oil down on the maze, burning it to ash with its defenders. But the Temple itself was of white stone, and could not be fired. They would have to batter that to pieces with cannon, and then dig Ilferth Simon and his guard from the rubble. *Unless we succeed.*

Aethal and the Wyrmguard, now back up to their full strength of twenty-four, advanced through the Garden Third at a trot. Eight of them were dressed in servant's uniforms from the Hydraxis, hastily scrounged to replace the ragged clothing they had been wearing when they had picked up the pistols. Reflexively, Aethal checked his right, and saw that Magnei was at least keeping up. Barely winded, the boy shot him a grim look.

"I told you, one of us must be with you," he rasped, eyes blazing with a determination Aethal had never before seen. "The Abbey is our place." *What makes him brave?* Aethal wondered. Even now he was unsure whether the boy's presence would be more help than liability. Malcoor had nearly ordered him tied up when he volunteered, but eventually had given in.

"You protect that boy with your life, Aethal Paaling," he'd said. *"I count his life only second to mine."* And then he had handed Aethal a treasure.

general malcoor values himself highly, commented Gun. Aethal snorted. Unfortunately, he could not fault Malcoor's reasoning. Nor his tactics. Only Maednac's Own were armed with Greater Rifles. Only they might have the strength to break the Temple Guard. The Wrackberg troops had supported the elite unit all through the siege, and Lord Vaughan's Westerenders had provided the confusion necessary to rout their foe. Now troops of both houses were restoring order around the city, manning the gates and enforcing the Discipline.

Aethal had seen Lord Vaughan when he had ridden into the Dragonmast, still half-drunk. But when Ardyth had reached him with news that she had broken Ilferth Simon's blackmail, and that nothing was left to him but revenge, he had taken it. His eyes had burned with a cold, fey light, and he had sworn to lead his men against the walls of the High Temple personally. Malcoor had refused to permit this.

Aethal's Wyrmguard had reached the edge of the Abbey's orchard. The smoke from the burning Temple grounds was streaming away in the west wind. Aethal shouldered Gun and looked to the walls.

Not a creature moved, either in the Abbey's yard or on its walls. Like the Temple, the Abbey was not designed for defense, and Ilferth Simon had not wanted to correct that.

Aethal beckoned to Magnei. He handed him a paper-wrapped package. "Inside this," he said. "Is a grain of *yasnuum*. It's one of two that Malcoor gave me. If you come to smell the most delicious scent of your life. If you find yourself suddenly and ravenously hungry, eat this. It will save you." Magnei nodded, his eyes wide.

"On the double," Aethal whispered to the Wyrmguard. "Get us over those walls." The Wyrmguard trotted forward. Over the muted crackle of flames, Aethal waited, his shoulder blades tensing, waiting for another Church sniper to shoot at him. In daylight, there would be no flash to give away a sniper's position.

But the shot never came, and their padded grappling hooks provided easy access to the walls. Still, they were not prepared for the sight that met them.

Bodies littered the courtyard of the Abbey. Magnei let out a cry of dismay, and Aethal felt his stomach knot. He bolted. Aethal cried out, "No, you damn fool!" and raced after him.

Magnei had reached the nearest staircase when Aethal caught him up. "They're gone!" Aethal hissed. "And there may be a hundred soldiers waiting below for headstrong young idiots like you to come down and join them. So stay put."

Magnei looked back at him, grief, fear, and anger mixed together in his eyes. "My brothers," he choked.

"My mother," said Aethal, "may be lying down there. Or in one of these buildings. And some may have escaped. Hold to that. As long as you can."

Magnei swallowed, sanity returning to his face. "Escaped. Hold. Yes. The Lord Warden. We must find him. Free him."

Aethal nodded. If any of the Guardians survived, the Lord Warden would be invaluable. But he did not speak his innermost thoughts, that the Lord Warden was the one man with religious authority that might challenge Ilferth Simon's own, and the one man Simon could not permit to survive.

***

There were bodies inside the Abbey as well, stabbed and hacked to ribbons. The Temple Guard had run wild here. Magnei led them, slowly, sometimes staggering with grief, through the corridors of the Abbey's living quarters. None of the bodies had weapons. The second time Magnei collapsed by the body of a friend, Aethal pitilessly dragged him to his feet.

"There is no time. No time, *Guardian*." Aethal gave the word an edge. "We must find the living, Guardian Magnei. Not the dead." But Aethal could not stop himself from searching the faces of the dead women as he passed them. At last, they passed up the familiar steps to the Lord Warden's offices.

Here there was blood, splashed on the walls of the central chamber whose six doors flanked the Lord Warden's office. Two Temple Guardsmen lay here with their foes, deep wounds in their chests. The six Guardians who had opposed them lay clustered around the Lord Warden's door. These had been shot. The door was broken in. Magnei dashed inside before Aethal could stop him and gave a high, wailing cry of grief.

Lord Warden Cledan lay in a pile of books, blood running from his split scalp. Magnei cradled the old man's head in his hands. In the relaxation of death, the man looked younger, and less careworn. Like a man who had laughed often in his life, but was now saddened. Saddened, but not surprised. Aethal could see from here how the skull was dished inward. Death had doubtless been instantaneous.

Aethal looked closer. The Lord Warden's torc, the dark glass that he had covered up so surreptitiously, was gone. *Did Simon do this himself?* he wondered. *He must trust some others with the secret of his Well-spawned eyes and ears.*

Magnei eased the Lord Warden's shattered head from his lap to the floor, cushioning it with a thick book, unmindful of the clotted blood smearing its cover. Abruptly, he rose. His face was white. He looked at Aethal and said in a voice as calm as the sea, and commanding as stone, "Come."

Magnei did not stop or slow for any other bodies. He did not stagger or stumble. Aethal and the Wyrmguard followed him from the building and to the Abbey's scriptorium, where Magnei led them past shelves of books and rows of copying tables. There were only two bodies in this room. One had tried to shield himself with a thick book. The spear had pierced it through. In a storeroom, amid barrels of ink, he stopped. He reached behind a single small barrel and pulled. In the floor, a trap door opened. There was a chorus of indrawn breath from below.

"'What has passed is past,'" he said.

A voice from below answered. "'What, then, shall we Wish for?'"

Magnei replied, "'Forgiveness and mercy. All else is vanity.'"

"Come down."

Magnei led the way down the stairs. Aethal followed. His eyes adjusted, and he saw himself and Magnei hemmed in by a circle of grim, tired folk holding half-spears. He recognized the man who had spoken. It was no man at all, but the Lord Warden's secretary, Karel.

"Magnei," she said, her voice toneless. "We did not know if you had been lost." There seemed a peculiar inflection in the statement.

"Never lost," said Magnei. "Only finding my place." He drew a shuddering breath. "The cost was great, Karel."

"Our father?" The question had little of hope in it.

"He is gone," said Magnei. "May God-Beyond-The-World receive him."

The men and women echoed, "May his soul find his God," and Aethal muttered the words with them, the traditional funeral response.

"Those above?" asked Karel.

"Some may have found another refuge," Magnei choked.

Several of the men dropped their weapons at this and bit back cries. "Ilferth Simon's arm is brutal," grated Karel. "And the judgment lies heavy on us."

Half the men choked out, "The judgment lies heavy."

"How many are here?" asked Aethal.

"No more than half," said Karel. "We knew we dared not hide more when the alarm was raised."

Aethal exhaled. Half was more than he'd hoped for, but now that his eyes were fully accustomed to the gloom, he saw that the woman was not lying, though many of the Guardians crowding the cellar were children. Still, there might be enough.

"I thought the Guardians of the Well were a militant order," he said, putting what he hoped was the right amount of dismissal and earnestness in his voice.

Karel's eyes blazed, and some of the men started forward, but she held up a hard hand. "The judgment lies heavy!" she snapped. They stopped.

"We are few where once we were many, Last Sword of Verlaen," Karel said, her eyes boring into Aethal's own. "We cannot fight when the enemy floods us with his numbers. Even so, our guards at the gate bought us the rest of our lives with their own, and they did this freely. We no longer Guard the Well. What would you have of us?"

Aethal let his smile broaden. "I would give you your revenge." He related the course of the battle to them, and the situation. "Break us into the High Temple from this direction, whence Ilferth Simon no longer fears attack, and we will have him," he finished.

Karel, who had listened to Aethal's story with a stony indifference on her face, shook her head. "That cannot be, Last Sword. We train to fight, yes. To defend the Well from those who would Wish there. To defend the world from Wellspawn. And to defend ourselves, at the last extremity of need. But we do not fight for revenge, no matter how we might burn for it. We do not stay where we are not wanted. We have been rejected from this place, as we were from our service before the Well at the World's Core. We will not break our oaths. We must go."

Aethal's fury rose. "Does it mean nothing to you that Ilferth Simon has used Wellspawn to geld and kill your own Lord Warden? That he has imprisoned you for years and now killed the half of you?"

"It means much," said Karel. "But not what you think it should, Seeker. We must go."

"What does it mean that Ilferth Simon uses Lotus as a weapon to destroy Verlaen? A Wish from the Well?" Magnei asked.

Karel stared hard at Magnei. "Weapons are used by men. Against men. Men are responsible, whether the weapons be Wished from the Well or no. Or should we fight for the Grassworms because he," Karel pointed at Aethal, "carries a Greater Rifle to kill his fellow men? We have discussed this before, Magnei."

"And you were wrong then, too, Elder Sister!" cried Magnei. "Listen to yourself. Lotus is not just a weapon, no matter how men may use it. It is a hunger. An infection. It will kill all of us, not just those Ilferth Simon seeks to dominate. It will kill him, too, and all of the fellow men we profess to protect if we do not act. Fear kills, Guardian!" And Aethal saw that statement strike home, though he did not know why. Whether he did or not, however, he would press the advantage.

"Guardian Karel, this is a matter of life and death for the world," pleaded Aethal. "I mean no disrespect to your oath, but is it truly worth such a price?"

Karel looked at him as a woman might an insect. "You do not even know the substance of the oath, Seeker. The last time a Lord Warden broke it," he said, "the world *did* die. You have no conception of what I fear," she said softly. She turned to Magnei. "Very well," she said. "Fear kills, little brother. I will give what you ask for, Last Sword. And in so doing, though I do not intend it, I will also be granting them their revenge. Whatever else we call it." She raised her voice.

"Guardians of the Well," she called. "I call you by your oath. The Lotus is upon us. Will you drink fire?"

The shout shook the floor's joists. "WE WILL!"

Up from the basement they climbed. Aethal tried to count, but lost it at around a hundred. There were at least that many more to go. All were leaving. Even the children.

"Who will watch these?" he asked.

"We will leave wet nurses for the babes too young to walk," said Karel, her hand on the ladder. "As for the rest, *we* will."

Aethal grabbed her arm. "But we're going into combat."

Karel simply looked at him. "Yes, Last Sword. We are. That is the Drinking of Fire. When there is Well-spawn to destroy, we all fight." Her eyes were wet with tears. "I told you that you had no conception of what I feared, and you recoil at this, the tiniest foretaste? Perhaps you should have listened to me while there was time. Now, we fight."

Aethal's grip tightened. "I've seen Magnei fight," he hissed.

Then Karel did the last thing Aethal expected. She chuckled. "Magnei is a very bad fighter," she said. "And came to us late in his life. It is one thing we have not as yet taught him. That does not change the Oath. We drink Fire." She climbed the ladder and was gone.

***

Aethal joined the Guardians of the Well in the anteroom of the Great Council Chamber of the Abbey. The sky was taking on the tired, hard light of late afternoon and Aethal knew that Malcoor would not attack so late as to risk fighting at night.

A great many men clustered around the scaffolding at the north wall, to the extreme right of the doors to the Chamber. There was a shout, and the wood collapsed, the tarp covering the walls rippling down. The mural was revealed.

Like the other panels of the mural, this one showed the Chamber of the Well in the Kalidranym. Whereas the first two panels had shown morning and noon, the sky of this picture showed night through the windows of the great vaults of the Kalidranym, and the cylinder of the Well's stones pointed upward like an accusing finger.

At the foot of the Well, in a Lord Warden's robes, lay a man whose eyes were glazed in death. A dagger was buried to the hilt in his chest. At the exit from the chamber, another man with a shaven head looked on sadly, and made the sign of blessing. In the sky, the moon shone down, covering the scene in unearthly light.

The moon? Aethal thought. He had never seen a Single Moon in the sky. But the ruined Kalidranym, and the dead man... it must be the Apostate Lord Warden, who drove the Guardians from their sacred trust. *How, though? The Moon was broken at the sinking of the Well. Why is it whole in this picture? And why was it veiled?*

He had no time to ask or hear an answer to those questions. Shouldering his way through the Guardians, he reached Karel. "We must go now," he said. "What is the report?"

Karel smiled grimly. "Ilferth Simon has guards on that door, but only four. He knows Malcoor has not have the forces to surround him, and he could move his men inside the Temple faster than you can move around it, were you foolish enough to try. This is the only door in the Temple's western face. As far as he knows, it is unthreatened."

Aethal nodded, and braced himself to give orders to the Guardians. *once again, we command not-soldiers,* Gun thought. Aethal grimaced. The weapon felt... Greater Rifles could not be unhappy, exactly, but they could appreciate fulfilling their function. This was not Gun's function. But Aethal could sense the difference in the men and women behind him. The Church's rape of the Abbey had been a haphazard, rapid affair. They had not had time to root out the survivors, nor had they broken the Abbey's armory and looted the weapons used in their training yards. There were enough real weapons to give every fighter a half-spear. Some bore other weapons. Knives, clubs, and killing tools Aethal did not recognize. And the way they held those weapons told Aethal that Karel's words had not been an idle boast.

If it weren't for the children, I could almost command these people with pride. Yet they were there, mixed in with the others. Some were as old as midshipmen, he supposed, but in the back, Aethal could see children as young as Sergeant Falk's son. And they had weapons as well. He swallowed. *We drink fire.*

The doors swung open.

Later, Aethal could remember little of the fight. From their vantage point at the Abbey gates, he had ordered the charge, and the Guardians had followed. He remembered using Gun to shoot one of the surprised Temple Guards, and seeing the muzzle flares as the remaining other three returned fire wildly. Then they were through the door and into the Temple. There was no battle cry, no roar of vengeance from the Guardians. They moved with speed and fought in silence, a focus of total control. It was almost like commanding the Wyrmguard, except for the snarls on their faces.

Aethal led a charge along a curving hallway. The man on his right charged a musketeer with a half-spear. He raised his gun, but the Guardian threw the spear, burying it in the Guardsman's chest. Ignoring the musket, the Guardian removed the spear and stabbed another Churchman in the belly. Aethal took up the musket and fired point-blank at a third man who was rushing to meet the charge. He dropped, and they fought on.

A child stabbed upward into a man wearing a black-and-silver uniform. The dying man thrust downward, pinning the boy to the floor. Both fell. A woman wearing the leaking pitcher rounded a corridor and staggered backward, most of her back blown away by a volley of musket fire. Aethal yelled for a charge while they were reloading and hacked at them with Gun's bayonet, scattering them. They fought on.

And suddenly, there was no one left to fight. Only the high, endless wails of the wounded and dying, and the stunned faces of the living, amazed to be drawing breath, realizing that it was over. Aethal called the Wyrmguard to him. Fifteen answered the call.

"You, Everwar," he said, pointing at one Wyrmguard whose arm was a mangled mass of blood. "Go and tell Lord Westerend's forces they may advance, but carefully. Take the worst of the walking wounded with you." The other fourteen followed Aethal to the Sanctuary, at the heart of the High Temple. The great black doors were aluminum-chased, with highlights of copper and waterforged steel. This was where the Church met in prayer. The spire of the Temple and its Single Moon stood at its pinnacle. From behind the doors, Aethal could hear a throbbing noise, which sounded like a voice, or voices.

In this room, the Conversant spoke with God. For an instant, Aethal paused. No man walked the Sanctuary except the Conversant. If he entered, would God act?

Aethal shook off the thought with a snarl at his own credulity. If God defended Ilferth Simon, then God was an evil bastard, and the world could burn.

He gestured to the doors. Goldhammer and The Lady's Demise pulled them open. Ilferth Simon's voice snapped into intelligibility: "...and you shall grow to reap eternal glory!" There was a cry of assent, of ecstasy, and the Wyrmguard stepped into the room.

There was a report of thunder. The voices cut off as though by a knife. And the two Wyrmguard fell backward out of the doors.

For a moment, Aethal's mind gibbered. *God has struck them down for entering His holy place.* But the spreading pool of blood beneath each of them was too familiar.

greater rifles. Gun snapped. *covering the door. elevated position inside. range approximately eighty to a hundred feet.*

The calm, logical assessment brought Aethal back to himself.

Aethal could see into the Sanctuary, now. It was richly carpeted, and metal vaults rose ceilingward, supporting the polished white stone walls and dome. On a central dais of black stone, Aethal could see Ilferth Simon, staring at him.

The Conversant's robes were torn, but the Single Moon shone from his chest. His face was a mask of ecstatic fury. Two men stood to his right, behind a large chest. To his left stood a carved chair of wood and bone and tooth. A man knelt before it, and behind him, at least fifty more, all in the uniform of the Temple Guard. They carried muskets and long, reverse-curved swords. They stared blankly through the open doors. They began to move.

Ilferth Simon smiled and raised his hand. "Hold!" he cried. "Do not fear the heretics, nor the evil that they bring. God shall not suffer them to pass the doors of this place." His smile grew. "I see you, Last Sword. You and your accursed Wyrmguard. They shall not guard that worm you call a king much longer." He gestured to the two men beside him, and then, almost casually, pointed at the doors.

The two men leapt from behind the chest, in a blur of speed. Aethal had only time to step back and raise Gun before they were at the doors. Flintmaw and Sparkhammer, faster than Aethal, interposed themselves, and there was a flurry of shots.

Flintmaw locked arms with his foe. Aethal could see five round holes in the Guardsman's chest, just beginning to bleed. Though his sword arm was caught by the wrist, he lowered it slowly, overpowering Flintmaw by brute strength. The edge came closer and closer to the Wyrmguard's neck. As if in slow motion, Aethal raised Gun. Then Flintmaw swayed back, slipped itself from the impossibly strong Guardsman's grasp, and struck upward. The bayonet on the end of the pistol slid up through the Temple Guard's chin and into his brain. The man sagged, just at the moment the other Guardsman slipped from Sparkhammer's grasp. In a liquid, flashing arc, the curved sword came around, decapitating the Wyrmguard. He turned to Aethal, and bared his teeth. Aethal saw the green strands moving in the mad Guardsman's eyes.

Greendel, Aethal thought in the frozen moment. *Ilferth Simon created the greendels.* Turned the Lotus-Eaters into weapons. Aethal heaved at Gun, but knew he would never bring the barrel around in time, never parry the blow of the sword that was lifting so fast above him.

Three shots rang out at once, and the Guardsman's head exploded in a shower of red and gray. Aethal stared, gaping. Stonelock, Flintmaw, and Carryon began reloading.

Now Aethal could see Ilferth Simon's face contorted in a paroxysm of fury. He signaled, and the man kneeling before the strange chair rose and sat in it. As he did so, it seemed to Aethal that his face changed, became sharper and harder. The Conversant reached into the chest and removed a handful of dark green leaves, silvery on the bottom. He raised them to the heavens. The men around him stared and sighed.

"Accept the Wrath of God!" he cried. He handed the leaves to the man in the chair, who took them and began tearing into them, eating in a ravening ecstasy. "Sow the leaf and you shall grow to reap eternal glory!"

So, the leaf and I shall go to sleep eternal... The words of the greendel Farnan had wounded at the Treeline weeks ago came back to him. *He misunderstood. It wasn't a plea for mercy. He died muttering his war-cry.*

Aethal looked at the Wyrmguard and they at him. Soon Ilferth Simon would have two or three score greendels, and they had already proven they were a match for Wyrmguard. They might kill the men before they were transformed, but even Wyrmguard could not charge through a door covered by snipers wielding Greater Rifles.

And if he called in Lord Westerend's troops to overwhelm them, he would be leading hundreds of men into a room full of Lotus.

Stonelock reloaded and walked calmly toward the door.

"No!" Aethal cried, but the Wyrmguard did not heed him. He stood beside the doors, where he could not be seen from inside the Sanctuary. Then he ducked his head just inside, for the briefest instant. There was a shot, and the slug spalled off the floor at Aethal's feet. He and the rest of the Wyrmguard backed away, taking cover from the possibility that one of the musketeers might shoot in defiance of his Conversant's order. Aethal could see with his last glimpse through the door that the first man had risen from the chair, and another man was taking his place.

Then Stonelock seized Aethal by the shirt collar. "Last Sword, we offer a new Compact."

Aethal looked at the man's weapon-ridden eyes in disbelief. The Wyrmguard was offering him a bargain? Now?

Aethal looked to the other Wyrmguard, but they stood as still as stone, their eyes fixed upon Stonelock, as though he were the only thing in the universe.

"What sort of Compact?" asked Aethal, finding his voice.

"When they go to the Well, and they Wish for the end of the Lotus," said Stonelock, unblinking. "You will take one of us with you. Is it agreed? Under the Compact?"

Aethal could only stare. "But why?"

"That is not under discussion. Will you take one of us with you? Yes or no?"

"What will you do?"

Stonelock stepped back. "I shall deliver Ilferth Simon to you." He turned to the rest of the Wyrmguard. "Stand ready." He said to Aethal. "You must follow." Aethal found himself nodding.

"Last Sword, yes or no?" demanded Stonelock.

Aethal nodded convulsively. "Yes. Agreed."

Stonelock walked through the door of the Sanctuary.

Two rifles spoke. The Wyrmguard staggered and stopped. But did not go down. He advanced and fired upward. There was a cry and a body fell.

"Last Sword!" cried Stonelock, and his voice was full of pain.

Aethal ducked into the room, looking up. There was a platform at the bottom of the domed ceiling, from which a crystal chandelier was suspended. On top of it, four snipers, one frantically reloading, another broken on the floor beneath. Two more snipers fired. The bullets smashed into Stonelock's belly and jaw. The Wyrmguard groaned and advanced again. Fired twice. Two more snipers fell, their rifles clattering.

Aethal dived for the fallen weapons. Stonelock should have been dead; dead and gone long ago, but was still on his feet. Aethal reached the first Greater Rifle and shouldered it. Its mind snarled against an unfamiliar owner, a cry without words, but Greater Rifles could not disobey their wielders. He sighted at the dais, and even the lightning reflexes of Ilferth Simon's greendels could not outspeed a bullet. The shot smashed the creature through the forehead and it dropped. Aethal cycled another round, sighted on Ilferth Simon. But the rifle clicked empty. It had not been reloaded. Two more shots punched out. These took Stonelock in the forehead, ripping away his skull above the hairline. Calmly, he fired twice more into the platform, and the last two snipers fell on either side of Aethal.

The waiting Guardsmen, now fully awake to what had happened, shouldered their rifles, A few shots rang out, bracketing Aethal. The rest of the volley would kill him.

Suddenly the air was split by the steady, even firing of Wyrmguard pistols. The last dozen Wyrmguard walked through the door, firing as they came. Every shot hit. The last of the Temple Guard fell, one by one. Three Wyrmguard fell, and three more staggered as heavy rounds from the Guard's muskets punched into them. But each of them had five shots, and not one Wyrmguard dropped before firing them. There were twenty of the Temple Guard left. Ten. Five. Aethal looked up. The last were falling. But now Ilferth Simon was shaking with rage. He yanked the last man from the chair and pointed at Aethal. Aethal swung Gun around, but the Lotus-thing was nearly on him, eyes blazing green and mouth open to rip like an animal.

The last five shots from the Wyrmguard lashed out in a continuous roll from behind Aethal. They hit the creature in both knees, both shoulders. It stumbled, convulsing its shattered joints. The last bullet passed squarely through its left eye, and it dropped.

Aethal looked back at what had been Stonelock. Its jaw was half-gone, and its eyes looked out at him with one last flare of sentience.

"Remember," it muttered, barely intelligible. Then it fell.

Aethal looked back to the dais, saw Ilferth Simon sitting on the chair, stuffing Lotus in his own mouth. He swallowed, looked at Aethal. "God's will lives in me. I can feel it. So will you. And all the world."

Aethal raised Gun. Fired. Ilferth Simon slumped in the chair, his skull shattered. The Sanctuary was empty of living men. Only he and the nine remaining Wyrmguard stood. Automatically, even mechanically, Aethal began the task of retrieving the Wyrmguard from their fallen mounts. He only paused when he reached Stonelock. He picked up the weapon by the barrel.

It was nothing he could have explained to anyone else. Maybe another owner of a Greater Rifle would have understood. But the weapon was quiet. Vacant. For the first time, Aethal took a Wyrmguard pistol by the hilt. There was no change.

"He is gone, Last Sword," said Flintmaw. "He will not return."

Aethal found his voice. "How was he killed?"

"He allowed himself to die." Flintmaw hesitated. "It can be done, with us. When our mounts are wounded, we... withdraw. Into ourselves. Otherwise, we share the death. The death of the mount. But we can choose this. To propel the mount beyond fear. Beyond pain. Even beyond death. For a little while. But then we are gone. And there is no returning."

"You hold his body in your hands, Last Sword. It is only a pistol now. You are the Last Sword. Do with it as you think he would have desired."

Aethal stared at the dead weapon. *My promise to him was worth his life. The life of something that could not die. Except by choosing.*

"Where did he go?"

"With the mount. Wherever it went."

There were running feet outside the room, and Aethal's head snapped up. "Wyrmguard! Let no man enter this room. And burn that Lotus."

The Wyrmguard obeyed. A young private of Maednac's Own saluted him outside. "My Lord! Warmaster Malcoor has taken the Temple. But he says he needs you; you and the Wyrmguard. They've found... God-Beyond-The-World, it's the dungeons, sir."

Aethal's heart sank. He forced himself to speak. "Have you captured any of the Temple Guard?" he asked.

"A fair number, sir." Aethal had five guns in his belt.

"Take me to them."

***

Malcoor was waiting by a dark stairwell when Aethal appeared, flanked by five newly-made Wyrmguard. He rose. "Last Sword," he said. "We've been combing the High Temple for holdouts. We found..." Malcoor hesitated for the first time since Aethal had known him. Swallowed. "We found many things that no one has suspected. I have had men opening the prayer cells of the bishops and priests. The ones behind the Sanctuary. Some were dead. Others... not quite. He's been starving them. So their prayers would be desperate enough to reach beyond the world."

Aethal's stomach knotted. "Do not let any of your men travel in groups of less than seven," he said. "You don't know what he might have been feeding them."

"I'm afraid we do. Not on this floor, not yet. But below. I sent... I sent three men. One came back."

Aethal looked beyond Malcoor to where a shivering private of Maednac's Own sat guarded by three of his fellows. Aethal walked over and gazed down, into the man's green eyes. Natural green. The man screamed upon seeing him.

"No, Last Sword! I didn't. I swear to God-Beyond-The-World I didn't eat it! I didn't!"

229

Aethal nodded, expression carefully neutral. "I will believe you. For now." To the guards he said. "Place him in a cell. In the Hydraxis. One week. It is Discipline." The guards nodded, and the man whimpered.

"Thank you. Thank you, my Lord. I almost... almost..." and he dissolved in tears, clinging to his captors.

He looked at Malcoor. "We will go."

"You will go?" said Malcoor. "There's Lotus." Aethal held up his hand.

"We will go with caution. Wyrmguard?" He turned to the five of them. "Set torches. Burn the Lotus. And give mercy to any you find. Report to me when you are done."

They nodded. After the torches were lit, the five Wyrmguard went below stairs. There were two sharp reports. Soon afterwards, black smoke curled up from the stairs. The smell of the Lotus made Aethal's mouth water, and he spat to clear it. He fingered his own packet of *yasnuum.*

A soldier approached Aethal. "Last Sword. A Guardian desires to speak with you."

It was Karel. Aethal nodded to him, glad the woman had survived. A chill thought struck him. "Is Magnei...?"

"Alive, and unwounded. He is not a coward, but he is also not a fool. He knows his limitations. Better than I do, it seems." She winced. Aethal could see a shallow, but long, gash running up her arm. "He very much wants to see what you have found in Ilferth Simon's secret chambers. He has long suspected that the Conversant kept artifacts of the Well, which are our responsibility."

"As do I," said Aethal. He reached into a pocket and handed two objects to Karel. One dark disc inside a silver torc, and another, larger one. "I found these on Ilferth Simon's body. You can use them to find the other spy-stones Ilferth Simon sowed along with the Lotus. Take this in earnest of all the rest."

"Surely that will be the decision of the new Conversant of the Church," said Karel, taken aback.

"The power of the Church is broken," said Aethal. "The new Conversant will need to build it anew, and it will be long in the building. I cannot speak for the King, but I think he would be interested in a Conversant more concerned with scholarship than with the Church's power and the Kingdom's piety. Perhaps yourself."

"I am no priest!" said Karel.

"No, you're a monk. But we can discuss that another time."

Flintmaw came up from the basement. His face, clothes, and hair were blackened, but he seemed undisturbed. The smoke was dissipating.

"The Lotus in the antechamber is destroyed, Last Sword. But you must judge the rightness of what happens next."

Aethal's heart sank. "I will come."

Malcoor touched his arm. "You shouldn't."

Aethal looked him in the eyes. "Someone must. Someone human."

Malcoor returned his gaze. "My niece has told me how you saved her. How you saved my brother, and the honor of our house. Whatever you need me to do for you, I will."

Aethal nodded. Then he turned and walked down the steps.

It was like walking into the aftermath of Hell.

Smoke clung to the walls and ceiling, obscuring the Wyrmguard's torches. Great troughs of clay smoldered in the heat. Only ash was left of the Lotus that had grown in the rich soil within. In the corner, two larger mounds smoked, bones protruding from them.

There were other devices, up against the walls. They, too, smoldered, the wood burned and charred. But it was obvious what sort of devices they had been. *The kind that are unnecessary when you command Lotus. Or think you do.*

Beyond, up a small flight of steps, were the cells.

"With me," Aethal ordered. The Wyrmguard closed ranks and followed. Aethal gestured. There were no keys. The Wyrmguard broke in the door.

He held the torch up.

In the darkness, a voice wheezed, "More, Lord? More?" The girl inside was emaciated, her flesh green. There was a pot before her that had contained Lotus, but the dirt was spilled, and she had even eaten the roots. Soil clotted around her mouth. She lunged desperately against her chains, screeching agonized laughing. "More, Lord?" Aethal gestured. There was a single report, and the thing that had been a girl slumped to the floor.

The row of cells stretched on. Aethal found in each cell a skeletal, cringing figure, wanting more. Some had green eyes. Others were gone much further, dark cords of Lotus bulging under their translucent skin, unable to speak, only to mewl pitifully and grab toward the light. Always the laughter. The report. The release.

It was the sixth cell.

The door banged open, but there was no sound. Broken plates lay against the door, and crushed Lotus leaves, harmless in the stink of the smoke. And a man huddled against the far wall. "Don't touch me!" he screamed. And blinked in the torchlight. His uniform was soiled, but only slightly frayed. The stink in the cell, of old urine and feces, was terrible.

"Farnan," Aethal whispered.

Farnan looked up squinting. He stared, uncomprehending. Then he said. "I heard you. Giving mercy to the others. Have you none for me?"

Aethal started forward. "Farnan, man, thank..."

"Get back from me! Are you fucking stupid?" The anguish in the cry stopped Aethal in his tracks. He stared at his friend.

"It was so small," Farnan whispered, the tears standing in his eyes. "Mixed in the food. The very first day. I never thought... never thought..."

Aethal raised the torch. Farnan's eyes. His blue eyes. His blue eyes, with a single thread of green in each of them. "But I knew," he whispered. "I knew the moment I swallowed, and the hunger began."

Aethal looked at the shattered plates, lying against the door. How much willpower had it taken for Farnan to reject every meal offered him? "We're getting you out of here," he said, mouth dry.

"You can't," said Farnan. "I can never leave. By Discipline. You are sworn to uphold it. Shoot me. Give me the mercy you gave Harry. Now."

"No!"

Farnan turned away. "You bastard," he whispered.

Aethal knelt and faced his friend. "Farnan, we are going to the Well. We are sending Malcoor to the Well to Wish for the end of Lotus. All Lotus, everywhere. You're not far gone, and I promise to take you where there is no Lotus, not anywhere around. You may yet live."

"You think I want to? The hunger, Aethal. The hunger is terrible."

And he has resisted it for five days. After *he was farmed. Truly, we need him.*

"You can survive," Aethal said. "I know you can. Take this." And he handed his friend the yasnuum. "It will ease the hunger. Make you safe." Farnan took the packet and opened it with trembling hands, and bit into the crumbling, brown square. He shuddered with relief.

"How... how very odd." He rose. Aethal gestured the Wyrmguard forward. They unfastened Farnan's chains. Farnan speared Aethal with a look.

"Where have you been, Aethal?" he asked.

Aethal wanted to say, "looking for you," but he couldn't. "Fighting the Lotus," he managed.

He offered Farnan a hand up, but Farnan scrambled to his feet, pulling his hands away. "I'm not hungry anymore," he said. "And yet, I am. But not for... that."

"You haven't eaten in five days. We'll feed you. Get your strength back."

Farnan nodded, and they walked out of the cell.

Outside the dungeons, the night had fallen. The moons, nearly full, were just rising. Yet all was dark.

Chapter Eleven

60th of Spring, 312 Exodus

The following evening, the Red Chamber beneath the Ophidian was full to bursting, the halls open to the cooling air. The ancient standards hung there again. Maednac's Ship and Trees. Wrackberg's Cannon and Isle. The Westerend's Fans and Towers. Even the five-masted Ship and Moon of House Skysil hung there, though Chancellor Pyk was the only one left in the capital of that House.

It darkened his mood, even as he looked out over the jubilant faces of the men who filled the Chamber. *We should not be celebrating,* part of him wanted to say. *Uncle Falaar is yet in rebellion, and the Westerend may be infected with Lotus.* But at least they had discovered where the Lotus in Ilferth Simon's Well-spawned glass was. A disused watchtower overlooking the Roaring Falls. There were fast, armed couriers riding there now. *The Grassworms are still advancing through the Grain Sea, no matter how many we have killed. We are not winning.*

But the men in this chamber had won their battle. And it would be foolish to deny these men their due. *They need a victory to celebrate.*

Maednac's Own stood, rank on rank, facing the king in their red-and-orange dress uniforms. Only about half were in attendance. The rest were dead or recovering from serious wounds. Behind them, even more decimated, and in a riot of colors, the various regiments whose shattered remains had been welded into the defense of the Hydraxis. To the right stood four score silver, green, and black-clad troops of House Westerend. To the left were nine hundred or so soldiers of House Wrackberg, in scarlet and black. Behind them, a throng of commoners in their finest.

On the great dais at the head of the Chamber, Aethal stood behind the king. Gun was at his back, but the Last Sword's curiously light weight was absent. Tonight, King Paitir held it.

Paitir touched the head of the man kneeling in front of him with the tip of the Last Sword. "Arise, Donar Falk, Sword of Verlaen."

The young man rose. Aethal could see the pride burning in his eyes, and the way he kept deliberately stopping his hands from rising to finger the hilt of the new short sword at his waist, the aluminum medal at his throat. Aethal looked beyond him, and saw in the ranks of the soldiers the echo of the young man's face in the grizzled features of his uncle. Water was standing in the Sergeant's eyes.

The young man turned and joined the fifty-three men who stood below the dais, facing the rest of the Chamber. The king turned, and handed the Last Sword to Aethal. Aethal stepped forward.

"These men have protected the King with their lives. They are the Swords of Verlaen." He looked over the heads of the young men. They were from the Bowl and the Fans. From the Wrackberg and the Madlands. Theoretically, he commanded them all now. It was Magnei who had reminded him that the Last Sword had once commanded a military order himself. The Swords were an old order, richer in glory than real fighting power. These were the first Swords of Verlaen to be inducted in a hundred years. That had been Aethal's idea. Glory was important, now that there was so little of it. Aethal finished the ceremony. "Swords. You are drawn in honor. Be sheathed where the King commands." He drew breath. "Or in death. The honored dead."

"The honored dead," the crowd rumbled back. And a seneschal approached, bearing a length of parchment. He began to read the names of the fallen.

There was a time, thought Aethal, *when the Conversant would have done this.* But that would not happen again for many long years. Aethal's father had made a definite point of that. To the king's left and to his right stood two empty chairs. One for the ghost of Ilferth Simon, thought Aethal, and one for Rolf Hlafen's. He had been hanged this morning.

To the king's left sat Chancellor Pyk, looking more lordly than Aethal had ever seen his uncle.

"The Chancellorship suits you, Uncle," Aethal had said, earlier in the day, as they were both attending upon the king.

"I'd never have thought it," the old man had replied. "Aethal, the King thinks we might be able to win your Uncle Falaar back to us with me as his Chancellor. I think he just might be right about that. With judicious reparations, we just might."

And King Paitir himself looked better than he had since Aethal's return to Maednac Serpiin, healthy and alert. To his right sat Warmaster Malcoor. Aethal suppressed a smile. Malcoor had sworn that this was the last time he would wear any uniform but that of an admiral. It was important tonight, but Aethal knew he was itching to command ships once again.

Aethal's blood ran cold at the thought. *And he will command that ship. And he will sail north to Wish in the Well. To Wish for all Lotus to die. And if he fails, what then?*

Then we all die, most likely. There was no more word of Lotus in Maednac Serpiin. The aluminum had melted and run off the spire, and the dome of the High Temple stood gutted and empty, like the shell of a primordial mollusc. Discipline required that any building where Lotus had grown be burned. Ilferth Simon's Wellspawn, which he had used to create the Lotus-fanatics had burned as well, Aethal had seen to that. Magnei had been fascinated when he had seen the thing, but even he had agreed. He had already discovered it in the Guardians' records.

"The Beast Throne of the Wish-King Gandobal," he had said. "Long thought to be lost. Gandobal Wished to make men as ferocious and trainable as animals. But his animal men were smart enough and fierce enough to kill their trainers rather than obey them. Gandobal could find nothing they wanted badly enough to obey him for. Ilferth Simon, though, had the Lotus to offer them."

And then the greendels had been fed a sleeping draught and shipped out beyond the Treeline with Ilferth Simon's missionaries, as part of their baggage. To the Grassworms, they had been proof that God was on their side against their hated, gun-wielding foes.

Aethal looked at Magnei where he stood at the king's left. He was now appointed as the Royal Liaison to the Guardians. However, Magnei, for all his learning, had not been able to answer the question Aethal had most wanted answered.

"Did Ilferth Simon bring the Lotus to Verlaen?" Aethal had asked. Magnei had searched the Conversant's inner office and carried away a number of thick volumes, but in the end had confessed that it was impossible to know whether the Conversant had planted the Lotus in Everview or simply taken the opportunity it had afforded him.

And so they had burned the High Temple. All buildings infested must be burned. Technically, that might include the Hydraxis as well, Aethal supposed. But no one had thought of that. The Wyrmguard had searched the palace and found nothing.

There was still no word from the Westerend. Lotus could still be seen in Ilferth Simon's accursed seeing-glass. But had any attended it? It could not be watched at all hours, even if men were set to do it in shifts. During Westerend's night, the glass went dark. Who would know if an agent of Ilferth Simon's pruned it? Ate of it? Aethal looked to Lord Vaughan, where he sat to Malcoor's right, with Ardyth beside him. His face was grim and taut with worry. He would be off home with his ships as soon as he could, Aethal was certain, but stayed this night out of consideration for his own men, and the king's.

There was no word from the Grain Sea and the Army trying to contain the Lotus there, either. Most especially, there was no word from any place in the Skysil domain. *If Malcoor fails, we all die. Just like the poor bastards in the cells under the Temple, with ropes and mats of Lotus growing under their skin. Into their hearts and lungs. Into their brains. Like Farnan.*

Farnan, of course, was not here. Could not be. Even if the *yasnuum* kept him from being a danger to himself or others, the Discipline could not easily be adapted for his special case. He occupied his own room, set aside for him by Aethal, in the Tree-King's Tower. Skraalen was here, and the old thief clutched the patent of nobility he had been awarded in its brass cylinder as though he would die with it still in his hand.

The seneschal finished the roll of the dead. There was a moment of silence. King Paitir rose again to his feet. "Now I proclaim a feast," he said, sounding tired. "To celebrate our victory. Eat well, with the thanks of your King!" There was a shout of approval, and servants appeared carrying large tables and benches, and space was made for them. A high table was set up on the dais, and all were quickly heaped with food. Aethal found his place across the table from Lord Vaughan and the Lady Ardyth. As wine was poured, Aethal felt a strong hand reach across the table and grasp his own in a firm grip. He looked into Westerend's pale eyes.

"Aethal Paaling," he said. "My daughter has redeemed the honor of House Westerend. Redeemed my honor." He paused. "And so have you. She says that you inspired her magnificent deed that served to bring me back... to myself. To be the Lord of Westerend again."

"The deed was the lady's," said Aethal automatically. "And your own."

Westerend cast down his eyes. "It was a fortunate scheme," he said. "But the good fortune of it was no fault of my own. You could have named it treason."

Aethal shrugged uncomfortably. It had been treason. It had also saved them from being the main course of a feast rather than honored guests at one. "I could do no less nor no more than I have done," he said.

Westerend speared him with a clear eye. "Oh, you could have," he breathed. "Many men have. I have come to expect both more and less at the hands of House Wrackberg," he said. Ardyth shot him an outraged glance, but he continued: "And now I have done both more and less myself. I find it passing strange that one Wrackberg should drive me to such depths, and another should come forth to pull me up from them again." He smiled, grimly. "With my daughter's help. A lesson I shall never forget: you work well together. Who knows what you could yet accomplish?" and he glanced at them both in turn.

The blush that blossomed in Ardyth's face, meeting Aethal's gaze, was a wonder to behold. And a terror. He babbled. "But, sir, we all might be dead a year hence."

Ardyth looked away, but Westerend frowned. "And tell me, young Wrackberg, just how that would change if there were no Lotus in this land, and only a civil war to deal with?"

Aethal, looking at Ardyth, found that he had no reply.

***

It was much later, and though the drink still flowed freely, the revelers had moved out into the courtyard. *"The man who won't buy his soldiers' love is a fool, when it's as cheap as wine,"* Paal had said to Aethal, once. And indeed, it was the Wrackberg's finest vintage that Paal had supplied. The king and the Lords Paramount had retired, but the yard of the Hydraxis had been turned into a miniature fair, with mummers, jugglers, and fools. Aethal and Ardyth walked apart, toward the Seagate, already repaired. Here, before Maednac's statue, again blazing with light, the first summer flowers, poking up early, waved in the breeze, their scents purging away the memories of blood and smoke.

Before them, Maednac Serpiin shone, its beacons relit. The Lotus patrols moved again through its streets. Now they were Skraalen's men. Well-armed, and paid. There had been no complaints about their behavior, and Aethal wasn't sure whether that was reassuring or terrifying. No flares rose. There were fireworks tonight, he remembered, and he had carefully checked them beforehand to make sure that there were no green starbursts scheduled.

It was Ardyth who broke the silence. "Tomorrow I will be gone," she said. "My father and I must leave for the Twin Fans. It is our duty."

"I know," Aethal said. "I think... I think you will find that it's all right. I don't think Ilferth Simon's men were the kind to... to act without orders. He'd never have tolerated it. But please," he said, aware that he was babbling, "Be careful."

"No," she said.

Aethal stopped, stared at her. "What?"

"No," Ardyth repeated. "It is not the time for being careful, Aethal Paaling. If I have learned nothing else these past two days, I have learned that, at least. My father was careful. Your father is perhaps the most careful man I may ever have known. There are times to be careful," she said, looking up at him. "But these are not those times. Only daring will stop the Lotus. My uncle understands this. So do you. Or you would not have done what you did. And I would not have ridden to get my father and his horse."

"There was no other choice, then!" said Aethal.

"And there is no other choice now," Ardyth said. "And so I say, Aethal Paaling," she said, standing on tiptoe to kiss him on the cheek, "do not be careful while I am gone. But be here when I return." To Aethal's amazement, she pulled from her ear one of the two earpins she wore. She folded it in his hand. "Do you know what this is?" she asked.

"Ivory?" he said. It was long and thin, almost translucent, and capped with a deep red stone.

"No. These are sea serpent teeth. Very young, of course," she said, at the look on his face. "A hatchling washed up on the beach near our summer estate," she explained.

"But the venom..." he trailed off.

"Yes. My grandmother showed me how to handle it, to treat the teeth, and draw out the venom, drying it up, until it blew away as dust. She pierced my ears with them. I thought my mother was going to kill her and then die of fright herself. Possibly not in that order." She laughed at the memory, then grew sober.

"Keep it for me," she said. "I'll be back for it." Footsteps approached them. They turned.

Firestrike walked into the glow of Maednac's statue. His shadow trailed away behind him. In his hands, he bore a Greater Rifle, its butt shiny and smooth except for the chevrons of lieutenant's rank and the crude beginnings of a carving in its lower corner. The wood was black, and its barrel blued.

"You found it!" Aethal cried.

Firestrike nodded. "It was discovered in the High Temple as we were preparing to fire the building. I recognized it as the weapon you mentioned."

"Crow," Aethal whispered, taking the gun. Its mind writhed under his, knowing it was in unfamiliar hands. But Aethal also felt a vague sense of relief from the weapon. It recognized Aethal as a friend.

it recognizes it is not being held by one of those, Gun corrected him.

"What has he found?" asked Ardyth.

"This is Farnan's weapon," said Aethal. He had not told anyone yet about Farnan, and his voice caught. He found himself telling Ardyth about Farnan and Crow. About the Phoenix Lancers' rifles. About Farnan's attempt to keep him from arrest. About finding him infected with Lotus in the Temple dungeons.

"I suspected where he had to be," he said. "I should have pressed the attack sooner."

Ardyth took his hand. "You did what you could; your men were exhausted."

"It wasn't enough." He held up the rifle. "He will want this back, though. I have to take it to him. I don't want him to think I have forgotten him." *Again.*

Ardyth looked up at him as if she were going to say something, and then changed her mind. "I'll come with you."

He shook his head. "You shouldn't. He's infected with Lotus. He'll be…" he blushed, remembering his own reaction, even in the heat of combat, to the girl in Everview. "…dangerous. More to you than to me."

She looked at him. "Aethal Paaling, I know what the effects of Lotus are. You've been telling people for a month now. And you have given him the *yasnuum*. I trust that my uncle told the truth about it. And anyway, you're supposed to have one other person along if you even suspect a case of Lotus. Discipline."

There would be a guard, of course. A Wyrmguard. And Firestrike would come with him, too. He supposed they would be sufficient to overpower her if she was wrong. And it would be nice to have someone along besides the chilly company of the Wyrmguard. "I'll be glad of it," he said. There weren't many of the revolvers left mounted, tonight.

"How is the recovery going, Firestrike?" he asked.

"Seventeen of the guns have been recovered and returned to the Armory of the Thirty," the Wyrmguard said. "Four guard the King. One guards Lieutenant Farnan. The rest are still missing."

Aethal nodded. Tomorrow, the Wyrmguard would be recruited back to full strength. There were enough captured rebels to ensure no shortage of mounts. Aethal had not yet told Malcoor about the new compact. He smiled.

They entered the Dragonmast just as the first fireworks went up. There was a shower of scarlet, and then a strange burst that seemed almost to glow black. *My father must have had something to do with the fireworks, too,* Aethal thought ruefully to himself. But the cheering was in earnest anyway.

They made their way to the staircase and exited along a catwalk, threading their way through the corridors of the Ophidian, through the eight-sided nexus of corridors outside the Red Chamber. Continuing, they left the Ophidian for the Tree-King's Tower, and began climbing stairs.

Farnan was nearly at the top. Aethal gritted his teeth. Apartments at the top of the Tree-King's Tower were an honor, of course, and they were comfortable.

But they were also very difficult to escape from. Aethal knew that, and he suspected Farnan did, too.

Even this high, the fireworks were audible. The glow of the reds and the blues, the purples and the golds threw strange shadows on the staircase where windows gleamed at the end of corridors. The next floor up was Farnan's. Aethal heard a groan. He stopped. The groan was repeated. "Someone seems to have had too much of my father's hospitality," he said aloud. Aethal stepped onto the landing and looked down the hall. Sure enough, a form was slumped against the corridor.

"You there," said Aethal. "Get up. Are you on duty, or lost?" The form did not stir. But two forms at the end of the corridor rose up. One leveled something at Aethal.

Aethal had Crow in his hands, and his reaction was instantaneous. He cocked the hammer and shot from the hip. The man pitched back, bowled over by the heavy slug. Aethal charged, Firestrike close behind. The Wyrmguard fired, and Aethal heard something buzz past his ear. Then there were only running footsteps.

"Go!" he shouted to the Wyrmguard, who took off to the left around the circumference of the tower after the other man. Aethal's eyes began to make sense of what had happened. There was a dead man at his feet, armed with a musket. A very short musket, as if the barrel had been cut down.

There was another volley of fireworks, very near.

Aethal's eyes adjusted further. The dead man was wearing a House Wrackberg uniform. The other man, the groaning man, had died. He had a stab wound deep in his chest. His belt knife was missing. Aethal looked up and realized that Ardyth was still standing on the staircase, mouth open in shock.

"Lady Ardyth! To me!" Aethal bellowed, but it was too late. There was a flurry of madly running footsteps, growing louder, and Ardyth screamed. A knife-wielding figure in grey-and-scarlet lunged past her and dove for the stairwell. A shot rang out, and Firestrike was there. He had run the man around the tower.

"Hold!" shouted Aethal, running to where Ardyth lay. "Are you hurt, milady?" he cried, hardly daring to look.

"No," she gasped, rising shakily to her feet. "He just took one wild swing. Missed."

"He wanted to get away." Aethal looked after him. Another man in a Wrackberg uniform. No. His heart stopped.

"What is it, Aethal?" asked Ardyth.

Aethal looked at Crow in his hands. "It could be nothing," he forced himself to say. "Gambling debt. Soldier's fight. Come on." He started upstairs.

"Shouldn't we follow him?" asked Ardyth.

"Perhaps. But I want to know more." Ardyth and Firestrike followed him upstairs. Flintmaw was waiting by the door.

"Didn't you hear the gunshots?" Ardyth said to the Wyrmguard's passionless face.

Aethal touched her arm. "He was ordered not to leave this post. "What did you hear?"

Flintmaw's voice was level. "I heard three gunshots, Last Sword."

From within the room, Aethal could hear Farnan, shouting. He spoke to Firestrike. "Do not let her in the room. Then to Flintmaw: "Open the door."

The door swung open, and Aethal stood face-to-face with Farnan, who was just picking up a stone vase to slam into the door.

"Aethal!" he cried, his features strangely expressionless. "What are you doing here?"

"Visiting an old friend," Aethal said, forcing his voice level. "As it turns out, with another old friend." He held up Crow.

"You found Crow," Farnan whispered. Then he shrank back. "It's no good. I'm farmed, Aethal. You remember what happened to Harry, with Dragon. Crow isn't my friend anymore."

Aethal tasted anxiety. He'd wondered about that ever since Falk talked to him about Dragon's character. Gun had provided no answer to his question. But Farnan was a very different man than Harry had been. It followed that Crow was a very different Rifle. His face hardened.

"You still know how to shoot, and we need you." Before Farnan could think, Aethal tossed Crow over. Farnan caught it with a look of shock.

Then he looked up. "You shot Crow!" He stared at Aethal in surprise, touched with outrage. Then that was wiped away, and wonder filled his face. "He's talking to me. It's... blurred. Like a whisper in a high wind. But he's talking to me."

Aethal let his breath out. *there is danger in this.* Gun slipped the words into his mind. *crow will bear farnan's burden of hunger. but the burden will not lighten.* No further explanation came forth.

"I had little choice," Aethal said to Farnan. "Here." He whipped out a handkerchief, knotted it, and spilled several bullets into it. Then he unhooked his powder horn. "Load," he ordered, taking Gun off his back.

"Why are you arming me?" said Farnan. "Freeing *me*?" He shook his head "It's likely nothing, but..."

"Last time we dealt with a case of likely nothing, we found a town overrun by Lotus," said Farnan, his voice dead.

Aethal looked at his friend. Farnan's stare was implacable and blank.

"I fear treachery," Aethal admitted.

"I don't, anymore," said Farnan. "Let's go." He looked at Ardyth and the two Wyrmguard. "I remember her," he said. "Why are we taking on Westerend's daughter?"

Aethal felt himself flush, began to babble. She looked into the room. "Is it safe?"

Farnan and Aethal stood out of her way. Seeing that the *yasnuum* was still effective, Aethal nodded to Firestrike, who released Ardyth. She walked past them to a pile of clothes piled on the bed. Aethal recognized them. They were

Farnan's House Wrackberg uniform. Aethal had ordered them made for his friend upon his rediscovery. But Farnan wore simple civilian clothes. Ardyth emerged, carrying the uniform's rapier.

"May I borrow this, Colonel?"

He bowed to her. "With a will, Lady."

"Take point," Aethal ordered Firestrike. "We must get to the King."

They were nearly to the bottom before they met the first patrol.

Firestrike rounded a corner in front of him. Aethal followed, and the four men in Wrackberg colors stepped out right in front of them.

"Stand!" bellowed Aethal. The men turned, raising weapons. Gun and Firestrike spoke at the same instant. The remaining two scrambled for cover. Aethal shouldered Flintmaw aside. "I said 'stand,' you Well-begotten fools! I am the Last Sword of Verlaen and Aethal Paaling, Heir of the Wrackberg!"

Aethal had just enough time to register one of the short muskets shoved around the corner before Firestrike picked him up and hurled him back. The shot ricocheted, and the Wyrmguard staggered.

Then Farnan was past them, screaming a high, banshee wail. He was at the end of the corridor. He turned, discharged Crow into a target on the floor, and then smashed at the man who'd shot at Aethal.

Aethal watched Farnan, then looked at Firestrike. His left shoulder was pierced by the bullet. Blood pumped from the wound, soaking his jacket.

"Last Sword," he said, calmly. "My mount is gravely wounded. I estimate it will lose consciousness in no more than five minutes."

Aethal nodded. "Understood." Farnan was coming back. He was breathing heavily.

"They're your father's uniforms, Aethal. You saw. All four."

"NO!" Aethal screamed once, hammering Gun's butt into the stone wall. But suddenly, the rage was gone. He felt himself go dead inside. Gun's influence, and Aethal was glad of it. The weapon was right. Why should he ever have trusted his father? Horror was just beginning to creep into Ardyth's eyes.

"Here is what we will do," he said, each word coming out as steady and flat as the shots of a Wyrmguard pistol. "We will make for the Ophidian. Farnan, Ardyth, and Firestrike, find the first man of Maednac's Own that you see. If I am no longer with you, have him take you, on Peril of the Well's Rising, to an officer. Have him round up as many men as he can and come to the King's chambers. Tell him the Last Sword believes," he took a breath, "That the Lord Paramount of the Wrackberg is planning to seize the throne. I will be there, with Flintmaw. Any armed man in Wrackberg uniform is to be shot."

Farnan nodded. Ardyth simply stared, but finally, she nodded, too. They set out. The hallway to the Ophidian was deserted. Now, Aethal could hear the difference in the bursts of sound. He looked over at Farnan, who caught his eye and nodded. "Gunshots," he whispered. "Under the fireworks?" Aethal nodded back. *The fireworks. Oh, God-Beyond-The-World, the* wine. Very good wine. He bet the Wrackberg troops had been served a different vintage.

They reached the Red Chamber. Now they heard other sounds. Shouts. And screams. Farnan nodded to Aethal and ducked inside. The huge room was deserted and eerily quiet. Aethal saw him motion for Firestrike and Ardyth to follow him.

"The kitchen door?" Aethal asked. Farnan nodded. The huge and rarely-used kitchen off the Red Chamber did have an outside door for garbage disposal. They might find the soldiers they sought outside. Aethal watched them go, then turned to lead Flintmaw back to the king's private chamber behind the dais.

There was the sound of thunder. Then running feet. Farnan burst back into the antechamber. "Aethal, it's alive with Wrackbergers out there."

Ardyth's eyes were wide with fright. "They saw us!"

Aethal looked around. "Come on, then."

There was a shout. "Stop there!" From the very door Aethal had been hoping to use, three men in scarlet and grey emerged, raising their truncated muskets. Farnan looked up and Aethal saw his smile grow fey.

"Farnan!" he shouted, but Farnan charged up the dais. Crow spoke once, and a man fell, shot through the heart. Aethal cursed and followed. A second man shot wildly. The bullet whizzed past Aethal's head. Then Farnan laid his face open with Crow's bayonet. The man fell, screaming. The third man smiled and raised his gun. Flintmaw's shot took him through the forehead. The Wyrmguard was still at the base of the stairs. "Run!" Aethal cried, as the door from the kitchen burst open, and Wrackberg soldiers poured into the Red Chamber.

The five of them dashed through the king's private parlor and into one of the main halls of the Ophidian. Before them lay the base of the mighty tower, where three staircases converged. Aethal put on a burst of speed and dove to the right of the big, arched opening. When he looked around, he saw that Farnan and Flintmaw were with him, while Ardyth and Firestrike huddled behind the left leg of the arch. Sighting around the door, Aethal fired back at their pursuers. Firestrike, Flintmaw, and Farnan did the same, and men sprawled on the stones.

Before Aethal could speak a word, he was interrupted by a yell from behind him.

Six Wrackberg soldiers leaped down the stairs behind them. Turning to meet the threat, Aethal saw four of them go down as fast as he could quickly count beneath the bullets of the Wyrmguard. Then he and Farnan were fighting hand-to-hand with the remaining two.

Out of the corner of his eye, Aethal saw Firestrike stumble. Reflexively, Ardyth bent to help him. Aethal ducked a sword blow and stabbed, punching through his attacker's ribs.

"The stairs!" yelled Farnan, turning his man "Aethal, get up these stairs and get to the King!" Aethal dashed up the steps.

"Come on!" he cried. Farnan felled his man with a blow, but Ardyth had led Firestrike to the foot of the stairs, out of harm's way.

The leftward stairs.

Running feet. Many running feet. The Wrackberg men in the hallway charged in, and parted Ardyth from Aethal and Farnan like a bloody tide.

Flintmaw fired into them, dropping two. Not fast enough. One ran at Ardyth, raising his musket, not to shoot, but to club her to the ground. She screamed and thrust with her sword. She gasped at the force of his impact and stumbled as he fell, her rapier buried in his gut.

"Milady!" Aethal cried. Ardyth looked up at him and went white. A dozen Wrackberg men faced her and the swaying Firestrike. She might as well have been on one of the moons. Only halfway through reloading, the Wyrmguard fixed his bayonet and backed her up the stairs, and Farnan, fighting to take every step. Then the other Wrackberg soldiers turned to face him and Farnan and Flintmaw. They raised their weapons. "Last Sword, surrender!" said one.

Aethal saw Firestrike, very pale now, knocked back by a shot, and fall, the pistol clattering to the floor. Ardyth watched it skitter at her feet. He had one last vision of Ardyth. She met his eyes. With her lips, she shaped the words, *Save the King!*

Before he could scream denial, she bent, and picked up Firestrike.

Her attackers froze. Aethal heard her fire three times, and then she vanished up the staircase, lost to his sight. "Aethal!" screamed Farnan in his ear. "Run! Now!" They fled up the stairs. A pair of badly-aimed musket balls chased them, and they were up and away.

***

The Ophidian staircase was like a tower reaching out of Hell, and seemed to drag at Aethal's feet in exchange for every step.

They were no longer alone, at least. There had been no Wrackberg patrols so high up in the Ophidian itself. On their way up, they had picked up two officers from Maednac's Own, who had been honored with rooms in the Royal Tower.

They had also picked up a half-dozen young servants armed with everything from spare weapons from the Ophidian's rooms to kitchen knives.

At last, Aethal, Farnan and Flintmaw reached the king's own chambers. Two Wyrmguard were without. Two more would be within. "Treachery," gasped Aethal. "Admit us!" The Wyrmguard, always at full attention, grew even more alert. They burst into the rooms.

They surprised a butler. He backed against the wall, eyes bulging. Aethal went past and into the king's solar, his men following.

King Paitir, Chancellor Pyk, Lord Vaughan Westerend, and Joseth Malcoor were sitting in the king's private parlor. The king was looking relieved, as Aethal had never seen him before. He was just shoving a drink at Lord Vaughan and saying, "...must try this, my Lord, they've outdone themselves."

"You're drunk, your Majesty," Pyk answered, with the first smile on his face Aethal had seen in a long time. "And I do have my own drink." All three men looked round at the entrance of the grim-faced soldiers.

"Treachery, Sire," Aethal got out. Flintmaw was right behind him, and the other two Wyrmguard in the corners of this room came to life as well. "My father. Wrackberg troops. They control the lower levels. Slaughtered your Guard regiment."

For a moment, there was only silence. "What?" the king finally said. "But I just saw him. I invited Lord Wrackberg to join us here personally!"

Malcoor's eyes narrowed. "You did. So where is he? You sent for him half an hour ago."

"Impossible," said Lord Vaughan. "Aethal Paaling, we'd have heard..."

"Fireworks!" shouted Aethal. And watched the awful light begin to dawn in the eyes of the old men. Westerend set his drink down. Paitir nervously ate from the bowl of nuts on the table. Malcoor went to the window.

"Can we..." Lord Vaughan stammered, "Can we retake the Hydraxis? With the Wyrmguard? We have five of them."

Aethal met his eyes and shook his head. "I've already lost one Wyrmguard," he said. His voice stuck. He knew that after his own attempt to betray Aethal and Farnan, Lord Vaughan Westerend looked upon the Wyrmguard as almost invincible. And now his daughter was the slave of a Wyrmguard pistol again. Aethal turned away. "Five is all we have," he whispered, cursing his own stupidity. There were sixteen more Wyrmguard quiescent and useless in the Armory of the Thirty, only a tower away. Sixteen Wyrmguard, to be bound tomorrow. He hadn't wanted to do that tonight, when they were all safe, when they were celebrating. Now, they might as well be on the Dark Continent.

"But even five..." began Lord Vaughan.

"Not a chance." The flat declaration came from the window. Malcoor drew his head in. "Look outside." Aethal, Vaughan, and the king walked to the window, drawn by the flat bleakness in those words. King Paitir simply buried his face in his hands.

Bodies littered the Hydraxis courtyard below. Many lay clothed in orange and red. Many wore commoners' garments, the best they had. No few wore green, black and silver. There were a few in scarlet and grey. Far too few, and most that wore those colors were still on their feet and armed.

"Where is my daughter?" asked Lord Vaughan, voice trembling.

Aethal opened his mouth, but could not make the words come.

A hand gripped his elbow. "Aethal. The King," said Farnan.

The king's hand scrabbled in the empty bowl of nuts he held in his hand. He looked about. "I'm hungry," he said absently. "What can we do, Last Sword? Can we escape? Reach the Army?" He paused. "Why am I so *hungry?*"

Aethal stared at the bowl, and his blood ran cold. He took it from his king's nerveless fingers.

"Did any of the rest of you eat from this bowl?"

"Why in the Well are you talking about that?" snapped Lord Vaughan.

Aethal gave the bowl to Farnan and clasped the king's hands in his own, staring deep into the wide, worried eyes. There was nothing to see there but blue-gray, but that proved nothing as yet. "Wyrmguard," he said. "Bring me the King's Rifle."

"Aethal?" said the king, his voice shaking. "What does this mean?"

"Lord Vaughan, Admiral Malcoor, Uncle Pyk. Answer me now," Aethal said. "Do any of you feel hungry?"

"We just came from a feast, Aethal," began Vaughan.

"No," said Malcoor, his voice hard and flat.

"Joseth, can you tell me what the Last Sword is doing?" Vaughan asked.

Goldhammer brought the king's Rifle. It was a beautiful weapon, shaped from teak and steelwood. Its name was Castlethorn. And it would tell him something, no matter what happened. Taking the barrel in one hand, Aethal held it toward the king. "Your Majesty," he said.

Paitir grasped the stock of the Greater Rifle. "Castle?" he whispered. "He's not... he won't answer." He looked at Aethal. "He won't answer!" Paitir cried.

Aethal stepped back. "The King has been farmed," he said. The words rang out like falling nails in the silent room. Gripping Gun, he cautiously sniffed the bowl in his hands. But there was only the smell of salt.

Then he looked at the drinks. The drink the king had been offering to the others. Just like Lotus-Eaters offered their leaf to any and all... so long as their own supply was secure. The king's glass alone was empty. "No one touch that glass," he said.

A Wyrmguard entered the room. "Last Sword. Your Excellency. There are men without who desire audience. They advance bearing a white flag."

"Who are they?" But Aethal knew before the Wyrmguard spoke.

"Paal Haerling, Lord Paramount of the Wrackberg," said the Wyrmguard, "and Aerhan Paaling."

In his seat, King Paitir lifted his head and stared through the Wyrmguard, through the door. Through the world and into some other place. Some more merciful place. He stared for a long time.

Finally, Aethal whispered, "Cousin Paitir?"

"Show them in," said the king, in a voice like nothing human.

The Wyrmguard answered the door.

In walked Paal Haerling, in his dress uniform of scarlet and gray. Behind him, Aethal's brother walked in. Both had swords and pistols at their belts. They were escorted by Knaad and Stren. They wore masks of red silk over their noses and mouths, and Aethal could smell the perfume from across the room. Paal signaled. Aerhan removed his mask and inhaled, cautiously, then nodded. Paal's expression was solemn. But Aerhan smiled, slowly.

Paal looked over the room. Then he pointed.

The butler bolted. Knaad and Stren were on him in an instant, pinioning his arms. He cried out once before Knaad slammed his head into the stone wall with a sickening crack. Stren held up a bottle, full of a clear, green liquid. It was infused with leaves. In the torchlight, they looked black.

"Lotus liqueur," said Paal, into the silence. The king fell to the floor, mouth gaping.

"In the King's favorite melon brandy," Paal went on. "I only just now discovered Ilferth Simon's plan: a fanatic, slipped into the Ophidian as a butler, sworn to work Simon's will from beyond the grave, and prove the will of God-Beyond-The-World upon Maednac's Line. Have I come too late to save him?"

"No," said Aethal, hearing his own voice from a great distance. "You have come just in time. As you intended." Aethal's hand tightened on Gun, though the weapon was empty. Paal saw.

"I need hardly tell you, I hope, that any sound of violence will trigger a full assault from my men outside. They know the tale, you see."

Aethal could not keep the raw anguish out of his voice, though he tried. "Father," he said, and the word was a curse. *"Why?"*

"Because the opportunity finally arose," said Paal. "The damage to Verlaen has been done, and I will allow no more. Between Ilferth Simon and the constant need to balance Westerend against Skysil, and trying to repair the decisions of your *Majesty,*" Paal bowed sardonically, "or get you to act at all, it is frankly a wonder that even half the Kingdom is left. But I shall preserve it. Unopposed, finally." He fixed Paitir with a stare. "In Breaking, We Build.

"Thirty years, Paitir. Thirty years I have built up Verlaen and watched you indulge your grief, your son, and your fantasies of replacing me. I am not going to watch you hand the keys of the Kingdom to the Skysils and the Westerends so you can wait for them to save it by Wishing in the Well and taking the responsibility from your hands. Rather, I will take it myself." He turned to a guard. "Bring him in."

The guard left and came back with another. Between them, his eyes glazed and his face slack, walked Crown Prince Eraad, armed and dressed in his House uniform. Paitir rose to his knees.

"Paal. Please. Please tell me you haven't."

Paal's face was a mask for all the feeling in it. "No, of course not, Paitir. The Lotus is far too dangerous a weapon to keep." To Paitir, he said, "But when I learned that Ilferth Simon possessed it, and what his plans for it were, I had to do something."

"You knew," said Aethal. "You prepared all of this. You could have stopped it. You *knew!*"

"I couldn't take the chance that Ilferth Simon might have had other fanatics. And I truly didn't know who had the Lotus until I came in, just now. I had to make certain I had both found it and its wielder."

"Are you lying to yourself as well? Or just to us?" asked Aethal.

"I also had to safeguard Maednac's Line," said Paal, ignoring him. "In case the Lotus had spread... further." Aethal heard Pyk's horrified gasp. *But of course, Aethal thought. He planned for that, too. Is he relieved, or disappointed that it only got Paitir?* "Therefore, I dosed Eraad with the *yasnuum,* to keep him safe. I may have overdosed him, but I wanted to make sure that the Prince's passions would not spoil our meeting. He is well aware that his future was in a delicate position, until now. You would have to make some sort of example of him, to placate the Skysils.”

“Indeed, Lord Wrackberg,” Eraad said, flatly.

The king closed his eyes against his son’s blank face. Aethal wished he could, too, but he had to keep alert, for any hint of an opening. His mind raced. *Eraad, what have you done? And what has been done to you?*

“Since I can no longer be the King’s Chancellor,” Paal said, “I shall be the new Lord Regent. As you are known to be farmed, Paitir, you will formally abdicate. The *yasnuum* will keep you alive while Grand Admiral Malcoor leads an expedition to harvest more. Eraad will be crowned king. A stable, wise and cautious king, who has, to the relief of all, cast off the impetuosity of youth, and will learn from his Lord Regent.”

A distant part of Aethal recognized the brilliance of Paal’s coup. But there was a way to thwart it. “Your Majesty,” Aethal said, barely realizing he spoke at all. “Give me but your command and these traitors shall not leave this room alive.” He locked his eyes on Paal’s. “And who then will rule Verlaen? Eraad?”

Paal met his eyes. “If you are determined to throw Verlaen into chaos to satisfy your sense of justice, then by all means, order the Wyrmguard to fire. But you know what will happen: my men will assault, fearing Lotus, and all of us in this room will be killed. Maednac Serpiin will degenerate into a panicked and leaderless civil war while the Lotus advances. Is that what your honor requires of you?”

Aethal’s throat tightened. No command came from the king.

Pyk spoke. “Lord Wrackberg,” he said. “My Lord Falaar will never accept Eraad as his king. Not after Telerat. You’ll make the breach with the Skysils permanent.”

“I think the Skysils will listen to reason,” Paal said. “Especially once I’ve led Eraad through the steps of enough apologies and concessions. But if I am wrong, what does that matter? The Skysils don’t accept Paitir now.”

Paal surveyed the room. "Since everyone in this room has been exposed to Lotus, Discipline requires that you all be confined for a week. At the end of that time, Lord Pyk, I will restore you to your office, if you so desire, as my Chancellor. Admiral Malcoor will leave, as I said before, and Aethal may retain his position as Last Sword, guarding both myself and King Eraad. Aerhan will be appointed Lord Mayor of Maednac Serpiin after his trial, where it will be found that he was the victim of a very clever deception by Major Varth, who slipped Admiral Malcoor into the Winery's secret cells without his knowledge on the orders of Ilferth Simon."

Aethal met his brother's calm, confident smile. "Aerhan threw Malcoor into those cells himself."

"Of course I did, brother," Aerhan said. "Father told me to. Aethal, you really ought to trust him. He does know what he's doing. If you had just kept your mouth shut when he asked you to that morning when you arrived, Ilferth Simon could have been exposed and defeated then. But we couldn't risk the King deciding that he needed a Chancellor who'd survived contact with the Lotus. Malcoor needed to go away. We were always planning to produce him at the right time."

Paal continued. "Lord Westerend will depart for home, his good behavior guaranteed by his daughter's new position." He beckoned. An order was passed, and Ardyth entered, Firestrike clutched in her hand. Lord Vaughan gave out a cry of anguish. Ardyth's face remained cool and unmoved. She was not really there.

A thought struck Aethal. "Firestrike. The King is infected with Lotus, and the Heir is not in his right mind. Will you still obey them?" It was grasping at straws, but he had nothing else to hold to. If his father knew that the Wyrmguard would not obey Eraad, would he reconsider?

For the first time, Aethal saw confusion written in a Wyrmguard's face. "The Discipline requires that we shoot those infected with Lotus," Ardyth's voice said. She looked at Paitir. "The Compact requires that we protect the Imperial

Governor. The Imperial Governor requires that we enforce the Discipline. Last Sword, we are uncertain what to do."

"I know what to do." King Paitir rose like a shattered mountain. His tear-stained face was no longer slack, but set in grim determination. He looked at his former Chancellor. "Thirty years, Paal. I knew you loved the power. But I always thought there was some love for me in that. Or for Verlaen, at least." Deliberately, he looked away. "Eraad." His son fixed him with a blank stare. "I don't know why you came to hate me so. Or how long they will let you live."

"Longer than you, old man," said Eraad. His voice was emotionless as iron. "Why?"

Eraad answered without rage. Like a statue. "You were so weak. And you were always in my way."

Paitir gave Paal a look. "And now a stronger man — your Heir, in fact — will be in your way."

Aethal inhaled, meeting Paitir's eyes. *No.* He understood. *Paal is not in your son's way. Eraad is in his.* Eraad's face only twisted in confusion. "I Wish you would die," he muttered.

"And I Wish you to live," Paitir choked. "In spite of it all. I truly do." He straightened. "I will do as you say, Paal."

"Good, your Majesty." Paal relaxed.

"But I have two things to do, first. Paal Haerling, of House Wrackberg. You have been taken in the act of treason, plotting to kill the King of Verlaen by omission. As King of Verlaen, I appoint myself your judge, and find you guilty."

Paal's head jerked up. *God-Beyond-The-World,* thought Aethal. *The Extreme Sanction!*

"Paitir!" Paal snapped, looking at the Wyrmguard. "Do it, and we all die!"

Paitir met his former Chancellor's eyes with something resembling pity. "I suspend your sentence of death," he said. "But you are personally attainted with treason."

Aethal went numb. Attainted. Title and lands confiscated. *I just inherited. Technically.*

Paal merely smirked. "If anyone ever finds out," he said. "And is believed. Really, Paitir, if the theater is over…"

"I am not finished," Paitir said. "Crown Prince Eraad. You have been accused of treason and murder for disobedience in the face of the enemy at Telerat. I appoint myself your judge, and find you guilty. You are also attainted."

"Paitir, what are you…" Paal began.

"And finally," Paitir rode over him, "I, Paitir, King of Verlaen of the House of Maednac, do in the presence of these assembled, relinquish my crown and my throne to Aethal, Lord Paramount of the House Wrackberg." He took a breath, and looked at Aethal. "Balance him, your Majesty."

Ardyth's arm rose, and Firestrike shot Paitir through the head.

Paal watched open-mouthed as the body hit the floor.

All eyes in the room turned toward Aethal.

Majesty?

The door broke open, and booted feet stormed into the room. Paal was surrounded by soldiers. "Back! Back," he screamed. "It's over. Don't shoot! And get out!"

The soldiers ground to a confused halt, then retreated. The only sound in the room was Paitir's twitching body.

"Paal." Pyk found his voice first. "Paal, let Aethal succeed. Your own son is the new King of Verlaen. Falaar may accept him. He's Skysil blood, too, man!"

"Yes," agreed Malcoor. "The Chancellor has the right of it. The troops will follow him." Lord Vaughan nodded, convulsively, tearing his eyes from Ardyth. "King Aethal will be a man of honor," he said. "The Westerend will accept him."

Paal stared at all of them. He tried to speak, once. Twice. Aethal had never seen him look so stunned. Now was the moment, before Paal could recover.

"I swear by my Gun and my Name," Aethal said, "that I will not confirm Paitir's judgment. You and Aerhan may be Lords of the Wrackberg in all honor, for the rest of your days."

Paal looked at him as though he had never seen Aethal before. Then he smiled thinly.

"Aethal," he said. "I'm sorry. I truly am. Once, I would have done almost anything to place you or your brother on the throne of Verlaen. But you are too much a man of honor for me to believe that I could be safe in your kingdom."

"I just swore you an oath," said Aethal.

"At gunpoint, yes. And how long would that oath hold? Would it hold when Lord Westerend was my father-in-law, and your Uncle Pyk was your Chancellor? When they reminded you, again and again that I was a threat to you? When Admiral Malcoor and the Skysils, and the Westerend all want my head? I have not survived all these long years by trusting to men's oaths, Aethal. I have done it by keeping them in my power. And I, to my lasting regret, have no power over you.

"My offer stands, Aethal. Abdicate. Let Eraad be king, and let us finish this. You cannot prove what Paitir said. Everyone here has good reason to lie for you. If you press this, I would have to have all of you tried on the charge of a conspiracy to usurp the throne."

"The Wyrmguard would tell the truth!" cried Pyk.

Paal snorted. "All six of them. Do you think the people will believe the word of the most fearsome Wellspawn we command? You are their Last Sword. You might be ordering them to lie."

"The Last Sword could never do that," Aethal said automatically.

"But the people will believe you could," said Paal. His voice was almost soothing. "They need to believe it. They need to believe that the person in power has a right to that power. Because they are frightened. You have no support. Now. You will abdicate, Pyk will be Chancellor, and Westerend will return home."

"You have to let my daughter go, Paal," said Westerend. "I've seen her enslaved to those things once before; I'll not see her suffer it again."

Paal shook his head. "I need her hostage to your good behavior, I'm afraid."

Westerend went white. "That you shall never have, so long as my daughter is bound to that monstrosity. King Aethal has *my* support. I will fight you to the death, and expose you and all this affair unless you let her go."

Paal gazed at him. "I see. You would destroy us all." He looked at the Wyrmguard. Then he said, "Aerhan?"

Without changing expression, Aethal's brother drew the pistol from his belt and fired. Lord Vaughan stared down at his shattered chest and fell.

With an inarticulate cry of rage and grief, Malcoor ran to his brother. Aethal turned to Flintmaw as if in a nightmare. "Why didn't you stop him?" he cried.

"We could not risk the life of your Heir, Your Excellency. You have no other."

"Get that away from him!" Aethal shouted. The Wyrmguard took the pistol from Aerhan and held him.

"Now that you have seen the futility of that," said Paal, who held up a hand as his guards burst into the room, "I beg that you will make me shed no more blood today."

Malcoor rose to his feet. "He's gone," the old man said in a small voice. "You killed him." He took a step forward, but before he could take another, Paal's guards and the Wyrmguard were all pointing weapons at each other. With an effort, Malcoor stepped back.

"You cannot kill me without killing the kingdom," Paal said. "And you will not do that."

Malcoor turned to Aethal. In the same voice Aethal had used with Paitir just minutes ago, Malcoor said, "What are your orders? Your Majesty?"

All I have to do is say it, Aethal thought. *And this man will die for me. Because I am the King of Verlaen.* The thought made no sense. *King.* He looked at Paitir. The King was dead. And yet he, Aethal, who had been the King's Last Sword, lived. *It was supposed to be the other way around*, he thought, dazedly. *What shall I do? Die for my people?* Paitir had done that. And nothing good had come of it.

then fight for them.

Gun's thought was ridiculous. He could not fight without dying.

"Firestrike," he said to Ardyth's expressionless face. "Can we fight our way free of Lord Wrackberg's rebels?"

She tilted her head. "No, Your Excellency. We can kill all your enemies in this room, but then we will all die defending you, and you will be killed or taken. None will be able to verify your claim except us alone, and we will be silenced."

Then how can I fight?

Aethal felt Gun drag at his eyes, the way it did in combat when Gun had seen a target he had overlooked. He found himself looking at Malcoor.

And then he understood.

"No, I won't," said Aethal, looking at Paal. "I won't kill the kingdom for you. Wrackberg." His voice seemed to be coming from somewhere outside himself. "But I will kill it unless you give it a chance to live."

"Your meaning?" asked Paal.

"I mean the Expedition to the Well goes forward," said Aethal. "I mean you let us go. Malcoor, Magnei, and anyone else we want. Ships to sail in. And I will go, too. We will leave and sail north. To the Dark Continent."

"To Wish in the Well?" scoffed Aerhan. "You're mad, or you think we are."

"Try me and see," said Aethal. "Brother."

"Out of the question," said Paal. "We will need all the ships and men we have to spare."

Aethal slowly began loading Gun. "You have until I finish this to change your mind," he said, ice in his veins. "But I suggest you consider. If you keep us here, you will have to explain what you are doing with us. Your guards can't watch us always." Powder. Ram. "You can't simply kill us without raising many awkward questions, and finally..." Bullet. Ram. "...there are other Wyrmguard, outside the Hydraxis. I can order them to obey you. Or not." Now he raised the weapon.

"Father," he said, sighting on Paal's head. "If you truly know me, then you know I will do this."

Paal seemed to look inward. "Agreed," he finally said.

"Father," protested Aerhan, "They..."

"Agreed. Aerhan." repeated Paal, in a voice of iron.

Aerhan dropped his eyes.

The negotiations for the Expedition took another hour. Paal would not agree to let them have ships of the Fleet, but all of Westerend's vessels were allowed to go, as many as could make the voyage. Provisions were released, grudgingly. A call for volunteers was permitted. Paal smiled at this demand, and allowed it with good will. *He knows he can get rid of the last of Paitir's loyalists this way.* It was to be published that the king had been farmed and had taken his own life rather than suffer, that King Eraad was to be crowned, and that Lord Vaughan had been killed upon discovering the Church's fanatic assassin, giving his life for his king. Pyk would remain as Chancellor, to try to win back the Skysils to Verlaen. That the post would be ceremonial did not need to be said. Aerhan would serve as Last Sword temporarily. The Wyrmguard would obey Paal and Eraad. Paal would have the Lotus removed from the Westerend with all speed. Ardyth of the Westerend would be confirmed by King Eraad as Lady Paramount, and remain in the capital as a guest. No one would know she was a Wyrmguard.

"She comes with us," Malcoor said, in a voice like death. "Or I don't guide your expedition."

"Impossible," Paal said. "If she goes with you, you will sail to the Twin Fans and raise a rebellion."

Aethal stared at Ardyth, who had — knowingly — given more than her life to try to save the king. Her face was carved of ivory, utterly unconcerned.

"I will not leave her here with you," he growled.

"It will do me no good to allow her to leave," answered Paal. "I will fight you here, first. She is my guarantee that you will leave, and send ships back with the *yasnuum.*"

"Not here," said Malcoor, stepping between them, and putting his hand over Gun's rising barrel. "All the ships you've given us won't hold enough *yasnuum* to stop the Lotus now, you Wellspawned fool,"

"I know that," said Paal. "But it will help. And you'll go there anyway, if only because you can get supplies. Refuse to send back help and you can hurt me. But you hurt Verlaen worse."

In the end, they had to agree. At Aethal's orders, Firestrike signed the orders to Captain Guilorum and the rest of his ships in the hand of Lady Westerend. Finally, it was over.

Malcoor whispered to Aethal. "There really isn't much chance we can succeed anyway. You do know that? Best to have things clear from the outset." Aethal nodded.

"But we must do what we can."

Then Paal said, "My men will escort you to the docks. Your belongings and provisions will be delivered. I need hardly say that it will be death for you to leave the docks before your launch?"

Aethal nodded. Malcoor and Farnan formed up behind him. "Flintmaw," he said. "You are with me." The Wyrmguard followed at his side.

"Just a moment!" cried Aerhan. "The Wyrmguard were to remain here! Where are you going?"

Flintmaw turned on Aerhan. "It was agreed under the Compact," he said. "I go to the Well."

"What compact?" demanded Aerhan.

"A new one," said Aethal. "The iron book in your quarters will explain the first one. I made this one just yesterday."

"You are not Last Sword!" shouted Aerhan.

"No," said Aethal. "I am the King of Verlaen."

"You abdicated!" Aerhan cried.

"Actually, I didn't," said Aethal. "I ordered the Wyrmguard to obey Eraad. I agreed Eraad would be crowned. But I never agreed to abdicate."

Aerhan looked at Paal. Paal looked as though he had bitten into something sour. "That can be easily remedied. Abdicate, Aethal."

Aethal raised Gun. "No."

"Aethal, I cannot let you remain King."

"You have the power, Wrackberg," said Aethal. "But I have the duty. You won't fight me for that. Not when it means losing everything. I know you too well for that. Unfortunately."

Paal sighed. "Go," he said, finally.

"Wyrmguard! Stop him!" ordered Aerhan.

It was Firestrike who answered, with Ardyth's voice. "The Last Sword may not order us to interfere with the King," she said. "You may not violate the Compact." Her pistol stayed by her side as though nailed there.

"Give me that sword," he demanded. Aethal didn't move, but looked at Paal.

"Make him give me the Last Sword!" shouted Aerhan, red in the face.

"The Last Sword is given or withheld by the Imperial Governor," said Ardyth. "And he is leaving for the Well. Your place is to go with him."

Looking horrified, Aerhan retreated. Aethal, Malcoor, Farnan and Flintmaw walked out of the Hydraxis and toward the docks. The war was over. Verlaen was lost.

Chapter Twelve

73rd of Spring, 312 Exodus

"He's not coming aboard my ship, and that's final," said Captain Guilorum, looking at Farnan.

The sky was whitening with the promise of dawn. Gulls cried and wheeled. At the sides of the *Lasses' Kiss,* men sweated and wrestled provisions aboard. Aethal stared hard into the captain's face. It was unmoved: "I'll dive in the Well, rather."

"Sire, be reasonable," said Malcoor. "Colonel Farnan may have been a fine soldier once, but he's a greeneater now. He's a danger to the ship and to all of us."

"Is he?" Aethal asked, patience fast running out. "The *yasnuum* will keep him from endangering us. We have enough to get to our first destination. There is no place for Lotus to grow except in him, and it won't grow while he's taking it. He can't feed himself Lotus while we're on board. There won't be any. Right?"

Malcoor nodded, face darkening. Three men were searching through every container before it was brought on board.

Farnan touched Aethal's shoulder. "It's as they say," he whispered, the green thread jumping in his eye. "I'm done. You should leave me. Or better yet, make a quick end to it, like you did with Harry."

Aethal drew breath. "Listen now and listen well. I am your King. I did not seek that duty, but it has fallen to me. That duty is to rule you, and it begins now.

As of this moment, this Fleet is my Kingdom. From this quayside to the Well itself. And Colonel Farnan is coming with us. Should I fall, Admiral Malcoor will command this mission. Then Farnan. Then you, Captain Guilorum."

The captain stared at him hard. "This is my ship, Sire, and I command it!"

"But it is *my* expedition, Captain. At sea, you command. No man doubts it. But we begin on land and we end on land. And that is my duty. By my Word."

He lowered his voice. "Your lord was killed by treachery. Your Lady commands you to follow me. You saw her orders. I am your only hope of vengeance, or of ever seeing home again. And as a practical matter, Captain, Farnan is ideally placed to be our scout in the Lotus-infested places of the world. He cannot be more farmed than he is. Which of your men would you rather place in that danger?"

Guilorum glared at Farnan. "He stays in his cabin then!" he spat.

"Unless I have need of him," said Aethal. "And I will have need of him. So will you. Mr. Farnan has stayed true through trials you could not guess at. Pray you never have to." Guilorum's mouth worked. Then he stalked away.

Aethal turned to Farnan. "I need you, Farnan. We need you. You're not done. Not until you're dead."

A mix of emotions swept across Farnan's face, but what won out was a watery smile. "Thank you, Aethal."

Malcoor lowered his voice even as Farnan went below. "You've just given our captain an excellent motivation to murder us all in our beds. You have a plan to prevent that?"

Aethal replied, "Yes. Before tonight, all of these men will know what my father did to their homeland."

Now Aethal could greet the solemn line of black-robed men and women that stood by the quayside. They were the only honor guard the Expedition would have. Conversainte Karel stepped forward. The only mark of her rank she bore was an aluminum Single Moon hanging from a chain about her neck.

Otherwise, she was the old monk she had always been. She motioned, and Magnei came forward, trailed by two Guardians bearing a chest.

"You will have my prayers, Seeker," said Karel. "How effective those will be, I do not know. But you will also have our books. All we could find about the Well, the Lotus, and the Dark Continent. You are taking with you the best of us."

Aethal bowed before her. "Thank you."

"I would that we could do more... Sire." Aethal raised an eyebrow. The Guardians had their own ways of discovering things. But he had known that since speaking with Cledan. He wished the old man had lived.

"You are needed here, Lord Warden."

Karel shook her head. "I cannot be the Conversainte of the Church and lead our order. There is a reason we have separated those offices. But the new Lady Warden would speak with you." He gestured to a tall, cloaked Guardian who threw back her cloak.

Kynthia Skysil approached Aethal, and tears shone in her eyes. She was much as Aethal had last remembered her: blonde hair fastened in a long braid, with deep blue eyes, and a faintly sorrowful face that was a bit more lined since Aethal had seen her.

"Mother," he said. No other words would come.

"Aethal." She took his hands in hers.

"I was..." he stammered. "I was worried. That you had been killed. In the fight."

"No," she said, dropping her eyes. "I was in no danger. Not of that, at least. You see, I was in the Temple. I have been for a very long time."

Aethal hesitated. "I remember Ilferth Simon said to me that if I wanted to see you, I should speak to him. Is that what he meant?" She nodded. "But why were you there?"

"I was betraying the Guardians to the Church. At least that is what Ilferth Simon thought. I helped him to use the Wellspawn he preached against. I was

Lord Warden Cledan's spy inside the Church. And…" She bit her lip, then said, "There must be nothing but truth between us. I was your father's spy, too."

Aethal swayed. "You helped him? But why?"

"Because there was need," his mother said simply. "You saw what Ilferth Simon was capable of. So did your father. I was uniquely positioned. Simon believed that I could not possibly be one of your father's agents. Because of our divorce. Because of your uncle's death.

"I was the one who told your father of the Lotus. And of Ilferth Simon's spy-stones. If I had been braver, or better, then I might have stolen one and had proof, but he guarded them as closely as he did his Lotus pits. And I never discovered those. I am sorry, Aethal. More than anything, I want you to know that. I owed you so much more than I gave. Because there was need. Because a Guardian's oath before God-Beyond-The World is to fight Wellspawn. Not men. Not even your father."

"You did not know what he would do," Aethal said. *I certainly didn't.*

"Aethal," said his mother. "I didn't live with your father fifteen years and not know what he was capable of. But I had to choose between him, and Simon. I hoped that I was wrong. But if I had to choose again. I would not change my choice. I cannot ask your forgiveness. I only wanted to confess to you, before we are parted, what I had done. Go, with the blessing of God."

Aethal dropped his mother's hands. "If it is in the name of God, Beyond-The-World or no," he said, throat aching with revulsion, "that you and Ilferth Simon have done these things, then I hope I may never hear His name again, any more than I may hear Lord Wrackberg's, who did them in his own name. He is not my father."

"But I am your mother, Aethal. Regardless of my unfitness for it. Regardless of my broken oaths, I am that. And I am very proud of you. My King." She bowed to him, and stepped back. "I Wish you success." She replaced the cowl over her face.

Aethal's voice choked. "And I Wish you nothing." Was it true? He himself did not know. He had found his mother, and lost her. The Guardians bowed, and withdrew.

Suddenly, there was commotion on the quayside. A Wrackberg officer stepped forward, leading a coffle of prisoners. "Crew for the Expedition!" he called.

Aethal walked down the plank. "What are these for...?" he trailed off. The third man in the coffle, giving no sign of recognition, was Sergeant Bedar Falk.

"For whatever you want, milo... that is, sir," said the Wrackberger, having the grace to look embarrassed. "Lord Wrackberg says that they have volunteered. Like the rest of you."

Meaning he'll shoot any you leave behind, thought Aethal. *Very well.*

"Volunteers?" asked Aethal, softly. Now he looked them over, Aethal recognized some faces. They were too young, and too old. The faces of men he had led against Ilferth Simon and his rebels. The officer nodded.

"Then these are men of honor!" Aethal shouted. "Why are they chained like criminals? Free them! Now!" The Wrackbergers quailed and leapt to obey. The young officer ducked, but Aethal caught him by the hair.

"Where are these men's weapons?" he demanded.

"I don't... gasped the officer, "don't..."

"They should have short swords, these men. At least half of them. They are Swords of Verlaen. If you do not give them back the honor you have stolen, I will have you shot! Understood?" The young lieutenant nodded and scampered away, terrified. Aethal wondered if the man would realize that Aethal's authority ended on the quayside. He doubted it. But it was worth it just to see the rise in the prisoners' chests.

"I'm proud of you men for volunteering," said Aethal, with a wry smile. "Get aboard and to work. Sergeant," said Aethal, as the man walked past.

"Yes, sir," said Falk, expressionless as ever.

Aethal groped for words, as he always did in the old non-com's presence. "I'm sorry you're here. But I'm glad to have you."

"Like the man said. We volunteered." Falk looked up the ramp. "Is it true, sir? Does Admiral Malcoor command this expedition?"

"*I* command it, Sergeant."

Falk looked at him. "Good. You can have this, then, sir." From under his tunic, he took a tiny flintlock pistol, and pressed it into Aethal's hands. Then he walked up the gangplank and began giving orders. Aethal shook his head and put the pistol in his belt.

***

The sun was cresting Verlaen Basin by the time the last crate was taken aboard, inspected, and stowed. Aethal stood on the quay under the gazes of his father's bored soldiers. Malcoor approached him.

"Your father's provisions are about like we feared. Few fresh fruits or vegetables. Not enough of anything. We'll have to trade at a Tidetown before we ever sail for the Empire's bones, let alone the Dark Continent."

"As you recommend," Aethal said.

The *Lasses' Kiss* was ready to go. But Aethal had learned from Captain Guilorum that this was only the cover name of the ship, the name of her merchant persona.

"What's her real name?" Aethal had asked.

"Malcoor's Revenge," Guilorum had answered.

"Subtle."

But that would not do, either. Aethal had asked Magnei for a name. A fitting name. Aethal turned to the man. "Do the honors," he said.

Magnei opened the wineskin and let the red liquid pour onto the sides of the ship. "I christen thee, *Phoenixborn*."

"Cast off," Aethal ordered, his eyes wet. *Well, what sort of man doesn't weep at the death of friends. The Phoenix Lancers are dead, and those who survived will never wear those colors again.* His face grew grim. *But then the flight of the phoenix always began with a death.* The three of them marched up the gangplank, and the ropes were loosened. The *Phoenixborn* and her fleet began to tack out to sea.

Aethal looked inland, to the statue of Maednac, his hand outstretched, and he seemed to be pushing them out into the bay. The sun turned the brass into liquid gold, and he looked a cheap ornament for the green hill on which the Hydraxis stood, alabaster in the dawn. Smoke still hung over the great palace like a haze. For the first time, Aethal felt it as an oppression, an evil instead of a great strength. It looked smaller. And he bowed his head to think of Ardyth, who was yet inside. *Forgive me,* he thought, holding tight to the name of the ship. *It is a promise,* he thought. *A promise to fulfill.*

A hand fell on his shoulder and he whirled. Malcoor was there. "Don't look back at the beginning of the voyage, lad. It's bad luck. Come away." His eyes were serious, but his voice was gentle.

Malcoor walked him to the starboard rail. The Wrackberg swelled at the mouth of Maednac's Bay. It looked like a canker, rising in its rotting, softened angles. Aethal tried to see the shapes of ships within the low mound, but as he had all his life, he failed. The sunken ships had melded and fused, and dirt and moss had caked them together in a low, round hillock, rising out of the sea. Aethal could now see a few of the old cannon that had laid them there on the shore, rusted and useless as the targets they had fired upon, so long ago. There were even a few stunted trees reaching hopeless limbs to the sky. Aethal remembered swimming from shore to the Wrackberg and back, so long ago.

Above, far above on the cliffs that extended their crescent around the bay, stood the real power of the Wrackberg. Twin towers rising a hundred feet above the *Phoenixborn* and her crew, bristling with iron cannon looking out to sea. One last glance back. Maednac Serpiin, city on a hill, and the Hydraxis thrusting up from a sea of grass. The smoke made the hill look darker than it was, a vision of the Lotus triumphant. Aethal shuddered and turned away.

They were fully in the shadow of the Wrackberg cliffs now. The gates of the kingdom, in his father's hands. Aethal felt a surge of fury. *I will break you if I can,* he vowed.

Then they were past the Wrackberg, past his father's towers. *I have left my home a hundred times, Aethal thought. But never by this road. Never by sea.* It was exile beyond imagining. The Serpiin Mountains stretched away to the west, an impenetrable sea wall. Captain Guilorum gave the order to turn. The sails flapped in the breeze, and the wind picked up. They tacked and set sail.

Aethal turned from Verlaen, from the last country of men on earth, to the bows of the *Phoenixborn,* and the sea. She was behind him. If she was to be saved, her only hope lay in the seas, and beyond them, in the most forgotten and darkest places of the world. In the Well.

To Be Continued...

Acknowledgements

This book has been in the works since before I got married, and so I would be remiss not to thank my wife, Katie, for offering support and encouragement while I struggled with it. I would also like to thank Ben Pittman and Ralph Seibel who were the first people to read it twice voluntarily.

Thanks to J.F. Holmes and Cannon Publishing for taking a chance on this monster and showing me that sometimes it's best to chop a monstrously-long novel in half. Others who deserve credit include Jim C. Hines, who saw the most awful of awful first drafts and gave valuable advice. Also to Kim Wiggans, Felix Savage, and a host of others, my most heartfelt thanks.

Finally, a huge appreciation to Michael Morton and Bill Erwin, without whom this work would be a mass of inconsistencies, both story wise and grammatically. No novel comes into being without excellent editors, and I am grateful for their hard work.

PLEASE RATE AND REVIEW THIS BOOK ON AMAZON!

About the Author

For the next book in this series, follow G. Scott Huggins on Amazon!

G. Scott Huggins grew up in Wichita, Kansas and now lives in Wisconsin. At a young age, he fell in love with the worlds of Pern, Tran-Ky-Ky, We Made It, and many more. He studied all around the world, and speaks both German and Russian. He is a graduate of the Clarion Writing Workshop (1997) and sold his first story in 1999.

When he is not writing science-fiction and fantasy, Huggins teaches history. With his wife, he is in the process of raising children and tolerating cats. His favorite authors include G.K. Chesterton, Dan Simmons, C.S. Lewis, Lois McMaster Bujold, Larry Niven, and Terry Pratchett.

More from Cannon Publishing

Join the Crew!

Sign up for our newsletter for the latest news on new releases and more.

Follow our authors at their Amazon Pages!

Shane Gries (Dragon Finalist)

Lucas Marcum

Al Hagan

James Copley

Jason Kyle

G. Scott Huggins

Michael Morton

Charles Hackney

Jon LaForce

Jason Weiser

Kal Spriggs

Brian Gifford

Charli Cox

Dan Kemp

Jonathan Shuerger

J.R. Wise

More Books from Cannon Publishing

Irregular Scout Team One

In July of 2016 a plague swept the world, and the civilization collapsed and fell. For a lone National Guard sergeant, a veteran of the wars overseas who had settled down to a new life, the nightmare began on a hot summer evening at the barricades. Orders and chaos, gunfire and being overrun, his unit dwindles away in the face of the infected. Months later, living in the ruins, the thud of helicopter rotors followed by a crash and the rescue of a downed pilot leads Sergeant First Class Nick Agostine back into the arms of the US military. From his experience comes the idea of teams, military and civilians experienced in dealing with the undead and barbarism of the wilds. The first Irregular Scout Team leads the way for Task Force Liberty to advance down the Mohawk Valley in Upstate NY, making contact with survivors and clearing out the infected with stealth and firepower.

Volume 1

Volume 2

Volume 3: Civil War

Volume 4: Bad Company

The Line

When the world descends into chaos and anarchy with an unbelievably swift plague, turning victims into ravenous maniacs, the soldiers of America's storied 1st Infantry are asked to hold the line. From the brutal streets of urban combat to the bloodied, desperate defense on the plains of Kansas, they fight a war against an unrelenting enemy who used to be their fellow citizens. As civilization falls, can they hold the line?

The Thin Dead Line
Dead Storm Rising
The Big Dead One

Fallen Empire

What's a soldier to do when the war is over? When he's only known conflict his whole life? Since time immemorial the solution has been to find another war, this time for pay. Whoever has the credits and wins the high bid gets the experienced fighter. Sometimes, though, the credits aren't enough to cover the price. Empires rise, but Empires also fall. The Terran Union has spent five centuries under the control of the alien Grausians, like a barbarian tribe under the thumb of Rome. Now, after almost two decades of civil war and succession struggles, the formerly subject races have settled back in their ancient territories to lick their wounds and re-arm, leaving hundreds of settled planets to exist in a political vacuum. Into that space steps the free companies, mercenary units that fight for gold, honor, power and glory. Veterans who can't get the wars out of their souls, new recruits looking for adventure, corporations with their own agenda. Join us in a 27th Century that echoes history.

The Irish Brigade

Overrun

Silent Violence

Doom Company

Athenaeum, Inc

The Professor has problems, and not just what decades of soldiering did to his back and his knees. His boss just died, leaving him as CEO of the extremely discreet intelligence contractor Athenaeum, Incorporated. His old buddy the Operations Director is a highly skilled Army Ranger veteran but his finance chief is slightly unhinged and spends her money on highly inappropriate work outfits. The surviving old men on the Board of Directors are stuck in the 1970s. Running Athenaeum out of an old Cold War bunker and keeping their roster of experts together is expensive, but the government contracts are drying up or going to bigger, flashier corporate players.

Door Number Three

Doubling Down

Off World

When nuclear war erupts on Earth, the American colony in the Alpha Centauri system is left stranded. As the new day dawns, a furious attack by the native inhabitants threatens to overwhelm the colony's defenses. It's left to the thin red line of the US Army's 9th Regiment to stem the tide and ensure humanity's survival in this harsh new world. From two time Dragon Finalist and author of the best selling series "Irregular Scout Team One" and "Invasion" comes a new tale that tells of the struggle for survival on a brutal planet.

Offworld: Ragnarok

Offworld: Expeditions

Cannon Fodder: Tales From the Gun Crew

Fifteen stories from Cannon Publishing Authors, each taking from the universes of their novels to bring you perspectives and deepen their world. From 27th century mercenaries fighting on distant planets and young soldiers riding with Arthur to defeat Saxon hordes, to enchanted weapons dealing damage in hands of Fae, we bring you the best of Science Fiction and Fantasy!

Valkyrie

Humanity engages in a desperate struggle with an alien species for this side of the Orion Arm. Space ships die in instantaneous bursts of light and turn into vapor, but on the ground Marines scream and lie wounded in the mud and blood, praying for the Valkyries to come save them. They aren't wishing for death and a Nordic goddess to take them to Valhalla, the wounded are praying for the men and women of the '348th Field Hospital MEDEVAC to dive through fire and hell to come save them. Because they know that ...Valkyries never die!

Valkyrie

Valkyrie: Rebellion

Valkyrie: Attrition

High Caliber Awards

The Cannon High Caliber Awards are an annual contest for new writers. In it we ask them to submit a novella length story of Science Fiction, Military or Fantasy genre to challenge their skills.

2024

2025

The Wishkiller Saga

While on patrol Captain Aethal Paaling discovers evidence that an ancient terror has reached the rich soil of his home: the Lotus, a prolific growth whose addictive leaves devour their victims from within turning their hosts into horrible, terrifyingly violent mockeries of humanity. Created at the dawn of history by the twisted power of a godly relic called the Well, the return of the Lotus may be a harbinger of even more horrors to come. Carrying the fatal news to the capital, Aethal discovers that even in the face of death itself, the Lords Paramount of Verlaen will fight to keep their secrets and their power. With only the guidance of his legendary Greater Rifle and the aid of the Pheonix Lancers, the soldier must find his way through the halls of a forgotten holy order and into deep dens of crime seeking answers. He must find the truth as quickly as he can, because the Lotus may have already taken root among those he loves… and fighting it may cost him everything, including his soul.

A Cold and Mortal Spring

When nine out of ten people in the world have died in a brutal plague, what do those who remain do to pick up the pieces? Does the creed, "Duty, Honor, Country" have a place any more if there's no country left? On his way across the devastated remains of Texas, Marine Corps veteran and survivor Eric Marten rescues a young woman from a vicious attack by men who have turned into savages. As Dani slowly learns to trust him, they try to stay alive in the deathlands that America has become, using all their wits to survive a post-apocalyptic nightmare.

90% Death Rate: A Post Apocalyptic Thriller
Angel of Death: A Post Apocalyptic Thriller
The Bloody Princess: A Post Apocalyptic Thriller

Hell Train

A single train carries what might be the last vestige of civilization through a hellish nightmare. A few hundred alive out of millions, lights going out all across what was once America as the possessed arose from the dead and murdered the living. A few hundred survivors travel across the country in an armored train, seeking some place to shelter in a fallen world. All that remains is a dystopian nightmare marked by rains of blood, impossible horrors, and portals to Hell opening in the skies.US Army Captain Jack Zamora is responsible for their safety, a self-imposed burden that wears on him every day. Fighting off undead, protecting the survivors, keeping the train running and supplied as his team desperately plans their next moves. Starvation and disease threaten. but it gets worse, because the ancient gods have sent their emissaries, horrific beings of myth and legend that walk the Earth. Things that can drain a man's very life essence or even that of an entire city.

Hell Train: All Aboard

Sometimes a hero isn't what you expect, and the one you need comes from the castaways of society. Nearly broken and at the end of his rope, former decorated scout pilot and prisoner of war, Red has finally accepted the inevitable. He and his kin have no future in the Human Confederation of Worlds, being gene mods and barely human themselves. With the help of his friend he flees Terra for adventure and fortune out in the reaches of the galaxy. Along the way he's dragged back into conflict that calls on all his piloting skills and he learns the deeper meaning of Kin, as his crew becomes his family.

Path to Freedom: The Path, Book One

More than a decade after the Confederated Earth Forces were defeated, their commanding general, a boyhood protegee, lives in exile and disgrace. His life on an isolated farm is forever changed when two strangers show up at his homestead, and the war comes crashing back down on him. The problem though, remains the same. How do you fight an enemy that is technologically superior and holds the high ground?

Invasion: Resistance

Invasion: Day of Battle

Invasion: Total War

The military experience is timeless, and echoes down from our past and into our future. Along the way, not everything is as it seems. Thirteen stories from established and new writers in the field of Military Science Fiction and Military Fantasy bring you tales of the terrors of combat and the even greater fear of the unknown in Cannon Publishing's first Bi-Annual Military Anthology.

Fifteen classic Science Fiction stories from both masters of the craft and up and coming new writers! A tyrannical United Nations pulls the strings of its colony worlds, ruling with an iron fist. Corporate interests take precedence, and brushfire rebellions smolder on the edges. One system, home to the only alien species yet discovered, with human allies throws off the yoke and calls itself Independence.

MECHA

Feedback from the slight pressure of a hand closing sends a powerful mechanical arm smashing into an opponent. A neural link hurls blustering plasma fire from your suit's shoulder mounted cannon. Your reactor levels scream with overload as return fire smashes into your armor, and damage alarms wail while you hurl your twenty ton body sideways for cover. You're a Mecha, a mechanical fighting machine with a human pilot. The guy that the infantry curse at in training and pray for in combat. The machine that the last hopes of your people ride on. The construct that strikes fear deep into alien hearts as they hear your turbines power up. The one able to pass through hell and come out the other side victorious, or die trying.

In the near future, massive empires rule the stars, and west of the Reach, they are battling for control of new systems. In the no-mans land between the front lines, Captain Nate Meric and the crew of the privateer Lexington fight for prize money, and loyalty to their ship and their friends. Beneath it all, though, runs a hidden dream. To see America restored, and take her rightful place among the stars.

Brian Corel, former slave, gladiator, ex-fiance to an Empress, exiled Captain of the Taland Royal Guard and now owner of the frigate *Widowmaker,* does the best he can to balance the lives of his crew with his own desire to live life as a free man. Skirting the border between being a privateer and an outright pirate, Corel stumbles into a war with a religious cult intent on corrupting the kingdom of an old friend and has to set things right while grieving over his lost love. Along the way he signs a dragon into his crew and has to risk everything to rescue his brother from the grasp of a demon that has destroyed an entire continent.

Chosen by the Sword

There are some things a PhD doesn't prepare you for, like running two feet of steel through the guts of a flesh-eating monster straight out of a nightmare, while ducking razor sharp claws. Or having the sword critique your fighting style while you do it. Dave Howard had a problem. Last week, he was out looking for a teaching job in the middle of a wrecked job market. This week he was neck deep in green blood and hellfire. Dragged into it by the very sword, his grandfathers' mysterious possessed blade, that was now walking him through hacking up a ghoul without getting his own head cut off. This wasn't exactly what he had gone to school for, and the University he had just taken a job with seemed to be anything BUT an academic institution. More like some kind of monster hunting bunch of weirdo nerds. Maybe his degree in Personality Psychology might be useful there, at least. The fighting though ... as he dodged another swipe of claws and awkwardly tried to follow the instructions the sword was screaming at him, he shot back at it, "Hell, I'm Canadian! Swordplay isn't in my cultural DNA!"

Beyond the Wall: A Novel of Post-Roman Britain

The legions are but a memory, the glory of Rome only a shadow of crumbling ruins and broken walls. A darkening tide of barbarism was washing across Britain's shores and the lights of civilization were slowly flickering out into darkness, only kept burning by the legendary Red Dragons cavalry unit. Led by their Tribune, Arthur, who serves no kingdom but goes where the fight is hardest and most crucial, they wage desperate battles to keep back the tide. The Red Dragons ride the length of Britannia to fight the invading Saxons, Scoti and Picts, wherever they show, from across the seas or down from the Highlands. At sixteen years old Peredur of Gwynedd has listened all his life to the stories of his father Pelinor fighting with Ambrosius Aurelianus. When word comes that his older brother has been slain in battle with the Saxons, his desire for revenge leads him to follow in his father's footsteps as a warrior, becoming a cavalryman with the Red Dragons. Along the way he may either find himself a warrior and leader worthy of Arthur or be left lying forgotten in the dust of history.

Two souls collide in the middle of a deadly war.

Sergeant Sylvie Lyons of Her Majesty's Royal Engineers wishes she'd listened to her grandda's advice and stayed away from the military.

USMC Sergeant Hondo Cassidy wants nothing more in life than being a Marine and fighting. Hondo and Sylvie find themselves thrown together when his artillerymen are assigned to provide security for her engineers deep in the desert of Afghanistan.. Amidst death, destruction, cultural misunderstanding and the inevitable that happens when you mix an all male unit of Marines with an engineer unit that is mostly female, Sylvie and Hondo find in each other a reason to live. That is, if they can survive.

Semper Die

The dead rose expecting a feast. What they got was a firefight.

Sergeant Alex Slaughter and the Marines of Alpha Squad were on a routine training exercise near Quantico when everything went silent. No comms. No command. No clue.

What they find when they return to base is worse than anything they trained for: a bioweapon has unleashed a zombie virus that has shattered civilization, and now they must survive the Collapse.

But as the squad pushes deeper into hostile territory—through the death-choked streets of Arlington and into the rot-stained corridors beneath D.C.—they discover that the undead aren't the only threat. Desperate survivors, rogue military units, and darker truths buried beneath the weight of secrecy will test their loyalty, their mission, and their very humanity.

Written by USMC veteran Jonathan Shuerger and set in J.F. Holmes's brutal and unrelenting Irregular Scout Team One universe, Semper Die delivers pulse-pounding action, authentic military detail, and a terrifying vision of what happens when duty and apocalypse collide.

Lock. Load. Semper Fi. Semper Die.

More From the Fae Wars

Get the full series!

Onslaught

What would you do if America and the world were invaded tomorrow by a relentless and brutal enemy? In an alternate 2015, a US Army Special Forces Team, part of the legendary black ops unit "Delta", is in midtown Manhattan to take out a Chinese spy and his handlers, sending a message short of outright conflict. All goes smoothly until they find themselves in a full blown shooting war through the canyons of the City. Portals from another world have opened in Central Park, making a way for figures out of historical nightmare to invade. The Fae, creatures banished from Earth thousands of years ago and now only part of our legends, have returned with Dragon fire, spell and sword to conquer and take revenge. The first volume of The Fae Wars covers Team Three, G squadron, Special Forces Detachment (Delta) as they fight their way off Manhattan and then join the defense of the refugees as the Fae assault the bridges. The fabled 69th Infantry puts up an epic fight against superior weaponry and then the war descends into the asymmetric hell that the Delta Operators know so well. Along the way they find new allies and old powers that come to their aid.

The Fall

For the first time in two hundred years an enemy has stepped foot on American soil and war has come to our cities. The US military is rocked back on its heels and driven into a fighting retreat as each defense line falls. The foe is unstoppable and ... Fae. Creatures from a legendary past who have come to reclaim the Earth in the name of magic and revenge. In the hills of Pennsylvania a ragtag, devastated army prepares to make a last stand against dragon fire capable of melting an Abrams tank and wizardry that stops fifth generation fighter jets in mid-air. Inevitably it comes down to shining steel verses human will, and Sergeant Oliva Acevedo transforms from a hospital clerk to a hardened fighter. Volume Two of the best selling "Fae Wars" follows the fighting retreat of the US Army as the Fae establish control of a shattered America.

Futures Past

Two thousand years ago the Fae were banished from Earth and they've spent that time plotting return and revenge. When their portals open around the world and start crushing the human's military with spell encased steel and dragon fire, it becomes a massive struggle between technology and magic. When the Fae Invasion hammers the West Coast, Captain James Powers and his California Army National Guard artillery battery is caught on its way home from Annual Training. In a running battle the unit is smashed by combat with orcs and elves, leaving their commander struggling to keep his people together and alive. Along the way a dying priest with a strange ability to see the future manipulates people and events to bring Captain Powers to his true calling as a Seer. As they run and fight, the humans gain new allies, Fea tinkerers who love all things mechanical and hate the elves. With their help they begin to take the war to the enemy in a brutal mayhem of ambush and assassination. Book Three of the Fae Wars series following the bestselling "Onslaught" (set in NY City) and "The Fall" (Pennsylvania)

Tales From the Occupation: A Fae Wars Anthology

Wars end, enemies are defeated and territories are conquered and the combatants have to return to a life changed. America and the rest of humanity have fallen to the Fae, ancient mortal enemies of mankind. After building their strength for two thousand years, the Elves have claimed their vengeance and now rule Earth with an iron fist and dragon fire. Down but not out, a human resistance is building, but first daily life needs to be lived. An anthology of stories exploring life during the Occupation in the best-selling Fae Wars universe.

Insurgent

Wars come and wars go. Eventually even the most belligerent of combatants will arrive at some kind of living arrangement, either through exhaustion or slaughter. Kill enough, down to the last child, and there will be no more war ... until the next one, of course.

In August 2015, the war started, portals opening up between their world and ours, allowing the Fae to return to our (or their) home world in blood, fire and magic. Conventional forces fought back as well as they could, but the invasion had been planned to hit us in the middle of our civilization. America's military was scattered overseas or concentrated in large bases that were quickly overwhelmed by forces that were dropped right in the middle of their units. The fighting was brutal and horrific, magic overwhelming technology. It took six weeks, and the President surrendered to spare the civilian population. A puppet government was put in place and the Fae started to divide the conquered lands into principalities run by their Great Houses, slowly turning America into a land of feudal slavery. Thing is, though, the Fae had lived in their exile for thousands of years, fighting wars among themselves and against various races that populated their new home. Pitched battles where there was a clear-cut winner and loser. They had never fought an insurgency and had no idea how bloody it could get. Major David Kincaid. United States Army 1st Special Forces Operational Detachment–Delta, soldier of a defeated but unbroken nation, was going to show them. If, that is, he can keep the faith. The follow up novel to the bestselling "Fae Wars: Onslaught" by J.F. Holmes.

Ghost

There are wars, and then there's War. The all-encompassing thing that is fought on many levels, and with many kinds of weapons, many kinds of warriors. Even ghosts.

Alex was no one, a man just trying to get by at his paperwork job at the new Homeland Security. A man grieving for his wife, who had died in the Invasion. Someone just trying to keep his head down while the elves appointed him to do the paperwork of putting their boots on the necks of a conquered American people. Thing is, even a nobody paper shuffling clerk has a weapon, one that had lit the fires of revolution in America hundreds of years ago. His mind, and his words. The internet was still up and running, somehow and someway, and Alex takes to his keyboard. Inspired by his hero Patrick Henry, soon the words of the "Ghost" start inciting attacks on the Fae and the District of Columbia rings with explosions, gunshots and cries of Freedom. The Resistance notices, and Alex is soon assigned a bodyguard and a handler, an ex-police officer who is running from her own hidden past. Together they work to keep the flame of resistance alive and escape from the tightening net of the Fae. The consequences are, as always, Liberty or Death.

Northwest Front

Fae Wars returns on a new front as war rages in the Pacific Northwest!

Corporal Erik Doherty isn't some kind of special operations super soldier; he's just an infantry grunt trying to get by in what was once the United States Army, now an enforcement arm of the Fae overlords. When orders come down from a chain of command more interested in boot licking their new masters than protecting American citizens, he has to make the choice. To serve and live, or run and die? Ashleigh Greene is a teenage girl with a price on her head, the Fae looking for retribution for the killing of one of their nobles. As her hometown burns behind her, she flees into the mist shrouded forests of the Pacific Northwest, her family killed by dragon fire and her world destroyed. On separate paths, each human comes face to face with a haunting legend that has lived for thousands of years. One that has been waiting, watching, and hating the old enemy that has finally returned. Together, they bring war to the Fae in a battle for honor and revenge. Book seven in the best-selling Fae Wars series!

Vendetta

The echoes of the Fae Invasion have died out in the Midwest when a new thunder rumbles across the plains. Tukor, former warband leader of the Red Arrow Clan, now rides with a motorcycle club of humans and orcs against his former masters. It's hard to tell which challenges Tukor more though; being the new chief of all the orcs in the free city of Wichita Falls, Texas, or being engaged to the tough and lovely human woman Misty.

Throw in an elven duke that's still pissed at Tukor for murdering his sons, a motorcycle club that'll follow the chief to hell and back, and a newly arrived orc matron determined to prove Tukor and Misty wrong about their future. The Fae occupation of the Midwest just got way more bloody.

Featuring orcs on choppers, magic ammo and a whole crew of Army SpecOps, the tale of Tukor and Misty is a front seat view of the occupation in the Southwest that no one expected, least of all Tukor himself.

Relics of Empire

In a world shattered by elven conquest, where magic crackles and dragons soar, the Navajo Nation stands as a defiant refuge. Living there is Ben Yazzie, a battle scarred Marine veteran who wants no more war—until a brutal encounter with elven oppressors at a remote gas station ignites a spark of rebellion. Alongside Maria Hernandez, a grieving widow fueled by vengeance, and a band of unlikely allies, Ben is thrust into a fight against an empire wielding arcane power and ruthless ambition.

As ancient ley lines awaken, unleashing chaos across the American Southwest, Ben uncovers a legacy of resistance tied to his ancestors and a mysterious relic from a forgotten era. Magic surges and the earth itself stirs, forcing Ben to embrace his destiny as the Coyote, the elusive and mysterious warrior leading a desperate stand against an otherworldly tyranny.

From the dusty trails of Arizona to the neon-lit chaos of Las Vegas, *The Fae Wars: Relics of Empire* is a pulse-pounding tale of courage, sacrifice, and defiance against overwhelming odds. Will the old ways and a warrior's heart be enough to reclaim a shattered land?

The rebellion begins here.

John Holmes

J.F. Holmes is a retired Army Senior Noncommissioned Officer, having served for 22 years in both the Regular Army and Army National Guard. During that time, he served as everything from an artillery section leader to a member of a Division level planning staff, with tours in Cuba and Iraq, as well as responding to the terrorists attacks in NYC on 9-11.

From 2010 to 2014 he wrote the immensely popular military cartoon strip, "Power Point Ranger", poking fun at military life in the tradition of Beetle Bailey and Willy & Joe.

His books range from Military Sci-Fi to Space Opera to Detective to Fantasy, with a lot in between, and in 2017 two are finalists for the prestigious Dragon Awards.

In 2018, he launched Cannon Publishing, www.cannonpublishing.us specializing in military science fiction, fantasy and thrillers, with an emphasis on works from up and coming authors.

Lucas Marcum

Lucas Marcum is a critical care nurse practitioner and an officer in the US Army Reserve. When he's not working, or performing his reserve duties, he can be found hiking, reading, attempting to perfect his soft pretzel recipe and spending time with his family.

James Copley

James Copley is a former Non-Commissioned Officer of the U.S. Army, having served over twenty-one years in both Active and Reserve/Guard units, variously trained as Infantry, Communications, and Ordnance specialties before finally retiring from the Army National Guard in 2016. During his service, he deployed four separate times, twice to Iraq and twice to Afghanistan.

He is currently working as a software engineer in Central California with his wife, two children, and two dogs. Reading was his number one passion from a very young age, and more recently he decided to try writing his own. Feel free to join him on his writing journey!

Charli Cox

Charli Cox is a best-selling Military Sci-Fi and Horror Comedy author. She also writes Sci-Fi, Alternate History, and Military Fantasy stories.

If you enjoyed Fae Wars: Northwest Front and want to see more stories about Ash and "Gunny," Cannon Publishing has you covered. Burnt Mountain and Sasquatch will be coming to your Kindle later in 2025. Also, please be sure to leave a review!

Representing #teamandmore, Charli's first published short story is in The Phoenix Initiative: First Missions from Chris Kennedy Publishing. She has stories in Bureau 42 and Express Elevator to Hell, also from CKP.

Look for Whistles of the Wendigo, an Alternate History/Military Fantasy novel set in the Joint Task Force 13 universe from Three Ravens Publishing, due to release soon.

Charli's previous experience has been as a Realtor, HVAC Business Manager, IT Office Manager, and freelance bookkeeper. Professional skills such as drafting strongly worded emails transition surprisingly well into writing fiction.

An animal lover and #boymom, she lives in SW Oregon with her Leg husband, two sons, an Arabian mare, and two Husky mixes who think they are hooman.

Learn more about Charli and sign up for her newsletter on her website. Hang out with her on Facebook, Instagram, and/or TikTok.

Jason Weiser

Mr. Weiser has been a government contractor for the last eleven years, and before that, a writer working odd jobs trying to get by. He has a BA in History from CUNY Brooklyn. Mr. Weiser released his first novel in 2025, with Cannon Publishing, but before that, released a short story in their 2018 Spring Military Sci Fi Anthology.

Mr. Weiser is also an avid wargamer and has been published quite a bit in the hobby, having most recently run "Military Miniature" magazine as it's editor in chief from 2021-2023. Before that, he wrote for EpochXperience (a division of SJR Research) as a contributing writer for their blog on wargaming and military history topics from 2020 to 2021.

He also wrote two scenario books on Cold War wargaming topics, "Red Star, Burning Streets" and "Red Star, White Lights".

Mr. Weiser encourages all his fans to visit Cannon Publishing at their website

Brian Gifford

A military veteran with more than 25 years of service in the U.S. Air Force and Army (in an order that would surprise you!), Brian is a lifelong science fiction and fantasy nerd of the highest order. A student of the hard sciences and the arcane arts of cybersecurity and IT alike, Brian has spent a lifetime accumulating his unique view of the world, which he now insists on sharing with everyone else. He is a husband in awe of the magnificence that is his wife and the proud father of three awesome sons, and looks forward to retiring from the military in the near future to focus on his family and his writing.

www.ingramcontent.com/pod-product-compliance
Lightning Source LLC
Chambersburg PA
CBHW071536110726
47908CB00007B/1900